VANISHED
THRONE OF FIRE

MORGAN VELA

CONTENTS

Preface   xvii

1. The Realms   1
2. Destiny   25
3. Fire and Ice   48
4. A Sacrifice   75
5. Breathing Fire   89
6. The Fire Realm   123
7. An Unwelcome Guest   156
8. Truth and Lies   182
9. Secret Liaisons   206
10. Reckoning   228
11. Power Lust   243
12. Mortal Allies   258
13. Whispers and Dreams   283
14. Redemption   307
15. Upherya   329
16. Abryas   335
17. Endings and Beginnings   337

Acknowledgments   363
About the Author   365
A sneak peek   367
Preface   369
Chapter 1   371
Also by Morgan Vela   391
Stay Connected   393

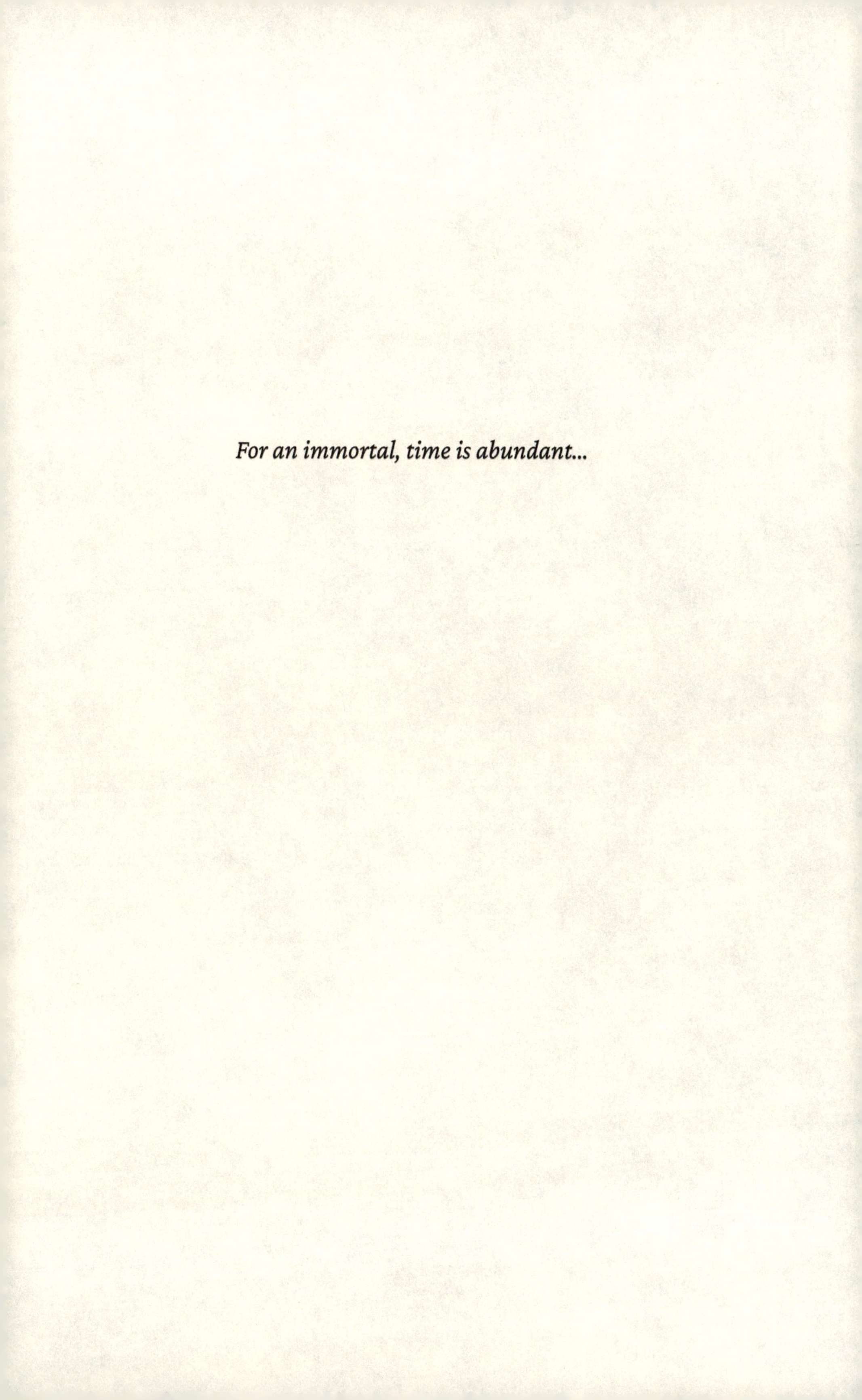

For an immortal, time is abundant...

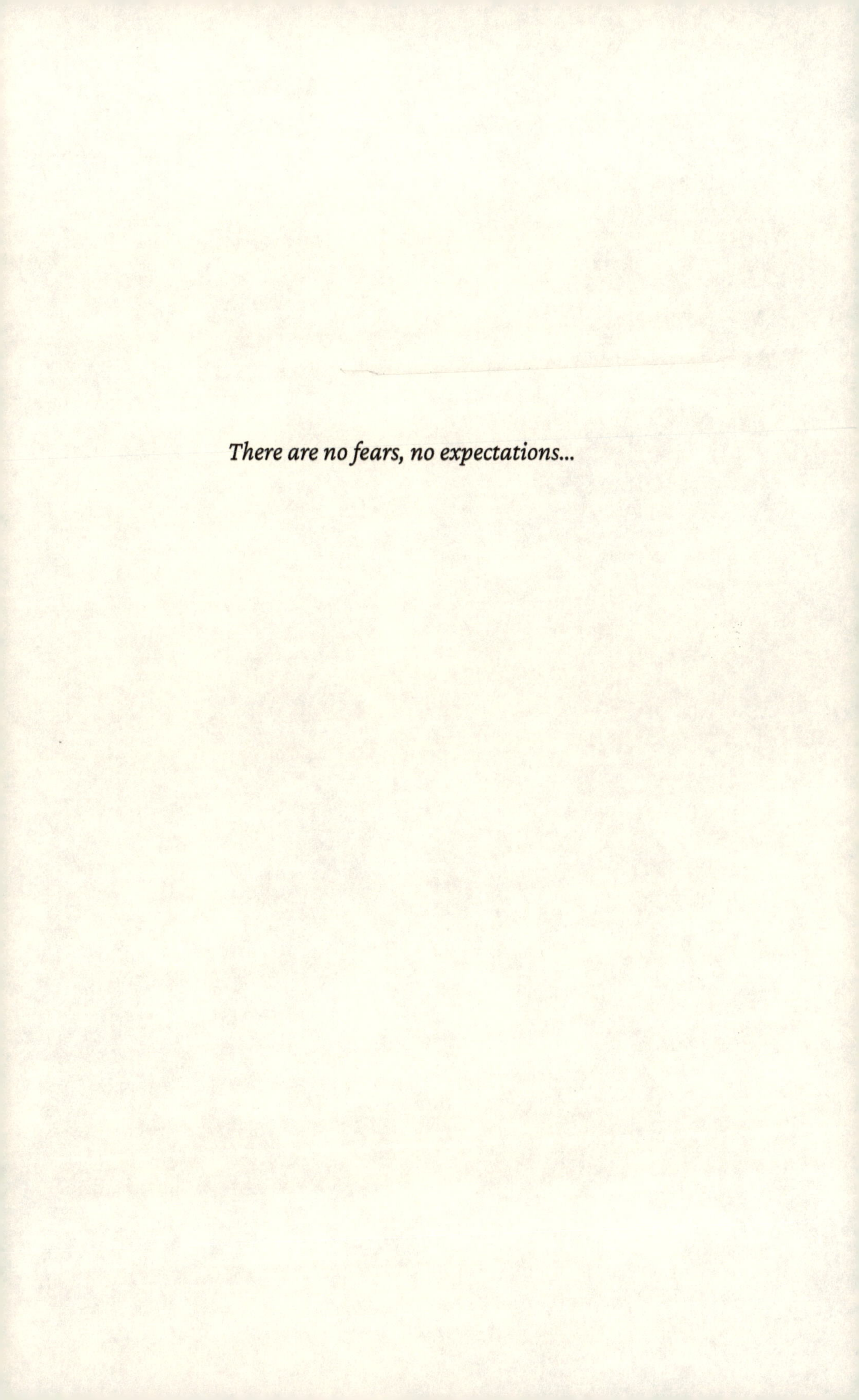

There are no fears, no expectations...

*I've lived within the boundaries of a world that consumes creatures far
more lethal than I and survived...*

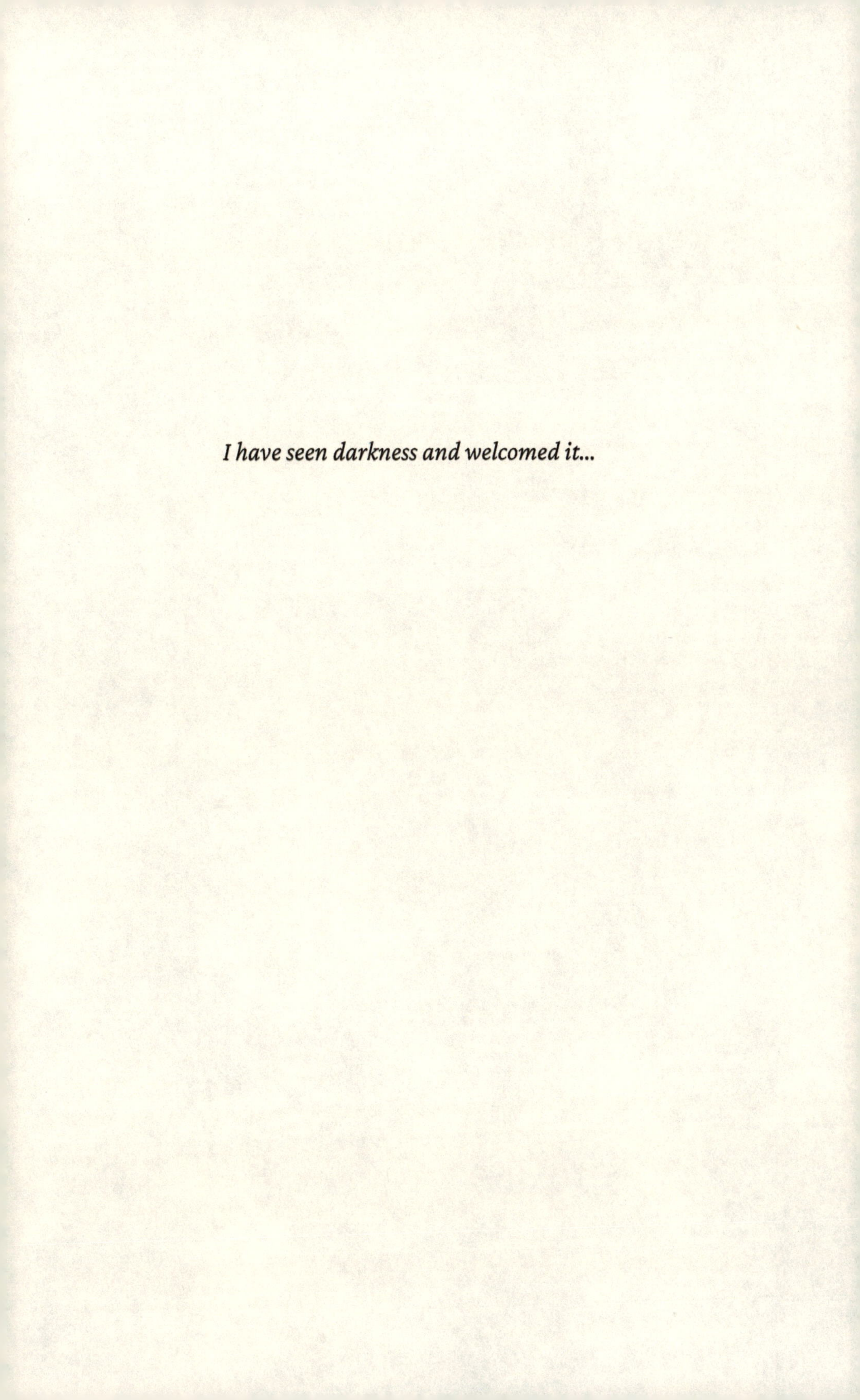

I have seen darkness and welcomed it...

Fire lives in my veins: eternal, indestructible, yet one look at her is all it takes to bring the monster to its knees...

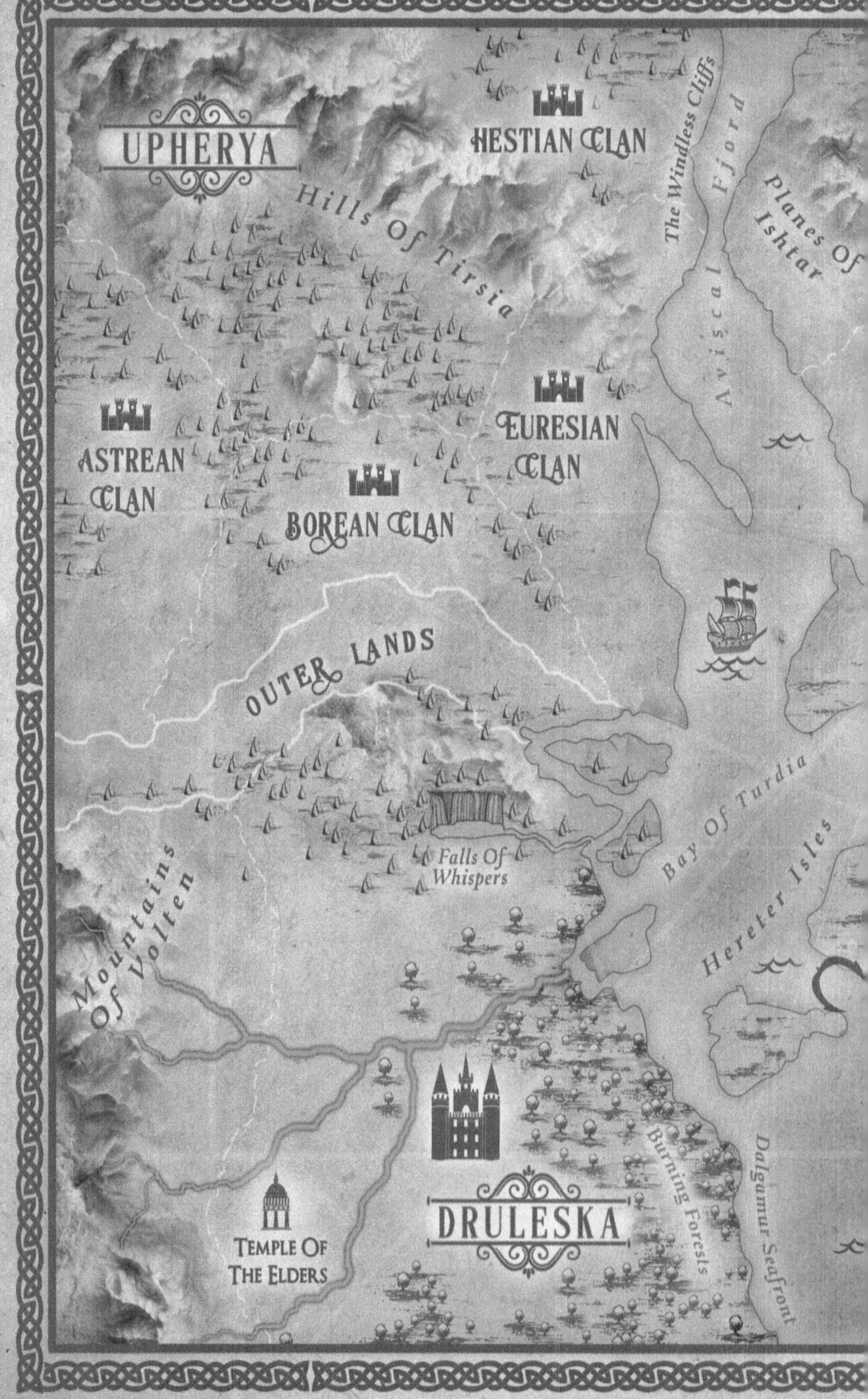

UPHERYA
HESTIAN CLAN
Hills Of Tirsia
The Windless Cliffs
Aviscal Fjord
Planes Of Ishtar
ASTREAN CLAN
EURESIAN CLAN
BOREAN CLAN
OUTER LANDS
Falls Of Whispers
Bay Of Turdia
Hereter Isles
Mountains Of Volten
Temple Of The Elders
DRULESKA
Burning Forests
Dalgamur Seafront

ABRYAS
THE FOUR REALMS
Graveyard Of The Gods
Grettos Cave
Shores Of Galnora
Shores Of Galnora
III
RUINS OF THE LOST
Sea Of Varenver
GLACIER PEAKS
Zodrox
SERFIER
N
W
E
S

PREFACE

The fates are on our side this time. For hundreds of years, the balance has been tilted by power and greed; no longer is there love and peace in the divided realms. It is our time to set things right. The fates and the elements have spoken, and tonight, I do my part.

Beautiful serpent... I know you will find the strength. Find the path where at rest we meet, and I will help you through. Give him all our love and passion, for he is our future, our destiny. He will love us as one, for we are one and the same.

Tell him. Beyond death, I loved him, and your love is proof of that. Cherish every minute and every breath, as I did in the flesh.

*Beautiful serpent, you are my rebirth, my soul…
together as one in life and death.*

*Embrace your destiny, for you are the chosen one:
the last and only pure blood.*

Isabel Adams Cromwell

I

THE REALMS

THE PASSING OF TIME CAN BE CRUEL. Every second is consumed by hopelessness. Every minute is a constant reminder of my failure. I cannot stop time and now spring is once again upon us, yet Drake remains the same: still, lifeless, frozen...

Isabel's letter, which served as my beacon of hope for months, now lay creased on the bedside table. Words that proclaimed me to be unique and powerful were now a reminder of my own deception. Words that had made me hope that the fates were on my side are proved contrary with every passing moment.

"Belynda... are you asleep?" My mother's worried voice came from the other side of the door.

"No. Come in." I sat up on the bed just as she peeked her head through the door, smiling. Yes, time had been cruel, but despite all the heartache, I was grateful for the time my mother and I had reclaimed.

The first few weeks had been burdensome, nonetheless. After so many years of believing her dead, getting used to the idea that my mother was alive was challenging. Still, the hardest was understanding why she had done it.

"Will you join us downstairs for dinner?" She sat at the edge of my bed; a gesture that felt natural now. Almost as if she had done it my entire life. "I made lasagna." She added in a poor attempt to persuade me.

"It will be good to get out of my head for a while," I admitted. "I'll come down." I forced a smile, but she merely stared at me, concern written on her face. I wasn't fooling anyone, only myself.

"There's my sensible girl," she gave me a peck on the head and stood, "don't be long now. Celest is setting up the table; you know how she gets." She whispered conspiratorially and winked.

Although time was unchanging for Drake, a few things had evolved in a year. Celest and I had grown much closer while my mother and Celest bickered constantly. Mostly, they argued over my care and what each thought was best for me. It was comical at times, though in others, not so much. They forgot I was an adult and could make my own decisions. However, I was grateful that Seymor had stuck around, seeing as he was the more level-headed of the lot.

As I reached the kitchen landing, I caught the brief exchange between my mother and Celest.

"Did I miss something?"

"Your Mother is being stubborn, as usual." Celest said. My mother scowled in return.

"Do I want to know what you two are arguing about now?"

"Don't worry yourself. You know better than to listen to

Celest." My mother answered, then strolled back into the kitchen: a subtle way of telling Celest that the conversation was over. Whatever their quarrels were, I had learned not to get in the middle of it.

"Is Seymor coming?" I asked Celest as she moved to sit across from me.

"Probably not. There was another collapse in the chamber." A cold chill traced my spine at the reminder of that dreadful place and how desperately I longed to forget about it. The decision to restore the Guardianship chamber was the one thing Seymor and I could not agree on. That hellish place was doomed.

"Was anyone hurt?" I felt sick to my stomach asking, after knowing how many had already suffered and died in that place — partly because of me.

"No. Thankfully not. But he sounded concerned about the reconstruction getting pushed back to clear the debris."

That place had witnessed too much loss already: the fires, the chaos, the bodies burned to a crisp. It would have stayed buried and forgotten under that mountain if it was up to me. Those horrible memories haunted my every move.

I closed my eyes, hoping to drown out the images. A year had past, and I could still feel that dagger piercing into me, my life slipping away, and the price Drake had paid for it.

No matter how the events of that day tormented me, it was a pair of frozen silver eyes that called for me, which often kept me awake: silver eyes begging to set them free. I snapped back to reality as my mother placed the hot plate in front of me.

"Well. Eat up."

"Thank you... It smells good." I took a bite, and it melted in my mouth. *You're eating... while he sits frozen at the bottom of that lake? While he could be hungry?*

I dropped the fork and shook my head, fighting against the destructive thoughts of guilt that ate away at me.

"Is everything alright?" Celest asked. Observant as usual.

"I'm ok." I pushed back and the sadness choked me.

"Belynda. You don't have to pretend. Not with us, child. We know how hard it is for you. We're not blind. We can see how every passing day without him destroys a little more of your soul. You are fading away right before our eyes. It's almost as if you've lost hope of ever getting him back." My mother's words were my undoing. I realized, then, that Celest wasn't the only one with a keen eye.

"Can you blame me? It's been a year. I have failed him." I wiped at the tears blurring my sight.

"You're wrong. Nothing is lost. We haven't stopped searching the old texts. I know we will find a way."

"How can, you be sure?"

"I just know. You are destined to be together, and I have faith in you and him. If you can't believe anything else, at least believe that."

"Destiny can be very fleeting and cruel. If our lives are in the hands of the fates, then nothing is ever certain." I said with a glooming realization.

"Then believe that bringing him back is possible. That the circumstances can and *will* change, and that this is not permanent. You will only fail him the day you stop trying." One thing I had come to realize was that my mother was always the optimist, and she always knew which buttons to push.

"I will never give up. That is the one thing I'm sure of."

"And neither will we." Celest placed her hand above mine and squeezed gently. "Now eat. Drake won't be happy to see you've turned to bones while he's been gone."

If there was one thing I had learned during my years of therapy, it was how reverse psychology worked. Nonetheless, I knew they were just concerned, so I indulged them and picked up my fork.

"How are things going in school?" Celest asked to change the subject. She knew how difficult it still was for Oliver and me.

"As best as can be expected, I guess."

The news of the mountain fire circulated in the media very briefly, and while I knew the connections of the guardianship ran deep, it was eye-opening to witness the extent of their power.

The death of those council members who had perished in the fire, including Oliver and Ben's fathers, was covered up. No one asked questions, but we knew... Ben knew too. Whenever he looked our way, the hate was clear in his eyes.

The few remaining members of the guardianship were bound to follow the covenant's law of secrecy. With Seymor's help, I came to understand why the need for secrecy was most important. The world wasn't ready to know. Ordinary people were not prepared to deal with the truth. Even if the council and its original purpose was now abolished, the guardianship's secrecy covenant provided this world with peace of mind.

The front door opened, and the sound echoed down the hall as we finished clearing the table. A minute later, a tired-looking Seymor stepped into the corridor.

"You couldn't stay away from my lasagna, could you?" My mother teased as he took one look at the already-cleaned table and smiled.

"Never... Did you leave any for me?" He said, smiling. Nudging against me playfully as he passed to take a seat at the counter beside me, while my mom treated him to a warm plate.

"Celest says there was a collapse in the chamber caves?" If I didn't know Seymor like I did, I wouldn't have felt comfortable hounding him while he had yet to take a bite of food. But I knew him; he was the most refreshing addition to this new family extension of mine. I was sure Drake would have much to say about that, recalling his aversion towards the man. But so much had changed since then. The Seymor I knew was very open, friendly, and — as my mother would say — too willing to indulge me with knowledge. Really, the man knew everything. Of course, there was one exception. He didn't know how to get Drake's human essence back.

"Yes, but they managed to seal it. The team has been working hard and we're hoping it will be cleared by morning. Then we're back on schedule."

"I still don't see why there's such a rush, or *need,* to fix that place." He would have rolled his eyes at me, but he was raised as a polite English man.

"You don't see it now because that place brings you memories you wish to forget, as it does for all of us. But doing what we do and knowing what we know... a place like the chamber is essential to protect the many secrets we are bound to keep. One day I know you will understand." He glanced between Celest and mother before taking a bite. "Any luck at the reliquary?" He asked, skillfully diverting the conversation.

"We think we've found something." My mother said hesitantly. I held my breath, hope blooming for the first time in months.

"Not really. We don't have anything solid yet. Felsia!" Celest admonished, scowling at my mother, but I didn't care.

There had not been a positive lead in months. A slim chance was still a chance, and I would take it no matter how insignificant it was.

"Why didn't you say something sooner?" I questioned my mother, but it was Celest who answered.

"Honestly, she shouldn't have mentioned it at all. We have stumbled upon a grain of salt. That's how inconsequential it is."

"Nothing is inconsequential when it comes to destiny. What did you find?" Seymor pushed for an answer — another reminder as to why I liked him.

"We've been researching the sacrificial tablets of Ora," Celest replied as if that explained everything.

"Oh. Well, then, I agree. That's not the path we want to go down. Felsia, it's certainly out of the question." He glared at my mother with finality.

"Why not? If there is the slightest chance, we must explore it." I argued.

"Trust me, child. Not the path of sacrifice. I think you can agree that enough blood has already been spilled."

Was he referring to an animal sacrifice? I hated myself for considering it, but Drake's life was worth it, even if the thought of harming something so innocent twisted something in my soul.

"I know I speak for entirely selfish reasons, of course, but surely sacrificing the life of an animal can't compare to the value of Drake's life?" The silent look that passed between Celest and my mother was not enough to deter Seymor.

"Indeed, it does not. But the tablets of Ora demand human sacrifices. I'm sure you understand…"

"Oh…"

"Yes. Indeed." He took another bite and glanced between the three women now staring at him, each with a distinct expression, and smiled.

As I lay in bed that night, I thought about the small finding my mother and Celest had made regarding the Ora tablets. I understood that a sacrifice of any kind — especially another human being for the sake of saving Drake — was out of the question, but I still wondered. What if that was the only option to be with him again? To return him to his human form and have his gray eyes look upon me as before... I could finally free him from his frozen prison.

There wasn't much I wouldn't sacrifice for him, but one life to save another was a line I wouldn't cross. I couldn't live with myself, and I knew Drake would understand. Perhaps I knew that better than anyone because I had witnessed his struggles; I knew his biggest battle was with his past and the decisions he had made in Xelraa. Those were the demons he fought, and he wouldn't want the same for me.

I would find another way. I had to...

THE SKIES CLOSED *above me like a red blanket of fire. The falling ashes stuck to my skin like demonic specks of burning frost. In horror, I observed the desiccated line of trees, or what was left of them, alight in embers. What sort of hell was this?*

The cinders stirred with the vortex of winds, and I held my breath as the giant beasts sailed through the fiery skies overhead. The dragons flew, twisting and turning in a dueling dance before crashing against what remained of the burning line of trees and turning them to ashes.

"Stop. Enough!" I called out to the beasts, but it was no use. Fearlessly, I ran toward the clashing dragons. My wrists were bound in shackles but it didn't stop me from grasping the heavy hilt of the sword between my hands.

"Please stop." I pleaded. A pair of grey eyes shifted toward me, but in that second, a cold breeze chilled my body, despite the fiery inferno

that raged on. The other beast spotted Drake's distraction and dug its teeth into his shoulder.

IT TOOK me a moment to realize the piercing scream was my own and not Drake's howl of pain. I gasped for breath, completely stunned by the darkness of that dream.

Since the day I left Drake frozen at the bottom of that lake, I had prayed for a vision from Isabel — some sign that would show me a way to bring him back. I had dreamed of Drake before, but this was different. It had felt so real that, even now, I could sense the burning ashes prickling against my skin.

It was a quarter past seven, and from the lack of sunlight, it looked like it would be another rainy day in Cummington.

I wrapped the robe around myself as I reached the kitchen. While no one was in sight, someone was up because the coffee pot was hot and half-empty. I poured myself a cup and went to search for my mother. I was still surprised she hadn't barged into my room after I screamed.

The lights in the study were on, and the door was slightly ajar. I pushed the door slowly and peeked in. Celest sat behind the desk, but didn't notice me. She seemed lost in her thoughts, her fingers mindlessly tracing the scar on her neck.

I knew exactly what she saw. She saw the ghosts from that day — the same ghosts that haunted me, too. Perhaps she saw the truth: that some scars couldn't be healed, even with time.

Watching her, I remembered that night when we returned to the house as if it were today. Everything felt dreamlike and I was shocked as I entered the house to find Leonor, Lily's mom, caring for Celest. I didn't know what to say. I couldn't understand why my psychologist was suddenly making house calls. I soon realized that the full spectrum of her qualifications was a secret, like everything else had been in my life. As Seymor explained in the haze of things, she was the guardianship's doctor, like her family before her. It could be Lily's future someday.

Though I was pleased to learn that Lily still remained in the dark. A selfish part of me had wanted a friend to confide in, but I was glad she was spared from the truth.

Celest cleared her throat, and I realized I had run away with my thoughts.

"Good morning. I see you found your way to the pot of coffee."

I smiled, bringing the warm mug to my lips. "I did. Thank you." I made note of the dark circles under her eyes. "Did you sleep well?"

"Not really. Your mother and Seymor decided to visit the reliquary early, so there was no point in staying in bed. Besides, I have to open the library." Well, that explained why my mother hadn't come running.

"To the reliquary, this early? Did they say why?"

"I shouldn't say anything else to encourage the subject, but I believe it concerns your mother's insistence on those Ora tablets. Seymor is determined to put her idea to rest, or perhaps he's just humoring her — whatever for, I do not know, nor do I agree. That woman has no sense."

"But why would she insist on that? Seymor clearly said that if we find an answer there, it would require a sacrifice. Surely she knows that's out of the question? Believe me, I've thought of nothing since. Even if it was the only option to get Drake back, he wouldn't want us to make that choice. Drake would understand."

As I said the words out loud, I knew deep in my bones they were true. He wouldn't want that.

"I know, but we are talking about your mother here. You know she is tenacious. 'No' is not in her vocabulary."

I snickered at Celest's accurate description of my mother. In the short time we had spent together I had reached the same conclusion, she did have a knack for recklessness.

"Don't let her catch you saying that." I teased, and Celest pretended to seal her lips and throw away the key.

"Did you need something?" She smiled, and I felt the heaviness of the dream looming over me like a bad omen.

"Yes, do you have a few minutes?"

"Always. Grab a chair." Celest's face transformed with concern.

"I promise it's nothing serious. I had a dream and I guess I'm just a little rattled and wanted to talk about it, that's all."

"A dream or a vision?" She leaned forward on the desk, eyes alight with interest.

"I'm not sure... a dream. I think."

I told Celest about the nightmare. The burning skies, the ashen forest, and the battling dragons.

"I can see why you would be troubled. And there was no Isabel?"

"No. Isabel hasn't visited my dreams since before... not since I freed Drake."

"Well, did it feel anything like your other visions?"

I thought about it for a moment.

"I guess they were just as vivid, but I saw no connection. Except for Drake. I know he was the Dragon that got hurt."

"You know... it doesn't necessarily have to mean something. It may just be a nightmare. After what you've been through and seen, it's only a matter of time before your subconscious starts playing tricks on you."

"You're right. I guess time will tell."

"Surely." Celest's smile was candid.

"Do you have plans with Lily, or will you stay in today?"

No. Remaining here meant dwelling on my thoughts — overthinking. I had done enough of that.

"Actually, I was thinking I'd come to the library with you."

"Oh! Well, I would like that."

"Yeah, I figured I'd check out some of those books that Mom and you keep insisting I read." Celest smiled.

"We're just looking out for you, you know..."

I did know that. The knowledge those books offered would be impractical for an ordinary human girl... but for me — the last pure-blood with the power to bend three elements and open portals to other realms — that knowledge was essential. So, I nodded.

"I'll change." I walked out with my warm mug in hand.

"Twenty minutes!" she called after me, and I rolled my eyes as I turned for the stairs. A date with books.

I SAT at one of the back tables, hidden amongst walls laden with old and dusty books. The information on the elemental realms was overwhelming, to say the least. I knew that learning to craft spells was important, but I didn't see the need to learn about other Realms or the creatures that inhabited them.

I flipped through the third tome regarding the Water Realm or 'Serfier' — its proper name as stated in the books. Serfier was the first elemental Realm created. I learned that beings that dwell in the water realm are known to possess many abilities, but it seems modesty was not one of them. Water Realm beings considered themselves superior to species in the other realms; the merfolk people, in particular, for it was them who ruled the underwater city of Serfier.

However, as I studied the illustrations of the Merpeople, I didn't find them to be superior, like the books claimed. They had narrow and scaly faces with deep sunken eyes and sharp teeth; all my childhood misconceptions crumbled as I beheld the real face of the Merfolks. Perhaps some part of me was biased, for I had never seen or judged Drake as anything less than human. But these people... these merfolk beings were the kind of monsters that lived in nightmares. Dark, creepy, and dangerous creatures that could delve into your mind for you to do their bidding. I shuddered.

The Realm's surface was described as a vast wild ocean dotted with tropical reefs and treacherous islands. The creatures inhabiting the depths of the Water Realm were accounted as powerful, magical, and mysterious— their strange songs and glowing apparitions a beacon to the brave and foolish alike. But the genuine marvel of the Realm rested beneath the dazzling surface of the ocean. A hidden kingdom. A landscape of sunken cities, icebergs, and mythical ruins, each with its own secrets and tales. The book referred to Serfier as the kingdom of the lost. Impenetrable by mortals and immortals alike. Those who had dared to brave its depths often found more than they bargained for — tales of forgotten gods, cursed relics, and unpredictable magic.

THE LAST VOLUME was filled with pages of every creature dwelling in the Water Realm; from water sylphs — tiny water faeries known to conjure enormous storms — to giant clams that could devour humans whole.

One particular fact I discovered was that Merfolk and Sirens were different. Although both were known for their mind control abilities, Sirens had seductive voices to lure and control, whereas Merfolk didn't require a deadly tune to slip into the depths of your mind. I had also never heard of Sea Witches, which according to the book, were powerful creatures that resembled beautiful human females. Their skin, said to be drawn upon like a canvas depicting all existing creatures of the Realm; their magic allowing them to shift into any of those creatures at will.

Then there was the Leviathan: a mighty sea entity said to possess the power to cause great destruction with its immense strength, forming powerful waves and storms... their most lethal ability being the power to control other sea creatures.

I MADE A GENERAL NOTE: everything in the water realm could potentially eat me or kill me. Serfier was directly connected to the fates, believed to also be a gateway between the mortal and otherworld realms.

"How's it going?" Celest appeared in the hallway, two more books in hand.

"Honestly? I don't know how I'll be able to remember all of this. Are those also for me?" My frustration must have been evident because she walked over and took the chair across from mine.

"No. These are for me." She smiled, amused, and I exhaled with relief.

"Really. I don't see why I need all this information about the realms. It's not like I'm going to open any portals."

"I certainly pray to the gods you never have to."

I felt my stomach flip at the thought of ever facing those

kinds of monsters. Then again, I never imagined I would meet a Dragon, let alone love one, and here I was.

"Look, no one expects you to become a mage, but you need to have some understanding of what lies beyond the human world. Your mother and I understand the great responsibility that rests over you, despite your short years. We only want you to be prepared to face anything. For this world and for the ones you know are out there. The ones you hold the key to."

"I know... I know." I added with resignation.

"How far along have you gotten?"

"I've got a general idea of the Water Realm..."

"Good. It's not my favorite, I must admit, but somehow the guardianship has always been interested in them."

"How so?"

"Have you ever wondered why your father didn't have a water elemental?"

Now that she mentioned it, I had wondered.

"Because he never found one?"

Celest shook her head.

"The guardians made it their mission to hunt them down to extinction. They believed the sacred book was stolen and brought into the human world by one of their kind."

I knew my father was despicable, but to hunt down so many innocent people was beyond the pale.

"Was it true? Were they the ones who took the book?" We still didn't know how the book, Isabel's sword or cup had gotten to the house. My mother didn't know, nor did Celest.

"No one really knows, but I think they must have been involved somehow to have the legacy persecute them in such a manner. Then again, the guardianship has always feared what they can't control. Many water elementals were able to manipulate the minds of others. I think the guardians felt threatened."

"Do you think they have any connection to why I can bend water so easily?"

Celest cocked her head to one side and considered the idea.

"I haven't thought about it before, but it is possible. After all, Serfier has always been known to serve the fates directly. It would explain your connection to water and why it is your strongest element."

I realized, then, that there was so much more I had to learn. Perhaps the books weren't a total bore. For a moment, I studied the illustration of the Merfolk people with a different perspective and slightly kinder eyes.

"Here," She picked a book from one of the piles on the desk and offered it to me. "Don't worry about the rest. You'll find all you need to know about the Air Realm there. It's actually my favorite." I flipped the small book and read the cover: *Upherya Air Realm*. "I've always been fascinated by how they live." She added, and her passion sparked my curiosity. The chair scraped against the carpet as she stood.

"Are we leaving soon?" I asked.

"Not unless you're ready to call it a day?"

I glanced at the book in my hands with curiosity and smiled.

"I think I'll stay a while longer and learn about your favorite realm."

"I'll leave you to it then." She walked away, obviously pleased by my change of heart.

CELEST WAS RIGHT. Upherya, the Air Realm, was magnificent. The illustrations made the experience all the more pleasant compared to the descriptions depicting the Water Realm.

The Air people appeared to live as free as their element, and I could see why Celest was fascinated by them. The mountains of

Tirsia seemed to kiss the clouds with white marble pillars crowning the peaks. It was simply beautiful. I could only imagine how breathtaking it would be to stand there.

The book often referred to those inhabiting the Air Realm as 'the wind people' and they seemed to live in clans — four clans, to be exact. The clans of the North, East, West, and South.

The clan of the North was known as the Hestians; the South belonged to the Boreans, the West housed the Astreans, and the East was home to the Euresians.

Unlike the other realms, which were ruled by a royal house, the Air people had a council that acted as the Realm's governing body. A council comprised of all the blood-name warriors of the different clans.

Air elementals, as I learned, were much like Drake: human shifters, but in their element form, they were fast flying creatures made of living air. They were known to be territorial, but above all, favored peace and living undisturbed. However, although they seemed a harmonious bunch, they could grow resentful when summoned for doing a mortal's bidding. They preferred to spend their time swooping and racing through the endless skies of Upherya.

The more I learned, the more tangible these other Realms and beings became. Particularly, the Air Realm which reminded me more of the human world.

I shut the book and the chair scraped against the floors as I stood. My muscles protested too, rigid and achy after hours of endless sitting.

Celest was overturning the library sign to close when I reached her.

I stretched my aching back and rubbed my tired eyes, catching the time on the standing clock.

"Where did the time go?" No wonder I was tired. I had sat at that table for almost seven hours straight. "Why didn't you call me? You could have closed almost an hour ago."

"I didn't want to interrupt you. Besides, there is always work to do here."

"Well, I'm definitely ready to go. I feel like I've run a marathon, although I've been sitting all day. I'm beat. I'm drained, my eyes burn..."

"Nothing a long bath, a good meal, and a good night's rest can't fix."

"Yes, that bath is calling me." Celest laughed and collected her purse from behind the counter.

"Did you want to bring any of the books home?" *By the gods, no...* I didn't want to see another book tonight.

"I think I've had enough books for today. But if you can recommend one on the Earth Realm from that pile mother and you compiled... I'll be grateful. The one you offered earlier was precisely what I needed."

She held up a finger, gesturing for me to wait, while she disappeared down the corridor towards the back corner where I had withered all day. She appeared two minutes later, a fat book in hand.

"I know you're done for today, but perhaps you'll be in the mood tomorrow. It's not small, but this has everything you need to know about Abryas, the Earth Realm." I held the heavy tome in my hands, grateful I didn't have to dig through another mountain of books to gather information.

Dusk began to set on the horizon as Celest drove up the hill towards the Manor. I glanced at the book resting on my lap and frowned at the task ahead... *Abryas... not today.*

• • •

THE NIGHT FELL, and there was still no sign of Mother or Seymor. I tried their phones a third time, but there was still no answer. I organized my closet to soothe my edginess.

The boxes and bags at the back of the closet sat untouched, beckoning me. Drake's clothes were mostly new and unwrapped. It had been a year since I was forced to leave him in that frozen prison, yet still I could not bring myself to open them. To smell them. To see if they held any trace of his scent. I was too afraid of what that small reminder of him could do to my sanity.

My cell ringing pulled me out of the haze. I ran to answer, hoping it was Seymor or my mother.

"Hello?"

"You're alive..." It was Oliver.

I knew he would have something witty to say, considering I had ignored his calls all day.

"Barely. I've spent the entire day at the library, buried up to my neck in books. I'm trying to force into my brain everything I can about the Realms."

"I know. It's a lot to wrap your head around."

"Wait. You actually studied the Realms? Mr. I'm too cool to pick up a book?"

"Not by choice... it was a requirement as part of the guardianship legacy, and I couldn't say no. Not to him..." The tone of his voice darkened, and I knew the painful memories of our father haunted him still. A cruel ghost.

There had to be a part of him that mourned. Despite how cruel our father had been, Oliver had been raised by him.

"Celest and my mother are nothing like our father, and I couldn't say no to them either," I added as a distraction.

"I have no use for it; you, on the other hand, are destined to protect the realms. In your case, it's wrong not to care." Wrong? How dare he.

"It's a good thing father forced it upon you too. After all, you were born and groomed to inherit his seat as head of the council, not I."

"I never wanted it." I heard the hurt in his voice, and I wished I could take my spiteful words back, but it was too late.

"I know. I'm sorry."

"I know you didn't mean it. I'm sorry too. I was only teasing you for not answering my calls."

"Then I take back my apology. It's your fault for provoking me when I'm tired and cranky." Oliver laughed, and I smiled, relieved at the ease of our newly formed relationship.

Lights reflected into the room, cast through the glass of my window; I jumped from the bed to see the car pull in front of the house.

"I have to go. My mother and Seymor are here."

"Wait, what's going on?"

"I'll tell you all about it tomorrow."

"Ok, so you're still coming over then?"

"Yeah. I'll see you." I rushed down the stairs.

"See you." Oliver's voice was cut off as I hung up.

I FLUNG open the door to a surprised Seymor.

"Someone's happy to see us."

I beamed with excitement as he hung his coat by the entry hall. I studied their faces, yet they gave nothing away. There was no sign they had been successful in finding a solution within the Ora tablets. Seymor was his usual neutral British self, and my mother looked tired.

"So... did you find anything? Is there any hope of using the tablets?"

"I'm afraid not." Said Seymor without preamble. The small hope I had allowed myself to have crumbled.

"But we will try it anyway." Said my mother and I felt the sudden urge to cry. I glanced at Seymor for confirmation — a sign that I had not imagined her words, but he grinned. For the first time in a long time, I felt a small swell of happiness.

"Granted... I don't trust it will work, at least not without a human sacrifice. But Felsia believes it can be possible if we offer another form of exchange. One that doesn't require taking a human life, and I'm willing to test her theory but nothing else." He stared at me. "I need you to accept that this is only a microscopic chance; it's not even a possibility. But know that, no matter the outcome, we will continue to search." It was clear what their worry was. They had seen the devastation and grief on my face over the last year; if this failed... they wanted to ensure I could move past it and not lose hope.

"I know that believing it will work is to believe in the impossible, but you wanted me to hope. So this is me being hopeful. It might be a long shot, but at least we're trying. Please, don't worry about me."

Seymor and my mother exchanged a glance as Celest reached the foyer.

"What did I miss?"

I beamed.

"We're doing the ritual." Celest looked between mother and Seymor with uncertainty.

"The Ora Tablets? I thought you said it was impossible." She asked, directing her questions to Seymor. It was my mother who answered.

"Never mind that now. I will explain everything, come." My mother pulled Celest down the corridor and towards the office while Seymor stayed behind.

"Aren't you coming?" Celest called out to him, but he declined with a subtle head movement.

"No, I think I've endured enough Felsia for one day. You can deal with her. It's her idea, after all. I'm just humoring her."

"You really have no faith that it will work?" I realized I was almost whispering as I looked up at Seymor.

"Child, I want nothing more than to make you happy. The last thing I want is for you to lose hope but I have studied the Ora Tablets; I have looked at this from every possible aspect and this... *notion* of your mother's that it could accept anything less than what it requires...I just don't see it."

"I understand. Thank you for at least trying. For being honest."

"No need to thank me. Really, it's all your mother. She is as tenacious as they come and would not take no for an answer. That's why I didn't feel inclined to follow them. I'm sure Celest is fighting the same battle I already lost, and truthfully, I'm exhausted."

He did look tired.

"Is everything alright at the chamber?"

"Yes, we're back on schedule after yesterday's cave-in, but I'm sure you don't want to hear about that." He smiled, knowing what my opinion was on the matter.

"Just because I don't agree with the decision to resurrect that place, it doesn't mean I don't care about you, the guardianship, or your work."

"I know you disagree with me now. But you will see its importance. One day."

"One day." I granted. Perhaps there would come a time when the ghosts and nightmares of that dreadful day would no longer haunt me.

· · ·

I LAID in bed with Isabel's letter, tracing my fingers over the words, written with skillful ink strokes — words I had imprinted into my mind, yet they had ceased to inspire hope. Closing my eyes, I allowed myself to dream. I dreamed of gray eyes staring back at me and a warmth that clouded my senses.

THE SKIES CLOSED *above me like a red blanket of fire. The falling ashes stuck to my skin like demonic specks of burning frost. In horror, I observed the desiccated line of trees, or what was left of them, alight in embers. What sort of hell was this?*

The cinders stirred with the vortex of winds, and I held my breath as the giant beasts sailed through the fiery skies overhead. The dragons flew, twisting and turning in a dueling dance before crashing against what remained of the burning line of trees and turning them to ashes.

"Stop. Enough!" I called out to the beasts, but it was no use. Fearlessly, I ran toward the clashing dragons.

My wrists were bound in shackles but it didn't stop me from grasping the heavy hilt of the sword between my hands.

"Please stop." I pleaded. A pair of grey eyes shifted toward me, but in that second, a cold breeze chilled my body, despite the fiery inferno that raged on. The other beast spotted Drake's distraction and dug its teeth into his shoulder.

I screamed in terror at Drake's roar but was relieved as he circled back with force, heading toward the other beast. He clawed at its wings, pinning it to the ground. I ran towards the burning forest edge and stopped a few feet from the dragons. Drake circled the beast, who appeared overpowered as it bowed its head. Drake roared, wings expanding above the fallen beast. He glanced my way, and I saw the monster yield within him. He growled yet turned away from the creature, sparing the beast's life. My body jolted, but I stayed rooted in place: silent. I stared at the sharp tail of the beast and the spike now protruding from my stomach. Pain seared through me as I watched the fire consume Drake's eyes. He turned with a fluid movement and took the beast's head. As my knees hit the ashen ground, Drake's arms held me.

"You promised..." I said, reaching to stroke his face.

2
DESTINY

OR SO LONG, I HAD PRAYED FOR A VISION. A sign that would prove it was possible to return Drake to his human form. But this vision... this *nightmare* had presented me with a darker reality instead. There would be no happy ending for us. *Was this what the fates had destined? More sacrifice?*

Drake once said the fates always had a higher purpose for twisting destiny the way they did. However, as I replayed the vision in my mind, I could not reconcile it with his belief. After all the pain and loss Drake had endured, how could the fates demand more?

I had to hang on to the idea of a future where it would be possible for us to be together again; I had to believe there would be another way. Any other alternative would be my undoing, and I needed to fight for him... for us. For now, I would hope and pray for my visions to be wrong.

The house was quiet, but it was still early. I put on a pot of coffee and took a cup back to my room. I fixed my bed and sat by the window with my laptop. I ran the search for 'Ora Tablets' on Google.

With endless resources on the web, I expected to find some form of information, even if it would most likely be presented as myth, but I was surprised at the results. *Nothing...* there was absolutely nothing on the Ora Tablets. That could only mean that whatever mysteries the Tablets contained, they were well guarded. There was a quiet knock at the door, followed by my mother's voice.

"Belynda, are you up?"

"Yes, come in." I closed the laptop just as she opened the door.

"I figured you would sleep in since it's Sunday. Celest and I were surprised by the freshly brewed coffee, but we figured it was you and not Seymor. We all know the kind of relationship he has with the kitchen."

I smiled while remembering his many failed attempts at cooking.

"He tries..."

"Perhaps he shouldn't." At her remark, we both laughed.

"Celest told me about the dream. Is that what's troubling you?"

"I wish it was just a nightmare," I confessed. "But the fates are turning those wheels and I have a feeling their plan is dark."

"Did you see Drake? Could he shift in your vision?" Mother asked.

"He did."

"Well, that's great news then," she smiled, but it didn't reach her eyes. "It means we can hope that the Ora Tablets will work. Perhaps we're on the right path." I wanted to say that, although the vision brought hope, it was also haunting. If Isabel had seen hope in her revelation... if an end with a new beginning had been the answer for her, then perhaps it was time I embraced my fate. I swallowed the knot in my throat and kept the horrific notion to myself. No one had to know. Only time would reveal my destiny.

"You're right. I'm just worrying for no reason. Are we ready to move forward with the ritual?"

"I wish I could say yes, but we're not. This magic is dark. We haven't dealt with it before, so Celest and Seymor are wary — perhaps overly cautious, in my opinion, but this is important. We only get one chance with the Ora Tablets, so we must do it right and take our time."

"Why do we only get one chance? How long do we have to wait?"

"A few weeks, at least. Perhaps more. Once the Ora Tablets are unlocked, the words are spoken, and the sacrifice is made. If it's not accepted, the tablets will break. Since we're attempting it without a human sacrifice, then we need to take our time to deliberate on the best alternate offering."

"What can I do to help? I feel useless."

"Nothing at the moment. Celest and I will take care of everything. You just worry about your studies and your added curriculum." She glanced at the book on the Earth Realm sitting on my bedside table. "You have enough with school and training. We can manage. Trust me."

"Ok, but if there's anything I can do."

"We will let you know. I promise." She added.

"We're heading out to the reliquary after breakfast as I want to get started. Today, Celest is helping, so if you need anything, call us?"

"I'll be fine. Oliver should be coming in a while anyways. I promised we could go spend some time over at his place."

"How's he doing?"

"He says he's alright, but sometimes I'm not so sure."

"It's understandable. Even if Stephen was evil and corrupted, he was still his father."

"Somehow, I think it's his lack of suffering which troubles him, even if he understands Stephen wasn't a good father." My mother stayed silent. I couldn't help sensing that she had taken my comment about Oliver's father to heart. I saw it in her eyes, turning my words over in her head — the fear that she wasn't a good mother after abandoning me for all those years.

"He will be alright." she finally spoke, forcing a smile. She walked to the door. "Say hello to him for me, and don't forget to call us if you need anything."

"I will."

My mother was not the monster my father was. She chose to leave me as she thought it would protect me, and while that had proven unwise, I knew she regretted it, and would lament it for the rest of her life. On the other hand, I was grateful. Thinking I'd lost her for all those years made me appreciate her more.

It was a quarter past noon when Oliver called to let me know he was outside.

He leaned casually against the passenger door as I descended the porch steps.

"Here," He tossed the car keys my way, and I caught them in one fluid motion. "Good reflexes. Come on, get in."

I stared at him, confused.

"You're actually letting me drive?"

This was his baby, and he had made it abundantly clear I would never be allowed anywhere near the wheel.

"Hershton, you're making me regret this. Go on. Get in before I change my mind."

He didn't have to tell me twice. I adjusted the mirrors and the seat, then backed out of the driveway with ease. Then, I sped down the road.

"Easy. Take it easy."

"Oh, hush. Stop fussing. You wouldn't have let me drive her if you didn't trust I could do it." I glimpsed his smirk as he turned his head to look out the window. Luckily, he remained relaxed, so long as I kept it within the speed limit.

I drove slowly through the winding road and into Oliver's property. Although my house was by no means modest, Oliver's place made the manor look like a cottage in comparison. No matter how often I visited during the past year, it always unsettled me. I couldn't place the emotion; it wasn't jealousy or envy. Perhaps it was knowing *he* had lived here, remembering that it was my father... *our father* who had built this empire.

As I took the last bend, the great stone walls flanked the rest of the way until we reached the gates. Oliver pressed a button and the metal doors opened.

"Keep your eyes on the road." Oliver growled. I rolled my eyes but complied. I just couldn't help it; the dense forest that lined the road was like something from a movie. The trees appeared to be thousands of years old with enormous trunks and branches which naturally met the trees on the opposite side of the road, forming a natural arch along the path.

The pebbled driveway extended ahead, as did the stoned front wall of the estate. There were fourteen windows on the second floor and fourteen on the lower level, lining the front of the property. Not to mention those facing the estate's East, West, and South side.

"Are you sure there is no royalty in your lineage?" I teased, and Oliver laughed.

"You forget it's your lineage too."

Yeah, I forget often, but this place reminded me; it reminded me of the guardianship, the legacy, the covenant. Somehow it made the supernatural world secretly kept from the rest, more tangible. This place was magical, like something out of a fairy tale book.

Our footsteps echoed around the grand entrance hall as I followed Oliver.

"No staff today?"

"Lately, we've been fending for ourselves on Sundays to give them a day off." I had no doubt by 'lately', he meant since Stephen's death. Stephen had not seemed like the 'fend-for-himself' type.

"Is your mom here?"

"She had Tyrus drive her to Worthington this morning." The frown on his face sparked my curiosity.

"I take it you're not pleased by that?" I asked. Oliver sulked.

"Honestly, I don't know how I feel about it." The boy was so confusing sometimes...

"What part exactly don't you approve?"

"Everything. They spend too much time together. That's the problem." I followed brooding Oliver down the corridor.

"There's nothing wrong with that. Your mom is young. I think Tyrus is a decent guy too and not bad looking for his age."

Samantha Radcliff was a beautiful woman indeed. Oliver took after her not just in looks but in personality. She was lovely and kind, unlike our father, which made me wonder what sort of hell she must have endured with him. If his own son had been such an abomination to him, I questioned how Samantha had faired. Oliver turned to me with a murderous look.

"What the hell are you rambling on about? I didn't say they were together... not like that."

"Well, seeing them together obviously bothers you, I figured..."

"You're wrong." He cut me off. Touché...

"Then what's the problem. Are you jealous?"

"No! Who would I be jealous of? Tyrus?"

"I don't know. You tell me. Something is obviously eating at you. Maybe the idea that they could actually have something?"

"Will you stop saying that!"

Oh yeah, that was definitely the issue. He just wouldn't admit it to himself. *Poor Samantha.*

"A word of advice... be kind. Something tells me you're not the only one who had a hard life. Imagine what marriage must have been like for her."

"I know." He admitted.

"Then, think for a minute. I'm not saying anything is happening... but if it is, don't you think your mother deserves to be happy?"

"Trust me. I know that. It's just hard, alright." There... finally. A semblance of recognition.

"I'm not saying it isn't. Only that you should be patient and kind. Besides, you know Tyrus. He's been like a father to you, hasn't he?"

Oliver grumbled, running his hand through his gold locks.

"You're right. I'll try. But for the love of God, stop talking about them. Now... what should we do today? Swimming pool, video games, or... gym perhaps."

"Gym... seriously?"

"Or not..."

"Last night, do you remember I told you there was something I wanted to tell you?"

"Yeah?"

"How much do you know about the Ora Tablets?"

"Never heard of them. Why? What are they?"

"Do you think Stephen might have had some information on them?"

"I don't know. Maybe. What do the tablets do?"

"All I know is that there is information about them at the reliquary. The tablets may finally give Drake back his human essence. Still, according to Seymor, they require a human sacrifice."

Oliver's face clearly signaled his disapproval of that method.

"Don't be daft. We're not going to sacrifice anyone."

"I didn't say anything."

"You didn't have to. I saw it in your face. Anyways, they want to attempt the ritual. My mother believes there might be a way to get the tablets to accept another offering."

Oliver seemed thoughtful for a moment.

"What could something that demands blood settle for?"

"Honestly, I don't know. That's what my mother and Celest are trying to figure out. Apparently, they only get one chance to use the tablets. If the offering is not accepted, the tablets will break."

"I've never heard of such magic, but I'll help however I can."

"Do you mind if we look through your father's things? Maybe there's something that can help." He was hesitant... "But it's ok if you don't want to, I understand."

"No, I want to. I just haven't been to his study. Not since before..."

"You don't have to. Oliver, it's normal to feel sad and mourn your father... No matter what kind of man he was."

"I..." He struggled to find his words, yet I could tell he wished to escape his burden. "I don't feel anything. That's the problem. Does that make me a bad person? A bad son?" he whispered, almost choking on his words.

"You are NOT a bad person. And feeling that way doesn't make you a bad son. Your father wasn't good to you; you don't owe him anything."

"That's what I keep telling myself, but then the guilt hits me. That's why I haven't found the courage to go in there. I don't know how I will react."

"You don't have to do it now, only when you're ready."

"No. I'm not a coward. This is important to you. Perhaps it's a good thing that you're here." He decided. "Come."

I followed Oliver down the lower-level corridors facing the back of the house. Right away, I knew which room was his study. If the opulent wooden doors weren't indication enough, Oliver's hesitant steps confirmed it. He paused.

"You can do this. I'm here."

He reached for the brass doorknob, and the door shrieked as he pushed it open.

The study was bathed in darkness. I took it all in as Oliver pulled open the curtains and switched on the lamps. It was exactly what I expected: a modern version of the guardianship chamber. Chandeliers dotted the ceiling and wooden shelves lined the walls; there was a massive desk — too intimidating for my taste — though Oliver seemed lost in thought as he stared at the empty seat behind it.

"Are you ok?" I nudged his arm, and he resurfaced out of whatever memory he was lost in.

"Yeah. It's strange. I don't feel comfortable in this space. I have this rooted fear in my stomach, afraid he's going to barge through that door any minute and catch us in here."

"But he's not."

"I know... I know." He walked around the desk and hesitantly picked up some of the papers on it.

"What is it?"

"Just papers from the accountant."

"Do you mind if I look around his library?"

"No. Go right ahead. I'll join you in a second."

THE OPULENT WOODEN shelves wrapped around the room; the golden patterns etched on the wine-red carpets reflected the lamp's glow, and made the room seem ominous.

I walked before the walls of books and browsed the spines, but none seemed important. They were regular books — the sorts you'd find in any traditional office or library. Nothing magical or out of the ordinary as I had expected.

As I moved my inspection down the shelves, I glanced at Oliver, who searched through the desk drawers.

"These books are all useless."

"Yes! I got it." Oliver held up an oddly shaped key. "Find the lair." He said, walking around the desk to browse the spines on the opposite shelf.

"What is the lair?"

He had completely lost it.

"It's a book. Trust me. It's called 'The Lair'. Help me find it."

We searched the endless walls aligned with books, spine after spine.

"The Lair... I got it!" Oliver was at my side in an instant. He pulled on the spine of a navy bound book, and the entire shelf shifted and moved aside, revealing a small passageway.

"If you have any chance of finding what you're looking for, it won't be out here. He kept anything of value in the vault. Come." Fear gripped me as I glanced at the stone walls of the barely lit corridor ahead. Oliver's mouth moved, but I barely registered his words, for I was back at the chamber, back to that day.

The golden reflection of the lamps reminded me of the

dancing flames of the chandeliers. I could smell Stephen; I could feel the blade piercing my side. My hand grazed the spot. Breathe. Breathe. I remembered Drake's voice as he surrendered his human essence to save me. It wasn't until I felt Oliver by my side that I realized I was hyperventilating.

"Belynda, you're safe. Breathe. It's ok. Just breathe." Oliver held me as my mind pulled from the abyss of that memory.

"Are you ok?"

I nodded my head but was unable to find my voice. "I don't think you are. Let's go back."

"NO!" I managed to say. "Just give me a second." I peered at the stoned walls around us, and took a deep breath. *Get a grip of yourself, Belynda. You are safe. You are strong. Nothing can harm you now.* I chanted those statements like mantras until the terror of those memories dissipated.

"Go on. I'm good."

Oliver eyed me with skepticism but didn't argue. We didn't have to walk far before we reached the arched metal door. Oliver inserted the odd-looking key into the keyhole, and as he turned it, the door screeched open.

"I was very young when I last visited the vault. But I never forgot it." Oliver spoke as though his mind was somewhere else. Lost in the memory.

As he stepped into the chamber, lights came on and automatically illuminated the space. We were surrounded by shelves filled with artifacts, books, and manuscripts.

"What's all this?"

"My father's treasures. Things he managed to collect of value throughout the years. Some from this world, some from others."

"I thought the reliquary held all the secrets and artifacts of the guardianship."

"We're talking about my father... he never liked to share much."

"Did the other council members know?"

"I don't think they did. At least not the ones who would have questioned him."

"What is this?" I stared at a glimmering orb that looked like a giant moonstone.

"If I had to guess, I'd say it's a Scrying Orb. Used for Spheromancy."

I stared at Oliver in complete astonishment.

"Like divination? Seeing the future?"

"Based on what I know, yes... or the past."

"And you actually think it works? I mean, if it did, don't you think he would have used it to know his future?"

"I guess, but this is just an instrument. Perhaps my father didn't have the gift to access the orb's power."

He didn't, but maybe...

"Do you think that I...?"

"Try it."

"I don't know..." I stared at the shimmering white ball, perched upon a silver pedestal. Afraid...

Hesitant, I reached for the stone and placed a hand on its cold surface. I glanced at Oliver, who watched expectantly.

"Is anything happening?"

"Nothing out of the ordinary." Then, I had an idea.

"No... wait. I see... your mother and Tyrus. I see them together... Happy."

"Seriously?" He pulled my hand away from the orb. "Who's being childish now?" he rebuked me while I laughed.

"I'm sorry. I couldn't help myself, really."

"It wouldn't kill you to show a little respect."

"I said I was sorry..."

"You know I'm right. You have no respect for any of this." He gestured to the items in the room, then. This was no longer about his mother.

"You forget I didn't grow up knowing about other realms and magic like you did. Forgive me if I find humor in some of it. Maybe it's my way of coping with the truth." He stayed quiet, his anger dissipating.

"You're right. I'm sorry. God, I'm starting to sound like my father."

"No, you're not. Just be patient with me. It will take me a while to fully wrap my head around all this supernatural stuff."

Oliver smiled, and I knew we were ok.

"Do you want me to try again?" I smiled. He rolled his eyes.

"Just concentrate this time. Think of the future or something."

I placed my hand back against the cold stone and glanced at Oliver.

"How do you know so much about this anyway?"

"I don't. It's just a guess. Now concentrate." I rolled my eyes but did as he said, staring intently at the shimmering orb. There were strokes of white marble in the stone that appeared to dance after a few minutes. Flickering back and forth. Mesmerized, I immersed myself in the void of white clouds. I was lost in the smoke, hot specks of burning ash landing against my skin.

Almost in ashes, the forest line before me dissolved as the Dragon's collided and crashed to the ground.

Frozen and silent, I stared at the harrowing scene unfolding before me. I saw myself in the center, frozen, as the beast pierced my middle with its pointed tail. Rage consumed Drake before he turned and took the beast's head. I stared past the solid planes of his naked back as he held me to him.

"You promised..." I heard myself say — I had heard it before. I watched myself reach to stroke his face.

The lifeless girl in front of me begged him with her final breath.

The ashes swirled in surrounding waves of white and gray, obscuring my sight. The waves moved and I felt water course around my feet as the voices sang.

"Only in death... only in death..." the wind whispered.

I BLINKED A COUPLE OF TIMES, staring at the orb in front of an anxious Oliver and me.

"What happened? What did you see?"

My death. I had seen my end just like in my vision. But I wouldn't speak of it. Couldn't. There was no point in having everyone carry the heaviness of that burden. I would live with it myself until the day came.

"Belynda." Oliver pressed. "Are you alright?"

"Yes. I'm ok. Sorry." I smiled reassuringly.

"What did you see?" he asked again with concern.

"Nothing."

"Nothing?"

"Nothing!"

"I don't believe you. Tell me." He pushed.

"Really, I didn't see anything I don't already know. I saw Drake. In the lake. Frozen..."

"Is that all?" He wasn't going to let it go.

"Yes, Oliver. Now drop it. Does it look like I need a reminder of my choices or his suffering?"

"I'm sorry. I only wanted to know what it was like. What it felt like."

"Like having a nightmare." I offered. "Now, can we see if we find anything on the Ora Tablets?"

. . .

THE CONTENTS of the Radcliff's vault had offered no light on the Ora Tablets. Still, it sparked curiosity in Seymor when I mentioned it that evening.

"I will speak with Oliver and the council to run an inventory as soon as possible."

"Perhaps, I can come with you when you do?" my mother asked, clearly intrigued. "I think we might find something worth offering amongst the relics there." Perhaps intrigue wasn't what motivated her, but determination to get Drake back.

"I'm sure that will be fine."

As I LAY in bed that evening, I rummaged through the future the orb had offered. It was the same as my vision, only I witnessed the dream through my own eyes. The orb made me a spectator to my demise. Whatever promise Drake had made to me weighed heavy on him, but it seemed important that he kept that promise. *Vital*, almost.

As sleep took me, a voice far and forgotten cooed, cradling me in my slumber.

"Only in death... only in death."

No AMOUNT of magic in the world could change my view. Mondays were still the worst. I was only glad there were a couple of months left to endure before graduation. Lily sat at one of the picnic tables under the oak tree and waved at me.

"How was your weekend?" I asked, taking a seat across from her.

"It was ok. Had practice Saturday. What about you?"

"The same. Nothing exciting. Went to Oliver's yesterday."

"Yeah, he did mention it, but I was tired. Did you guys do anything fun?"

"Oh, nothing much. We did some fortune telling, the normal stuff."

Lily laughed.

"Yeah. I guess I didn't miss much then." If only she knew how far from the truth she was. While it was her mother's decision not to bring Lily into the guardianship, I wasn't sure I agreed with the choice. Look what it had done to me. A part of me thought she was better off not knowing, not having to worry about this whole other world. However, a more significant part of me recognized it would make things much easier for us all if she knew. It would undoubtedly help her understand why Ben suddenly changed so much and decided to end things with her. Finally, she could understand why Oliver and Ben had drifted apart and why he and I had grown closer. It would undoubtedly stop her pestering comments about Oliver and me and her notions that I had a thing for him and vice versa. But for now, we had to respect her mother's wishes. Lily would know when the right time came, according to her mother. Whenever that was... I had no idea.

"No, you didn't miss anything, actually."

Ben walked across the lawn and didn't even glance our way. However, I didn't miss Lily's lingering stare, following him until he disappeared into the main building.

"Notice any change?"

"No. He's still brooding and cold. Won't talk to me or anyone. He hasn't been the same since Oliver and his dad's accident."

"Give him time. He will come around." I lied. That would likely never be the case for Ben. He despised us; he blamed us for his father's death, and I guess I *was* partly to blame. But he had betrayed Oliver's friendship and what little trust I had given him. Siding with Stephen made him just as guilty for what had happened.

"I don't know what hurts more... Ben's indifference or seeing him and Oliver. It's like they want to kill each other at times. They almost took to fists Saturday after football practice."

"They did? Oliver didn't tell me." Then I recalled I didn't answer his calls all day Saturday.

"Oliver doesn't share much. You should know him by now." She was right, but somehow, I felt our bond had breached that wall.

At lunchtime, Oliver brought over a lunch tray as he regularly did. I picked up a sandwich from the tray as we sat at the back of the cafeteria, away from prying ears.

"Where is Lily?" Oliver asked, taking a bite of his pizza.

"Doing make-up work for last week. By the way, she mentioned something happened between you and Ben on Saturday. Why didn't you say anything?"

"Because nothing really happened."

OLIVER

Ben tackled me to the ground with more force than was necessary for the game. A part of him wanted nothing more than to plunge my face into the ground, and I was ok with that because a part of me wanted to hurt him just as much. For betraying me, for being such a coward, but above all, for blaming me.

"You forget it wasn't just your father that died. Mine did too."

"Do not pretend to care. You fail to recall that I was there. I know whose side you took." Ben pushed me, but I would not fight back. Not

here. Not with everyone staring. He was sworn to secrecy under the covenant, as was I, but I still had Seymor to answer to. Even if the guardianship laws were abolished, there were still rules to abide by. One was, without question, to steer clear of any confrontation with Benjamin.

"You know nothing of how I feel, and yes — I chose the right side. The side of justice, no matter the cost. Unlike you."

I shook my head, attempting to dispel the memory of my discussion with Ben.

"Really. Nothing happened. We said some things, but that was it. I walked away."

"What did he say?"

"The same as always. Ben's angry and trying to take it out on the world. He blames me for my choices. Perhaps I was at some fault, but not for helping you."

"I know it's hard not to blame yourself. I do it too. Constantly. But the bottom line is it didn't have to get that far. Stephen crossed the line the second he sent that man to attack me at the fair, then by kidnapping Celest and — let's not forget — committing murder. We both know I would be rotting in the cemetery now if it wasn't for Drake."

"I know. Trust me. I'm not blind like Ben is. I wouldn't have gone against my father if it wasn't for knowing the kind of monster he was. I lived with it myself."

"Don't let Ben get to you. He's angry like you said. It's easier to avoid him. School is almost over. Soon he won't be a problem anymore."

"I don't know... I think Seymor should keep a better eye on him. He's bound to secrecy by the covenant, but he's angry and unbalanced. He could bring about a lot of trouble if he opens his mouth just to piss them off."

"They have enough power and connections to deal with him if it happens."

"It's still a risk."

"Maybe. But why worry ourselves about it?"

"I guess. Though Tyrus feels the same way, and the instincts of that man are never wrong."

"Has he brought it up to Seymor and the council members?"

"He's given his opinion, but most of the council thinks Ben will abide by the covenant. Seymor is giving him the benefit of the doubt."

"Seymor is wise. I'm sure he has reasons for not keeping a tight rein on Ben."

"I hope so."

BELYNDA

I was glad that Seymor arrived on time for dinner. Lately, it was rare to have him sit with us.

"When will you be taking the inventory at the Radcliff's?" I asked as I took a bite of meatloaf.

"Tomorrow. Felsia and I will head up there, and Ren will meet us."

"Will everything be taken to the reliquary?"

"That's where it belongs."

"And Samantha and Oliver are ok with that?"

"Oliver understands, and Samantha thinks it's for the best. I would go on a limb to say she seemed rather pleased to get them out of the house."

"She has no ties to the guardianship; I'm sure having them

under her roof reminds her of the life she was forced to endure with that monster. I pity her." My mother added.

"Have you and Celest found anything else on the Ora Tablets?"

"We have the ritual carved. Celest is searching for some items and ingredients we're missing. The delay we are foreseeing is finding the perfect offering."

"I hope you find something of worth tomorrow."

"I hope so too. It would mean moving ahead with the ceremony much sooner than expected."

It had to work. If not with the Ora Tablets, then some other way; we would soon figure out how to give Drake back his human essence. I had seen him in my dreams and in the Scrying Orb, returned to his human form. I was no longer afraid of being unable to keep my promise.

"You can leave your plate. I'll do the dishes." Celest offered.

"Are you sure? I don't mind."

"Yes, don't worry. I'll give her a hand." My mother offered.

"Good, then I'm off to shower and possibly start the book on the Earth Realm. Goodnight."

AFTER MY SHOWER, I did something I had been too afraid to do for the past year. I brought out Drake's things from the back of my closet and placed them on the bed. The few items still had a trace of his scent. I smelled the collar of one shirt, and it felt like breathing for the first time. His scent swam around my head, slipping into my very soul. I put on the t-shirt and climbed into bed with the large book that had been resting on my night table.

'Abryas: The Earth Realm.' Strangely enough, this was the Realm from which the legends of the leprechaun sprung. I smiled. Was nothing a myth anymore?

Mountains covered the Realm; rolling hills and lush forests were home to the legendary gnomes, pixies, goblins, and trolls. However, it was the house of the Elves who ruled Abryas. The Elven house was ranked by King Herod and his Queen Leiwen. I allowed their strange names to roll off my tongue; it was weird to say them out loud, knowing they were real — or at least I hoped they still were. The portals to the realms had not been opened in centuries, so there was no telling how accurate the information was. According to the book, the Earth Realm was always at conflict with the Wind Realm.

Abryas was known for its prosperous land filled with green meadows, vibrant wildflowers, and forests full of ancient trees. The royal court was described as powered by magic. A mystic beauty, the book detailed, where ancient magic and rituals filled the air, and the lands themselves whispered the secrets of centuries past. The royal house brimmed with a sense of mystery, imbued by a magical energy that flowed through the Realm.

I knew nothing about the Elvin people, but the book described them as strong and loyal to their leaders, families, friends, and the land itself. They took pride in their realm.

One of the depicted images was of a Cave Gargoyle: an amphibious humanoid creature that inhabited the deep dark dwellings of the Earth Realm. They often guarded secret artifacts; their thick, scaly skin was almost impenetrable, and their long, sharp claws could slice through the toughest rocks. In the image, the stones hovered above the Gargoyle's grasp, creating lighting. The book said nothing about it, so I wasn't sure if it was a power they possessed or a depiction of one of the artifacts it usually guarded.

I was surprised to learn that Dragons weren't exclusive creatures of the Fire Realm.

Abryas apparently had Earth Dragons: powerful, wise, and

ancient draconic creatures providing sage advice to those who dared befriend them.

Then, there were the fascinating spirits of Earth. These beings inhabited the depths of the Earth Realm, apparently made of pure energy. While invisible to most creatures, the spirits can be seen by those who can alter their spiritual eyes. These spirits of Earth possessed powerful magical abilities which could help them manipulate and shape the atmosphere of their domain, creating powerful storms and shaking the ground beneath them. Their weakness was shiny objects. *Gems.*

As I read, I marveled at the realization that this was real and not some fantasy book I had picked up for pleasure.

The book offered an illustration of Ishtar, a sandy desert. There was also an image of the lowlands, the graveyard of the gods, where giant statues were erected in honor of the ancient gods.

I PLACED the book back on the night table and sat by the window, thinking of the millions of people out there living their lives, going about their days without a clue of what was truly out there. Unaware of the other worlds and creatures they thought only existed in myths.

For the first time, I truly understood the importance of maintaining the secret covenant. Humans were not ready to know the truth. If the veil between them were to be breached, no covenant in place could keep the lie from the human world at bay for long. And it was my duty to ensure that the portal to those realms remained closed.

I wasn't sure how much of that remained in my power. The fates had predestined my demise at the hands of that Dragon. If that was my fate, it could only mean that a breach was unavoidable, and I wouldn't be around for long to contain it. Whatever Isabel had foreseen long ago for my destiny was no longer in the fate's plan. Yet I didn't care what happened to me. My only unfinished business was to give Drake back his human essence. Perhaps he was never meant to make such a sacrifice for me; maybe I had been destined to die that day in the council chamber by my father's hand. It almost seemed ironic that Drake, a fire creature, had sacrificed himself to save me, only to have another Dragon claim my life.

At that moment, I understood the depth of the promise I had forced him to make. I could not allow him to sacrifice himself for me again. No matter what happens, I would make him keep that promise.

3

FIRE AND ICE

THE BUS HORN RESOUNDED IN THE distance. I stirred under the covers, unable to dispel the relentless noise. As I opened my eyes, everything cleared as the sunlight slipped through the windows. I was late. I jumped from the bed and scurried to the window in time to watch the bus leave. *NOOO.*

"Good morning, sleeping beauty." Seymor sat at the counter with his laptop, sipping his coffee.

"Not so good for me. I just missed the bus."

"You can take my car, if you like. I'll ride with Felsia."

I thought about it but then remembered what a nightmare student parking was.

"I'd rather get a ride, if you guys don't mind. The school is on the way to Oliver's house anyways."

"Sure,"

"Seymor, are you ready? Good morning sweetheart." My mother said, kissing my cheek.

"As ready as I can be. But we're stopping along the way to

drop her off in school."

"I can take her," offered Celest as she stepped into the kitchen. "I saw the bus leave. I figured you'd need a ride."

"WHAT ARE YOU UP TO TODAY?" I asked Celest as I clicked in the seatbelt.

"I'm heading to Northampton. I need to get some items for the ceremony."

"From a magic store?"

"Yes. A friend of ours owns a shop there."

"Does her name happen to be Selene?"

Celest faced me, surprised.

"Yes! Did Felsia tell you?"I laughed.

"No, but it's a small world. I've met her before. She sold me the ingredients I needed to cast open the portal."

"I'm sorry you had to carry such a burden on your own."

I knew speaking of the past would reopen those wounds.

"That's in the past. You did what you thought was best to protect me. So, forgive yourself already, and let's forget it ever happened." I offered, and she smiled in agreement.

"You've become so wise." She said, smiling.

"I don't think I've had much choice." With the kind of life I had, I was forced to grow up. "I wish I could come with you." I added. I hoped she didn't think I was using the moment to guilt trip her into agreeing.

"I don't know... I'm not keen on the idea of you missing your classes."

"I'm doing well in school. Besides, we only have a little over two months to finish. We're not even into finals yet. All we do is plan for prom."

She glanced at me, still undecided.

"Please..." I begged. Anything to get out of school, even for a day.

"Oh... alright. I don't think it will do you any harm. But you must promise to make up any work you miss. Agreed?"

"Cross my heart."

FELSIA

I couldn't remember the last time I had stepped foot in Radcliff Manor. It seemed like forever ago.

The butler opened the door, guiding Seymor and I into the parlor. Tyrus stood guarded, like usual, by the window while a very impatient Ren sat with Samantha.

"About time," Ren remarked without preamble.

"Ren. Samantha. Our apologies. We ran into a bit of traffic." Seymor offered.

"That's alright. Ren was just telling me about the process your team has made at the chamber."

"Yes. We're getting there. You should stop by some time; I'll show you around." Samantha smiled politely at Seymor's offer, but it was clear she wouldn't be calling for a tour anytime soon.

"Felsia, it's good to see you."

"You too, Sam. Is Oliver around?"

"No. He's already left for school."

"Oh, that's right. I completely forgot."

"Well, shall we do this today?" Ren interrupted impatiently.

"It's always nice to see you too, Ren." I teased, merely to annoy him. Tyrus smiled behind him. "Hi, Tyrus..."

"Felsia." He dipped his head once.

"Right this way, please." Samantha let us into the vault. The Manor had undergone many improvements since I had last seen it. Stephen's study was precisely what I had expected, his pretentious personality reflected in every surface. The partition of a bookshelf panel revealed a barely lit passageway. Ren whistled as we stepped through the archway.

"I'm not surprised that he would keep a place like this. He was a narcissist; no offense, Samantha." Ren spewed without thinking.

"None taken." While she didn't seem offended, she did look mortified. After all, the man had been her husband.

When Samantha inserted the key and pushed open the door to the vault, we all froze. Belynda had mentioned the vast collection but seeing it with our own eyes was different.

"Well, I did not expect this." Ren was the first to enter the chamber, and the further he walked, the more display cases came to life, lighting up along his path.

"Did you know about this, Sam?" Seymor asked, clearly stunned.

"Not about this." She gestured to the collectibles. "We were never allowed in here. We never thought."

"It's ok, Sam. Seymor only asked as protocol. No one blames you." I added. She forced a smile but was clearly uncomfortable, likely by Ren's earlier comment and now Seymor's assumption. Though I knew he hadn't meant anything by it.

"If you guys don't mind, I'll give you some space to work. Please call me if you need anything."

"Thank you." It was Seymor who answered this time, seemingly ashamed for upsetting her.

Seymor and Ren moved separately, inspecting, and cataloging the items along the shelves.

I was glad for the space. I didn't have to search long before I found it. When Belynda mentioned the Scrying Orb, I had to see it for myself. The gift of sight was the one ability I had inherited through my guardian blood, and it was perhaps why Belynda was special herself.

My future had been chosen. Preordained by the fates. I had envisioned it countless times since the moment Belynda released the fire-bound. I accepted my fate, but I had to see what the Orb could offer.

Hesitantly, I cupped my hands around the cold stone and watched the pearly lines sway the deeper I stared. *You know what I want to see. Show me.* I compelled the Orb with my thoughts.

The moving ripples parted like crashing waves before I found myself in the woods. Staring at my surroundings, I felt my destiny solidify. Everything would be as I had foreseen. All would be well. Things would occur as they were destined to.

"Show me."

This time, the words escaped my lips. The lines on the Orb blended and twisted once again until I found myself in an ashen forest, watching her life slip away as the fire specs fell against her cream skin. Heaviness settled on my chest. My visions were right. The Orb had revealed nothing else except what I already knew. It was not a sacrifice. An end for a new beginning was the answer. Not a sacrifice. I understood, then, what Isabel had meant all those years ago. It wasn't the end. It couldn't be.

"Felsia! Felsia!" Seymor's voice rushed at me like a bullet train down a tunnel. I blinked, staring at my hand, and then at Seymor.

"Are you alright?" He asked, his face etched with concern.

"I'm fine. I'm sorry... I was curious." I admitted, but he didn't seem convinced.

"Felsia, you look like you've seen a ghost. I swear by the gods if you are lying to me..."

"I promise. I'm ok. I was just curious, but I didn't see a thing." He stared at me until Ren complained from behind.

"These things won't catalog themselves; you know?"

Seymor picked up his clipboard and returned to the back with Ren while I fought to swallow the knot lodged in my throat. No one could run from fate. We were no exception.

BELYNDA

As we entered the city limits of Northampton, I began questioning how much I was allowed to say in front of Selene.

"Does she know?"

"Not about the Guardianship," Celest confirmed.

"She doesn't know about this other world, yet believes in it?"

"Selene is one of many out there that don't need proof to believe that there is more."

"I guess a part of me always felt there could be more, but I was never inclined to follow those thoughts like she does."

"She's not just a believer," said Celest. "She has gifts too."

"What kind of gifts?"

"She's very intuitive and has an uncanny way of making people feel at ease."

"Yes, I noticed that" I recalled the woman's odd comments about my aura, "she said I had an old soul."

Her words hadn't made sense then, but they did now.

"Well, she wasn't wrong about that. Was she?"

"No. I just didn't know it at the time. I thought she was crazy."

Celest laughed as she parked in an empty spot outside the store.

"She's definitely not that."

"I know." I smiled, blushing.

Everything was exactly as I recalled. The chimes hanging from the door resounded, and we were assaulted by incense as soon as we entered. A second later, Selene appeared through the sun and half-moon curtains draped at the back.

"Celest! It's so good to see you." The woman floated around us, offering Celest a quick hug.

"It's been a while, I know."

"And who is this?"

"This is Belynda. My niece." Selene studied me with eager eyes, evidently trying to place the familiarity of my face.

"We've met, actually. I bought a few things from you last year."

Her eyes lit with recognition.

"Yes, yes. I remember you. You've grown a bit since, too."

I smiled politely.

"Come. Sit." She ushered Celest and me through the curtains to the back of the store and into a small, cozy nook filled with candles, crystals, and a scattering of Moroccan pillows.

I didn't know why, but I felt instantly at peace. Celest handed her a paper with the needed items while they chatted away. At the same time, Selene rifled through her cupboards and shelves, gathering an array of things. I leaned my head back against the pillows and pretended I was floating.

"Your light is blinding, child. Much brighter than when I last saw you."

Startled at the unusual remark, I sat bolt upright.

"Yes. We think she's special." Celest added, playing coy. She knew just how special I was.

"Would you like a reading?" The woman looked at me but then turned to Celest, as though silently asking for permission.

"It's up to her." Celest offered, watching me for an answer.

"I... I don't know. Yes, I guess." I held Celest's gaze for reassurance, but she gave a gentle nod of encouragement.

"I can step outside if you need me to." Celest offered.

"No, stay!" I exclaimed, and Selene laughed.

"Don't worry, child. You're perfectly safe here. They're just cards." She pulled a worn deck from a drawer in the small table at the center of the room, then motioned me to join her. I took the chair next to Celest while Selene shuffled and parted the cards before me, separating the deck into three portions.

"Pick one stack." She instructed, and I gestured to the one to my right. She gathered the stack in her hands.

"Pick another one." This time, I chose the one to my left. She picked it and placed it under the one already in her hands. Collecting the last bundle at the table, she added it last to the pile. For a moment, I had the urge to laugh, yet remembered Oliver's reproachful expression as he told me about my lack of respect for the supernatural, and I instantly sobered. Though as I watched Selene spread the cards around the table, I realized my need to laugh wasn't for lack of faith or belief. Ironically, I knew there was nothing she could tell me about my future. I knew the road I was destined to take until my very end.

I glanced around the scattered cards and instantly panicked. The death card... Selene must have clocked my expression.

"Don't worry about this; nothing is ever as it seems."

If only that were true.

"The Ace of Wands is upright in your house," Selene said, "this could mean a fresh start. Perhaps a decision will take you down this new path. Perhaps a trip, far away... Yes. That's it... Accepting this path will align you with your highest self. You must trust the process."

I nodded, completely lost but nonetheless intrigued.

"However, getting to that path will be a struggle for you. The nine of swords is reversed in your immediate future, usually indicating an event that triggers inner turmoil. Dark thoughts and negative emotions will weigh down on you. You must stay strong, no matter what difficulties you face. You must believe there is always hope."

I had hope, hope that I would help Drake. Beyond that... I knew where hope would lead me.

"The wheel of fortune smiles upon you. The fates are working for you: life cycle changes, destiny, karma, a turning point. That's your future, so do not despair. The elements will all align to help you."

I froze when she mentioned the elements, but Celest was unbothered, so I relaxed.

"Finally, here is the one everyone fears, but I assure you it is without reason. The death card usually symbolizes a spiritual transformation. An end to a new beginning." As she said those words, something clicked. An end with a new beginning... that is the answer! Not a sacrifice. *Is that what my death meant? A new beginning? For whom?* Isabel had sacrificed herself for a purpose, yet my vision of my death seemed far from a sacrifice.

"I don't understand. What exactly will be ending?" I asked.

Selene rested the cards on the table and motioned for my hands which I offered without question. Tracing her fingers along the lines in my palms, her eyes took on a faraway look.

"What is it?"

"It's strange. Your lifeline is short here, yet not here." She touched the line on the opposite hand. "I've never seen anything like it."

That was my cue to stop, and from the look on Celest's face, she agreed. I pulled my hands back.

"You asked what is ending, but I'm afraid I have no clear answer." Selene continued. "However, I see a new you. So perhaps some parts of you must die to allow the new to be reborn."

"I'm sure by dying, you mean shedding habits and such, not in the literal sense?"

"Yes, of course! It's unlikely that the card represents a physical death." I didn't miss the added 'unlikely', but who was I kidding? I had expected nothing less. Selene had only reaffirmed my worst nightmares. I didn't have much time left.

CELEST WAS quiet for most of the ride back, yet it wasn't awkward. It felt nice to lose myself in my thoughts.

"I hope you're not giving much thought to what she said."

"No. Not really." *I lied.* The truth was I didn't want to think about it, but her assertions had solidified my worst fears. *Death was coming.*

IT WAS a quarter past nine in the evening when Seymor and my mother arrived. She peeked into my room as I lay in bed reading more about Abryas.

"Can I come in?"

"Yeah." I sat up and placed the book on the nightstand. "I was just reading."

"Celest told me of your little adventure today. Are you ok?"

"It was... interesting. But I'm ok. I've decided that whatever the future holds, it's in the hands of the fates." The words rang true, then. There was no fighting against the path that was destined. If death was the price the fates had set, then I was certain no magic could fight against it.

"What about you? Did you find anything useful today?"

Mother smiled, and I felt my heart soar with hope.

"You did, didn't you?" I probed, and her beaming smile was my confirmation.

"Let's just say your father was a very resourceful man."

"What did you find?"

"We will offer the realms as a sacrifice."

I was lost. How could they possibly offer the Realms? They were worlds; it was not a tangible offering easy to provide. The confusion must have been evident on my face. "Not the Realms themselves, of course." Mother amended. "We will offer a piece of each," she added as if that clarified everything.

"A piece of each Realm? That makes no sense. Do you have a piece of each?"

"We have the Waters of Isilium from the Water Realm. Winds from the hills of Tirsia. Blue Fire from the burning forests, and the Sands of Time." Her face lit up with wonder and veneration as she spoke.

"Do you actually have these objects?"

"We do. The items are invaluable, without a doubt. If they are not the perfect offering, I don't know what will be. These are rare relics, indeed. Each one has a unique power. We don't know how they came into our realm, even less into Stephen's hands, but if they are the real relics... no other offering will compare."

I had so many questions, but only one seemed to take priority.

"What sort of powers?"

"We only know of their value through the manuscripts of the legacy. No one has ever seen them work, but the Waters of Isilium are said to enable anyone to breathe underwater. It's a well-guarded gift from the Merfolk people." Remembering what I had learned about the Water Realm and the Mer people, I could not imagine how their sacred water had come to be in the guardianship's hands. The realm was said to be impenetrable.

"I assume the special winds are from Upherya?"

"They are. The legends say winds of Tirsia allow you to fly."

"How exactly do they do that?"

"They give you wings."

I was at a loss for words.

"But the powers are only temporary." Mother added. Of course, there would be a catch, but regardless, it was incredible.

"What about the Blue Fire and the Sands of Time?"

"The Blue Fire is from Drake's Realm. A rare gift indeed. The blue flame allows you to shape-shift."

"Into a fire Dragon?" With this revelation, my mind added another list of questions for Drake, to ask once he returned.

"You can take any form with the Blue Flame." Mother explained.

"Is it possible that the Blue Flames could allow him to shift into his human form?"

My mother considered the idea.

"Perhaps, but it's not a permanent solution. It would only allow Drake to shift temporarily. He would have to consume Blue Fire, and like I said, it's rare. Even in his Realm."

For a moment, worry consumed me. What if Drake shifting in my visions was only a product of Blue Fire? What if I hadn't been able to give him back his human essence?

"What is it?" my mother asked, perceptive of my sudden shift in mood.

"It's just I hoped we could succeed with the Ora Tablets... After seeing him shift in my visions, I allowed myself to hope that this was the way forward. But now... I don't know. What if what I saw was only thanks to Blue Fire?"

My mother touched my face and smiled warmly.

"It will work..." She whispered, so low I looked up to her.

"You don't know that."

She smiled candidly and dabbed away a tear that had escaped my eyes.

"Belynda, we all have a purpose in this world. Mine is to be here now. I can feel it in my bones; this is what is meant to be, no matter the sacrifices we must make along the way. There is always a way, I promise you." She seemed so passionate in her conviction that I wanted to believe her. I had to hope I could offer Drake his human form before Death claimed me. I smiled.

"Tell me about the Sands of Time," I said to lighten the mood.

By the time I went to bed, my head was flooded with images of magic waters, winds that gave me wings, Blue Fires, and Sands that according to my mother, could freeze time. But the prospect of moving forward with the ritual made my heart soar. According to Mother, if all went as planned during the next full moon in three weeks' time, we might finally use the Ora Tablets and hope for a miracle that could return Drake to his human form. However, now that the possibility of getting Drake back was tangible, I faced another conundrum. His mind-reading abilities would be problematic if I planned to keep my visions secret. I had to find a way to block my thoughts from him...

FELSIA

The full moon was almost upon us, and still, I could not find the words to put onto the paper.

"Are you even listening to me?" Celest asked, tugging me from my muddled thoughts.

"I'm sorry. What were you saying?"

"Nothing of importance, but I'm starting to worry about you. You've been acting strange lately. Is everything alright?"

I wished I could confide in her, but the burden of the truth was not hers to bear.

"I'm just worried about Belynda. I hate to think how devastated she will be... she's lost so much. If we fail..."

"She knows this is a long shot."

"Even so. Haven't you seen her lately? How happy she looks. It's like she's come back to life over the past few weeks."

"Belynda is a lot stronger than we think. You know she is."

I did know that, but my heart ached knowing the suffering she had yet to endure before the end.

"Your friend was right about one thing. Her path will not be easy."

"There's something you're not telling me. You've seen something. A vision?"

"The Scrying Orb," I confessed, though she didn't need to know the Orb had only confirmed what I knew already.

"Felsia, you're worrying me. What did you see?" The terror in Celest's eyes was enough to make me pause. No... I couldn't say more. This was not the time.

"I only saw what the Orb wanted me to see, but I understand now why Isabel's prophecy spoke about sacrifice."

"I don't understand. What are you saying?"

"I'm saying that it won't be easy. Belynda's destiny. The road she must follow is filled with pain and sacrifice. Belynda and others will have to make sacrifices along the way, all for the greater good." I spoke. It was all I could say, and I prayed it was enough to satisfy Celest.

"What can we do to help her, Felsia? There is so much resting on her young shoulders. I feel useless. It's not fair."

"I know that too, but I made the mistake of leaving her once, hoping we could change her fate, and we both know how that turned out. We cannot stop the ripples of time. I don't know what's to come, my friend. But I feel better knowing she has you by her side to help her through it."

"She has you and Seymor as well," Celest added with a forlorn look.

"She does." And she would have Drake. I knew that much.

BELYNDA

The house was bustling, and it had been for the past few weeks while the final preparations for the rite were enforced. Even though the assistance of the other council members was unnecessary, Seymor insisted on their presence. He argued that coming together, after so many years, would help solidify the true purpose of the guardianship. It would demonstrate the guardian's true purpose: to help and assist the realms rather than punish, deceive, or enslave. Ren stayed at the town's Inn, for which I was grateful as that man was as insufferable as they came. Although Seymor found Ren's candor to be a quirk of his personality, I was sure many council members disagreed, gaging by the constant looks of displeasure between them. Sylvie, who had been a champion of my cause last year, had arrived two nights ago from Denmark and had been offered a guest room in our home. Despite my brief encounters with Sylvie, she was polite and kind, and made a pleasant addition to the already full house. Sylvie was also much younger than Celest and my mother, perhaps in her late twenties, so it felt nice to have someone closer to my age to speak to.

Oliver and Tyrus had also helped. Oliver offered land on his estate where the ritual could be done privately, since the chamber was still out of commission, while Tyrus oversaw security and provisions for the day. I visited Oliver's place, too, using it to my advantage by practicing mastering the elements in private.

With everyone busy, it became my mission to use the time I still had to do something useful. Under strict supervision from Seymor, alongside my mother's guidance, I familiarized myself with the contents of the sacred book and the spell to open the portals to the realms.

Thanks to my mother's help, now I, too, felt confident in preventing Drake from reading my thoughts. While my practice remained in theory, since we had no one with Drake's ability to test it, my mother was confident it would work. All it took was a simple knot spell. I touched the endless knot sigil weaved into my bracelet. Its purpose was to prevent others from stealing my energy, while also stopping them from reading my thoughts without consent. Or so I hoped.

A part of me felt guilty for even considering such measures against Drake, but it was necessary. My mother had understood the necessity to keep my thoughts private. Still, it was for his own preservation. I couldn't allow him to see my fate and live with it day after day. If he knew, I would never get him to make that promise, then all of this would be for nothing. He would sacrifice himself again without a second thought. The dreadful images of my death invaded my thoughts more often now. Every day that passed, I questioned how much longer it would take. That was the real reason why I had to block myself from Drake. I didn't trust my mind to prevent the awful reality from surfacing.

THE SITE at Radcliff Manor offered for the ritual was perfect and secluded, but it also required some work: overgrown shrubs covered the space in which the circle would be cast. I called on the earth, sensing the ground's energy flow from the soles of my feet and course through my body. By my will, the vines parted and coiled, twisting away from the ground. Its tendrils became curtains, which hung from the surrounding tree branches.

"Impressive..." Said Oliver, leaning casually against one of the ancient trees that graced his property.

"It is, isn't it?" I willed the last of the shrubs out of the way. Left behind was a perfectly manicured circle of grass, surrounded by trees and curtains of vines. I smiled at Oliver, proud of my work.

"What else am I useful for?"

"We're done for the day. Go home. Rest. Save your energy for tomorrow."

That was the problem. I couldn't keep still. *This was it.* This was the moment I had been waiting for, yet I felt consumed by anxiety rather than excitement.

"I don't know if that'll be possible."

THE SUN WAS an orange ball of fire resting low on the horizon as I watched Oliver drive from my porch.

"How did it go?"

Startled, I spun to face Sylvie who sat on one of the porch swings.

"It went well. The grounds are ready. Everything looks perfect."

"You're nervous."

"Am I that obvious?"

She frowned, and I slumped beside her in the swing.

"You can control water, earth, and wind," she said, "but you must stop trying to control everything else around you. Time and destiny are their own masters. They will play the game as they please. Remember that."

I pondered Sylvie's words, and a wave of peace washed over me.

"You're right." I sighed. "But how do I shut my mind off?" Tilting my head back, we rocked slowly.

"I'm afraid I can't help you with that. I usually resort to wine to numb my thoughts, but you're not of legal age so I strongly advise against it." She added, and I couldn't help but laugh.

"Yes. That's definitely a hard pass for me. I think I'm going to turn in early, shower, and try to get some rest. See you tomorrow?"

"Bright and early." She confirmed as I turned to the front door.

I was glad for the reprieve from the visitors. In this night, of all nights, I needed peace and quiet. I needed the comfort that came with snuggling under the warmth of my covers while wearing Drake's shirt. If all went according to plan tomorrow evening, it wouldn't be the fading scent of his shirt lulling me to sleep, but his arms instead. I grinned, imagining his smoldering silver eyes.

With my eyes closed, I visualized every step of the ritual. Although my mother had insisted initiating the rite herself, my role was not any less vital. Retrieving Drake from his frozen prison at the bottom of the lake and ensuring discreet transportation from the mountain to Radcliff Manor, where the rite would take place, would be no easy task. It had been so long since I had faced him in his Dragon form. I feared what being subdued by my gifts may have done to him. *Would he hate me for it?* I had to remind myself that, beneath it all, was Drake. He had been capable of reasoning once before; this time would be no different. He would do what was necessary for us to be together again.

STRANGELY ENOUGH, I slept like a rock, eventually awakened by the bustling in the house and the waft of brewing coffee. Seymor sat at the kitchen counter with an older man. I had seen him several times in the past few weeks and remembered his face from the chamber. He had been another member of the council to vote against Stephen, alongside Ren, Sylvie, and Seymor.

"Good morning."

"It is a good morning indeed." The older man said, seeming genuinely pleased to see me.

"Belynda, this is Victor. I don't think you've ever been formally introduced."

"It's a pleasure to meet you. I never had the opportunity to thank you for your support. I'm glad you're here today."

"The pleasure is all mine, my dear." The older man extended his delicate hand, and I took it politely. "I'm glad I get to be a part of this. I'm an old man; this is the first time I feel like I'm fulfilling the true guardianship's purpose."

Seymor patted the old man on the back and smiled with candor.

"You and I both, my friend. You and I both..."

"Is my mother up already?"

"I don't think she's gone to bed yet," Seymor said with a worried frown, and I felt my throat close with panic.

"Is everything alright?"

"Everything is as planned. Felsia is just being Felsia. Over effective, over dramatic. The usual."

"She's going to be exhausted tonight."

"Don't worry about your mother, child. She knows what she's doing."

"I know."

SYLVIE AND CELEST were placing boxes into the back of the SUV, but my mother was nowhere in sight.

"Need a hand?" I asked, leaning on the porch rails.

"Those were the last of them. Even with the full moon, we'll need the extra light." Celest said.

"You slept in," Sylvie noted.

"I did. Surprisingly. Have you seen my mother?"

"I'm afraid you just missed her," Celest said, closing the trunk. "She's gone to the Manor to ensure everything is in place, so I'm afraid you won't see her until this evening."

"Seymor said she didn't sleep."

"She's just being overly cautious. Did you need her?"

"No. I just wanted to check in on her and make myself useful. I'll feel restless until it's time to leave for the mountains."

She placed her hand on my cheek with a warm smile.

"Everything is under control, but I suggest you find something more appropriate to wear. It's freezing in the mountains, especially during the nighttime. Sylvie and I are heading to the Manor, but I will return with Oliver and Tyrus to collect you."

I watched the sun light filtering through my bedroom window disappear. As promised, the large cargo truck pulled into the driveway at dusk, and I watched Oliver help Celest out of the vehicle.

As I reached the landing, Oliver smiled.

"Someone's ready." He commented, mocking my hiking boots and snow jacket.

Celest disappeared down the hall towards her room, returning a few moments later wearing a thick jacket and boots.

"She would be a fool not to. It will be freezing up in that mountain."

I smiled back at Oliver, who only wore jeans and a shawl collar cardigan. He rolled his eyes.

"I'll survive. Let's go. The roads are slippery. It will be a slower trek up the mountain road with the cargo truck."

Oliver was right.

TYRUS HAD to take the winding roads with extra care. Most of the snow had melted, and the trails were extra slippery. The truck's headlights pierced through the eerie darkness of the desolate mountains.

"Once we reach the next bend, we'll have to pull up and continue on foot. That's as close as we can go." Tyrus added, breaking the silence. We could not even get a car close to the lake, let alone this truck. We knew a small hike was unavoidable.

As I jumped from the truck cabin's warmth, the piercing cold felt like prickling knives against my body. I glanced at poor Oliver, who cursed as soon as the cold air hit him.

"Here." Tyrus pulled a jacket and a pair of boots from a compartment on the side of the truck, handing them to Oliver.

"Thanks. I owe you one."

Tyrus smiled and patted him on the back.

THEY LED the way through the snow and the maze of trees, breaking the darkness with their lanterns. If Tyrus hadn't taken the time to visit beforehand and map the area, I wasn't sure we could have found our way.

"We're getting closer. The tree line breaks up ahead."

My heart pounded with each step I took.

I froze as we broke out of the trees and into a clearing, staring at the sight ahead. The crystallized lake extended beyond us: a pale blue blanket illuminated by the shimmering glow of the full moon.

Celest took my gloved hand, urging me forward.

"We shouldn't delay. They are waiting for us."

I approached the glimmering edge of the crystalized lake, glancing back towards my companions who thought it best to keep their distance.

Kneeling on the frozen surface, I removed my gloves. I had practiced changing the water's form countless times, but still hesitated. My eyes scanned the icy rock, following its pearly surface until halting at the center, where I knew Drake resided. My palms burned against the cold ice, but I did not care. It was a small price to pay.

Calling on the element wouldn't be enough. After all, it had taken a spell to ensure the ice remained solid during the warmer months.

"Water that binds. Water that moves. Break away on the white surface moon. Water that yields and shields. *Aqua cedit et scuta. Regressus. Regressus. Regressus.*" A crack spread across the ice like a thunderbolt over the lake's surface. Fissures broke as roots extended across the solid mass before me. Chunks of ice separated down the path illuminated by the moonlight, and my eyes followed expectantly as the center of the lake imploded.

Shards of ice, water, and smoke erupted towards the night skies with the force of a vortex. A creature's cry erupted. Drake was stealthy, his lethal shadow breaking free from the icy prison. He moved fast through the wall of water and smoke, disappearing in the veil of darkness above the trees.

"Drake!" I cried, warm tears streaking down my face. I began to panic as I studied the skies and no longer saw him. "Come back! Please." I begged.

The cracking ice drowned my voice, but I knew he could hear me. The question was, would he listen?

I heard the whoosh of the wind before my eyes caught his

silhouette. Drake circled the clearing before taking a sharp turn and diving directly toward me.

"Belynda, move!" Celest shouted from her spot by the edge of the woods. But I couldn't. I wouldn't. I was frozen like the shards of ice that remained broken over the lake's surface. I closed my eyes as the whistling wind touched my face.

"She's out of her freaking mind!" Oliver's angry voice, and the fact that I wasn't dead yet, gave me the courage to open my eyes, and as I did, my breath caught in my throat. The beast rose before me, wings expanded to their full length as they fluttered behind him. He was here, finally free, and suddenly I couldn't breathe.

I fell to my knees, overcome with emotion, and for the first time in a year. I didn't hold back; my pain, my frustration, and my happiness tore from me as I sobbed. Right then and there, I promised myself never to imprison him again. Willing or not, it was still a prison. If we failed tonight, I would make sure he returned to his home where he could be free, no matter the cost. I wiped my face with my sleeve and smiled while looking at him.

The Dragon turned towards the lake, a rain of fire erupting from its deadly mouth without warning. Whatever ice remained over the lake's surface disintegrated in seconds. In a way, it felt like he was slaying his own demons. Though if that's how he felt about his prison, how did he feel about his jailor?

"Forgive me..." I whispered, and the beast roared, ceasing his fire. As the hot bubbling waters settled, the Dragon turned towards me for the first time. Fire still clouded his silver gaze.

"I missed you," I whispered, extending a shaking hand toward him. My heart felt heavy as he roared again, lowering his head to my outstretched hand. I didn't miss the battle in his eyes. Drake was in there. The fact I was still alive was proof of that. But it wasn't without effort. The fire fought for control.

"I know you're still in there. Somewhere..." I whispered, and the beast heeded. "It might be possible to regain your human form."

The beast's head snapped back, and I saw it again: the fire in its eyes as golden flames fought with silver until the latter was the victor. I knew it the moment I saw myself reflected in his shimmering gaze. He nudged his nose against my trembling hand.

"Drake..." The knot lodged in my throat was unbearable. I found release as salty tears touched my lips, and the warm breath of the beast warmed my skin, drying the tears away. "There is a possibility it won't work." I admitted, moving my fingers over his warm skin, and he grunted beneath my touch. "If we fail... I give you my word this won't happen again. I will make sure you are free. That you return home." My throat constricted at the idea of losing him again.

The Dragon backed away, returning to its full height. It flapped its wings, sending dirt spirals around us. I knew that he understood every single word and wasn't happy about it.

"Belynda, we need to go." Celest reminded me from afar. The beast lifted its head, regarding her for a moment with recognition. "Hello, Drake." Celest offered, and I could hear the kindness in her voice.

"I know you understand." I ran my hand over his peculiar skin, and he settled down once more. "We must get you to the site of the ritual. Everyone is waiting for you there."

A low grumble erupted from the back of the beast's throat. I wasn't sure if it was a response to my words or my touch, but he seemed pleased, so I continued. "We can take you there without the risk of anyone seeing you, but you have to follow us to the road's edge. Can you do that?"

The Dragon rose and propelled itself into the night sky.

"I think he understands." I said, turning towards Celest and the boys. "Tyrus, show us the way back to the truck."

We could hear the beast's wings whooshing above the tree-tops as it followed us to the road's edge.

Tyrus and Oliver opened the large metal doors of the shipping container as the Dragon landed near the line of the trees. The container was big, but Drake was much larger. Asking him to be confined to a metal box after releasing him from one prison didn't seem fair, but it was the only way.

"Drake, we need to get you in the trailer. I know it will be uncomfortable, but it's the only way we can get you there."

The Dragon flapped its wings and hovered at the trailer's entrance before landing on the ground. It placed its gigantic head inside the container before springing back with a loud roar, backing away to the line of trees.

"We didn't account for this." I turned to Celest. "He's still struggling to contain his fire element. I can't force him to get in that metal box."

"There is no other way. How else are you going to get him to the Manor?"

That was a good question.

"Well, he can fly, can't he?" joked Oliver.

"We risk exposure." Celest said, watching me with caution.

"What if it's the only way? If he stays low enough, flying just above the trees, he can go by undetected."

We all glanced at Tyrus.

"Don't look at me. But the way I see it, you won't be able to get him in there. So flying is his best chance. It's clearer up here in the mountains, but lower down there are cloud banks. If he can be guided, I trust that he can make it without exposing himself."

"He can do it. I know he can." I said, pleading with Celest.

"I pray to the gods he listens to you. If he is seen... I don't want to think about the mess we'll find ourselves in."

Tyrus and Oliver closed the doors to the container while I approached the restless Dragon.

"Easy. It's me." I raised my hands slowly and took measured steps closer to him as I spoke softly. "I will not ask you to get in there, but you must fly and promise to stay low. No one can see you, Drake. You know what the exposure of your kind means to the mortal world."

The Dragon huffed and without warning, snaked its long and stealthily sharp tail around my waist. Fear gripped my body.

"Wait. What are you doing?" I yelped, in full panic, but the beast ignored my pleas and gargled almost as if it were laughing.

The Dragon twisted the tail over his head and placed me on its back, right atop its spine, and wedged between the wings.

"Oh no... No. Drake... No!" I shrieked, though the last thing I saw was the horrified look on Celest's face as Drake propelled himself into the night. My cry of terror did not stop him. I felt the beast's power and muscles activate beneath me as it ascended. He soared higher until he passed the top of the trees and glided gently over the foliage. I clasped the spikes on its back, hanging on for dear life. I wasn't sure where I got the courage, but I didn't close my eyes. If he was allowing this, I had to be brave. At the very least pretend, even if I could feel every muscle in my body petrified with fear. The one thought that helped me breath, was knowing he wouldn't risk hurting me. The Dragon kept its body steady as the darkness surrounded us.

"Stay low, Drake. Find the truck, follow it."

The Dragon circled back above the forest's edge until spotting the truck in the distance. Once I saw the barely visible taillights of the trailer, I felt the tension slowly dissipate. Drake was in control. Drake was with me. He understood.

His warmth was so comforting, not even the sharp lashing of the wind against my skin bothered me up here. I rested my cheek against his skin and ran a hand over the edge of one of his wings.

"I missed you so much," I whispered, and the Dragon slowed. Once again, he circled back until we found ourselves trailing the truck's tail lights, maintaining a close distance. As we left the mountains, we found ourselves surrounded by a blanket of clouds. "Drake, we can't lose them."

He didn't circle back this time, so I prayed his sharp senses were enough to guide us in the right direction.

The moon was high in the sky as we watched the truck veer into Radcliff Manor. This time, Drake followed the path to the house as we remained above the arching trees. Without my guidance, he rounded the estate until the lights and the gathering below were visible. I held on tight as the Dragon descended, anchoring myself for the landing. Yet he was stealthy as its talons reached for the ground, and once again, the Dragon wrapped his tail around me, lifting me effortlessly from his back and placing me gently on the ground.

4
A SACRIFICE

THOSE GATHERED WATCHED DRAKE and I with genuine curiosity, yet no one dared move an inch. The only one brave enough to disregard the daunting beast was my mother, who pulled me into a hug.

"Mom, I'm ok." She was crying... "I promise I'm alright, really."

"I know you are. You are my strong girl; never forget that. I'm just a little emotional, that's all." She glanced at the Dragon behind me and smiled.

"Your highness," She said, bowing her head to Drake. "Thank you for keeping my girl safe. I know you will take good care of her."

The Dragon roared and extended its wings, an indication that he understood my mother's words. Hushed conversations began to erupt around the circle as those present appeared more at ease after my mother's exchange with the Dragon.

"It's almost midnight." My mother announced. "Please have him step to the center. We must cast the circle around him." I donned the black ceremonial cloak my mother offered me, before joining the council members in the inner circle.

Drake followed me into the circle, but he was restless. It was clear he still distrusted the guardianship and being surrounded by so many was not helping.

I ran a hand over one of his front legs.

"It's going to be ok. I promise."

The beast glanced at me momentarily before its vigilant eyes returned to the black cloaks surrounding him.

Lanterns hung from the trees around us while the moon bathed the circle with light now that it was positioned straight above us. Oliver, Tyrus, and Celest remained in the background outside the marked circle. The rest of the council members: Meerim, Thomas, and Felix, whom I had come to know, but not by choice, did not have an active part in the rite either. Having taken sides with Stephen, ensured they remained on the sidelines as witnesses only, a courtesy offered by Seymor. If it was up to my mother, they would not be here. Yet my say in the matter would have weighed on Seymor's decision, so I had chosen to stay neutral. A part of me agreed with him that making allies was better than keeping enemies, although witnessing Drake's uneasiness made me question if it had been a good idea at all. If I remembered the roles they had played, then Drake must too. He grunted each time he caught any of their stares, confirmation that he had not forgotten nor forgiven their actions.

REN WALKED AROUND with my sword in hand, casting the circle's boundaries. My mother stood in the center, facing the large flat rock. The one I had fun shaping and manipulating to serve as a working altar. The candle and incense were lit before she added the salt to the water, used to consecrate the circle. Ren and my mother walked clockwise around the circle's perimeter, cleansing the ground that would seal the rite space.

Like a composed dance, Seymor took a stand and faced the North, calling on the element of Air.

"*Te voco protectorem et spiritum specularum Aquilonis, prodire testem, hunc ritum custodi et custodi. Attende voluntatem meam. Omnia grata.*"

Sylvie followed, standing on the East to call on the element of Earth.

"*Te voco protectorem et spiritum specularum Orientis, testem prodire, hunc ritum custodi et protege. Attende voluntatem meam. Omnia grata.*"

The older man, Victor, took a stand and faced the South, summoning the Fire element.

"*Te voco, protectore et spiritus specularum austri, prodire testor, hunc ritum custodi et custodi. Attende voluntatem meam. Omnia grata.*"

Drake's fire roared to life as his element was invoked. The Dragon flapped its massive wings, but no one dared move as the circle was cast. I laid a hand upon his front leg, beckoning Drake to stay, to remain in control. Once again, I witnessed the fight behind his eyes as he struggled with the darkness warring inside of him.

"You can do this. I need you." I whispered. The beast within him retreated as his eyes returned to the light silver, I'd come to know so well. "That's it. I'm here, Drake. I'm right here." I saw myself reflected in his eyes as I took my place facing the West. I was tasked with invoking water, for it had become my strongest element.

"*Te voco, protector et spiritus specularum occidentalium, prodire testor, hunc ritum custodi et custodi. Attende voluntatem meam. Omnia grata.*"

. . .

TYRUS, Celest, and Oliver took cover as the elements crashed over the skies, descending outside the circle's boundaries while we remained protected within.

Once again, I was witness to the grandeur of the elements and how nature became wildly unbound by their presence. It was nothing less than magical. The skies flashed silver with every roar of thunder, yet with every strike over the trees above us, Drake's restlessness increased. Following my mother's request, Ren took my stand on the West quarter, so I could return to Drake's side. Darkness appeared to be taking over him; neither my words or my touch seemed enough to stow the fire within him.

"We need to hurry..." I begged my mother. "He's fighting it, but I don't know for how much longer."

Mother unveiled the stone tablets which rested on the altar. Behind her, a cauldron scorched above the fire pit.

"By the fire and the stone," To the cauldron, she offered the crystals, herbs, and powders which had been gathered. They had one purpose... to unlock the Ora Tablets.

Once the tablets were revealed, they would be ready to accept the offering... that was the first challenge, ensuring the first part of the spell worked. If we failed to ignite them, it all would be over soon. I held my breath as my mother spoke to the Ora Tablets.

"*Per ignem et lapidem elementa spectantur. Secreta et desideria innumerabilia, tribue nobis. Cedant nostri vocati. Invocamus iubemus. Potentiam tuam nobis revela.*"

"*Invocamus iubemus.*" All voices became one as all who were present began to chant.

"*Per ignem et lapidem elementa spectantur. Secreta et desideria innumerabilia, tribue nobis. Cedant nostri vocati. Invocamus iube-mus. Potentiam tuam nobis revela!*" This time, Mother's summoning was stronger.

"*Invocamus iubemus.*" The united chant made the hairs on my arms stand.

"*Per ignem et lapidem elementa spectantur. Secreta et desideria innumerabilia, tribue nobis. Cedant nostri vocati. Invocamus iube-mus. Potentiam tuam nobis revela.*" Mother continued.

Thunder roared above us, swallowing the foreign words.

"*Invocamus iubemus.*"

The stone altar exploded with light. Everyone shielded their eyes, and the silence that followed was soon replaced by gasps. My mother had done it. She had unlocked the Tablets. The bright stones shimmered above the altar like blinding beacons, even the Dragon at my side seemed lost to their luminosity.

"Bring the items forth." My mother called to Seymor first, who had stood post at the North. He approached the altar, and from his robe, offered a small leather-bound pouch.

"Winds from the hills of Tirsia."

Sylvie followed, offering a small brass box, which she, too, placed on the altar.

"Sands of Time."

Victor followed, pulling the dark Cerulean-colored stone from his vest.

"Blue Fire." As he placed it on the altar, the Dragon roared in protest, recognizing the relic from his Realm.

At last, I approached the altar and brought forth the delicate glass bottle I had been entrusted with.

"Waters of Isilium," I whispered before returning to Drake's side.

"The price is a human vessel; in return, we offer the power of the Realms. Waters of Isilium with its influence of change and immortality. Winds of Tirsia, providing the powers of freedom and hope. Blue Fire is the catalyst of life over death and the Sands of Time granting eternal wisdom. Accept our offering. Grant the fire-bound your hallowing blessings." The blinding light swallowed the items as my mother placed each above the tablets.

This was it. The moment we had all waited for. I glanced at the Dragon beside me, stroking his scaled face. It would be alright. The tablets had to accept the offering.

"*Suscipe sacrificia nostra. Largire ignem ligatum benedictionis tuae. Occupare sacrificium.*"

The eeriness that followed was haunting as even the elements retreated from their assault on the circle's boundaries.

"*Occupare sacrificium!*" My mother called into the night. "*Suscipe sacrificia nostra. Largire ignem ligatum benedictionis tuae. Occupare sacrificium!*"

"*Occupare sacrificium!*" she bellowed a final time, and the altar shook. The trembling of the ground extended beneath us all.

"NOOO! You will accept this sacrifice!" My mother screamed.

I stared in horror. She had warned me this might happen, but I never believed it would... The tablets were breaking. It was over. All was lost.

Everything quivered: the earth, the trees. Even the wind seemed to whistle, then intensified as the ground parted beneath the altar. We had been so close... I held on to Drake, overcome with terror. *I had failed him...*

"I give myself. Take what you need..."

"NOOO!" Seymor's cry stifled my mother's voice and I stared in confusion as he rushed to her side in time to catch her slumping body.

Time suddenly halted as I fought to understand the scene unravelling before me.

My mother lay on the ground. Seymor and Ren were by her side while Victor and Sylvie released the elements. A frantic Celest fought against Oliver and Tyrus to force her way into the circle, all while the blinding light of the tablets took hold of the Dragon, who I clung to with my life. He became a blinding star, and I, too, brightened as I couldn't let go. Anchored to him, we were swallowed by power. Lost in the light. For a moment, I felt the absence of his presence, but then a warm hand reached out to me and caressed my face.

"Go to her." The strangely familiar voice beckoned through the mist. "Say goodbye," the voice beseeched.

I took a step back, then another, until I was no longer melting into the light gripping Drake.

"Belynda!" The terror in Celest's voice brought me back to my senses as I finally understood what was happening.

"NOOO!!!" I rushed to my mother's side and gripped her cold hands, but my eyes could not believe it. This woman with graying hair and fragile hands was not my mother, yet I recognized those eyes of sapphire-blue. She stared back at me, drained of life and youth.

"Mom." I cried. She offered me a weak smile.

"Don't be sad." Her words only made me weep harder.

"You can't leave me. We haven't had enough time." I pleaded.

"Do not be afraid... only in death will you find your true powers."

"Mother, please. Don't speak."

"My beautiful child. Be strong. Don't fear for me. This is how it was meant to be. I'm ready."

"NO! Give her back!" I screamed as her eyelids fluttered closed. "You cannot have her!"

Without thinking, I turned to the Ora Tablets and allowed the Earth's power to fill my body. Draining, consuming everything around me. I became one with the Earth, the trees, the stones... My body vibrated, as did the ground around us. I fed off its energy, capturing their life force until something inside of me snapped. Power exploded from my body, raw and unyielding, targeting the tablets until nothing was left of them but dust. The light dissipated before me, but as it did, my legs gave up, and my world sank into darkness.

DRAKE

A stroke of light painted the horizon as I stared out the window to watch the last of the council depart. Someone else in my place would offer, at the very least, a sliver of gratitude. Yet I couldn't. We wouldn't have found ourselves in this mess if it weren't for the guardianship and their rules. No, I couldn't forgive so easily. Doing so felt like a betrayal of Isabel's sacrifice and to the loss of my home, and all the family I had ever known.

But would she understand? I wondered this as I glanced at her sleeping form.

The price her mother had paid for my sake, for hers... I knew it was mainly for Belynda's sake, but nonetheless... I didn't deserve it. I wasn't worthy of her sacrifice. Perhaps I had been destined to live with the monster: an atonement for all the wrong I had done. No. I couldn't forgive. Couldn't forget... but why did it feel wrong? *You know why...* the monster inside jabbed at my misery. *You don't want her to hate you...*

I sighed and moved to her side. Sitting at the edge of her bed, I traced a finger over the moon-kissed skin of her cheeks.

For an immortal, time is abundant. There are no fears, no expectations. I've lived within the boundaries of a world that consumes creatures far more lethal than I and survived. I have seen darkness and welcomed it. Fire lives in my veins: eternal, indestructible, yet one look at her is all it takes to bring the monster to its knees.

She rested. Unconscious. Fragile. Her face as pale as the moon's surface. My dark heart blazed as she stirred. Slowly, her eyes fluttered, adjusting to the glare of the bedside lamp until focusing on me.

With dreamy eyes, she lifted a hand, and her fingers traced my jawline.

"If this is a dream, I don't want to wake up." Her words warmed my soul, and I smiled, taking her hand, and bringing it to my lips.

"I don't think your imagination is as good."

Her face lit up with realization, and tears filled the corners of her eyes.

"Drake?" she whispered. Pushing herself off the bed, she locked her arms around my shoulders.

She wept as I placed my hands on her back, breathing in her scent and allowing it to saturate my being. I knew it before, and I know it now. My immortal life meant nothing without her.

"I missed you so much." She slurred; her face pressed against the collar of my shirt.

"I have died a thousand deaths every day since I last saw you. I would do it again if it meant I could be here with you."

This was my truth. I could not live in a world where she didn't exist. She pulled away, and I tucked a loose strand of hair behind her ear.

"What happened?" She swallowed, and the haunted look in her eyes tore something inside of me. "My mother?"

How could I tell her that the Ora Tablets had taken what they needed from her mother, and all because of me?

The soft knock at the door was my salvation.

"I'll be right back." I touched her chin and blurred to the

door. I stared at the woman standing there, but I didn't know what to say. Instead, I stepped aside and allowed her to pass. After all, she was the reason I was standing here now.

"MOM!" Belynda bolted from the bed. Again, something primal stirred inside of me at seeing her so undone: the need to protect and comfort her, but this was her mother's time.

She cried, clutching to the woman, who had aged a decade overnight. I had listened in on their theories, but they had yet to understand why the tablets had spared her. Her mother believed the Ora tablets had taken only a few years of her life because the items offered held significant value. The others had a different theory. They believed that Belynda had infused the tablets with the Earth's power, and somehow, this forced them to yield and comply before meeting their end. I felt particularly inclined towards this idea, considering the tablets were made of stone and likely Earthbound.

"I'll leave you." I offered, closing the door behind me to allow them some privacy.

The foyer was quiet, but the steady breathing from the living room confirmed I wouldn't be alone. A young woman sat on the couch with a book in her hands. Sylvie was her name if I recalled correctly. I cleared my throat, making my presence known, and she jumped. She clutched the book to her chest like a shield, as if that could somehow save her from the monster now standing before her. Something inside of me recoiled.

"My apologies. I was on my way out." I added curtly.

"But it's freezing outside. Come take a seat in the kitchen. I'll put on some coffee."

I hesitated but decided to follow, slightly amused that she would think the cold was of any concern to me.

"It's been quite a long night. I couldn't sleep." She rambled as she moved about the kitchen, maneuvering one of their modern artifacts. She was nervous; perhaps a human wouldn't have sensed it, but I could. The uneven rhythm of her heart and her breathing was an easy giveaway.

"I saw Felsia on her way up. I take it Belynda is awake?"

"She is." I offered.

"Here. Sit." She said, placing a steaming cup on the high table. Reluctantly, I took a seat.

I drank the strong liquid in one go, and as I placed the cup on the table, I caught her watching.

"I'm sorry. I didn't mean to stare. I just... I realized what I said earlier about it being cold outside, with you being... you know."

"A dragon." I offered, but my intention was clearly to mortify her.

"Yes. I'm sorry. That's going to take some getting used to. But I'm glad... *we* are glad you're here."

The woman didn't know when to keep quiet, but I decided I liked her. She was foolish but brave.

"Thank you for the coffee." I forced a smile and left the kitchen with human speed. But once I was out of her sight, I blurred to the front porch, and closed the door behind me.

The sun had yet to fully break through, but I was restless. The fire in me had dominated my senses for far too long to be content with slumber. My Dragon ached to be released, to take to the skies and spread its wings.

The monster had been a companion during my time in the Dark Realm. I had grasped its darkness as an escape from what had been lost... a way to survive. But he had been free to rule, then, to devastate as he saw fit. For the past year, the Dragon had been a prisoner by my choice, and now the monster remained beneath the surface, whispering, and clawing at my reasoning. Begging to escape. I couldn't fight it. If I wanted to remain here, I had to find a way to appease the fire. Otherwise, I would be consumed, and we would all burn.

The overgrown grass whipped against my chest as I ran through the field toward the woods. It was probably not the best choice to release my fire, but the exposure of a flying Dragon would surely be more difficult to contain in a human world.

My hands shook as I broke through the edge of the trees. The roar that tore through my lips roused the sleeping forest. It was a warning for each creature as they scurried away to safety.

I removed my clothes, and the black lines came alive as ripples of smoke broke over my skin. The darkness seeped from within, and I found relief as the fire exploded in my veins. I allowed my fearless companion to take a breath.

Igne Draconis… Easy, I beckoned the darkness as my claws dug for control into the roots of the trees. Finally, I could breathe.

Branches snapped in protest as the wings extended high above, thrusting into the Air, and breaking through the foliage of the trees. It was liberating. I no longer felt like I was suffocating inside my own fire. The monster needed this. We needed this. I needed it…

The sun rose over the horizon as I glided stealthily above the trees. I returned to the mountains, where I could soar through the still-white peaks unseen.

There was no trace of my frozen prison, only the agitated waters of the lake and my distorted reflection as I flew above it. Now that my soul companion was free to soar, I could think. It was easier to make him yield when I surrendered to his wants. Easier to make him listen. Yet the creature's restlessness bit back every time I thought of returning to human form. It wasn't ready, so I freed myself and allowed him unrestricted passage.

When the sun began to set, I knew Belynda would be worried.

As I returned to the forest edge, the monster felt sated. It meant I could hide the blunt edges of myself. It meant I could be human, perhaps even summon a speck of gratitude towards the old woman.

I slid the pants on and stared at the dusk as I did the buttons on my shirt. Belynda would be worried. An explanation was in order, but would she understand?

How could I describe the battle inside of me? She knew this world was not made for someone like me, but my human essence had made it a possibility for me to stay. Now I wasn't so sure it would be safe. For her. For those around her. For this world... not until I could ease the fire and retake control of my human side.

BELYNDA

Celest and Sylvie prepared dinner and refused to let Mom lift a finger, even though she looked as healthy as a horse. The years taken had clearly aged her, but her spirit was intact. Celest, Sylvie, and my mother filled in the pieces I had missed. Apparently, as the Ora Tablets disintegrated to dust, I had lost consciousness while my mother regained hers, and Drake returned to his human form. Sylvie seemed to be the most enthusiastic narrator, and I knew it was because she was in awe of Drake. She told me that no one had saw Drake move, but somehow, I was in his arms before I reached the ground. My mother said he never left my side when he carried me from the circle. He refused to let go of me in the car, pinning me to him as if I were his anchor. She said he was in a rather odd mood; every attempt to speak to him was met by the same brooding silence. Eventually, they gave up and allowed him to carry me to my room, where he had remained since earlier. No one dared disturb him.

Drake's behavior was unusual. Something was wrong. The

Drake I knew wouldn't have stayed away, not when I had just gotten him back. No one said a word, but I knew the question on everyone's mind. *Where was he?*

Had he stayed by my side because of some mistaken sense of duty? Was it possible he hated me for his time spent under the icy surface of that lake? Did he regret saving me?

We sat in the living room, and I kept my mother company. However, her constant attempts to ease my mind had me realizing that she thought it was I who needed the comfort and reassurance, not the other way around.

She reassured me he only meant to give us space. He would be back. However, hours passed, and slowly I began to lose my mind with worry.

I excused myself and stepped outside to the porch, attempting to conjure up reasonable explanations for his absence. However, each theory made my heart sink further.

My mother was alive, and I had Drake back. However, our victory felt hollowed, for nothing had been gained without loss. Years were taken from my mother's life, and Drake... appeared the same, but he wasn't. Something had changed in him as well.

5

BREATHING FIRE

T WAS STRANGE, BUT SOMEHOW, I sensed his presence before I noticed him standing on the porch steps. He blurred before my eyes, taking me from the swing and into his arms.

Breathing was always easier with him; the way he held me, the way his eyes worshipped my face with longing... it eased away my worries. He didn't hate me.

He pressed my body against the verandah while his eyes smoldered, analyzing my face as his fingers grazed the nape of my neck.

Leaning in, his lips burned a trail from the base of my ear to my chin; his nose skimmed against my neck and up my cheek. My lips parted with a sigh as his thumb sketched over them, my body was resurrected by his touch. I was burning alive, became a bursting bright star, the moment his lips brushed mine. They probed, and I welcomed them. Tasting him, breathing his fire in, and becoming undone. His lips were urgent, and I didn't hold back. His hand anchored me in place as he pressed his hips against my thighs, but it wasn't enough. I clutched his shoulders as he grasped my behind, positioning me on the verandah rails. With ferocious need, his lips struck against mine as his tongue plunged deeper. His fingers dug into my cheeks, squeezing me tight and pulling my core flush against his firm primal need. A needy heaviness began to form between my legs as he pressed himself between my thighs. It was a need foreign to me, yet devastatingly familiar beneath his touch. My fingers dug into his shoulders as my hips rocked against him. I wasn't sure what I wanted, but I needed more. All of him. My hand reached between us to trace the strain in his pants, and as my fingers grazed the stiff ridge, he roared.

"Fuck love..." He broke away, holding me at arm's length. His jaw tensed and his eyes closed as though in pain. "I'm sorry." My breathing steadied, and his eyes found mine as the pain subsided. "Forgive me. I got carried away." He whispered, his voice raw with desire.

"Hey..." I placed a finger under his chin. "It's ok."

"Is it?"

"Always. With you, always."

He kissed the back of my hand, then my lips.

"You deserved better. An explanation, at the very least, before being ravished."

"I don't need explanations. I just need to know that you're ok." He took a step back and eased me off the rail.

"What if I'm not?"

My heart dropped as I searched his eyes.

"Whatever it is, we will figure it out. Together." He turned away, unable to meet my eyes, and for the first time in a long time, I was afraid. "Speak to me. Please." I begged.

"Not now. Your family knows I'm here and they're growing impatient."

"They can wait." I couldn't. All my earlier worries had flooded back to haunt me.

"Later. I promise." He whispered. He leaned down to brush his lips against mine and the corner of his lips turned up into a smile.

DRAKE WAS RIGHT; Celest, Sylvie, and my mother sat in the living room. While they attempted to appear casual, their unease was noticeable even to me; Drake must have sensed it a mile away.

"Good evening." His deep voice boomed, echoing throughout the room. My mother smiled in greeting, as did Sylvie. Celest was the one who stood and came to us.

"I'm glad you're back. I'm happy to see you are in better spirits."

She must have been referring to the catatonic state he was in this morning. He offered an apologetic smile.

"It's good to be back." Instinctively, he pulled me closer to his side, and every woman in the room smiled, making me blush.

"It's been a long night and an even longer day, it seems. I'm sure you'll want to rest. Why don't you let Belynda attend to your dinner? We can catch up tomorrow."

"I would like that. Thank you." Drake glanced at Celest, before his eyes shifted to my mother. I had the distinct feeling he wanted to say something, but decided against it. "After you..." He excused us and followed me into the kitchen.

"What do you call this?" He asked as I piled his plate with lasagna.

"You've never had pasta before?"

He speared a piece with his fork and graciously took a bite. He savored it and smiled before taking another.

"I've never tasted anything like it, so I can't say I have. Not back then, anyhow. Things might be different now." I didn't miss the way his brow creased with his last remark.

"I'm glad you like it. Would you like something to drink? Perhaps some wine?" I offered, aware I wasn't old enough, but there was no point in depriving him.

"Only if you'll join me,"

I laughed, but he just stared.

"I can't. I'm not of legal age to drink spirits."

He dropped his fork, and I glimpsed the amusement flash in his eyes.

"That's absurd."

"That's the law." I smiled. "Besides, I don't care for it, honestly." I poured him a glass and enjoyed how he inhaled the red liquid in one fluid movement. "I take it you've had wine before?"

He placed the empty cup in front of me.

"In theory, yes. But truthfully, the taste I remember was more like pond water. This was exquisite."

"Would you like another one?"

"No. Thank you. You intoxicate me enough as it is. One of us must keep their wits."

I laughed, momentarily forgetting the worry still weighing on my chest. As usual, he was trying to distract me, and it was working. I watched him eat every last mouthful of food. It had been a long year, yet he hadn't changed a bit. Not physically at least, though I knew he had in other ways. He wasn't going to talk about it. Not yet anyway. I wondered if I looked different to him.

"What is it?" He asked, catching me staring.

"Nothing. You haven't changed."

He smiled.

"The advantages of immortality. But you have." His voice warmed as he reached a hand over the counter to study a strand of my hair. "Your hair is much longer." He abandoned the strand to run a finger down my cheek. "Your skin is pale, which tells me you haven't been out much," he said this with a sadness in his tone. "Yet you've never been more beautiful." His fingertips now traced my bottom lip.

I held his wrist and gently bit the tip of his finger. His eyes changed so fast, darkening to black before returning to their usual grey hue.

"Are you ok?" I asked, as his eyes scanned over my face.

"Do you have any idea what you do to me?" He said. The depth of darkness oozing from him made my core ache.

"Tell me," I whispered. I probed the darkness and it felt exhilarating. The energy around us shifted, just like earlier outside. He growled as he stood, creating distance between us.

"I need a shower." He said and vanished before my eyes. Not so easy...

I trailed upstairs, and the water in the bathroom was already running. I was certain he could hear me, but I didn't care. If I was going to die, I would make sure I didn't take a single second of our time together for granted. Even if that meant going against his ridiculous notion that my virtue was something to be 'preserved'.

Curiously, I reached for the doorknob, and it turned beneath my fingertips... *should I?* Before I could talk myself out of it, I pushed open the door. The bathroom was filled with steam, but I could make out his reflection against the mirrors in the mist. His back was to me, hands splayed against the walls while the scorching water fell down his back. Surely, he could hear me, sense me... but he didn't move, so I pushed the door further, and as some of the vapor escaped, I froze. The tattoos on his back and arms were no longer inked on his skin but swirled around him like wisps of moving black sand.

"Drake…" His name was a whisper on my lips, but it made him turn. His eyes were black like before, and it took them a moment longer to return to normal.

"Belynda, go!" He commanded, but I didn't move. I couldn't. Instead, I closed the door behind me.

"I'm not going," I stated, and his eyes morphed to black again, simmering under the surface, before returning to grey. I took a step closer to the glass door that separated him from me. He didn't move. It was as though he was gathering every ounce of self-control to fight whatever demon possessed him.

"Belynda…" He warned with a growl as I reached for the frosted door. As I pulled it open, the water droplets bounced off him and onto me, but he remained still. Hesitantly, I outstretched a hand towards his shoulder, and the black sands recoiled. Slowly, they dissipated altogether, and solidified against his skin. His grey eyes pierced through me, but there was no battle inside them now, just desire.

I ran my hand down his arm, and the fire in his eyes burned. He turned to me, and I became lost in the glistening arc of his chest, his stomach, and his rigid sex, which was taut like the rest of his granite-sculptured body. He caught where my eyes had rested and growled.

"Belynda, I beg you. Go."

"No." I challenged.

"You're clearly overestimating my self-control."

I trailed a hand over his chest as the water cascaded down the smooth surface of his skin. The muscles on his abdomen tightened as I continued the path down. I searched his eyes, but the fire burning in his gaze only encouraged me further. Hesitantly, I allowed my fingers to glide over the hard yet smooth surface of his taut sex, and for the first time, the fire creature shivered. I took it as encouragement, and closed my hand around him, caressing his length with a firm but gentle grip. Drake inhaled and threw his head back.

I was inexperienced on all accounts, but every sound he made was confirmation that I was on the right path.

"You will be the death of me." He growled as he pulled me into the shower, covering my body with his. He pressed me against the wall.

"I'm all wet." I giggled, but the humor was lost in the fire that blazed behind his eyes.

"Are you wet?" He whispered in my ear as his fingers found themselves on the crease between my thighs. I gasped, and my legs almost buckled, but his body held me in place. As his fingers stroked and teased the fabric of my pants, his rigid member rubbed against the wet shirt clinging to my stomach.

"Drake…" I gasped as a strange pressure intensified inside of me.

"That's it, love. Let go." He claimed my lips, drinking from my mouth as the water cascaded over us. "Come for me." His teeth grazed against my chin, and my world exploded. I rocked against his hand as the last pieces of myself shattered.

I felt sated, and breathless but he was restless. His naked body towered over me, pining me with his unyielding desire. He wasn't finished. I placed my hand around the smooth skin of his sex once more, and he lurched in my hands.

"You want to know what you do to me?" He whispered, bracing his hands against the wall. "Like this…"

He grazed my ear with his teeth and placed one of his hands over mine, tightening the grip as he thrusted into my hand. He let go, but I kept a firm hold as his drives increased. "You drive me crazy. All I want is to bury myself in you. Break you. Claim you as mine in every possible way." His breathing peaked while his thrusts increased with every branding word. "I am no saint, love," he whispered against my lips. "I will fuck you in every possible way, and you will scream my name when I do."

My core pulsed at his brazen words. The promises they held. They urged my boldness, so I allowed my fire to coax him.

"Is this what you like?" I teased, tightening my hand around him and gliding firmly up and down his length. He sucked in a breath and grabbed onto my shoulders, anchoring himself to me.

"Yes, love. That's it." He threw his head back as his thrusts became urgent, unraveling. "Belynda..."

My name became a grunt, rooted deep in his chest as the last of his thrusts brought him over the edge. He rested his head against mine and kissed my lips tenderly as he jolted in my hand and over my stomach with the last of his resolve.

I LAY in the warmth of my bed, relishing in the memory of every touch, breath, and word shared between Drake and me. He had ignited a fire in me that still burned bright. My heart skipped as he walked into my room with his devastating smile. An immortal god, shirtless, with his hair still dripping wet. I couldn't look away, but the distance became unbearable as his eyes met mine.

"I think it might be best to put the guest room to use tonight." He said, staring out the window.

"Who's being absurd now?" I said, and his eyes shifted to me.

"I think you've exhausted every ounce of self-control I possess for the night. So, unless you want to see the house destroyed and possibly burned to ashes, you will not fight me on this."

There was no humor in his words. I stood up and walked to his side, clasping his hand, and pressing it against my cheek.

"Will you tell me what's wrong? Please?"

"I'm losing control of my fire. Every time I'm in human form, I feel it clawing inside me, trying to break free."

"I know after the Dark Realm it was difficult for you, but was it like this?"

"No. This is different. My fire lived free in the Dark Realm. It was an effort then to adjust to my human form and the emotions, but it's different now."

"How…" The suffering etched into his face made me frown.

"Belynda, all those years, I was able to live in my fire form… this time, it wasn't free to roam. It was imprisoned under a wall of ice. Dominated by its opposite element. It doesn't want to be confined, not even to a human body. It gets restless." He sat on the windowsill and ran a hand through his wet hair. "If I cannot give it what it wants, it will consume me. It could be dangerous… for you, for everyone. If I can't give it what it wants, I could expose our kind to the human world, and that is the lesser of the evils…"

I couldn't think clearly. I was no longer worried… I was terrified. What did this mean for us? I kneeled in front of him, wrapping my hands around his shoulders, and burying my face in the crook of his neck.

"What can we do? There must be a way. I will do anything."

He pulled back, bringing his hand to gently caress my face.

"The only way is for me to return home. To Druleska." His words were whispered, yet it felt like thunder ripping deep into my soul and tearing me apart. I tried to hold back the tears, but as they pooled over my cheeks, Drake wiped them away. "It would be temporary. Only until it's contained and sated, then I will return. I promise."

"NO!"

"There is no other way."

As I stared into his eyes, everything became clear. Selene's words recited in my head, puzzle pieces coming together.

The Ace of Wands upright in your house—a fresh start. A decision. A new path... far away...

The Nine of swords reversed in your immediate future... turmoil. Dark thoughts, negative emotions.

The wheel of fortune... life cycle changes, destiny, karma, turning point.

The fates had rolled their dice, and once again, the verdict was against Drake and I. Our destiny was mapped out, shaped, and bent to their will. Free will was merely an illusion, and I could do nothing to change it.

The death card—a spiritual transformation. An end to a new beginning. A new you. Some parts of you must die to give way for the new to be reborn...

My path was clear. Death was coming for me, and I would face it head-on. There was no point in running. No point in hiding. *The Fire Realm awaited.*

"You're not going without me." I stared into his eyes with resolve. "If you go, I do too."

He stared at me with an odd expression.

"You would come with me?"

"Yes."

His eyes seared through me.

"Belynda, you don't owe me anything. I saved you, and I would do it again."

Did he think I would follow him out of guilt? I pulled out of his arms.

"It hurts me that you think you're worth so little to me, as if I would only follow you out of responsibility. Seriously, Drake."

"Please don't be mad."

"I'm not mad; I'm disappointed that you still can't see the truth. I cannot live in a world where you don't exist. Where you go, I go."

He stared into my eyes, and a spark of hope flickered on his face. He tugged me to him. His body was so warm, it melted the chilling fear creeping into my heart.

"I will speak with my mother tomorrow."

"How do you think they will take it?"

"It doesn't really matter. I will open that portal with or without them, but something tells me they will understand. After all, it's for the benefit of protecting the covenant."

"I meant how will they take the news of you leaving?"

"I'm sure they won't be happy, but it's my decision."

"What about your life here? School, your friends?"

"Drake, you're more important. School will be over in a few weeks, and as for my friends... Oliver will understand. And Lily, well that's more complicated, but it will all work out. I know it will."

His eyes studied my face with adoration before his lips found mine. Lifting me from the floor, Drake sat me on his lap as his fingers made trails from the base of my spine to the back of my neck. His lips melted with mine in a fluid dance, each of us giving and taking. I giggled as I felt his arousal beneath me.

"Are you sure you still want to take the guest room?" I asked, teasing. I stirred over him, and he growled and kissed my neck.

"Yes, now more than ever. But first I'll stretch my wings; it will be safest if the fire is quiet before I return."

"Is that why you were gone today?"

"I should have explained before leaving like that. I'm sorry."

I kissed the corner of his lips, and smiled.

"I'd rather you behaved badly more often."

He ground his hardness against my behind, bit my shoulder, and then stood despite my protests.

"I better go now before it's too late. Leave your window open. I'd rather not have to explain my late adventure. Not tonight, at least."

"Go. Please be careful and remember to stay low."

"I will. I promise." He kissed my cheek. "Don't wait up." He said before leaping effortlessly from my window and disappearing into the darkness.

Now that he was gone, I allowed myself to cry: for his pain, the thought of leaving my home, but most of all, I cried because I realized what going to Druleska meant. *The materialization of my visions.*

Something Sylvie said had stuck with me...

You can control Water, Earth, and Wind, but you must stop trying to control everything else around you. Time and destiny are their own masters. They will play the game as they please...

And she was right. I was done trying. Fighting. Whatever happened from now on was in the hands of the fates.

Tomorrow I would speak with my mother and Seymor about opening the portal. The longer we delayed, the more Drake suffered, and the more risk of exposure the covenant faced. They would understand. They had to. But no matter what—Drake and I would be going through that portal.

I woke up wrapped in a blanket of warmth. I stirred, and realized Drake was holding me. His lips were parted, sleeping peacefully beside me. Sleep wasn't a necessity for him; still, doing so helped his kind hone in on their element. He looked tired, this internal battle taking its toll on him. He never moved from his position as I closed the bedroom door quietly behind me.

School would need to wait today. There were more important things to address. Seymor and my mother sat with their coffee mugs at the kitchen table. At the same time, Celest and Sylvie moved about making pancakes, and from the smell, bacon too.

"Need a hand?"

"Good morning to you." Celest beamed.

"Don't worry, I've got it covered." Sylvie said. "Did you sleep well?"

"I did." I smiled, and she winked.

"Mom, Seymor, I know it's early, but I wanted to speak with all of you before Seymor left."

My mother turned to face me.

"When you start the day with 'we must speak', I shudder, child," Seymor said playfully. He abandoned his newspaper, and I braced myself. Soon, no one would be laughing. There was no easy way of saying it, so I got straight to the point.

"I need to open the portal to Druleska. Drake and I are going back to his home."

There was a clatter as a pan fell to the floor behind me, but I kept my eyes on my mother and Seymor.

"Have you lost your mind?" Celest was next to me in a

moment. Based on Sylvie's expression, she thought the same, too.

"What has brought this on?" Seymor asked. "I know you. You would never make such an impulsive decision, not unless there was a valid reason."

Seymor never disappointed me; he was the more levelheaded of the adults in my life.

"He was imprisoned under a wall of ice, constantly dominated by his opposite element. His fire doesn't want to be confined. You saw it the other night when he wouldn't get in the truck. But it's not just that, he's restless, even in human form."

"That is still no reason to jump to such a hasty decision," Celest said.

"He has a hard time controlling his fire. Even in human form, trying to fight the constant urge to shift is unbearable. It will consume him if he doesn't give in and lets his fire out. I won't allow that. I can't see him suffer anymore."

"How did this happen?" my mother spoke for the first time. "Could the spell and the Ora tablets be the cause?" Concern was etched on her face.

"No. I don't believe that's the cause. But if Drake cannot find a way to free himself without restraints or the constant fear of exposure, then we need to leave. If he doesn't, he fears what the fire will do. It could be dangerous for everyone. It could break the covenant and expose his kind to our world or worse."

"What could possibly be worse?" Sylvie murmured as she took a seat beside me.

"Oh—it could always be much worse," added Seymor. "Or have you forgotten what he is? If his mind is lost to the fire... he could devastate cities in the blink of an eye."

"This is a foolish idea." Celest protested. "Please, tell me you are not all seriously considering this."

"We can't fight what is meant to be." My mother said with a look of defeat.

"You have all gone mad. After everything you have sacrificed, you will let Belynda go. Alone into a world, she doesn't know?"

"Letting her go would be a sacrifice for us all. But she is old enough to make her own decisions. We must stand by her no matter what." Everyone's eyes turned to Drake, who stood silently on the threshold of the dining room. Celest returned to the kitchen without another word. Clearly, she would have no part in this. I understood her concern, but it wasn't a decision I took lightly.

"My apologies for not being here earlier." His disapproving eyes burned into mine. Drake was a gentleman; I was sure some part of him felt that he had to be present with me when I broke the news to my family.

"I'm sorry. I hate seeing you struggle. It had to be said, I couldn't wait."

He walked closer and brushed his fingers gently under my chin before taking a seat at the table.

"Celest is right about one thing, though. I hope you both reconsider this decision as well, for her safety." Although he said both, Seymor was staring directly at Drake. "You don't know how much your world has changed. There is no guarantee that you will be safe, let alone her."

Drake kept his eyes fixed to the table, but I knew he agreed.

"Drake has no say in what I do." I cut in. "I understand the risks, but I've already made my decision. I'm not here to ask for permission. I'm here to tell you that I'm doing this with or without your help."

No one spoke but Drake.

"He is right. I have been gone for far too long. Your safety is not guaranteed if you come with me." I glared at him.

"Are you saying this because you don't want me to come? Or because you're being honest?"

The muscles on his jaw tensed.

"My life begins and ends with you, I want you with me always even against my better judgement."

"Then there is no need for further discussion." I peered at the faces around the table with resolve. "I'm going."

"You don't know what you're saying." Celest argued. "That place is nothing like the human world. You would be alone. Without your family. Belynda, I beg you."

"You forget that is still *my* home. I understand your concerns, but I assure you, I would die before I let anything happen to her." No one dared argue with him; we all knew he would sacrifice himself to save me, not that I would ever allow him to do so again. That was a promise.

"Well. I will inform the rest of the council today. Felsia, are you well enough to work on portal spells with Belynda?"

"Belynda has no trouble opening portal gates. She's a quick learner." Mom said, winking at me.

"I take it you did more than just knot spells over the last few weeks."

My mother smiled at Seymor.

"She has the knowledge she needs, but we will go over it. She will be ready; I'll make sure of that." The certainty of what followed terrified me. I was closer to my end, yet the worse was the weight of the secret. But no one could know... It was for the best.

CELEST, Sylvie, and Drake hovered on the veranda at the back porch facing the woods.

"Remember what you learned. You already opened a portal

once. Just say the words and draw on the energy of the elements you control. Once you speak the magic name of the door, it will open."

"Do you want me to actually open it?" I questioned, glancing at Drake.

"There is no better time than now. Don't worry; you can close it the minute it opens."

"How do we know what will be at the other side of that gate?" Celest warned. "Felsia, the risks..." Although most still disagreed with my decision to accompany Drake back to the Fire Realm, no one voiced it except Celest. She never missed the opportunity to remind everyone what a terrible idea this was.

"She won't leave it open long enough to allow anything to pass. Trust me, there is no danger." Mother smiled at Celest. "There shouldn't be," she added. Celest threw her hands up, shaking her head.

I looked at my mother, who nodded encouragingly. She was teasing Celest. If she thought opening the portal would present a real danger, she would not allow me to open it.

"Here goes nothing."

With my hands extended before me, I listened to the elements. Water came first. I always felt its force before others. Then came the Wind; it moved my hair, and I captured its breath, letting its power fill me. Lastly, I reached with my mind for the Earth. Grounding myself, I called for the hearts of the trees, beckoning their roots. There was no connection. The vibrations I usually felt were dormant.

Mom had said I didn't have to summon all the elements to open the gates. So, I focused on harnessing all the power of Water and Air, willing it inside of me. I spoke the magic words for the gates to Druleska.

"*Dimittis Voltrattis.*" I felt a strange pulse as I called the name of the magic gate, but nothing happened. *"Dimittis Voltrattis."* I willed the bound power to flow from within me, but once again, I failed.

I glanced at Drake who offered a reassuring smile, clearly noting the disappointment on my face.

"You can do this!" My mother encouraged me.

"I don't know if I can. Something is missing. I can't feel the Earth's power."

"You don't need to control the elements to open the gates. All it takes is the power you possess already; otherwise, you wouldn't have been able to bring him back. You can draw it from the elements you control, but the power is within *you*. If you cannot feel the Earth, try summoning it first."

I reached for the power beneath my feet, urging it forward to find my connection to the trees and Earth, but it was no use. Before, I could sense the energy simmering beneath the ground, but there was only silence now, as if the threads of magic that had once connected us had been severed somehow. *I felt nothing.*

"I can't." I glanced at my mother and Drake with unease. "Why can't I summon earth?"

"Is it possible your power was drained by the Ora Tablets?" Sylvie offered. Both she and Celest turned to my mother for answers.

"Honestly, I don't know. You did draw an excessive amount of energy that day." She was right. Half of the trees on the Radcliff estate had withered, paying the price for my anger.

"The power of the elements is endless. They are summoned from emotions, anger, happiness, pain, sorrow, fear, and love," Drake explained. "If you don't confront whatever it is that is holding you back... not only, will you be unable to control the elements, but you won't be able to draw on the power you require to open the gate. Try summoning any of the other elements." Drake urged.

Though as his words sunk in, I realized the truth. I was afraid. I didn't want to admit it, but deep inside, I was frightened. I couldn't shut my emotions off like a machine. One thing was watching your own death, another thing entirely was willingly following the path that would lead you to it. I knew what I had to do.

I summoned Air, and I felt the Wind caress my face. Willing it to materialize, I extended my hand, but Drake was right. Nothing happened.

"You're right, but it felt different than when I summoned Earth. The energy is there with Air; I just can't seem to connect with it."

"Do it again." My mother urged.

I tried again, this time with water. I allowed the pulsing in my veins to increase, sensing the currents flowing from deep within the Earth. It was alive, coursing like ripples of white and blue behind my eyes, and when I dared to look, I watched it flow before me, and I beamed with relief.

"I did it. But I think that's because it's my strongest element."

"That discards Sylvie's theory, then. If you can't summon Air or Earth, then Drake must be right. Something is holding you back." Celest said. "How about, instead of harnessing your power from the elements, you try focusing on an emotion." She glanced at Drake, and I knew what she had in mind.

Closing my eyes, I dug deep into the feelings I had for him. My love, devotion... our bond. I reached deep inside for that connection we had shared from the moment we met. However, no matter how hard I tried, a part of me felt hollow. It was the part that knew what was coming and the suffering my secret would bring. Especially to him.

"I'm sorry." I mouthed to him, and he moved to stand beside me.

"This is not your fault. You tried."

I had tried, but it wasn't enough, and I knew why. I was too afraid. *But how does one stop fearing death?*

"There might be another way." Mother added.

"No more sacrifices." Drake cut in, and my mother dismissed him with a wave of her hand.

"Who's talking about sacrifice? I meant it can be possible with the help of the council members."

"It's not enough. You know that." Celest said.

"It could be if we had help from the elementals. If we can combine Belynda's magic with the elementals, we just might be able to open the gates."

"What happens if we succeed? How can they return if Belynda cannot open a portal from the other side?"

Celest strode towards us. She looked tired. Everyone remained silent, for no one had the answer. I wanted to say it wasn't necessary, but I held my tongue. There was no need to open a portal. I wouldn't be returning. My fate was sealed to Druleska, but they didn't need to know that, and I'd make sure they wouldn't.

"We will cross that bridge when we get there. Now, how do we find the elementals, and most importantly, will they be willing to help us?"

"Finding them won't be a problem. They took Stephen's downfall as an opportunity to start a new life without someone exploiting them for their gifts. Seymor allowed it, but I know he could easily track them if he wanted. As far as helping... I don't know."

For the first time, I wondered about the kind of life the elementals must have lived; the water elementals were hunted down. Persecuted. Used for their powers. Had their decision to serve my father been a choice or an obligation? In the end, they chose to protect one another; their loyalty was to each other before anyone else.

"Please speak with Seymor and see if he can locate them. But if we do this, it will be their choice. We are not my father."

"We wouldn't have it any other way," Sylvie said before disappearing into the house, Celest and my mother following in her wake.

Drake hugged me from behind, and I allowed my body to be sheltered in his warmth.

"I want to get out of here. How about I pack some food and we go up to the mountains? You can stretch your wings."

He kissed my neck, and I melted into him.

"Will we be flying there or driving?" He whispered, his nose skimming along my ear.

"I think I'll take my chances driving."

His laughter warmed my insides.

"You don't trust my flying?" He teased.

"I do. I just don't know if it's wise, with your fire out of control and all..."

"Belynda, all it wants is to be free. I would never hurt you." I heard the pain in his voice, so I spun to face him and outstretched a hand toward his face.

"I'm not afraid of you. I was only thinking of you. I don't want you to feel hurt or uncomfortable because of me. Honestly, it's still light out, so I also worry about the exposure."

"Then it's settled. We wait for dusk, and we fly."

"I said I wasn't scared of you, not that I wasn't terrified of heights."

He laughed, and I grimaced in anticipation to our adventure.

"Seriously? I thought you were braver than this." He taunted. His voice darkening.

"I know what you're doing. It's not going to work."

"What if I begged? What if I promised to misbehave..." He whispered, and my stomach twisted, though not out of fear of flying.

"You really don't play fair."

"I told you last night I was no saint and I intend to keep my word." He turned me around and my heart raced as he took my bottom lip between his teeth. The corner of his lips pulled up into a smile and before I could recover, he vanished before my eyes.

Before returning to the house, I attempted to call on the elements again but failed, except with water. Clear ripples flowed before me, forming strange patterns, and separating into millions of water droplets that twirled around me. I laughed as the droplets followed my steps until I was back on the porch and allowed them to fall.

I wouldn't let today's setbacks take moments away from Drake and me. Tonight would be ours.

My mother understood when I told her of my evening plans with Drake. Celest? Not so much. She didn't outright object, but clearly, she wasn't happy. Not since I revealed my plans to follow Drake into the Fire Realm.

I packed sandwiches, fruit, and cheese for us and a bottle of wine for Drake. Though I questioned if that was a good idea, considering he was the designated driver, or pilot in this case. I smiled, trying to squash the nerves. I placed two blankets in the bag as well before showering. At quarter to seven, Drake strolled into my room, his hair still wet and fresh clothes on his body.

"Ready?" he asked; the room lit up with his smile. He was clearly excited about our escapade. I was too, but the thought of flying had my stomach in knots.

"As I'll ever be." I beamed, trying to match his excitement, but he knew me so well.

"You're scared, aren't you?" He laughed.

"Terrified. Now let's go before I change my mind."

I draped the book-bag on my back as we left the house, then Drake lifted me into his arms. The Air whipped against my face as he ran through the grassy fields. I closed my eyes, enjoying the lashing of the wind. I was close to the ground, in his arms, safe. Now flying... that was a whole other thing.

Once we were under cover of the trees, he released me, and I followed him into the deeper part of the forest. Silently I watched him as he removed his shoes, socks, shirt, and lastly, his pants which came off with his briefs. There was enough moonlight filtering through the trees for me to see every line, every smooth granite surface of his body. He was perfect. He collected his clothes and handed them to me with a grin.

"What?"

"Nothing. Just your face, love." I made to punch his arm playfully, but he caught my hand swiftly and brought it to his lips, pulling me closer.

"I like it when you say that." I admitted, intoxicated by the warmth of his naked body so close to mine.

"What? Love?"

"Mhhh. You only do it when you're being bad." His laughter echoed through the quiet forest.

"You seem to have quite a lot of theories about me. If I recall, you accused me of having wicked thoughts when my eyes lightened, and now I have bad intentions when I call you love?"

"Yes. Those are my theories, and I'll prove them to you."

"I'm looking forward to that."

He quickly pecked my lips. As I placed his clothes and shoes in the bag, he created distance between us.

"Is this really necessary? Can't you just run us up the mountain instead of flying?"

"But where's the fun in that? Besides, you said I could stretch my wings, did you not?"

I rolled my eyes.

"Fine."

His laughter was drowned by the buzzing of his tattoos as they came to life. For the first time, I watched Drake's body transform before me. I recalled a time, not too long ago, when we joked about this moment. Yet now I realized his worry had not been for fear of hurting me, but for what I would think of him.

I was in awe. Drake was magnificent. Equally beautiful, both in human and Dragon form. Strong and lethal.

The lines became ribbons of black sand floating above the surface of his skin. They grew and circled his body like an orb of darkness. Then, his entire body began to glow, pulsing in a fiery orange blaze until no skin, flesh, or trace of human Drake remained. Only darkness and fire. The light exploded, and the majestic beast flapped its wings in his wake.

"I don't know if I will ever get used to that."

The beast snorted; it was definitely laughing at me.

The Dragon wrapped its tail around my waist, and I shrieked as it lifted me effortlessly, placing me above him as it had done before.

"Please take it easy on me," I begged as the Dragon propelled himself from the forest floor. I closed my eyes as we ascended. I didn't trust myself to keep from screaming. It wasn't until the Dragon found a steady glide that I allowed myself to look. Only darkness surrounded us. The moon, however, was big and right above us. It felt so close, like I could reach out with my fingers to touch it.

I relaxed a little and ran my hands over the skin at the back of the Dragon's neck. The beast grunted. That sound I understood. It liked my touch.

When the Dragon dipped in a sharp descent, I tensed again, taking hold of the spikes at its back, only this time, I didn't close my eyes. My heart thumped as I watched the treetops draw near. The second he touched down on ground, a wave of relief coursed through my body, and I dissolved into a fit of laughter as adrenaline pumped through me.

I recognized the place as I stepped out of the forest edge. I didn't think he would ever want to return here, but I realized there were not many choices when he was bound to remain inconspicuous and out of sight.

The lake extended before us, and the moon's glow radiated a long shadow over the water.

A blaze of fire broke from the Dragon's mouth, startling me, but he was simply lighting a pit to offer some light and warmth.

Without warning, the Dragon took off into the night sky like a bullet. Flying with me on his back was like driving on the slow lane.

He looked so free and lethal as he cut through the night with blinding speed.

While he did, I set up the blankets, and kicked off my shoes to lay and watch him. He soared under the veil of stars for some time until eventually, he returned. This time, the Earth shook as he landed. The Dragon roared, and the darkness and fire swallowed the beast.

Drake walked towards me in all his naked glory as the last of the black lines settled against his skin. He stared at me with a grin as I studied him. He seemed comfortable naked, but why wouldn't he? He was an immortal God. He liked being watched. He slipped on his pants, not bothering with the rest of his clothes.

"You are extraordinary; did you know that?" I said as we lay facing each other.

"I'm glad one of us thinks so." I managed to punch him this time, and he laughed. "You know you only hurt yourself, love."

I narrowed my eyes at him, which only made him laugh harder.

"What's to eat? I'm famished."

I dug through the bag and took out the sandwiches, cheese, fruit, and wine. I had brought water for myself.

When he said he was famished, he wasn't kidding. He devoured his food in record time.

"Should you be drinking all that wine? Considering you're the designated driver and all?" He smiled, and his eyes scanned my face.

"I got here just fine, and I was already intoxicated enough because of you."

"I'm serious, Drake."

"You have nothing to worry about. Immortals don't get drunk. Not from this, anyway."

"They don't?" He shook his head. "Then why drink at all?"

"Because it tastes good, but only special brews can affect us the way this would affect a human."

"What kind of special brew?"

He smiled mischievously.

"I'll let you try some when we return to Druleska."

"What makes you think I'm interested in trying it?"

"I know you're curious. I can see it in your eyes."

I smiled, and he rolled his body above mine. His lips teased against my neck, slowly, and then my chin as he kissed and nibbled until claiming my lips.

I could taste the wine on his lips and tongue as it clashed with mine. He rolled on his back, and I was in complete control as my knees came to rest either side of him. His growing need pressed against my core. He hiked my dress up to my thighs, rubbing circles above my knees as he pressed closer.

I sat back and monitored his face; his eyes were wild as I ran my fingers over his stomach and chest. He sat up, and I held on to him as his lips burned a trail from my neck and down my right shoulder. He lowered one of my dress straps, then the other, until it fell between our bodies, exposing my white silk bra. He growled as his lips moved over the skin above my breasts.

"Stand. I want to see all of you."

I pushed back and did as he asked. His eyes roamed my body as I moved the dress from my hips, allowing it to pool around my feet. His eyes scanned my body.

"You are a goddess." He leaped to his feet; a predator ready to hunt its prey.

He walked around me, assessing, his fingers gracing my skin from my navel to my back. Finally standing behind me, he deprived me of his body but teased me with the grazing of his fingers. Over my back, my shoulders, my behind... when his hands took hold of my hips and pressed me to him, I sucked in a breath.

"You are so eager, love. But I'm going to take my time with you." He pulled aside my hair and kissed the side of my neck. His hands held my hips, locking me flush against him, and moving my body against his hardness.

It was madness. I wanted this burning to be eased, but no solace would be found unless I drove him over the edge as I had done in the shower. With a fire I didn't know I possessed, I turned in his arms. Taking his hand, I slipped one of his fingers into my mouth, and sucked, locking my eyes with his. I licked and teased until the strain in his pants felt like granite against me. His eyes burned, and his hardness pulsed against my stomach. I could work with this.

Eyes dark, his lips parted as he stared at me silently. Slowly, I kissed his chest and his abs, and before he knew it, I was on my knees as an offering, ready to worship him.

"What do you think you're doing?" His voice was lower… darker, and his eyes were wild.

"I'm taking my time too."

The fire in his eyes burned.

"Show me." His darkness beckoned as he eased the buckle from his belt. If he thought I would tremble, he was mistaken. I was burning alive and the fire made me brazenly reckless.

I reached for the button of his pants, and then the zipper. His lips parted with anticipation as he watched me.

His sex sprung before me, taut and glistening smooth. The fire-breathing Dragon shivered as my fingers closed around his warm skin. He moved my hair to the side while his eyes dared me to take him. My fingers tightened around him and glided from the base to tip.

"You are wicked… I'm burning for you." He growled with his devastatingly teasing smile. I wasn't done. I leaned in, and he sucked in a breath as my lips grazed his taut, smooth skin.

"Fuck, love." His hand moved to the back of my neck, encouraging me to take him on, and I did. He was big and rigid inside my mouth. Warm and soft and wonderful.

My tongue danced around him, teasing, sucking, and he was lost, but so was I.

Moisture formed between my legs as I welcomed him deeper into my mouth. He drove his hardness in and out then with slow, measured thrusts, as a feral growl escaped his lips. He lifted me in his arms and, in a second, had my body pinned against a tree. He lifted one of my legs to wrap around his waist while his hardness pressed against my core, just over the thin material of my panties.

"I wanted to take my time, but you had to go and tease the fire..." He ground against me with desperation. "I don't know if I can be gentle."

"Don't be," I whispered close to his ear, and he groaned, digging his fingers into my thighs. "Take it, please. My soul... my innocence. It's yours."

His fingers were on my folds, and I heard the thin material of my panties tear apart while his other hand tore at my bra. He stared at my exposed breasts, the fire burning in his eyes.

"You are so beautiful and wet." He grinned as his fingers glided between by folds. "Did you like taking me into your mouth? Tasting me?" His fingers continued their slow assault. "Tell me..." His voice was lust filled as his lips probed against mine.

"Yes." I sucked in a breath, as his hardness pushed against my stomach.

"What do you want? Tell me..." His lips moved over my breaths, as his tongue teased. His grunts of pleasure vibrating against my skin.

"I want you. All of you."

"You want me inside you?" One of his fingers slipped inside of me, just barely and I jolted against the wonderful sensation.

"Yes. I want you inside me." What was he doing to me? He could ask for my life at this moment... and I would gladly give it up as offering if only to be pulled from this precipice.

"Do you want me to fuck you? Is that it? Tell me..." His lips glided over my cheek before taking claim of my lips.

He took his hardness in his grip and guided the tip against my throbbing folds. I inhaled, driving my hips forward to meet him. He teased my entrance, and I felt the pressure build inside me.

"Drake, please do it." I couldn't take it anymore...

"Say it. Tell me what you want. I want to hear you say it." The darkness in his voice made my body tremble.

"Fuck me, please. Hard..." I gripped his shoulders as his single thrust tore through me.

Drake's lips drowned the cry from my lips. My fingers dug into his skin as the sharp pain seared through my insides, and he stilled inside me.

"I know you asked for hard. But not yet..." He drowned my face with feather kisses. "I promise the worst is over." Covering my lips with his, I found the discomfort easing as the kiss deepened.

I moved my hips against him, and he eased himself out gently then back in but not all the way. He felt so tight around my walls, I wondered if I would ever be able to take all of him.

"Is this, ok?" He asked, tracing his thumb over my bottom lip as he pushed a bit deeper. I sucked in a breath, burning to sheath him completely, but worried, he would break me...

"Yes." I responded. As the sensation became bearable.

He took his time and moved in a slow rhythm. In and out, teasing, pacing his thrusts as his eyes burned into mine. My hips met his as the wonderful sensation started to build inside me. He must have known I was ready because his thrusts grew deeper, faster, and harder. His eyes became pools of darkness as he watched our joined bodies.

"Are you ready for more?" He pushed in deeper and pain pierced through me. I braced my hands against his chest and he became still.

"Did I hurt you?" He withdrew a little, but I tightened my legs around him making him halt.

"I'm ok. Slowly..." I urged him, guiding my hips to meet his.

His fingers found their way to the apex of my folds and they teased. Soon, the discomfort disappeared, and was replaced by an urgent need.

"More?" His eyes darkened, as I meet his thrust allowing him to health himself almost all the way this time.

"So tight..." His lips parted in a breath as his eyes blazed.

He lowered my leg and turned me around to face the tree. He kissed the back of my neck and shoulders, and I felt his hardness slip between my folds. He eased himself from behind and took my breasts in his hands, encouraging me to meet every one of his thrusts.

"You are so wet for me." A sigh escaped my lips as my hands clutched the tree. "Is this what you wanted?"

"Yes, but I want to touch you." At my breathless request, he turned me around instantly and, once again, brought my leg up around his middle.

"Take what you want."

I stared at his taut sex, glistening, waiting, and his eyes burned into my flesh. I reached my hand and guided his stone-hard ridge to my folds, sinking into it, inch by inch, taking him into me. Allowing him to fill me almost completely time. His hands gripped my thighs, and I moved against the body of this sleek God as his eyes worshipped me. My hands trailed over the muscles on his chest, and they tensed. His hips drove up in one swift movement and my cry filled the night.

"Drake..." I sucked in a breath.

"Now you are all mine love," he teased and I felt him smile against my ear. "Every inch of me belongs to you." His hardness pulsed inside of me, as he pushed all of his body against mine, branding my back against the tree's bark, but I didn't care. The darkness needed control. He became savage as he tore into the depths of my soul with each thrust.

"Drake…" I cried out as the pulsing inside me increased. Pain and pleasure. His fingers found themselves to the apex of my folds, teasing as his relentless thrusts pulled me closer to the edge.

"That's it. Let me feel you, love. Don't hold back." His words made me come undone. My hips rocked with the wave as his thrusts shattered the last of me.

"Fuck." He ground out his teeth, filling me. He was at the precipice; I knew it when the darkness in his eyes took over, and his thrusts were suddenly hard and unyielding. "By the fates." The tattooed lines on his skin came alive as he impaled himself into my very my soul, and his warmth filled my insides. His tremors rocked us, and his eyes became bright once more.

"You will be the death of me." He kissed my lips breathlessly and eased me to my feet.

My BODY FELT SORE, achy, but wonderful all the same. I beamed, as I picked up my torn panties and bra from the ground and stared at him as he slipped on his pants.

"What am I supposed to do with these?"

He laughed wholeheartedly, and it made me smile.

"Burn them." He walked towards me and took them from my hand, tossing them into the fire. "I like you better without them anyways." He walked closer and his fingers ran over my exposed breasts, then trailed lower, running them between my still sleek folds. "Easy access." He teased, kissing my neck, and I shoved him away, smiling.

"Will you hand me my dress?" He picked it up and eased it

over my head, helping me into it as his fingers graced my skin teasing everywhere they touched. He was insatiable... the thought made my core ache, but I didn't think I could take him again. Not tonight.

"Something else is different." He assessed my face, tucking a lock of hair behind my ear. "I didn't notice yesterday because I was too distracted, but earlier when I asked you to tell me what you wanted... I probed your mind, but I couldn't see."

"I thought you said it was almost impossible for humans to guard their thoughts against you?" I teased, and he inspected me with interest.

"How did you do it?"

I smiled and lifted my wrist, pointing at the bracelet my mother and I had weaved with the spell. I watched his face transform from curiosity to confusion.

"Why?"

While I knew he would question my motives, I couldn't tell him the truth.

"Drake, I'm yours: mind, body, and spirit, and that will never change. Is it too much to want to keep the little things to myself?"

"Belynda, I would never violate you like that. Not intentionally, at least." He smiled, realizing he had admitted to doing so a moment ago. "In my defense, I was overcome with need."

I laughed. He was incorrigible.

"Drake..."

"Belynda, I do understand." I smiled and touched his face, knowing that understanding and acceptance were two very different things.

"This might not be the best time, but there is one thing I must ask. I know we haven't talked about what happened in the chamber with my father." He turned around and found his shirt, clearly distracting his mind from the memories of that day. "I know what you gave up for me." I paused, and he turned to face me.

"And I would do it again. I've told you. I would die a thousand lives before I let anything happen to you."

"I don't want you to. That's the problem."

"It's my life. My choice."

"Please listen to me." I snapped and turned around, fighting to contain my emotions. He was in front of me in a moment.

"Please don't be upset." He begged.

"Then promise me, please." I whispered. "Promise you will never do anything like that again." I stared into the depths of his silver eyes, hoping to convey the importance of my request without making him suspicious.

"Belynda..." His jaw tensed. "I don't know if I can."

I pushed away from him with unbreakable resolve.

"Promise me, Drake, or I will never forgive you for it." While I hated saying it, I had to force his hand somehow.

"Why are you doing this?" His brows lifted in confusion.

"I don't want you or anyone else to make sacrifices for me, for us. I would never forgive them or myself for doing so." I pleaded, and I watched his resolve begin to crumble before me. "Say it, Drake. I need you to say it. To promise."

"I promise." He whispered, speaking the words as though he was signing his own death sentence. I kissed him on the cheek and smiled, even though something inside me had broken. My fate was sealed with that promise, and there was no going back.

LOCATING THE ELEMENTALS WASN'T as easy as we had hoped, but Tyrus managed it. I never doubted him, though. Strangely enough, everything seemed to be culminating for me, as if this chapter of my life was ending.

School was out. Lillian was excited to go tour different universities, which meant she would be busy for most of summer. Once she left, it would be easier for her to forget about me, at least until her mother decided to reveal the truth. Then she would probably resent me for having lied to her, but by then, I would be long gone. I accepted that with a heavy heart, but it was as it should be.

Oliver and I spent the first week of summer mostly at his place, where Drake had more privacy and freedom to roam and free his fire, which occurred more often now.

"I don't think I'll ever get used to watching him do that." Said Oliver as he joined me in the meadow. I was watching Drake soar high through the trees.

"I'm still having a hard time believing it myself," I admitted as he streaked above us.

I glanced at Oliver, unable to pin his expression.

"What is it?"

I knew him well enough to know something was on his mind.

"Do you really have to do this? I mean, look at him. Isn't this exactly what he needs? We can find a way for him."

I lowered my eyes and shook my head before returning to watch the sky.

"It's not enough. Drake doesn't talk about it much, but I think it's about much more than freedom. He fears losing control. Even if he doesn't say it, what he did that day…" I glanced at Oliver. "He's ashamed of it."

"I don't judge him for what he did. Our father deserved it." Oliver said, and he was right. Stephen deserved it.

"I know you don't, but his conscience is punishment enough. Even if he doesn't show it."

"Is there no way to convince you to stay?" My brother asked with a saddened look. It hurt me to leave him.

"I'm afraid not. He's been away from his home for too long. A thousand years is a long time." I said, and Oliver glanced up at the soaring Dragon.

"I know, but he's immortal. He has eternity to return home to see his family. We don't have much time." He was right. I knew that better than any of them.

"I'm sorry, Oli," I said, unable to find the words to convey I understood. Yet I still chose to spend whatever time I had left with Drake. He nodded and leaned back on the lawn chair.

I WASN'T sure if Drake's restlessness was attributed to the elementals' arrival or the promise, he made to me on the night I became his. Since forcing him into making that promise, I had caught him staring on countless occasions, studying me, almost as if he could sense something wasn't right. But I smiled, and his worries seemed to ease when our bodies connected at night. As did mine.

TONIGHT, however, he seemed remarkably at ease as he lay across my bed. He had spent the day roaming the skies, and his fire was sated.

"Should I pack?" I asked, glancing at Drake through the mirror, propped upright with his hands behind his head.

"Pack?" Drake lifted his head, his face a mask of confusion.

"For Druleska? Should I take a bag?"

He ran his fingers over his mouth, trying to contain his laughter.

I turned from the mirror to look directly at him.

"What?" I asked. This time, he no longer tried to hide his amusement.

"You should definitely not bring a bag." He said, laying back down with a huge smile on his face. I had to know what was so funny.

"Why not? What's so funny about that?" I asked, leaning against one of the bed posts with my arms crossed before me. I waited for him to enlighten me.

Drake pushed himself up and braced his arms against the bed to look at me.

"Perhaps because you're not going on vacation. You're traveling through a portal to a magical world where you're the *only* human. You will stand out just by being there. Trust me, you won't need it."

"But what will I wear?" There it was again... that smile.

"Definitely not those jeans. They're a distraction enough as it is." He jostled himself in a blinding move and pulled me to lay on top of him.

"Stop it." I laughed, hitting his chest. "I know you're trying to distract me."

"No. You're the one distracting me with these." He pressed my hips closer to him by tugging on the belt loops of the jeans. He pressed his lips against my neck, and for a moment I forgot what we were talking about.

"Trust me. I will make sure you have something suitable to wear." He whispered. The way his voice darkened as he said it told me enough.

It was so easy to get lost in him when we were alone. I could no longer recognize the innocent girl I had been before I met him. Every time his eyes burned like they did now, something ignited in me.

I STARED AT THE CEILING; Drake's arm was wrapped securely around me while he slept soundly.

This would be the last night I slept on my bed. The last time I stared at the bed's canopy like I had done countless times when recovering from one of Isabel's dreams.

That seemed like so long ago. I was no longer the weak, insecure girl who opened that portal.

Tomorrow, when we marched through those gates, I knew what I would be leaving behind: my home, my family, my life. But a part of me clung to the thought that Drake and I would be together, the only thought that provided me comfort. Whatever time I had left, I would spend it at his side.

My bond with Isabel and the fact that Drake and I were destined to come together made my choices that much easier to live with. For my family, too. But it didn't make saying goodbye to them any easier.

MY HANDS WERE clammy as we drove up the mountains toward the chamber entrance, where everyone waited. Drake took my hand and kissed the back of it, likely sensing my distress.

"You don't have to do this. I will understand if you want to stay." He whispered, and I stared at him as if he was mad.

"You're not getting rid of me that easily." I teased and felt his hand relax in my grip.

KEEP OUT. RESTRICTED AREA.

The signs warned from a mile before. The entrance to the chamber was a remote building heavily guarded by fences. Not to mention there was a slew of guards and checkpoints to cross before entrance was permitted.

Drake pushed the glass doors, entering before me. The building was clearly a façade. The corridor extended in two wings to both sides. However, our prize was straight ahead toward the elevators, secured by the guard's standing post.

I stared at the faces in the elevator, a knot forming in my throat as I realized this would be the last time, I ever saw them if we opened the portal today. And we would. My mother, Sylvie, Celest, Oliver, and Tyrus were oblivious to our imminent goodbye.

The doors opened into the antechamber. The light from the chandeliers blinded us momentarily. Seymor put in a lot of effort in restoring this place. It was still majestic but bore no resemblance to what it had been before. The high pillars supporting the vaulted ceilings were no longer made of stone, but the purest marble. The room was opulent and seemed lighter, more open, and modern. It certainly made the ghosts from the past seem less haunting.

Amirth was the first one I spotted. I noticed her jet-black hair was cropped short, but she didn't seem hostile as she approached Drake and me while the others stayed behind.

"Belynda... Drake."

"Amirth." I greeted. Drake remained silent.

"I wanted a chance to speak. To apologize..."

I cut her off with a wave of my hand.

"Water under the bridge. We should be the ones thanking you for agreeing to help us."

"Nonetheless, what we did..."

"I know why, and who you did it for. I understand how important family is. I would do anything to protect mine."

She glanced at Alexia and Rache, smiling.

"Yes, though they can be a pain in the ass sometimes."

I laughed, and she did too. Drake remained stoic as usual. He was a tough nut to crack.

"I'll leave you a moment."

I watched him walk toward my mother, and I was curious to know what he had to say. Amirth spoke, distracting me.

"I know I have no right to ask this, but we were wondering if we might come with you and the Dragon?"

That I had not expected.

"Amirth, I don't know if that's a good idea..."

"Please. I know it will take some time for you and the Dragon-bound to trust us, but we don't belong here. We want to be free just like him. To be ourselves. We have nothing to leave behind. No family or friends, we only have each other."

"Believe me, it's not about trust. I would never stand in the way of your freedom, but we don't know what awaits us on the other side. Drake says I will be safe, but even he can't guarantee that. Are you willing to put your family in danger?"

I knew my fate. Understanding Drake the way I did, my loss would consume him. I couldn't allow them, in good faith, to come with us. "But I promise. I will come back for all of you when it's safe."

"How will you open the portal?"

"All it takes is energy. I know the magic words. If I don't over-come whatever is holding me back, I will find plenty of energy to draw from on the other side. I promise. I will find a way."

"I will hold you to that promise." She offered her hand, and I shook it with a heavy heart, for I knew it was a promise already broken.

Only some of the guardians were present this time. It was a special request I had made to ease Drake from any discomfort.

With everyone gathered, it was time to make my rounds.

"Sylvie." I gave her a hug. "Thank you for being like a sister to me."

"You know I hate that you're doing this. Stop. You're going to make me cry." She pushed me away and disappeared towards the elementals.

"Ren. Thank you for everything. Even for being a pain in the ass." His roar of laughter echoed around the chamber. He offered me his hand and smiled.

"Take care, will you?"

I nodded.

Oliver and Tyrus flanked Celest, and as I approached, Oliver pulled me into a hug, lifting me from the ground.

"Put me down, you fool."

Drake glanced our way briefly before dismissing us, returning to his conversation with my mother and now Seymor.

"You don't have to do this." He said as he placed me gently on my feet. I glanced at Drake at the same time his eyes met mine.

"I want to go. Stop worrying. I'm going to be fine."

Tyrus offered me his hand, and I shook it.

"If you need anything, I'll be at your service."

I smiled. I had grown quite fond of Tyrus.

"I know. Thank you." Celest looked like she was about to cry. "Keep an eye out for this one, will you?"

I nudged Oliver and stole a glance at Celest, who was dabbing away her tears.

"Celest. You'll make me worry if I leave seeing you like this, please."

"Come here," she said, hugging me. My heart ached. I fought the tears and the knot forming in my throat. "Please take care. Don't do anything foolish. Stay with him and I know he will keep you safe." She pulled away and cupped my face.

"I love you, Celest. I really want you to know what a good mother you have been to me. I'm going to miss you." She cried and pulled me back to her. "Your cooking mostly." I added, trying to lighten the heaviness that had settled between us before I broke down too.

"Gosh, you've turned me into a sobbing mess. I don't know what I will do when you're gone."

"You will be fine. You've got the library to keep you busy and my mother and Seymor for company."

"And this is not goodbye." She added, so unaware of the finality of this moment.

"Not goodbye." The knot in my throat intensified, so I smiled and excused myself.

Drake, Seymor, and my mother had spoken about the energy required to open the portal. Seymor agreed that if Drake joined in, we could draw power from him, too.

Seymor gave me a hug but said nothing, not even a goodbye. But I could tell it cost him a great deal to remain collected.

"Felsia, I'll give you a moment. Drake, why don't we go get everyone in position?" Drake glanced at me before following Seymor.

I stared at the lines of gray in my mother's hair, the sacrifice she had made to get Drake back.

"Child, come here." She pulled me in, and I felt the warm tears break free, unable to contain them any longer.

"I'm sorry. I know I'm a mess." I attempted to smile, but I couldn't.

"Don't cry. This will be a new life for you. Do not be afraid."

I was afraid. So very afraid. I had accepted my fate with a heart of stone, but knowing I would never see her or any of my family again shattered every morsel of my strength.

"I know." I swallowed the pain roaring through me. Drake watched us with an uneasy expression, and I smiled although I was dying inside.

THE CIRCLE WAS DIFFERENT; everyone held hands. There was no boundaries or a ritual to follow; it was just a group of individuals. Friends that had come together for a purpose. I smiled once I noticed even Tyrus, Oliver, and Celest had offered. Any amount of energy we could channel, no matter how small, would help. I closed the circle, taking Drake's hand and my mother's.

A fire circle ignited in the center as Drake and Rashe allowed their energy to flow. Air followed, offered by Alexia, then Earth from Amirth, and I drew water last. The four elements danced together, unbound, as every person in the circle focused on extracting white energy from their bodies. A sizzling bolt of white power.

"*Dimittis Voltratti.*" I spoke the magic name, and this time, a burst of blue tore through the open space with ease.

"You did it." Drake said, looking down at me.

"*We* did it." I corrected, peering around the circle. I couldn't have done it without them.

"Are you sure about this?" He asked, his eyes searching mine. I nodded, not trusting my voice.

"Very well." Drake released my hand. "I'll go first. You may follow when you're ready."

He took three steps forward, and as his body met the light, he was gone. I took a step, but my mother's hand gripped mine, pulling me back.

"Belynda," She whispered, "Remember what she said in her letter. Only in death."

I pulled away, staring into her eyes; they said everything that words could not. Everything she had not dared speak aloud before. *She knew, but how?* I wanted to ask, but too many eyes watched us.

"Do not be afraid."

Tears ran down my face as I took one last look at all the faces around me.

"I love you, Mom. Goodbye." I turned and dived into the light before I crumbled into a million pieces.

THE LIGHT DISAPPEARED behind me as Drake pulled me to him. I cried for myself, for us, and for those we had left behind. My mother knew... Somehow, her words had given me hope, until I glanced at my surroundings. I felt the knife press against my throat. This was my vision. As clear as day. This was where I would die.

"What is this place?" I asked as I stared at the forest. A fire raged before me, and I studied the white specs of ashes that rained from the sky.

"These are the burning forests of Druleska." He smiled, a nostalgic look in his eyes. All I felt was sadness.

"Do they ever stop burning?"

Drake turned to me.

"No. Their fire is eternal. Welcome to the Fire Realm." He ran his fingers over my cheeks, wiping away the ashes that marred my face.

"Let's go. It's only a matter of time before the Dravonis sense that a gate was opened. They will come looking for us."

"Who are the Dravonis?"

"The royal guard."

DRULESKA, the Fire Realm, was nothing I had ever imagined. Mountains peaked in the distance, their summits lost to the darkness of the horizon: an angry battle of gray skies and thunder.

"What time is it?" He glanced at me, though this time he didn't smile.

"I'm sorry. I should have prepared you for this. I realize you don't know much about my home. Here in Druleska, we live in almost perpetual dusk. Days are distinctly lighter than night. Yet you will never see the sunshine in our Realm."

No sun? I stared, fighting to put a smile on my face.

"I will adapt. I'm not much for going out anyways." He squeezed my hand and turned to me.

"I'm sorry. I know this is a lot more than you bargained for, but you must promise to be honest with me." He lifted my hand and touched my woven bracelet. "I would hate for you to be unhappy if only to please me."

"This is not your fault, remember? It was my choice." I looked up at the sky and frowned. "Yes, the idea of perpetual dusk is not something I'm *thrilled* about, but like I said... I will adapt." I smiled, and though it was clear Drake didn't fully believe me, he reluctantly accepted my words.

"We will be faster if I carry you, at least until we reach the outer parts of the kingdom."

"Why not fly?"

"We're already showing up unannounced. I don't want to draw unnecessary attention to us. I think it's best to keep a low profile until we have reached the castle, and I can speak with my father."

"You mean *that* castle? *That's* your home?" Drake laughed.

"Where else would the royal family live?"

"I've never been inside a castle before. What's it like?"

"Towers, dungeons, and everything you've ever read about in those earthly books. Including the Dragons." He winked, and I smiled. "Even though you shouldn't believe everything they say."

"Which parts should I not believe?"

"The fairy tale part. There are no such things as happy endings."

"Don't say that!" I punched his chest.

"It's the truth. Happiness is only temporary. Some can attain it for longer than others, but in the end... there are no happy endings."

"I don't like this new theory of yours," I huffed, crossing my arms. Simply infuriated. "I don't want to hear any more about it."

He smiled and lifted me into his arms as if I weighed no more than the shirt on his back.

• • •

He wasn't kidding when he said there were towers; I was sure he wasn't joking about the dungeons, either. The tip of the towers disappeared into the clouds, all interlinked by a bridge of stone arches. The castle looked like it had experienced the weathering of the elements and time, yet there it stood.

"Are those... Dragons?" I asked, pointing to the distant sky.

"Yes. Likely officers of the royal guard."

From where we stood, they looked like birds gliding and circling the fortress. The closer we got to the castle, the more magnificent they became. Yet they weren't the size of Drake in dragon form.

"Why are they so much smaller?"

"Like I said, they're guards. Royals are always larger and much more lethal. Those born into the crown also have distinct spikes on their heads, separating us from the rest. The Dragons chosen into the guard are there to serve only, and they would never dare go against a Royal Dragon. Not while we take form, at least. They know it's a death wish."

Yes... I recalled Drake's spikes. Staring into his eyes, I realized there was so much I didn't know. How would I survive here? Would his parents welcome me or hate me? My stomach twisted in knots.

When Drake finally placed me down, I spotted pebble roads up ahead, yet they were beaten, dirty, and old. There were houses too, some made of straw, others of stone. This part of the city required a helping hand. Drake must have clocked my gloom as I glanced around.

"It wasn't always like this but controlling a kingdom and its people is hard. Those that seek to thrive live better. Those that don't... they stop living, and this is where they end up."

I nodded and clutched to him, trailing behind as he led us down the alleys. The stone roads twisted and turned in countless directions up the mountain; I wasn't sure we would ever make it to the castle gates. However, as we ascended, the small stone buildings, stores, and market tents became livelier. People stared at us with genuine intrigue.

Soon, we had a trail of them following us as we weaved through the markets and tents filled with strange trinkets and foods.

"Drake..." I glanced at the multitude of people that followed.

"It's ok. Just keep walking."

"Why are they following us?"

"They recognized me, that's all. They are likely wondering how I escaped Xelraa and why I'm here with a guardian." I clutched his hand as his words left his lips. "It's alright. They wouldn't dare hurt you."

"How can they tell?"

"The same way I could sense it the first time I saw you. It's in your blood." He explained, "All guardians are what we call blood witches."

I turned to him with questioning eyes.

"I thought you said it was my essence?"

The side of his mouth quirked into a conspicuous smile.

"Oh yes, but that privilege is only reserved for me. Your soul is bound by Isabel's. I was particular to her scent for obvious reasons, so I recognized it in you immediately." He glanced at the growing crowd and frowned. "To them, your essence holds no meaning, but your blood... *that,* they recognize."

I stole another look at the many curious faces trailing behind.

"I don't think they like me very much."

"They don't know you. But once I claim you as my mate, they will respect and protect you like any other member of the royal family."

Claim me as his mate?

I stopped in my tracks, and he turned, glancing between me and those approaching.

"What do you mean *claim* me as your mate?"

"Belynda, now is not the best time to have this conversation. You trust me, don't you?" He assessed my face, and fear flashed across his eyes. "I am yours, body, and soul. Is that not how you feel?"

"I do. You know I do. I wouldn't be here if it were otherwise." He visibly relaxed, then.

"We will speak of this no more now." He took my hand. "Come. We're almost there."

THE SMELL in the air was intriguing. It was a strange combination of saffron, spices, and cinnamon.

Drake noticed my interest was piqued and promised to bring me back once we were settled.

"Your highness..." An elderly man's face glowed with veneration as he addressed Drake. He tried to kneel, but Drake held his arm to stop him.

"Really, there is no need." He whispered to the man before ushering me along. "Let's hurry up." He urged as people began closing in. Little by little, murmurs of the prince's return echoed around us.

"Are they all Dragon shifters like you?"

"No, Dragon shifters are rare, few and far between. That's why when one is born, they are usually called to serve the royal family. There are also Phoenixes and Fire Hounds. You might spot a flame sprite, but they tend to hide, especially from humans. There are giants too, but you won't see them here. They live in the mountains of Volten, and it's best not to get in their way."

I was intrigued by these people... these creatures who stared back at me, likely feeling the same. How long had it been since they'd seen a human?

"You told me before there were no humans here in Druleska, but are there any in the other Realms?" He smiled and graced my cheeks with his fingers.

"No, love. There's nothing as beautiful as you." I knew we were close as the castle became more opulent. A shadow towered above.

The thumping on the stones made me halt at Drake's side. Right outside the castle gates, a barricade of soldiers stood, forming a line. They were dressed in black and red leather armor, a dragon insignia stitched on their chests. They stood, unmoving, clutching spears with tips that blazed with fire. We watched as more guards joined, parading before us. Surrounding us.

"I'm the Prince. Put your weapons down now. I demand to see my father, the King." The guards didn't move. They didn't even blink.

"I do not believe it." A deep voice broke through the line of armed guards, and a man seemingly ten years older than Drake strolled towards us. "Is it true... Is it really you?" The man said, staring at Drake. I didn't realize I was squeezing his arm until he spoke.

"Dagasti..." Drake said curtly but offered his free hand. The man shook it, smiling, then pulled Drake into an awkward embrace, forcing me to release him.

"Is that any way to greet your uncle? How is it possible?" he questioned, glancing at me with curiosity. "A mate? A human mate? No, wait..." The man closed his eyes and lifted his face, sniffing the air. "Much better... a *blood witch*..." His eyes pierced Drake, whose hand reached for mine again. His grip was tight. "I see history repeats itself."

I knew he meant Drake and Isabel; based on what I had just learned... being a guardian born also made Isabelle a blood witch.

"Trust me. I will not make the same mistake again." Drake released my hand, and I felt him stiffen at my side. "Unlike Isabel, this one is of no consequence to me."

I froze, not sure what was going on.

"But I would appreciate it if you extended her some courtesy as my guest." Drake added.

His uncle glanced between us and smiled. What kind of game was he playing?

"Good. Then I look forward to getting to know her better." He regarded me up and down, eyes hungry like some sick predator. "That is if you don't mind sharing, of course..."

I froze, unable to speak. I glanced at Drake; I felt my face burn with rage at this man's audacity. Even worse was the shock that Drake would allow it.

"You know I do mind..." Drake said, surprisingly calm. He had to be playing along for a reason. He had to... "But if she changes her mind... and *wishes* to entertain you, I will not oppose it."

I was sure everyone could hear my heart thumping in my chest. Drake surely did because he reached for my hand and brought it to his lips. He kissed it and winked at me. This was all an act... Yes. He was bluffing, but why I did not know.

"Very well. I'm much more intrigued to hear how you managed to breach out of Xelraa."

"It's a long story, but I will tell you about it over dinner. Now, if you don't mind, I'd like to see my father." Drake said with finality, and the man lifted his brow, staring at Drake with an odd expression.

"I'm sad to say that won't be possible." Drake stiffened beside me, and the man seemed anything but sad. "Your father is gone I'm afraid."

Drake's hand trembled against mine, yet his grip was tight, as though I was his anchor keeping him afloat. I circled my thumb over his skin, trying to help him find control of the darkness threatening to burst free.

"How?" Drake managed to say through gritted teeth, gathering every ounce of his self-control.

"You will find much has changed. It was your father's search for peace that drove him and your mother to their graves."

"My mother?" Drake roared. Every last morsel of restraint vanished.

"I'm sorry." His uncle said. Drake dropped my hand and turned around.

In a moment, a blanket of darkness consumed Drake. I had watched him transform before, but not like this. The fire burned through his clothes. Fire exploded around him with the deep roar of the beast.

"Easy there..." His uncle warned. It was too late for warnings.

"Drake, please..." I pleaded, but my pleas met darkness and I knew he wasn't listening. The Dragon rocketed into the skies, leaving me behind. Alone. I stared after him... how could he leave me like this? He was hurting, and I could not reach him...

"Let him go," His uncle said. "It will do him good to spread his wings a bit. Come, I'll have your rooms prepared." I stared behind Drake's uncle, unsure if following him into the castle was a good idea. Without Drake here to protect me, I was easy prey for this man. But I had nowhere to go, so I sucked in a breath and marched behind him.

The walls and towers of the fortress stretched above as I followed the man and his guard through the gates into the castle.

There was obviously bad blood between Drake and his uncle. Something told me to stay clear from him, yet my mind still tried to understand why Drake wanted him to believe that I was of no consequence to him. Even worse, why would he insinuate that I was some piece of property that could be shared?

I glared at the man's back, fighting against all irrational thoughts while reminding myself that this was a different world. Perhaps this kind of hostility and behavior was acceptable. Regardless, I decided to keep my guard up. Something about him made my skin crawl, and my instincts were usually right.

I TRIED TO KEEP PACE, but I found myself distracted the moment I entered the castle. The grand entrance and high vaulted ceilings were breathtaking. In awe, I gaped at the stone pillars; four winding staircases, crafted of stone, led to the four wings above. I quickened my pace, it would be too easy to get lost here.

He pushed open a pair of doors, and we entered a large dining room. It was enormous. I had never seen anything quite like it. There was little time to focus on the details as I clocked Dagasti's glare.

He pulled at a cord from the wall and sat at the head of the grand table. A minute later, a burly woman strolled through the door.

"My lord. You called?" The woman glanced at me, then back at Dagasti.

"This is..." He looked at me, and I realized we had not been properly introduced.

"Belynda. My name is Belynda."

"Rommina, make sure she has what she needs: a room, clothes, food. The food can be brought up to your room, if you prefer to rest?"

"Yes," I responded quickly, hoping my eagerness to escape wasn't apparent. "Yes, please. I'm tired. Thank you."

"Very well. Make sure the prince's chambers are also made."

"My lord?" The woman froze at his request. The news of Drake's return had clearly not spread within the castle walls... yet.

"Just do as I said." And his refusal to explain made it clear he wasn't as pleased by Drake's return as he pretended to be.

"Yes, my lord. Right away. My lady, will you come with me?"

Drake's uncle clearly ran a tight ship here. I followed the woman through the winding halls and corridors. I stared at the paintings on the walls, losing myself as I spotted Drake's silver eyes.

"My lady, right this way."

"Just Belynda, please."

"Yes, my lady." The woman hurried down the hallway, and I smiled. I guess that would take some getting used to.

She climbed the stairs without breaking her stride. I, on the other hand, fought to catch my breath.

The woman stood by a door at the top of the stairs, waiting for me to reach the landing. As we entered, I stilled. It was magnificent. The room was circular, surrounded by an open balcony. There were no doors, no windows, only open sky... gray skies, but still sky. I marveled at the Realm below me. Despite the darkness and gloom, Druleska was magnificent.

"I will have supper brought up right away, my lady. Would you like us to prepare the tub?"

"That won't be necessary." I had made sure to be clean and presentable to meet Drake's parents, yet the woman glanced at my jeans and jacket and frowned.

"I will have clothes brought up, but I'm sure you will find some nightgowns in the wardrobe." She signaled to two wooden doors, which I assumed were the closet. I smiled politely.

"Thank you, Rommina."

"My lady." She curtsied and left the room.

What had I gotten myself into? And where the hell was Drake! I glanced down at myself and sighed. There was nothing wrong with my clothes... but I could see why Drake insisted I didn't pack a bag. These people were stuck in medieval times.

I threw myself onto the massive bed; it could easily fit five people or more.

How would I ever pass the time here? There was no televisions or phones, let alone electricity. Candles lined the stone veranda of the balcony and every stone surface in the room.

As I investigated, I came across a small alcove: a chamber pot of sorts. Another small room adjacent to it had a huge metal tub. No showers. No toilets... I grimaced.

A soft knock on the door startled me.

"My lady, may I come in?"

"Yes, please."

It was a younger girl this time, perhaps a couple of years younger than me. She placed a silver tray on the table and curiously turned to face me.

"My name is Tolly, my lady. Do you need help changing?"

I looked at the young girl, then the room, and everything started to sink in. How would I ever adapt to their customs? I didn't need a maid or anyone to help me dress or undress. Druleska was stuck in the past. Drake's uncle, who apparently now sat on the throne, was a sick man. And Drake... wasn't here when I needed him.

"My lady... are you alright?"

"I'm sorry. Tolly, is it?" I said as I sat at the edge of the bed, allowing the magnitude of today to sink in.

"Yes, my lady."

"Please. Just Belynda... I would feel better if you called me Belynda."

She clutched her hands to her apron, clearly uncomfortable.

"My lady, that's not allowed. You are a guest of the King here."

I raised an eyebrow. So, he did call himself King...

"I won't tell if you don't." I smiled conspiratorially, and she did too. It appeared the only way to stay sane in a place like this was to make friends, something I had never considered.

"Ok. Belynda?"

"Yes. Much better. Thank you. Oh, and Tolly, I don't need help dressing or undressing. I can manage on my own."

I stood and walked to the balcony, already yearning for home. "I've done it all my life, after all," I whispered.

"My lady... *Belynda*." She corrected. I smiled, pleased. "Is there something else I can get you?"

"No. Thank you." The girl made for the door. "Tolly, wait. Has Drake returned to the castle yet?" Her eyes widened.

"My lady, do you mean the prince?"

"Yes. Have you seen him?"

The girl's cheeks turned beet red.

"No, my lady... no." I could tell she didn't feel comfortable answering.

"Tolly, it's ok. You can speak freely here."

"No one has seen him. There is talk among the castle staff that the true King is back, but no one has seen the young Prince."

"Will you do me a favor and inform me if anyone does?"

"My lady... are you saying the rumors are true? That the Prince is back to claim the throne?"

I smiled at the girl.

"He is back, and I am his guest. But as far as taking back the throne, I do not know."

I had not thought about it. Would Drake want to stay here? Would he want to rule? It was his right. Once I was gone, it would undoubtedly give him a sense of purpose. "Thank you, Tolly."

"Belynda." She curtsied and left the room. I made a mental note to eradicate that blasted bowing too.

The food was surprisingly good. The stew was delicious, as were the puffed pastries. I took a sip of the liquid in the cup, and a strong whiff of alcohol invaded my mind. I coughed, then heaved. I assumed that's what Drake meant when he said wine tasted like pond water.

I thought about venturing out into the castle, but I wanted Drake to offer me the tour. Besides, something told me it wasn't a good idea, not until I managed to speak with him so he could explain what the hell was going on.

Since I was confined to this tower for the time being, I snuggled under the inviting covers and closed my eyes, waiting for Drake to appear.

I wasn't sure how long I slept, but the gray skies looked the same when I awoke, and I wondered what time it was. If Druleska lived in perpetual dusk, how could one function? How would I know when to go to dinner or when to sleep? Then, I remembered Drake's explanation that they didn't require sleep like humans did. Perhaps that wasn't a problem for them, like it was for me.

A loud knock had me out of bed.

Tolly stood at the door, a bundle of clothes in her hands.

"May I come in?"

I smiled, pleased that she was trying to drop the formalities.

"Yes. Please."

"I know you said you wouldn't require my assistance, but perhaps you would like my help choosing something appropriate for dinner? I hear the prince is attending."

I sat up as she placed the clothes on the bed. I wasn't hungry, but I wouldn't pass on the opportunity to see Drake.

What was so wrong with my clothes? It wasn't until now that I saw what Drake found so amusing when I had spoken of packing for Druleska. Clearly, my clothes were offensive. Glancing at my outfit, then at the pile of dresses on the bed, I sighed in defeat. I knew nothing of Drake's home or their traditions, and it wouldn't hurt to adjust if I wanted to fit in.

"Actually, I think I might need some help after all. Thank you."

The girl's face brightened.

"How about this one?" The dark blue dress was beautiful; it had short sleeves, yet wasn't what I had hoped for.

"What else have you got there?"

Next was a red corset top, which pooled to the floor from the waist. Not only did it look mighty uncomfortable, but I suspected red might be too much. The last thing I wanted was to draw more attention to myself.

"No," I said at once. "Do you have anything less... exotic?" She looked confused by my request. "Something more my style." I motioned to the jeans and t-shirt I wore, but Tolly smiled.

"No, my lady. We do not."

"Let me guess. Pants are only for men..." Her timid smile answered that questioned. "It's ok. I should have known better." What did I expect? I strolled out to the open balcony and stared at the horizon. Something was different. It was definitely darker. Tolly ignited the candles on the balcony, and then the ones inside the room.

"Would you like to look at the other dresses?"

"Tolly... Drake mentioned Druleska existed in eternal dusk. How is that possible? How long was I asleep for?"

"You slept most of the day. I figured. You were exhausted and didn't dare wake you. The prince's description was quite accurate. I'm afraid our days are not bright and warm like other realms. But we do have nights, and it will get darker soon."

"I'm curious; how do you tell time?"

"Our days are as equally long as our nights. I don't know much about the human world, but I've heard time is measured differently there. We follow the solstices."

Perhaps they weren't so different to us. If I recall correctly, the solstices marked the four seasons like the calendars in the human world.

"Thank you, Tolly. I think I'm going to wear the dark blue one." I doubted the rest of the selection was any different.

"Excellent choice, my lady. Are you sure you don't need assistance?" I assessed the long dress, realizing I would likely be unable to put this device on myself.

"Actually, perhaps it's best if you do help me. I don't really know what I'm doing." The girl smiled and pulled some garments from the closet. I removed my jeans, jacket, and shirt, feeling a little self-conscious about having a stranger help me dress. She gaped at my lacy underwear and bra.

"Those are beautiful."

"Thank you."

"I'm afraid we don't have anything like that, but if you'd like, I can take those from you later this evening and have the seamstress make you a few new pieces to wear. She's a good friend of mine."

"I would really like that. Thank you."

The dress was beautiful and fitted as though it had been tailored just for me. It hugged my shoulders, uplifted my breasts, and tightened my waist and hips before flowing to the floor. The sleeves were short, almost off the shoulders, and the deep plunge between my breasts was scandalous, yet all the dresses seemed to be cut similarly. In the end, I had to discard the bra altogether. It just wasn't right. So, I asked if the seamstress could make a minor adjustment to the new pieces, like removing the shoulder straps.

The midnight blue glinted beneath the glow of candlelight as I walked around, feeling the smooth material glide around me.

Tolly offered me flat slippers, but I chose to keep my boots. No one would notice them anyway.

When the skies were closed in darkness, painted by streaks of lightning illuminating the clouds, I decided it was time to find Drake.

After tripping several times over the hem of my dress, I learned that I had to descend with grace.

Despite the lack of electricity, I was surprised at how well-lit the castle was. Candles were everywhere, planted in the lanterns and chandeliers that dotted the castle. The court was magical at night.

My footsteps echoed against the polished floors of the galleries, yet this time, I was able to stop and study the portraits closely.

The painting of the boy had to be Drake as those eyes were unmistakably his. There was another one with his parents, who, to my surprise, appeared young and beautiful too; then there was another of Drake, highlighting the man I had come to know. Dark, handsome, and mysterious.

Drake was immortal, yet seeing portraits of him as a young boy to adult made me realize I had no idea how their aging process worked. He had not aged one bit from that last portrait to now.

I tried to remember where I needed to go. Sadness creeped in, however, as I glanced around the empty halls. Drake should have been here.

I wandered through the corridors, turning left and right. In my search, I found a library and my mind automatically sprung to Celest. She would have loved to explore it.

Closing the double doors behind me, I continued down the illuminated corridor, trying to find my way until the sound of dripping water caught my attention. I followed it until reaching an open terrace. There was a fountain with gargoyle-like statues sputtering water. I walked to sit by the fountain's border, dipping my fingertips into the stream. The water was surprisingly warm compared to the chilled night air.

Beautiful... I spun, startled, yet found no one.

"Hello... is someone there?" I glanced around, but it was as if the voice was a lost echo on the wind or perhaps my imagination. The hairs at the back of my neck prickled, and I couldn't escape the sensation that I was being watched. I gathered my dress and ran back through the throng of corridors.

The dining hall doors rose before me, and my heart leapt with relief. Then as I reached for the door, the voice echoing from within warmed my insides... Drake.

He sat opposite his uncle at the other head of the table and stood as I walked in.

"Belynda..." He strolled to my side and took my hand, guiding me to a chair that was too far from him for my liking.

"You look exquisite." He leaned down to whisper while pulling back a chair. His fingers graced the back of my neck before he returned to take his seat at the head of the table, which was far too excessive if you asked me. While I knew it was a compliment, the Drake I knew would have said I looked beautiful. Something told me he was still playing a part in front of his uncle.

After being gone for so long, I had anticipated his return home would be difficult, but it felt like an island separated us now, and I didn't know how to breach its walls. Maybe it was the news of his parent's death, or the freedom he had regained from returning here, or perhaps it had to do with me being his mate. I had never anticipated how hard this change would be for me; I had a whole new world to acclimate to, and Drake hadn't been here to guide me through it.

I stared at him as he sipped silently from his cup, and whatever was laced in the liquid was clearly starting to affect him. He traced his finger around the rim of the chalice, his eyes darkening as they shifted over the line of my breasts. His gaze seemed to undress me slowly, but that wasn't like Drake. Not while his uncle was present in the room with us.

"How are you doing?" my voice broke as I attempted to reach him.

"Fine." *Fine?* He was anything but. His eyes shifted to his uncle. "I apologize for this morning. Losing myself earlier..." He was apologizing to his uncle? But what about me...?

"It's understandable. You seem more yourself now that you've had time to process your loss and sort out your thoughts."

Was that how it seemed to his uncle? He obviously didn't know Drake as well as I did. Or perhaps it was the opposite, maybe I was the one who did not know him at all. Something pierced my soul, then. The realization that I had known him for a year or so, when Dagasti had known him for lifetimes.

There was no way Drake could have processed the loss of his parents in one afternoon. He was hurting, he had to be. But why was he acting so harsh and so cold towards me?

"I'm curious to know what has brought you back now. Do you seek to take your claim to the throne?"

His uncle was not one to beat around the bush. Drake took a measured sip from his cup before placing it firmly on the table.

He glanced at me for the briefest moment before addressing his uncle.

"No. That's not my intent. Besides, it looks to me like you're doing a good job. Much better than the one I could have done. Nonetheless, I'm at your service if you require my assistance in any court matters." Somehow, I doubted that, but Drake never saw his own worth.

"Thank you. Though I can't take all the credit. It was your father who forged this empire, after all." Dagasti's words solidified the permanence of his rule.

"Yes. He did, didn't he..." Drake's fists tightened, but it was only briefly before he managed to compose himself. He glanced around the high castle ceilings with a look of melancholy.

"Very well, if it's not the throne you seek, what has prompted your return?"

Drake leaned forward, his hands on the edge of the table.

"It was impossible for me to remain in the human world. You know how they fear exposure." He was lying to his uncle...

"Yes. The guardianship and their convenance... I remember it well."

"Then you understand I had nowhere else to go."

"Yes. What I'm intrigued to hear is how you managed to escape Xelraa. Or did the blood witches have something to do with that?"

Drake glanced at me and brought the chalice to his lips. When the cup was lowered, he was smiling.

"She did it," Drake confessed, shifting his gaze from me to Dagasti.

His uncle turned to me with keen eyes.

"Interesting..."

"She paid the price for it, though." Drake drank from his cup again. "Her magic is useless now." Dagasti frowned.

"Well, that is definitely bad news. Is that why you decided to keep her as your pet?"

I glanced at Drake, unable to utter a word.

"Something like that."

His words cut deeper than he would ever know. He must have been playing some type of game with his uncle, but the way he looked at me... The way he said those words... I wasn't sure of anything anymore.

"Well, you are welcome to stay for as long as you'd like. This is, after all, your home."

I wasn't so sure the invitation extended to me.

I ATE my dinner in silence, feeling out of place. When I was done, I excused myself, and claimed I was tired. Drake made no move to follow, so I left him and his uncle alone.

I was no fool, with his parents gone, Drake had to earn his uncle's trust, but his games had started before he realized his parents were dead. His reasoning for treating me like a worthless possession of his had to be good.

Knowing Dagasti was occupied with Drake, I began exploring the castle's many hallways and winding staircases, yet everywhere I went, I felt like I was intruding. The fire people were not as candid as I would have thought. Then again, I was a stranger: a human, a born guardian or blood witch as they liked to call us. I saw no reason for them to like or trust me, especially knowing what the guardianship represented to this Realm and the others.

By the time I reached my chambers, I had a loose notion of the castle's layout. The lower levels of the East wings appeared strictly for staff, and likely situated the kitchens, though I had not ventured that far following a series of disapproving looks.

The South wing led directly to an opulent room and in the

center were two imposing chairs: the throne room. I didn't linger long.

In the lower levels of the North wing was the library and many other unoccupied rooms. It made me wonder why I had been set up in one of the towers if there was so much more space down there. Perhaps the towers were reserved for special guests? Dagasti had instructed Rommina to prepare Drake's chamber, too, and I found myself wondering where his room was. Would he come to me tonight, or would he choose to stay on his own? He certainly had a lot of explaining to do. I wanted to be angry with him but I knew there must be a good reason for his behavior. His lies.

I tried to get out of the dress, but there was no way to reach the clips at the back. I could barely move in it as it was. I pulled on the rope by the bedside, and a few minutes later, Tolly was at the door.

"My lady?"

"Belynda." I corrected her, and she smiled apologetically.

"Do you need help with that?"

"Yes please. How anyone lives wearing this day and night is beyond me."

Tolly laughed, seemingly much more comfortable in my presence, as I was in hers too.

"Do you know where Drake's chambers are?" I found myself asking, and her cheeks turned crimson red. She likely wasn't used to anyone addressing him so informally.

"Yes, my lady. The prince's chambers are in the West tower."

"Why the towers when so many rooms are available in the lower wings?"

"The royal family has always occupied the towers, my lady. It makes it easier for them to come and go." As I glanced at the lavish balcony, I realized what she meant. It was easier for them to shift and fly out. Yet I wasn't one of them, unless... the easy accessibility also extended to me. A dragon could fly into my room at any moment...

"My lady, is there a reason why you asked about the prince's chambers?"

"I was just curious. I haven't seen him much since we arrived. Why?"

"I... it's not my place to say, but I hope you're not planning on going to his chambers unannounced, my lady."

I glanced at the girl's mortified expression in the mirror as she tied my nightgown.

"Is there a reason why I shouldn't?" I turned to her. "His uncle knows we're... *together*," I added, not wanting to say mated. That term sounded so primal.

"It has always been the prince who orders who visits him and on which nights, my lady."

What in the world was she talking about? Is that how they did things here? Could that have been why his exchange with his uncle was so debasing to me yet natural to them? Whatever he had done, whichever way he had lived his life before, that was back then. Not now.

I walked to the balcony, staring at the thundering skies and fires illuminating the city beneath me. Who would visit him? Were there others? *No...* There couldn't be. He was just pretending.

"Tolly, has anyone else visited him?" As I asked, a hole opened inside my heart.

"No, my lady. No one. You've just arrived and the prince has barely been around. Many of us have not even seen him. In fact, many do not believe he's back." As she spoke, I felt the hole in my chest repair itself. What was wrong with me? I had nothing to worry about. But if that were the case, perhaps I should be thankful. It would mean he could move on quickly and perhaps my death wouldn't cut him as deeply as I feared it would.

Tolly said goodnight, and I slipped into bed. I couldn't tell the time, but I was exhausted: a sign it was way past my human bedtime.

I closed my eyes, thinking about Drake, and about what lay ahead. I had to speak with him. If he didn't come to me tonight, I would go in search of him tomorrow. It wouldn't hurt to explore the castle some more, to discover what lay beyond the four stairs in the grand entrance and what resided on the second floor. Perhaps I'd find Drake's room if I was lucky.

Whatever Tolly said did not apply to me. Things were different now. Drake would not care if I visited him, and he certainly would not be calling anyone else to warm his bed.

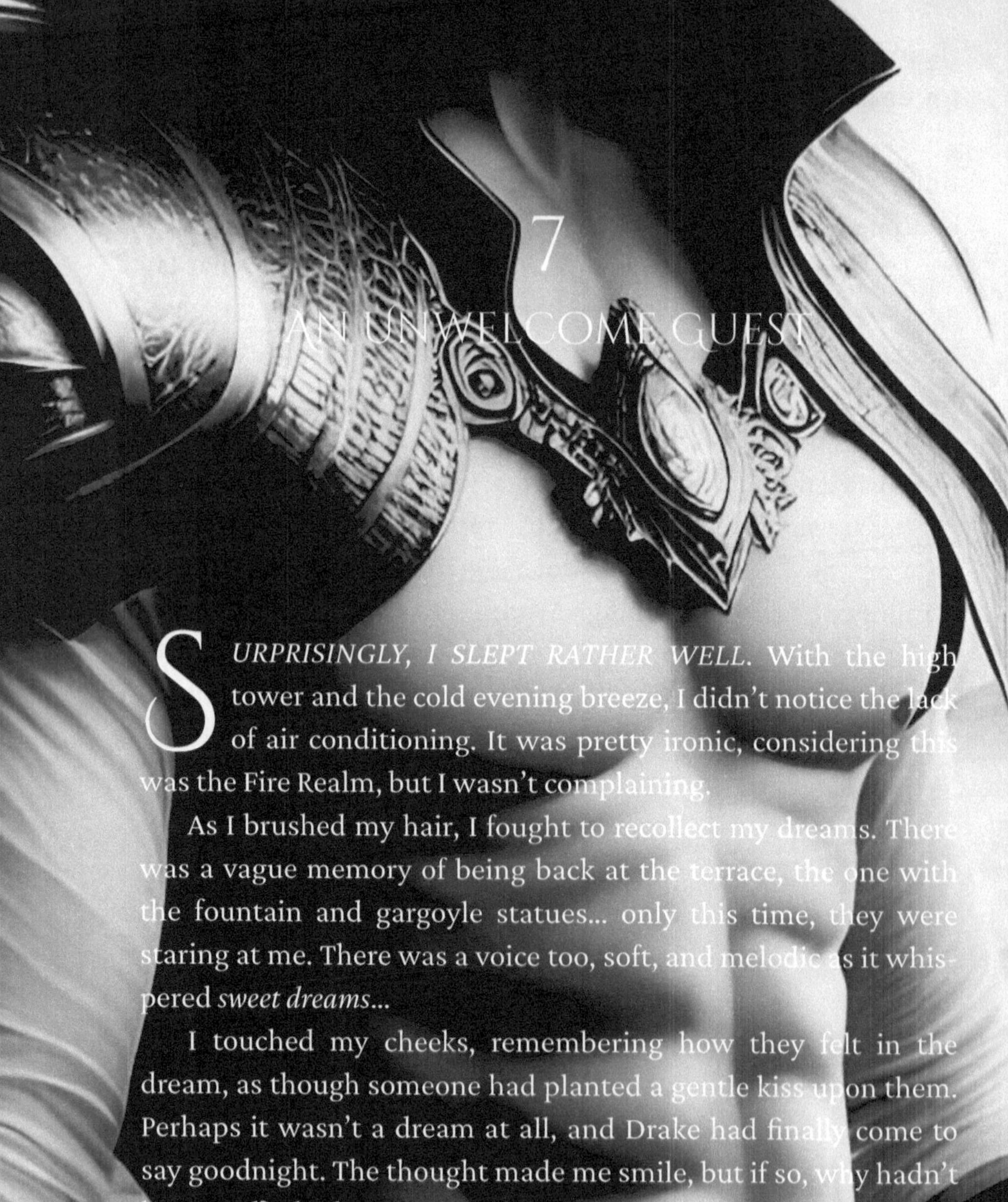

7

AN UNWELCOME GUEST

SURPRISINGLY, *I SLEPT RATHER WELL.* With the high tower and the cold evening breeze, I didn't notice the lack of air conditioning. It was pretty ironic, considering this was the Fire Realm, but I wasn't complaining.

As I brushed my hair, I fought to recollect my dreams. There was a vague memory of being back at the terrace, the one with the fountain and gargoyle statues... only this time, they were staring at me. There was a voice too, soft, and melodic as it whispered *sweet dreams...*

I touched my cheeks, remembering how they felt in the dream, as though someone had planted a gentle kiss upon them. Perhaps it wasn't a dream at all, and Drake had finally come to say goodnight. The thought made me smile, but if so, why hadn't he stayed? I had to speak with him. If we continued on like this, I would lose myself in this place before my time came.

Tolly brought a basin of water, and I cleaned myself as best as possible. I wasn't sure what I would do without her. She helped me into a dark purple dress this morning; it puffed a bit on the shoulders and pushed up my breasts, but I could breathe easier in it, so I was instantly sold.

"Thank you for washing my things last night."

"It was no problem at all. I'm glad you liked the pieces my friend made for you. She said if you needed anything else to let her know."

"I still can't believe she did these so quickly."

"There is a lot one can accomplish when sleep is unnecessary." She was right. It was so easy to forget I was the only human around here.

"Either way. Don't forget to thank her for me." The quality of the undergarments far exceeded the expensive types sold in the human world. The materials were smooth and luxurious. While things were still rocky as I settled in, it wouldn't be long until I asked her to make me pants, too.

Finding my way to the dining hall this time was easier. As I approached the doors, I heard voices. Dagasti... and another I did not recognize. The door was slightly ajar, and I didn't want to be impolite by barging in, so I knocked before pushing on the heavy doors.

"Come in." Dagasti's voice resonated through the doors.

"Good morning. I apologize for the intrusion. I didn't see Drake this morning and thought he might be with you." I asked, not daring to intrude further. Dagasti sat at the head of the table, and on the opposite chair, where Drake had sat the night before, sat another man, his back stiff.

"You're awfully attached to him, aren't you?" Dagasti said as if I were Drake's leech. I wanted to respond but bit my tongue. "I believe he went off early this morning. Why don't you join us? Have some breakfast."

I wasn't used to all the ordering about, yet something told me refusing him would cause a scene, so I accepted out of fear.

The man sitting at the other end of the table stood as I took the same place I had last night.

"You're not staying?" Dagasti questioned.

"I'd rather not." The man responded curtly. I could feel his eyes burning into me. Was I the cause of his hasty departure? Could these people degrade me anymore? I was done letting them think I was a puppet they could use and treat as they pleased. I wouldn't cower under their eyes anymore. I had done nothing wrong.

For the first time, I felt like myself since arriving here. I allowed myself to survey the man, challenging him, though his eyes fought back. Daring me. I didn't look away. Who the hell was he? He appeared different from the fire people; his clothes were finer, dressed in lavish midnight-blue pants; his white-collar shirt was crisp and neat, nothing like I had seen the fire people wear thus far. No, he definitely didn't fit in this place. These people, I noted, preferred to dress in leathers of black, reds, and dull grays. No, this man didn't fit here; he was just like me. Yet he appeared pretty comfortable, despite my presence unsettling him. Perhaps he thought himself too superior to share a table with a human? He was young, proud, and strikingly charming. He knew it, too. I had no doubt about that.

I needed to get out of this place. Since we had arrived, I had barely seen Drake, and everywhere I turned, I felt like an outcast. Suddenly, I couldn't breathe. I shot up, the chair legs scraping against the floor and echoing in the dining hall.

"Actually, if you'll excuse me... I seem to have lost my appetite." I stood up and strolled past the man, no longer caring what anyone thought, least of all Dagasti. It felt like I was in some sort of nightmare that I was desperate to wake up from, but never could. Wiping my tears with the sleeve of the dress, I decided I was done feeling sorry for myself, and went in search of Drake.

I WAS in the grand hall by the entrance, about to explore the second floors, when the castle doors swung open. Drake... a knot formed in my throat at the sight of him.

"Where have you been?" I asked, "I haven't seen you! And you've barely spoken to me since we arrived. Do you care to explain what the hell is going on?"

He closed the distance but hesitated as he stood before me.

"I'm so sorry. Please forgive me." He took my hand and kissed it, and I was desperate to bury myself in him.

"Speak to me. Please." I begged.

"Belynda, it's not easy. You already understand my fight for control; it's why we came here. But now that I am back and my father is gone, I have a part to play. I'm not proud to admit it, but I can't show weakness. Not in-front of my uncle or any of them."

"You are *not* weak."

"But I am. Dagasti sensed it the second he saw us together. I see it in the way he looks at you. My uncle is not to be trusted." He whispered. "He suspects you are my weakness, and I don't want that to become leverage for him or anyone to hurt you. Do you understand?"

"So you're avoiding me and being cold towards me because you don't want people to see how important I am to you?" The hole in my chest suddenly gaped open once more.

"It's not like that... I only want to protect you. Belynda, with my father gone... I'm a threat to them. My uncle has been nothing but welcoming, but my father did not raise me to be a fool."

He sighed, running his fingers through his hair. There was so much more he wasn't saying. What was I doing...? I was supposed to be here for Drake, this was as difficult for me as it was for him.

"Is that why you didn't tell him the real reason why we're here?"

"Yes. My uncle cannot know."

I touched his face, and he took my hand and kissed my fingers.

"I'm lost here without you, Drake…"

"I know. I'm sorry. But it will be ok. I promise."

"Do what you must to control your fire and keep us safe. But please… do not abandon me."

"I would never abandon you. I love you."

"I love you too."

He looked behind us, took my hand, and guided us into a door under one of the staircases. Closing the door behind us, he pinned my body against it and devoured my mouth. His lips melded and branded themselves to mine, and for a moment, I forgot where we were. He cupped my breasts and grunted.

"Last night at dinner, I fought the need to jump over that table like an animal and tear that beautiful dress right off your porcelain skin." I sucked in a breath as his lips burned a slow path down my neck.

"Why didn't you come to me after?"

"Last night, I drank too much. I wouldn't have been gentle… I cannot allow myself to get lost like that. Not with you."

"Yes, you can."

"No, love. I could hurt you, and then, I would never forgive myself."

I cupped his face as his eyes searched mine.

"Tonight," I said and smiled. "I still have these…" I took his hand and glided it under my dress to the breach between my thighs; his fingers grazed the lacy material of my panties. He sucked in a breath and gently bit my shoulder, hands caressing my behind over the soft fabric. I felt his smile against my skin.

"I'm afraid they won't last past tonight. I think I much prefer these to those undergarments I'm sure ladies still use here."

"That won't be a problem. I already had some new pieces made, and they are even more *exquisite*." I used the same word he used last night, teasing him. He stared at me in awe, and his laughter filled the empty room.

"You've only just arrived, and you've already managed that? I can't wait to see what you can do in a month, a year... a lifetime."

"As long as it takes, I'm here for you."

I stared into his eyes. I was a mortal; we both knew a lifetime was impossible. Even a month or year was uncertain for me, but he didn't know that. All he had to know was that I would love him until my last breath.

"I did promise to show you the town. How does a walk sound?"

I beamed up at him and kissed him with force.

Drake took my hand, guiding me out of the room and across the great hall.

"If it isn't the prince of the Fire Realm himself." Drake and I froze, as the man from earlier in the dining hall descended the winding stairs. The man's eyes scanned my dress, and Drake squeezed my hand.

"What are you doing here?" Drake asked, abandoning the formalities. Perhaps he was an unwelcome guest. "What happened to the realms being at war?" Drake questioned, taking measured steps to meet the men at the landing of the stairs.

"Dagasti and I have come to some agreements. But I won't bore you with the details. I see you're *busy*." My cheeks burned as his eyes fell on me. His inspection made Drake's grip tighten.

"Don't let me keep you then," Drake said curtly, dismissing

him. Yet I got the impression he wanted to take me away from him as fast as possible.

The man smiled, and a cold chill slithered down my spine. I stared at his retreating back with curiosity.

"Who was that?"

"No one you want to know." Drake turned towards the South wing.

"Where are you going? I thought you said we'd go for a walk?"

"Belynda, I must speak with my uncle. The walk can wait."

He disappeared down the corridor before I could protest further. What happened to not abandoning me?

I took measured breaths to collect myself as I looked at the castle gates and the town streets beyond. I wasn't a coward. They wouldn't dare harm a guest of the royal family. I tightened the cape around my shoulders as the guards opened the gates. At least I wasn't a prisoner.

A little boy crossed my path, and I noticed the green scales patterning his face. I wondered what he was. I stopped at the blacksmiths who forged their weapons, staring in awe at their strength and skill. I felt odd here; I could feel it in their stares and whispers.

I pulled the hood tighter around my shoulders, as if that could shield me from their unfriendly stares.

Not everyone was hostile, though. An old man behind a market cart was smiling kindly at me as I approached.

"You may take some." He offered me the satchel of strawberries when he caught me looking at them.

"No. Thank you. I can't." I couldn't pay for them. I had no money. Heck, I didn't even know what form of currency they used here.

"Just the same. Here." The old man pushed the small bag into my hands, and I smiled, taking one and biting into it.

"Mmmm, it's delicious." It really was. Fresh and ripe. "Thank you for your kindness." I made a mental note to return with money and repay the old man.

Drake was right about the perpetual dusk. He had been serious when he said Druleska never saw sunlight, though a part of me had hoped he was exaggerating. I grimaced as I surveilled the gloomy skies. These people lived under a constant haze of gray.

The markets were buzzing with life, and though I had never enjoyed the social aspects of the human world, being here made me feel almost at home. At the very least, I wasn't alone and locked up inside those castle walls.

The rain fell in a slow drizzle, but no one seemed to mind. I did. Pulling the cape around my shoulders, I kept my head down as I weaved through the throng of people to find shelter.

My boot caught on the edge of my cape that dragged through the mud. All I saw was a metal cart filled with wood as I dove headfirst toward it.

As firm hands pulled me back with force, the carriage trailed out of sight. I tried regathering my bearings, and froze... I was pressed securely against a man's chest, my hands clung to his shoulders for support. I sucked in a breath and instantly released my hold of the man. I lowered my hood to offer my gratitude, but as I stared into those eyes, I could not speak. His hands remained against my waist. It was him...

I stepped out of the man's arms, attempting to escape the depth of his eyes. They were the deepest blue I had ever seen, like the darkest part of the ocean during a storm.

"What? No thank you?"

No one you want to know... Drake's words from earlier whispered in my mind. His words brought me to my senses.

"I was perfectly fine. You didn't have to bother. Good day." I shielded my face from the rain again and quickly turned down an alley, but I could feel him following. I should have run faster but I was no coward, so I stopped and turned to face him.

"Stop following me." I snapped, yet the insufferable man merely grinned.

"What makes you think I'm following you? Perhaps you're in my way."

I scoffed and turned in the opposite direction, but halted again as his laughter followed in my wake.

"I thought you were on your way? Or perhaps you're stalking me."

His dark and melodious laugh seemed to attract attention.

"That's an interesting assumption. I'm merely trying to assist someone that is clearly lost." As if...

"I'm not lost. I'm perfectly capable of finding my way back."

"Are you now... point the way then." He challenged. With a jerk of his chin, he grinned. Oh, how desperately I wanted to erase that look from his face. I peered at my surroundings and realized I had ventured so far out that I had no idea which way to go. There was a castle tower in the distance, so I offered a triumphant smile and pointed in that direction. His laughter brought even more curious eyes to us.

"Let me guess. The tower gave it away?" He mocked, and I crossed my arms.

"You are no gentleman, sir." Furious, I looked up at him as the drizzle increased, bathing my face.

"I never claimed to be." He bit back, and slowly the smile faded from his face. He seemed even more beautiful as rain droplets trailed down his dark hair and over the sharp edges of his cheeks and chin. For a moment, I felt the urge to reach out a hand and touch his face...

"You shouldn't be out alone. You're not safe, and he is too trusting." His words broke whatever spell he had put on me, and I stepped away from him.

"From you. I'm not safe from you!" I said. He didn't deny it. Instead, he smiled, eyes assessing my face. Whatever trance I had been under seconds ago vanished. I felt my hand shake as I fought the urge to smack the grin off his arrogant face. Why are all immortals so overconfident? Perhaps their unnaturally good looks gave them a warped sense of superiority.

"I could be dangerous to you, but I think you're safe today." What the hell did that mean? He walked away before I could demand an explanation. In shock, I stared at his retreating back, but then his pace slowed, and he turned to me.

"Oh, you were right... just follow the tower." He called out, winking at me before disappearing down an alley. *Insufferable.*

I was left with many questions, but the most important one was who the hell was he?

He could be dangerous to me, but not today? What was that supposed to mean? Would he pose a danger in the future? Could he be the one to face Drake and end my life? Had I just stared into the eyes of the man who would bring about my downfall?

He and Drake obviously had their differences. I thought of his words, saying Drake was 'too trusting'. Drake was being anything but...

The more I thought about it, the clearer it became. I would have to stay clear of their conflict. Whatever it was, I could see myself getting caught in the middle.

But what if he was right? What if I was in danger?

DRAKE

Perhaps allowing Belynda to come had not been such a good idea after all. Being without her would have been easier to live with than knowing the dangers lurking around every corner she walked. I could do absolutely nothing about it.

I sensed we weren't safe the moment Dagasti welcomed us and not my father or mother. I hated myself for my behavior. She didn't deserve this, not after everything she had given up following me here. But I had no choice. If Dagasti realized how much she mattered to me, that I was willing to sacrifice my life for her... he wouldn't hesitate to hurt her in every possible way just to get to me. It was why I was forced to lie about her powers, too. Technically, she was powerless, but he didn't have to know why or how temporary that might by.

My confrontation with him had not eased the tensions either. On the contrary, he had made it abundantly clear that Callix was a visitor, and any hostility between us would only strain their negotiations.

A part of me had burned to call him out and demand my rightful place, but I knew what that would mean for Belynda and I. Taking a claim to Druleska's throne would anchor me to a life in this realm, and something told me Belynda would wither away here. I had to play the obedient nephew well if I hoped to deter his interest in Belynda. I didn't know what he was up to, but I would find out.

I was trapped in this place I once called home. Yet I could not seek the one thing that gave me comfort. *Should not...* especially if I hoped to keep her safe. However, I needed to see her, even for a moment...

I knocked on her chamber, but I let myself in when there was no answer. My uncle had offered her the best accommodations, and for that, I was grateful.

"My lord. I'm so sorry. I didn't know there was anyone here." The young girl bowed and kept her head down.

"Where is she?" I demanded without pleasantries. My tone, I noted, was perhaps a bit harsh, but I was playing my part. The part that was expected of me as the prince of the realm.

"My lord, I have not seen the lady since this morning when she returned for her cloak."

I gripped the stone rails of the balcony as my eyes scanned the city below. She would never change. She had no sense of self-preservation, not even in a completely different world. Did she not realize how fragile she was amongst these people? My fire hummed with ire, but I pushed it down. Taking a deep breath, I allowed myself to take in all the scents, tasting them and discarding them as none were hers. She was out there without me, and I had to find her.

As I reached the grand hall, the castle doors opened. Cold air streamed in, her scent trailing with it... she was trembling.

I closed the distance, uncaring who saw us, and pulled her into my arms. I allowed my fire to blanket her, but as I did, I noted the subtle hint of his scent mingled with hers, and I stopped breathing altogether. My fists tightened, and I pulled away.

"What happened...?" I demanded. Her eyes met mine briefly, but she looked away. Her lips tightened in a thin line. She was angry...

"Nothing. You were busy. I went for a walk." She strolled past me, heading for the North tower, and I followed. I couldn't pry. Wouldn't pry. She would tell me. Wouldn't she?

"You won't do that again. Promise me."

She kept her pace, ignoring me, and the darkness burned. I seized her arm, making her halt.

"So, I'm a prisoner now?" She bit back, and I took a breath to collect myself. Though as I did, I smelled him again, and something primal snapped inside of me.

"You are not a prisoner, but you will be if you cannot promise to remain inside for your own safety." I snapped. The hurt in her eyes tore open my soul.

"What's happening to you? I don't recognize you anymore." Her eyes clouded with unshed tears, and I watched her disappear up the tower stairs.

I did not follow her. I couldn't move, afraid of what I would do or say. She was right about one thing, I didn't recognize myself either, though I wasn't sure if the fire was to blame this time. *No...* Jealousy and madness clouded my judgment, and if I was not going to get the truth from her, I would get it from him.

He was gone. All traces of Callix had vanished, and I was left to drown my thoughts and this rage inside of me with wine. I could picture him with his hands on her. She was mine... the bottle shattered against the wall, and the darkness inside me roared. I tried to drown the thoughts, but they were asphyxiating. Why didn't she say she was angry with me? The darkness sank its claws deeper into my burning soul, reminding me I was to blame.

There was a blaze inside of me that needed to be released. I pulled on the service cord and called, even against my better judgment. The servant, whose name I had yet to bother remembering, came a few minutes later.

"My lord. You called."

"Bring an odalisque."

The girl stared at me, unmoving.

"Did you not hear me!" I roared, and the servant girl ran from the room, terrified. I could do this. I would satisfy my fire and regain control of myself. If not that, at the very least, it would make me feel better for her lies. I punched the mirror, and it shattered into a million pieces before my feet.

I thought of the many ways I could take her, yet none were gentle. I burned to claim Belynda now and make her plea for release, tormenting her would be my form of revenge. I stormed to the balcony, trying to ease my burning soul though I couldn't. All I saw was him holding her, kissing her, and branding her body with his hands. What was worse, I pictured her response to his touch...

I punched the stone wall. What the hell was I doing...? This was not the way ordinary people dealt with their emotions. I was overreacting. Overthinking. But the monster taunted me, reminding me I was to blame for abandoning her. She wouldn't have craved another's touch if I had stayed by her side. The monster reminded me I was beyond redemption, so I might as well enjoy the darkness while I burned in hell for my sins.

There was a soft rasp at the door.

"Enter!" I thundered impatiently.

She was a slip of a girl. She reminded me of Belynda. *Nooo!* The fire inside me roared. It didn't want to think, only to feel. *To forget.*

The gown's thin, almost sheer material, flowed down her breasts, and a feral growl escaped my lips.

My eyes traced the length of her long legs as I imagined Belynda bent before me as I buried myself in her. The monster rejoiced.

"Come." I beckoned, and she obeyed. Why couldn't Belynda listen when I asked her to? I only wanted her to be safe... The monster inside me burned. *Take her, he urged.* Sink yourself into her mouth and forget your misery.

"On your knees," I commanded, and she did as I said.

My hand moved to trace her skin, but I stopped myself when images of Callix stroking Belynda's face came to mind. I was consumed by jealousy, and the monster sneered. This would be enough to forget, I reminded myself as I loosened the belt. I anticipated how good it would feel to release my fire and frustration inside her mouth.

"Look at me."

Her eyes found mine, and when I saw the monster reflected in them, pieces of me shattered like shards from the broken mirror. *What the hell was I doing?* This girl didn't deserve this. I was a monster, and Belynda deserved so much better. I turned around and closed my eyes, but I could feel the last of my control vanishing.

"No," I said to myself as I took a step away from her.

"Master. Have I done something wrong?" What was wrong with me... I turned to face the innocent girl before I did something I would regret.

"Leave now."

"Master..."

"Just leave!" I thundered, fighting to stay in control. As the chamber door closed behind her, I allowed the darkness to take over me as I plunged from the heights of the tower. You could have your freedom tonight, but I would be damned if I allowed my fire to consume whatever was left of my soul.

BELYNDA

The encounter was enough to make me retreat to my chambers. It certainly crushed any plans I had to explore the rest of the castle. I was beyond upset at Drake and didn't feel like humiliating myself further in front of Dagasti, so instead, I asked Tolly to bring dinner to my chamber.

I was restless. I had never argued with Drake before, and it was eating me inside. Sure, he was an idiot for insinuating he could keep me locked in here, but I knew he wanted to protect me. Though it was the way he went about it that upset me. His demands. Since we arrived, it was as if this place was transforming him, and I had to do everything I could to keep him afloat.

The water spilled over as I stepped into the tub. I sank into its warmth, and it felt amazing.

Tolly added petals, salts, and oils to the water, but her mind seemed elsewhere.

"Is everything alright?"

"My lady?"

"You seem distracted."

She looked down, avoiding my eyes.

"You don't have to tell me if you don't want to. I understand. I only wanted to know if you were ok, that's all." Her face looked torn with guilt.

"I'm ok. It's not me, really. I just…" She looked away and hesitated, measuring her words. "I heard the master called for a visit to his room."

Her words trailed out of her mouth, and she glanced away, embarrassed. I stared at the girl before me, yet without really seeing her.

"When?" I whispered. A deep-rooted ache tore through my chest.

"This evening. Just a while ago."

I closed my eyes as if the action would stop my heart from shattering into a million pieces. How could I save him if he was fighting to break away? Had something changed? Did he not want me anymore?

"You can go, Tolly. I'll manage on my own. Thank you."

"My lady..." I saw the worry on her face.

"I'll be alright. I promise."

She bowed and left the room, leaving me alone with my misery.

THE COLD WATER dripped from my body as I finally found the will to move. I tightened the nightgown in front of me and sat on the edge of the bed, staring into nothingness. How could he do this after all our promises to each other? My soul ached, but a part of me refused to shed a tear. I was... furious, overcome with rage. But I could not bring myself to close my eyes.

The once-open room appeared smaller, almost as if the tower walls were slowly conspiring to cave in on me. I slipped a robe over my nightgown and descended towards the main hall, bare-footed. I passed the portrait hall and found myself searching his eyes. My fists clenched, and I ran down the corridor. I couldn't look at him.

As I passed the stairs, I hesitated. Curiosity got the best of me and I lifted my nightgown, taking the stairs to the second floor. The castle was awfully quiet at this hour, and I was glad because I needed to be alone. I just had to be in motion to keep myself distracted. Anything to keep me from remembering Drake's betrayal.

A red carpet with golden trims, rolled along the floors of the corridor. The glow from the lanterns made the hall look eerie. Every door I passed was closed, yet it was late enough that I didn't dared to peek inside.

Once I reached the end of the corridor, I turned around to

explore the opposite wing, but halfway back, there was a noise up ahead and I panicked.

I pushed myself against one of the pillars, hoping no one would see me. Peering down the hall, there was no sound... no movement. I picked up my gown and crept quietly down the corridor, and back towards the stairs, but I froze when I noticed a door slightly ajar.

A servant perhaps... I attempted to slip past them, then realized that if their hearing abilities were enhanced like Drake's. I might as well stroll in there and make my presence known.

I tiptoed and glanced inside as I passed the open door. Candlelight danced against the walls. There was a mirror in the distance and a shadow inside. I held my breath for a second. It was him... shirtless. His smooth skin glowed against the candles. I couldn't move, instead watching the taut muscles of his back tense as he reached to the floor for something.

His gaze went straight to the mirror when he stood, and I moved away from the threshold. I panicked and hurried down the corridor, wondering if he had seen me. He had looked directly in my direction when he glanced in the mirror.

No... I shook the thought away. He couldn't have. If he had, he would have come after me. I was sure of it.

I descended the stairs and made for the library, wondering what he was doing back at the castle. After seeing him leave, I didn't think he would return. Not after his hostile encounter with Drake this morning...

The library was covered in darkness. Clearly, it didn't get many visitors. I opened one of the curtains, and the light from the thunder offered enough clarity for me to find the lanterns and light them up.

I scanned some of the sections, trying to find a book to pass the time, but most of them were in a language that was unfamiliar to me.

Returning yet another volume back in its place, I yawned, and felt the day's exhaustion catching up to me. I dowsed the fire in the lamps and returned to the solitude of my chambers.

THE GLOOM of day dressed the sky, and the bed felt empty and cold. A part of me had hoped it wasn't true. I had waited for Drake to march through my door all night, but he never came. No. He had turned to another instead and something inside of me had shattered.

I stared at my reflection in the mirror. My somber expression was an odd contrast to the beautiful sky-blue dress.

"I can barely breathe."

"I'm sorry. Here. Is this better?" Tolly asked, loosening the strings on the back of the dress.

"Much. Thank you."

"I can have breakfast brought up if you prefer to stay in, my lady?" I turned away from the mirror and put on the slippers.

"That won't be necessary. I will go down shortly. Thank you, Tolly."

She smiled and excused herself before leaving.

He was mistaken if he thought I would wither away in this place. I would pick up every broken piece of my heart, march into that dining hall, and look him straight in the eyes. I would not cower when he was the one who had wronged me.

THE CORRIDORS and galleries were busier with staff this morning, cleaning and polishing everywhere. When I entered the dining hall, I was surprised to find it empty, though I wasn't sure if I felt relieved or disappointed that Drake wasn't here. I pulled the service cord and took my seat. A few minutes later, Rommina appeared.

"My lady. Good morning."

"Good morning, Rommina." I decided it was useless to insist she dropped the formalities when she had ignored all my requests to do so.

"I will have breakfast served right away." She announced.

"Rommina," I called after her, and she paused by the door. "Will Drake and Dagasti be joining me?" She was clearly displeased by my lack of formality when addressing them, but I was making a point.

"My lady, I'm afraid the Prince and Lord Dagasti broke fast at dawn and left the castle on errands."

I didn't understand. Drake said he didn't trust his uncle, yet was now out running errands with the man. He made no effort to come to me, to even explain or apologize or tell me of his plans. There was no point in trying to understand or excuse his actions. I was nothing to him.

"Is there anything else you need, my lady?"

"No, Rommina. Thank you."

If he was cold enough to forget our bond so quickly, what made me think I was important enough to be considered in his plans? My stomach twisted. What had happened to us? To him? I had not changed. The pain I felt inside was proof that I still loved him, even though his betrayal had shattered something inside me.

Did he not love me anymore? Was I not good enough? *Stop it!* I shook the thoughts away as a servant walked in with a platter of food.

The girl placed the plate before me alongside a silver cup. She curtsied before leaving, without saying a word.

I stared at the food before me, fighting to push down the knot forming in my throat. Eating alone reminded me of how much I missed my home. My family.

I picked up the fork and forced myself to swallow a few pieces of egg and toast. However, I couldn't stomach much, not between the corset and the knot in my throat.

Tracing my fingers over the smooth marble tabletop, I realized this was the first time I could appreciate the room's details. The elegant table hosted space for fourteen guests; the chairs had intricate wooden carvings on the back, supported with armrests. Very medieval.

The grand chandelier that usually floated high above was lowered close to the table today, likely to replace the burnt candles with new ones.

I pushed back from my chair and surveilled the rest of the room. Erected on both sides were four enormous pillars lining the stone walls.

Evenly placed between those columns were golden Dragon statues towering a few meters high. Hundreds of candles rested at the base of each statue upon layers and layers of melted wax.

Gray skies blanketed the kingdom, but the three opulent glass windows covering the North wall offered a panoramic view of the mountains and their peaks as they disappeared through the clouds.

The room was majestic, but something told me it had once been even more magical.

I had no idea what to do to occupy my time. The servants moved to and from the castle corridors. Once again, I ended up back at the library. The books provided a strange comfort, and the smell of old wood, polish, and dust offered a piece of home. Nostalgia beckoned me to this place.

I glanced at the library's second floor and decided to try my luck there today. I took to the first section and pulled a few random books, yet I could not understand them.

I moved the rolling stepladder to inspect the higher shelves. I examined it before climbing to ensure it was secure. It proved sturdy enough. Discarding my slippers, I pulled up the hem of the dress and climbed the ladder.

I was right. They kept foreign language books above eye level and the native ones within reach. A book on phytology wasn't something I was remotely interested in, so after studying it briefly, I placed it back. Most of the books in that section were related to botany so I tried my luck on the next section, moving the ladder and climbing again to reach the top shelves.

The first one was an alchemy book, and though it wasn't what I was looking for, I glanced through it. I placed the book under my arm as I descended, but the hem of the dress caught under my foot, and before I could clasp my hands on the rails, I was flying backward.

I watched the roof of the library float away from me as I fell, almost like slow motion as my life flashed before my eyes.

My body jolted, but I never hit the floor.

"We have to stop meeting like this."

Sapphire eyes searched my face, and it took me a moment to collect myself and realize he had saved me yet again. I wondered how he always seemed to be near when I needed him.

He made no move to put me down, and for a moment, I felt content being in the stranger's arms. But something deep in my chest twisted as I remembered Drake, and I sobered up.

"You can put me down now."

He hesitated, staring back at me, then lowered my feet to the floor. He steadied me, holding me close.

"Thank you," I said, putting some distance between us.

"Anytime." He offered politely, surprising me, for I had expected some snide remark.

I walked back to the first section and picked up the slippers I had discarded, not bothering to put them on. I could feel the stranger's eyes burning into me, silently studying me. I ignored it.

He turned the book that had fallen in his hand and smiled.

"Alchemy? Interesting choice." He said, and I got the distinct feeling he was baiting me.

"What's wrong with it?"

"Nothing. It just doesn't seem like something you would be interested in."

I stared at him.

"What gave it away?" I asked, intrigued to know how he had reached such an assumption.

"Your face." He said. "I was actually sitting down in that corner when you walked in." He pointed to the lower level. "I didn't want to startle you, but I was curious. Botany was obviously a hard pass, and by the look on your face when you decided on this one, I gathered it wasn't your ideal choice, but just something you'd settle for." I stared at the blue eyed God before me. I wasn't sure whether to feel offended for his apparent stalking of me or grateful for the fact he was. I hated to think what could have happened to me.

"Sadly, you're right," I admitted, and he smiled. "I haven't had much luck."

"Let me guess? Novels and Classics?" He crooked his head to the side and ran his fingers over his chin, lined with a shade of stubble.

"Am I that predictable?"

"Truthfully, it was just a guess." He smirked. "I think it is a common preference amongst ladies."

"Perceptive... I take it you know a lot of them?" His grin widened and something told me I had played right into his trap.

"Yes, I know a lot of ladies."

I felt my face turn red from embarrassment.

"I meant books." I stammered, clearly affronted, which seemed to amuse him even more.

"Oh. I know quite a few of those too." He teased.

"Clearly, modesty is not one of your abilities." I bit back and marched barefoot down the carpeted stairs, unsure why his comment had irritated me the way it had.

I didn't have to turn around to know he followed closely behind me. Strangely, I could feel his body levitating toward mine like a tethered string. It was an odd sensation. When I reached the lower level, I noticed his grin had morphed into a frown.

"Don't leave." His words and heavy tone made me pause. "Just wait here." He motioned with his hand before disappearing into the back shelves. He returned a few minutes later with three books. "Here."

As I took the books from him, I couldn't help staring into his sapphire eyes.

The books were ancient.

"They are not Pride and Prejudice, but I think you'll enjoy them."

I stared at him in surprise.

"You know Jane Austen?"

He smiled.

"I don't, but I know a bit about the human world."

"But how is it possible that you even know who Austen is? Her work only goes back two centuries or so. And how can you know so much about the human world if the gates to the realms have been closed for a thousand years?"

I didn't miss how his jaw tensed; his entire demeanor changed at my observation.

"You can go now. I think I'd like some privacy." I frowned, confused at his abrupt change, and my eyes narrowed.

"Why are you refusing to tell me the truth?" I snapped, and he closed the distance between us in an instant, towering over me with a stern look. His eyes studied my face, and I watched the muscles on his jaw slowly relax.

"Just go," he whispered. "Before I do something, ungentlemanly."

I glared back at him defiantly. What the hell was that supposed to mean? Did he think that would intimidate me? Fine. If he refused to tell me the truth and would rather be an ass, then two could play at that game.

"Actually... I think I'll stay and read." I smiled up at him before marching to one of the sofas. I dropped my slippers on the floor and propped my feet on the couch comfortably; all the while, his eyes burned into me.

I opened one of the books and scanned the first page, trying to ignore him despite the fact he still stood there. After a minute, I glanced at him, and sure enough, he had not moved an inch. He stood in the same spot, hands in his pockets. His white crisp shirt was unbuttoned, halfway down his chest. I swallowed, remembering how he had looked the night before without it. The taut muscles of his back... I shook the thoughts away and shifted my eyes to meet his.

"Is there a problem?" I asked and I noted he fought to conceal his smile.

"Not at all. Make yourself at home."

"I will." I retorted and went back to scanning the book's pages. Though I couldn't concentrate knowing he was still there. I fought hard to block the strange sensation within me and kept reading. After a few minutes, that odd feeling was gone, and when I looked up, so was he. I frowned.

His refusal to explain how he knew about the book and the human world only urged me to find out more. If the gates had been closed for a thousand years, there must have been some connection that allowed access to the other Realms.

He was right, though. I forgot about Drake. I found myself wrapped in the love story within the pages of the book. For the rest of the day, I chose to forget where I was and it was all thanks to the unwelcome guest.

8

TRUTH AND LIES

RULESKA'S DAYS OFFERED little light, and as the last of it slipped from the windows, I knew it was time to return to my room. As I crossed the entrance hall, I froze, clutching the books to my chest. Drake slowed his pace, and we both hesitated. I couldn't meet his eyes, not while knowing what he had done. When he took a step towards me, I whirled around and disappeared down the corridor towards my chambers. A part of me wanted him to follow. To beg for my forgiveness. To offer an explanation. An apology. But he didn't, and perhaps it was for the best. I wasn't sure I was ready to forgive him. I didn't know if I could.

DRAKE

For an immortal creature that required no sleep, I had felt exhausted since arriving in Druleska. I was certain it had everything to do with Dagasti's lies, and now worse, my fight with Belynda.

While I knew I had been brusque, I only wanted her to be safe. It didn't help that his scent was all over her. But even so, my actions were wrong. By the fates, the dark feelings had consumed me to a point where I could have taken that girl, possessed her without an ounce of remorse and all for the sake of revenge. My soul was sick, dark, and tortured, but at least I still possessed a shred of self-control. If I had followed through with it, I would have never forgiven myself, and I was certain Belynda would not have, either.

I fought the urge to fly into her balcony last night and beg for her forgiveness, but I couldn't even look at myself, not after what I had almost done.

Today, I had to stare into the face of evil once again and pretend. Dagasti was lying. He pinned my parents deaths on the other realms, though everyone I had spoken to thus far seemed to have contrasting versions of events. Nothing made sense. Even the elders refused to speak of it, holding their tongues out of fear.

My uncle seemed to show a particular interest in Belynda's gifts. I noticed it the moment he realized precisely what she was. A guardian. A blood witch by birth. That's why I had lied. It was a good thing that Belynda's powers were dormant, somehow, and that Dagasti believed she had lost them for good. The less attention I drew to her, the safer from him she would be, even if all the lies and hurt in her eyes tore at my soul, little by little.

My uncle was shrewd and despicable. I knew he questioned my arrival, and her presence here, so I was fighting my hardest to dissuade him. I wanted to send her back through that portal the moment I realized he wasn't to be trusted, yet we were trapped here and I had to find a way to keep her safe. I could only do that if I made them believe she wasn't important.

The moment he came to greet us outside the castle gates, I knew something was wrong. With my father gone, and Dagasti on the throne with the guard supporting his claim, I realized, protecting her was my priority.

If I admitted to offering my human essence to save her, he would slay me in an instant to claim Belynda for himself. No immortal would ever make such a sacrifice, not unless they had a powerful reason. If Dagasti found out how important she was to me and the extent of her powers... I dreaded to think what he would do.

I had to play my part well enough to convince him otherwise. At the very least, I needed him to believe I'd lost interest in her. If I managed to do that, perhaps he would be willing to trust me enough to confide in me his plans. However, I feared Dagasti was no fool.

I took a deep breath as I pushed open the doors to the throne room.

He wasn't here yet. He did it on purpose, a way to flaunt his power, and I hated to admit how much it vexed me. He had no right to sit on my father's throne.

I looked at the grand chairs, now empty with nostalgia. This was where I had last seen my parents, the time I had told them I would take responsibility for my relationship with Isabel and for breaking the rules of the guardianship. Neither of them were happy about it, but my father understood I was honor bound to do the right thing. I didn't know what 'right' was anymore. I wasn't even sure my father would recognize the man I had become.

"Always punctual. Like your father." Dagasti remarked, but it wasn't a compliment. He despised everything my father had and possessed, aside from the throne, of course.

"Ready to go?" I asked, hoping to finish this dreadful business to learn more of his plans.

"Yes. We might as well." He strolled past me, and I followed him out of the castle to the horses that waited in the courtyard.

"Do we really need the entourage?" I glanced behind us at the line of guards.

"We can never be too careful. Can we?" He was definitely no fool. The trail of guards was proof he didn't trust me, and he was wise not to do so. It was only a matter of time before I found proof that he was the one responsible for the death of my parents. And when I did, I would see his immortal life extinguished before me. He would pay. I would make sure of it.

I trotted ahead, and I felt his eyes burning into my back. It was clear that if he could do away with me, he would. I wouldn't make it easy for him... but I did wonder what was stopping him. Perhaps he feared that doing so would cost him the guards and the people's loyalty.

BELYNDA

Morning came and went, but I refused to leave my chambers. I had three books to pass the time. However, a voice at the back of my head was probing, taunting. There was another reason for hiding away in here. I didn't want to run into... him. Not again.

Tolly's face was marred with concern when she brought in supper that evening.

"Are you sure you're alright?"

"Yes. Don't worry about me. See? I have these to occupy myself with." I said, attempting to ease her mind.

"Very well. Please ring if you need anything. Anything at all." She insisted before leaving my chamber.

I sighed, closed my eyes, and placed the book on the bed beside me. What was the point of our relationship, our *love*, when all we had to show for it was heartache? Was this what the fates had destined?

The street carts burst with vibrant colors as herbs and spices filled the air. I was transported to the first day Drake and I arrived in Druleska. I followed the alleys and stone paths, acutely aware I was in a vision. I discovered it was easier to identify them when I paid close attention. The surrounding sounds seemed muted, not crisp like my recurring dreams, yet it was accompanied by a strange feeling of weightlessness.

One thing I had learned was that the visions always served a purpose. I glanced at passersby's in search of my message. I wasn't sure who I was looking for or what I was meant to see, but I could feel the pull. It was another sign that this was a vision and not a dream. That odd feeling inside of me was like a compass, guiding me on the right path to follow.

The market's vibrancy faded, and the pleasant scents transformed into a putrid stench as I neared the city's limits... where the forgotten lived.

I felt drawn to the dwindling house the minute I passed it. My feet moved closer without hesitation, and I knew I was meant to see whatever lay within those walls.

The blue doors of the little stone house opened, and a woman stepped out. There were mud stains on the hem of her gray dress. She pulled on the hood of her cloak and closed the door behind her. As she passed by, she glanced up briefly as though she could see me, and I froze when I stared into her eyes.

I LOOKED around the empty chamber; the candles still burned bright. I moved to the opulent balcony, and watched the city below, knowing the lady from my dreams was somewhere out there, and I would come to find her. Tomorrow... but first, I had to be certain. There was only one way to confirm I hadn't just imagined her.

I slipped a robe over my nightgown, and like the night before, descended down the silent tower. Yet tonight, I had a purpose. I tiptoed as I reached the entrance hall and scurried down the corridor toward the galleries. There was no servant in sight, and I was glad for it.

I paused before the massive portrait and pulled the robe tighter to block the cold.

Staring into Drake's silver eyes, the same eyes of his mother stared back at me. The same eyes that haunted me since I woke from that vision. While I could have forgotten the face, I could never forget those eyes, not in a million years. She was alive somehow, and I was unsure why she had chosen to remain in the shadows. I had to find her, that much I knew.

I burned to run to Drake and tell him what I had discovered, but I didn't have the courage to look him in the eyes without hurting. I would have to tell him, but not until I found her. Not before I was sure.

"It's a bit late to be wondering about the castle halls, isn't it?" I turned, startled by Dagasti.

Every hair on my body stood on alert. Something inside of me told me to run, but I remained still. I didn't miss the way his eyes scoured over my body. Unconsciously, I pulled the robe tighter, hoping to disappear.

"I'm sorry, I didn't think there was a curfew," I said defiantly, and his laugh chilled me to my core. He took a step towards me, and I held my breath.

"You know if you ever grow tired of him... you can always come and warm my bed." His fingers skimmed along my jaw, and I could hear my heart about to jump out of my throat. "I'm no fool. I know you must be very special for him to have brought you along. Imagine what you and I could do together." His fingers moved over my shoulder, draping my robe to the side. I felt my body tremble. He paused and glanced down the corridor before dropping his hand.

"Looks like I'm not the only one restless in this damn place tonight." The blue-eyed god glanced between Dagasti and I, and if I hadn't been trembling, I would have smiled. I had never been happier to see him. I took his presence as my chance to step out of Dagasti's reach.

"What are you still doing here?" Dagasti barked. "I thought our business was over." Sapphire eyes glanced at me then Dagasti before offering him a dazzling smile.

"It is. I just thought I'd extend my stay. Your library is much more extensive." Dagasti's eyes narrowed in his direction.

"Books? Do you peg me for a fool?" Sapphire eyes raked over my body, and my face flushed crimson red.

"Books and other pleasures, of course. Your staff is always very accommodating," He glanced at me briefly again. "and charming." he added. I felt Dagasti's eyes on me, but I did not dare look.

"Yes. I understand the fascination." Dagasti said without

humor. "Just don't overstay your welcome." The blue-eyed god smiled, clearly not intimidated by Dagasti.

He tucked his hands into the front pockets of his pants, and when Dagasti realized the man had no intention of leaving, he turned and marched from the galleries.

As soon as he was out of sight, those sapphire eyes darkened, and his smile vanished.

"Are you alright?" He asked, eyes searching my face. I glanced away, embarrassed.

"Yes. I'm ok." My gaze moved elsewhere, but I could feel his stare burning into me, studying every move I made as though trying to decide if I was telling the truth.

"Thank you again." I said, "It seems you're always around at the right place and time. I don't know if I should be worried about it or grateful for the divine intervention. But thank you, nonetheless."

He smiled.

"What are you doing alone at this hour anyway? Did you forget your way to the library?"

"No." I glanced at the portrait behind him. "I just couldn't sleep, so I thought I'd explore the castle. No one is about now, so I don't get any servants glaring at me, reminding me I don't belong here."

His brow furrowed.

"They're not wrong, you know."

"This is Drake's home."

"I think even he knows that's no longer true," I was angry with his assumption, but he continued. "He should have never risked bringing you here."

"Coming here was my choice," I said, an edge to my voice.

"Let me guess, follow him against all odds, even if it puts you in danger, even if it means *death*." His eyes bore into me. For a moment, I remembered that was exactly the sentence that awaited me.

"I'm safe here. Drake will protect me." I said, though not believing it myself. He looked at me, shaking his head and I lowered my gaze, trying to shield the lie from my eyes.

"Remember when I said I could be dangerous?" I glanced back up at his words.

"Yes," I whispered, not daring to say another word.

"There are worse dangers lurking in these halls." His eyes stared into my soul. "I would advise you to stay in your room... but something tells me you won't listen." He smiled as though enjoying some inside joke. "Just be careful." He said, all traces of his smile gone before he turned abruptly and disappeared down the corridor.

DAGASTI WAS A SICK MAN. I shuddered to think what he would have done had we not been interrupted. Something he said stuck with me, the comment about power-seeking. I realized then why Drake had chosen to lie about my powers. I had underestimated Dagasti, but so had Drake. He clearly was no fool, and something told me I had not seen or heard the last of him yet.

Now more than ever, I felt trapped in this place, unable to confide in the one person that promised to shelter me from the evil lurking about. Whenever I thought about running to him, I remembered what he had done, and the hollow feeling in my chest returned.

Regardless, I would have to find a way to speak with him. But not tonight, not until I was able to find her. First, I needed proof that his mother was alive.

. . .

When the guards opened the gates, I took a breath. Drake hadn't acted on his threat to keep me locked up like a prisoner.

The town was buzzing, but I was in a tunnel, lost in my thoughts. I was alone in a different world, away from everything I had ever known. Drake, the only one I could trust, had torn my heart and fed it to the crows. I could find a way to go back and leave him here... but the thought of leaving him sickened me. No, I couldn't. I wouldn't. My fate was sealed to his, and to this place.

I strolled past the shops and alleyways to a part of the city that had seen better days. Beggars roamed the streets, and the walkways reeked of death. I was close.

The small stone house was just as I envisioned it, only smoke broke over the chimney. I hesitated by the door, hand poised and ready to knock. Though I was unsure of what to say, but the door opened before I could decide. A woman stared back at me. There was no confusion. She looked exactly like her portrait.

Her eyes widened in surprise before she peeked outside, looked around, and took my hand, pulling me in.

I was too stunned to speak. This was Drake's *mother*.

"Were you followed?" Her eyes desperately searched mine.

"No. No one knows I'm here." I confirmed, and her expression shifted from fear to bewilderment.

"How did you find me? Does my son know?"

I didn't miss the manic edge in her voice when she mentioned him.

"No. Drake doesn't know. Not yet. I had to be sure first."

"Then how did you know where I was? That I was alive?"

"I had a vision."

"Of course... You're a blood witch."

I wasn't sure what I was, to be honest.

"I guess I am," I admitted, and she surprised me, smiling and pulling me into an embrace.

. . .

THE HOUSE WAS modest and clean, with a fireplace that I used to warm my hands.

The woman removed her veil, her silver eyes following me as I moved about the small room.

"He chose you as his mate." She said. I wasn't sure if it was a question or a statement. "I can sense he is part of you."

"That's what everyone seems to call us here, not that I'm fond of the term. But I guess we are, in a way, soul mates."

The woman smiled. She was beautiful, just like in the portraits.

"I don't know how to address you." I said. I wasn't sure if your highness was appropriate, but I didn't want to risk getting it wrong, not with her. She was important to Drake, and now to me.

"Kylram... just call me Kylram." She offered while I tried to process that she was here. Alive...

"Why have you allowed everyone to believe you're dead?" Why would she choose to live like this when she could have ruled the realm?

"I am dead." She said with overwhelming sadness. "I was dead from the moment Dagasti took my husband's life, perhaps even before that. In truth, I started to fade the day my son left us." Kylram admitting that Dagasti was responsible for the death of Drake's father's wasn't a shock to me. I was sure Drake suspected as much.

"But Dagasti said..."

"Forget anything Dagasti said." She snapped. "He believes me dead, but that is for my safety." While she claimed to be dead, there was fire in her still.

"What happened?" I asked, taking a seat by the fire.

"He saved me, you know." She stared into the flames, eyes lost to the memory. "He gave up his life to save me. "A tear escaped and rolled down her cheek, but she quickly swiped it away. "I'm so sorry. It feels like yesterday."

"I'm sorry too. I can't imagine what it must have been like to lose your son, your husband, and your kingdom." I offered.

"Tell me about my son." She said, facing me with eyes full of adoration.

"I'm sure you know Drake better than I do. You've had lifetimes together; I've only had a short while."

"Something tells me he is not the same boy he was a thousand years ago. Even for an immortal, I can't begin to imagine what he lived through in Xelraa."

"He doesn't talk about it much, but I know the choices he made there changed him. He thinks what he did to survive makes him unworthy. Even though he would never admit it, I can sense the constant battle he faces with himself."

"Something tells me you're just what he needs, and you know him better than you think."

I thought back to our time together before arriving here. Perhaps that was true then, but now? I wasn't sure I knew him at all. I thought he loved me, promising to never do anything to hurt me, yet at the first opportunity, he snapped my heart in two.

I smiled at his mother. She did not need to know of my suffering or our current differences.

"He saved me too, you know," I confessed, and she lit with pride. "It seems he is more like his father than he dares to admit."

"Tell me about it, please. I want to hear it all."

I found I could not say no to this woman, so I told her about our time together. How it all started, my visions, the truth about

Isabel and our bond, my family, and the guardians. I admitted how her son gave up his human essence to save me and how being subdued by water had affected him once his essence was returned.

"That is the real reason why we found ourselves returning to Druleska. He needed to regain control of his fire and couldn't do it in the human world. Not without the risk of breaking the covenant and exposing himself."

"And you followed him here without knowing what would await you?"

I thought about the decision I had made. Despite recent events, I realized I would make the same decision again if necessary. The truth was: I loved him. I didn't think anything would ever change that.

"Sometimes we do stupid things for those we love. The truth is, I couldn't live in a world where he didn't exist." I found myself confessing. I felt the truth of my words settle in my body. Drake's mother smiled fondly at me.

"Thank you for being brave. For saving my son and bringing him back home. I can never repay you for that."

I shook my head.

"Knowing that you're alive is reward enough. I think this is what your son needs the most right now, to know he is not alone."

"He isn't alone. He has you too."

I nodded, not sure if I mattered to him anymore.

"Dagasti said Drake's father tried to make peace?" I said, though it was more of a question. I was trying to pull myself out of the suffocating emotions threatening to drown me from the inside out.

"He did, but the realms are not to blame. The truth is he sent his assassins to have us killed. The blade that claimed my husband's life was meant for me, yet he took it to save me. The last man standing begged for his life." Her eyes narrowed to slits. "I had never killed before, but I took my time with him. After he confessed, I felt no remorse for taking his life."

She was so strong, and I saw Drake mirrored in her as she spoke.

"After learning of Dagasti's betrayal, I knew I would never be safe in the castle again, so I let him believe his plan had succeeded. But the unfortunate girl found next to the king was not me. She was one of the servants who perished in the assault. I traded clothes with her and scarred her face; I hated myself for it, but it was necessary. She was dead and her body served a greater purpose."

"I don't understand. I thought it was impossible to kill an immortal." I said, "That means Drake could be in danger..."

"It's hard to kill us, yes... impossible? No. Every immortal creature has its weakness. For us, it is weapons forged from blue fire stones. There are spells, too, potent enough to serve the purpose. For Drake's father, it was a dagger forged of blue fire-stone." She opened a small box that rested above the fireplace mantle. Nestled inside was a small blade that looked like it was made of glass.

"What about the war?"

"There was a time when your world was open to our realms freely, even before the guardianship came to be. But the realms have suffered since."

"But humans don't know of your existence."

"They don't believe we're real. Only myths and legends, but every story has its beginning. Where do you think the children called elementals come from? Some chose to remain in the realms, others stayed behind in the human world."

"Are you saying there are still elementals or half-humans here in the realms?"

"Yes, there are a few descendants, but the bloodlines have become less pure over time. I believe the only human trait left is their mortality. They age and die like any other human would."

A part of me felt better knowing I wasn't the only mortal on this side of the portal.

"So, the war started because of the guardianship? Because the portals closed?"

"In a way, it did. Even though Drake sacrificed himself for his mistakes, it wasn't enough."

"It wasn't his fault."

"I know. And his father knew it too. We never judged whom our son loved. We would have never demanded such a sacrifice, but we should have stood against it, and we chose not to. When the guardians threatened to close the gates, guilt drove him to make that decision. He thought his choice would somehow make amends, and perhaps it did for a while, but when the portals closed permanently, blame turned to our realm once again."

"We can fix this. The guardianship is not what it was before. We have the power to open the gates again. Bring back peace." Perhaps this is what Isabel had spoken about in her prophecy. I was meant to restore the balance to the realms.

"Child, it might have been the conflict that started the war, but it's not the only reason for it now."

"Then what is?"

"It's complicated. Dagasti fights for control of the other Realms. He has the ludicrous notion that we are the strongest element. He believes Druleska is meant to rule over them. Upherya fights to defend its people and their borders from Abryas and the assault from Dagasti's army. He was always a snake after power, but my husband was blinded by their blood ties. Serfier used to be one of our only allies; however, anyone who betrays my son, or sits to make plans with Dagasti, is considered a traitor in my book."

"There must be something we can do?"

"Yes. Once Dagasti is removed from the throne, we can make amends. Starting with the people in the kingdom of Upherya. If we can persuade them to put down their swords, we can approach the elven king for a truce."

"What about the Water Realm?"

"Honestly, I don't know what they want or who they fight for. Callix has always been a mystery to me. But as far as trusting him... I don't know."

"Who is Callix?"

"The Lord of Serfier. He rules the Water Realm. He is powerful and directly connected to the fates. His kingdom is impenetrable."

"If what you say is true, then Drake needs to know... You are proof enough of Dagasti's betrayal. You cannot hide anymore. He could be in danger." I said, beginning to pace.

"Yes. I knew the moment had come when I saw you standing at my doorstep. But I have one request, if you don't mind."

"Anything."

"I would like to be the one to speak with my son. I'd like to be the one to explain."

So many thoughts swam in my head. The fates never made anything simple. Yet as I glanced at the woman before me, I felt at peace. For a moment, I managed to put aside the pain of Drake's betrayal. If I was going to die here, I would be content knowing he had his mother. She could help him find his way.

"Thank you for everything. I will find a way to bring him to you. I promise."

The woman gave me a quick hug.

"It's getting quite late. I will have one of my Ifrit guide you back to the castle gates. Or as close as possible without raising suspicion."

"I know the fates have strange ways of going about things, but I thank them for guiding me to you," I said in earnest.

"So do I, child. So do I."

BASED on what I had read on Ifrits, they were supposed to be demonic spirits of sorts. But I found myself following a creature that bore a striking resemblance to a dragonfly. We journeyed down roads and alleyways to the castle. Then before we reached the open gates, it disappeared into the night sky.

The eerie darkness of the castle did not help my unease after all the information I had acquired. Dagasti was a murderer, a liar, a sick man, and I had no time to waste. Drake could be in danger.

I went in search of him, but I didn't have to look very far. I found him in the dining hall with a decanter of wine, brooding.

"There you are." He said, pushing back from his chair. He took a deep breath as he closed the distance separating us, and the darkness surrounding him eased.

"Do you have any idea how worried I was when I went to find you, and I couldn't?"

I wanted to say that he shouldn't have left me alone in the first place or that he didn't seem concerned the night he... *No*. I wouldn't be the jealous, emotional human girl... so, I held my tongue.

"I'm sorry. I lost track of time. You went to find me?"

"I did. But your scent died in the market. It vanished.

Belynda, if anything had happened to you…" I wondered how he had lost my scent, though I was glad for whatever the reason.

"I hate this." I motioned between us. "This fighting. The distance that has built between us since we arrived. The lies…" I whispered the last part, and he took a step to close the space between us. I stepped back. I couldn't let him touch me. Not yet. His eyes bore into mine, pleading.

"Are we going to be ok?" He asked, and my soul ached to ease his mind.

"We will." But not tonight. I remembered Kylram's request to be the one to tell him, and I realized that leaving the castle now, and in his condition, was not the right move. Besides, I felt the exhaustion of recent events catching up to me. Physically and emotionally, a heavy weight sagged on my shoulders. Turning away, I left the dining hall and was glad he didn't follow.

Tolly brought dinner to my chamber like she had the night before, but she was in better spirits tonight.

I caught her smiling in the mirror's reflection as she eased the ties of my dress.

"He didn't do it." She blurted impatiently, and I turned to her, clutching the dress to my chest.

"What do you mean?"

"He didn't take the girl. Didn't touch her." My heart pounded like a wild animal.

"How do you know?"

"Everyone knows, my lady, or the staff at least. They talk of nothing else." My soul soared with happiness. I wanted to scream with joy. The heaviness in my chest melted, light and happiness filling the space left behind. I hugged Tolly and she laughed, sharing in my bliss.

"He loves you, my lady."

I turned to look at my smiling reflection.

"Tolly. Bring the red dress." My cheeks flushed a crimson red as I plotted my next move.

DRAKE

The darkness eased as I watched her walk from the room. She was safe; that's what mattered. I allowed myself to breathe in her scent again, and the beast rejoiced. She hadn't been near him, yet her rejection had hurt even more than if she had.

I had to pull myself together, leave this place and return to the human world. She said we would be alright, but I didn't think that would be possible. Not while we remained here. I needed her. The fire inside me burned, and I roared as it clawed to be released.

I LOST myself in the cover of the night, gliding between the strikes of thunder and light. As usual, by the time I had reached the seafront and returned, the monster felt sated. But not tonight. Something was off. I dove for the West tower.

The candles on the balcony wall were lit, yet the servants knew better. They knew I preferred the darkness. My sharp eyes snagged on a beautiful girl with porcelain white skin; she stood there, and the fire blazed. She had come to me, despite the darkness. I flapped my wings, easing my landing on the balcony, and watched the beast transform in the reflection of her eyes.

My fire still burned, but I didn't care. I closed the distance between us and claimed her lips to calm my thirst. She kissed me back, and her urgency matched my scorching fire. We needed this.

I tugged on the lace covering her breasts, and the material gave way with ease. Her giggle was like a melody for my starved soul and my lips scorched her skin as I branded myself across her neck and breasts.

"I'm burning for you," I admitted, lifting the dress to her waist, and pressing myself to her core. There was no gentleness, no pleas, no words. I lifted her and buried myself in her.

I took and claimed, and as I plunged inside her, my darkness roared. She clung to my shoulders as her back pressed into the stone wall of the balcony. The monster wasn't satisfied. I tore what remained of the dress, and the pale skin of her breasts glinted under the candlelight. I licked the valley between them, and her back arched as an offering to the darkness. The deeper I went, the closer I came to the light. She was tight and smooth around my hard throbs.

I released her from the wall and turned her, bracing her hands against the balcony. Easing hard inside her warmth, I was home once more. I gripped her shoulders, my hands tracing the smooth skin of her back as I rode into her. Without remorse, I claimed, I took, and broke into the tightness. The beast didn't stop until she screamed my name. My soul burst as I finally saw the light, and I stilled in her, releasing all my agony as I filled her with my fire which trickled, glistening down her legs.

BELYNDA

I didn't care if it was his way of punishing me. He had me. I found my release and felt him come undone, and it was as though the walls he had built crumbled too.

He lifted me into his arms and carried me into the bath chamber. He touched the water in the tub, and steam rose from it in an instant. Tearing the rest of the dress off me, he then eased us into the water.

"I'm sorry for how I acted. The truth is I was... jealous." I admitted.

"Jealous?" He turned my chin so that he could look at my face.

"I know you had another visit your chamber." His arms tensed around me.

"I promise you. Nothing happened." He paused. "But it could have, and I'm sorry. I admit, my soul turned dark when I caught another man's scent on you. It was the night you came back from town." He knew... of course, he knew. How did I not think of that? "Did he hurt you?"

While that was all he asked, I knew his soul burned to know more.

"No. I was only saved from a carriage accident. That man just happened to be there at the right time. That's all." With that, his tension slowly dissolved.

"I'm sorry I was rough."

I smiled, pressing my back into him.

"I'm not." He sucked in a breath, while another part of him hardened, pressed against my behind.

"You really don't play fair." His teeth graced my ear; his dark raspy voice made my core ache. "Are you sure you want this?" His hand moved in the water, parting my thighs while his fingers teased at the apex of my folds. "I just took you like I owned you, ravishing you like a savage, yet you want more?"

I sucked in a breath as his fingers intensified their assault.

"Y-yes." My confirmation was all he needed. Lifting me out of the tub, I braced my legs around his middle. He stormed to the bed, the water vaporizing from our skin.

"I'm going to take my time with you."

I closed my eyes, lost to his touch. His lips gently brushed my collarbone. "And when I'm done teasing you... I'm going to claim what is mine." His nose skimmed the valley of my breasts, and I arched my back, offering myself to him, and his touch. His lips. His hands.

He kneeled on the massive bed and laid me down before him. His eyes studied my face, before devouring my body like a man starved.

His lips burned a trail down my stomach; his hands parted my legs, and he positioned himself there. Mischief glinted in his eyes as he teased, kissed, and nibbled the inside of my thighs, making me writhe with anticipation.

When his fingers found my folds, I was breathless. Then, I felt his lips brush my core, and I was on fire.

"Drake..."

"You are so ready for me, love..." My body throbbed against the rhythm of his skilled fingers.

When I felt his tongue swipe at my entrance, I lost all control.

"That's it. Let me taste you." The desire in his voice and the assault of his tongue brought me over the edge instantly.

My body slacked against the bed, yet his eyes raged with desire.

"Oh, we're not done yet, love. Not even close." All it took was those words before I felt something tighten in my core again... I didn't know how it was possible, but I wanted him. I ached for him.

"I want to play, too," I said, and darkness flashed in his eyes.

"Is that so?"

I pushed myself up, crawling to him until he lay flat against the bed with his hands behind his head. His desire-filled eyes studied my every move.

The dark lines moved above his skin, and his eyes shadowed as I trailed my fingers above his chest. Wherever my fingers touched, my lips followed. His abs tensed as I eased myself lower, my breasts brushing against his already-taught length. He sucked in a breath and made to move.

"No." I smiled, pushing him back down. "You had your turn," I said. He growled, eyes burning into me.

When my tongue brushed along the length of him, his body jerked.

"Fuck. You have no idea how good that feels."

I licked the moisture at its peak and closed my lips around him, licking, tasting, sucking... My fingers tightened around him. He jolted in my hand as I took him deeper into my mouth, his breath hitching.

"You are a sight." He whispered, eyes darkening with desire. "Watching that beautiful mouth of yours take me in..." He groaned as his fingers weaved in my hair, urging me to take him deeper.

"That's it, love. Take it." The back of my throat burned; I couldn't take him all, even if I wanted to. "Do you want to taste me? Is that it?" His jaw tightened as his hand urged me on. Faster. "Fuck, take it." His body lurched forward. "Take it all." His warmth spilled into my mouth, but I didn't stop. He tasted salty and tangy. Drake beamed, relaxing beneath my touch before pulling me over his body.

"Did you enjoy that?" I asked, and the grin on his face intensified.

"I don't know if enjoyment is the right word. I don't think any words can describe how amazing that felt." He kissed my lips, and I smiled.

"I never knew making love could be this intense," I admitted, and I felt a slight blush creep onto my cheeks.

"Oh, there is so much more to explore." He whispered, pressing my body to his. I felt him throb and thicken against my leg.

He pulled me up, bracing my thighs at his sides as he guided his stiff sex to my entrance.

Slowly, I eased down onto him as his hands grasped my hips. I met his every thrust, moving, teasing, circling as he buried himself deeper into me. As we found our release together, I realized that no matter what, everything would be alright as long as we had each other.

9

SECRET LIAISONS

THE SHEETS WERE STILL WARM, BUT Drake was not in bed. Glancing around the room, I spotted him on the balcony, fully dressed. I draped a sheet over my shoulders, and his eyes turned to me as I reached the archway of the balcony. His eyes glowed silver and bright and his smile warmed my insides.

He pulled me into his arms, trapping me against the balcony wall, as he brushed his nose along the back of my neck. He seemed happier today, lighter somehow.

"Is it getting easier?"

"Easier?" he repeated.

"To control the fire, I mean." His lips twisted into a smile against my skin.

"I do feel strangely at ease today." He kissed my neck. "What do you say we skip breakfast? I owe you a visit to the town. There is much I want to show you."

I stared at the city below us and smiled, content to have the old Drake back. Visiting the town would ensure I made good on my promise to his mother.

"I have nothing to wear."

I glanced at the shreds of my red dress scattered on the balcony floor. The rest was probably in a heap somewhere in the bath chamber.

"I'm sorry for that." He was anything but sorry given how his voice vibrated against the nape of my neck. "I seem to have a bad habit of tearing your clothes."

"I take it that it's not a good idea for me to walk back to my chambers wrapped in your sheets?"

He growled.

"Unequivocally."

"Then you will have to fetch my maid. Tolly can be trusted." I said, and he turned me around.

"You should trust no one."

"I don't. But she has proven to be a friend. She helped me get into your chambers last night without being discovered."

"Very well. Stay here." He kissed my cheeks, then my lips, and smiled. "I will send her your way." He pressed me flush to his body and lifted my chin, so my eyes met his. "I will meet you down at the courtyard." He said, releasing me. "Don't be long."

As he left his chambers, I picked up the shreds of the red dress and any other evidence of our escapades from the bath chamber.

I had finished washing myself when I heard Tolly in the main chamber.

"My lady?"

"Thank you for coming." I smiled, a gesture she returned, too, when she saw me wrapped in nothing but a blanket.

"I take it you had a good night?"

I beamed.

"You could say that. But I'm afraid the red dress didn't make it." I giggled, and she laughed too.

"Something tells me it was worth it."

"It was. Thank you for being a friend. For helping me and coming to my rescue." I said with sincerity.

"I'm glad to help. Not everyone has treated me with the kindness you have." She offered. "Now, let's get you dressed. He gave another instruction, which was 'be quick'. So, we better not keep him waiting."

THE STREETS DROWNED with murmurs as Drake and I made our way through the cobbled paths. However, today, many offered their respects, bowing and smiling, unlike the sneers I had received when venturing on my own. I informed Drake of the old man that had offered me the bag of strawberries, and he made it his mission to find and reward him for his kindness. Drake followed the scent of strawberries to search through the different merchants as I could not remember the location of the old man's cart.

"There he is." I pulled on Drake's arm, and as we neared his post, the old man smiled, remembering me.

"You're back." The man clutched his hat and bowed when he saw who hovered behind me. "Your highness."

"Please, there is no need for formalities." Drake said, extending his hand. The old man stared, surprised, then shook it.

"I understand you were generous to my mate, and I wanted to repay you for your kindness."

"There is no need. Seeing her smile was reward enough for an old man like me."

"Nonetheless, thank you."

"It's been so long since we've had a human walk these roads. She reminded me of the old days. And of Rilka."

"Was that your wife?" Drake asked.

"Yes." The old man confessed, his mind somewhere far away.

"You had a human wife? How?" I asked.

Drake smiled at my curiosity but allowed the old man to tell his tale.

"Many of our kind and those of the other realms chose human mates in the old days. Before the gates closed, that is. I had a son and a daughter. My son was born human. He took after his mother, but my daughter Ross—she was special. She was a fire elemental. When the gates closed, they chose to stay in the human world with their mother."

I glanced at Drake, suddenly ashamed of the guardian legacy I had inherited.

"And you couldn't stay with them in the human world?"

The old man glanced at Drake.

"I would have stayed with them for as long as their human lives would have allowed, but only elementals were permitted to remain in your world because of their human blood. After so many years, I lost hope of ever reuniting with them. Now, I'm simply an old man, happy to see a friendly human face."

"I'm sorry to hear that. Truly." I didn't know how much time I had, but I vowed to do everything in my power to restore the connection of the realms to the human world, if it was the last thing I did.

Drake pulled a small leather pouch from the inside of his vest, handing it to the old man.

"No. I couldn't." The man refused.

"Please take it. It would make me very happy." I insisted. "Please."

Finally, he accepted the coins.

"Thank you. Please, come back anytime. I am at your service." I smiled fondly at the old man before we went on our way.

"My father used to walk these very streets with me. Our people loved him. He was a good king." Drake spoke of his father with melancholy. I wasn't sure if it was our conversation with the old man that had brought it on, but it was clear Drake missed his father. I desperately wished to tell him his mother was alive, but I had promised to bring him to her.

"Can I ask you a question?"

"Just one?" He teased, just like he had when we first met. I rolled my eyes.

"When I saw your family portraits back at the castle, it got me thinking. You aged from a young boy into a man and while I know you're immortal, you don't seem to age now. I guess I don't really understand how it works." His pace slowed and he brought my hand to his lips.

"As immortal children, we age the same as humans. Yet when we reach maturity our aging slows, and eventually, stops. But we can choose to age at any given time, especially when an immortal has children. It gets complicated when your offspring begins to look like your sibling rather than your child. That's often when immortals choose to age. At least, that's how it is for Dragons in Druleska. There are species of this realm and others that actually pride themselves on their eternal youth."

"Like who?"

"Phoenixes choose not to age. You also have the Elvin people, and I cannot recall ever seeing an old face in that kingdom; things might have changed since I was last there, though."

"How old are you then?"

He laughed, pulling me along.

"Don't ask me that question. I'm not sure you really want to know."

"Tell me," I demanded, but he carried on, guiding me through the crowds of the market. While it didn't bother me how old he was, he didn't seem willing to share, so I chose not to push him.

"Wait. This way." I pulled on his arm.

"Where are we going?"

"Come. It's a surprise. You'll see." He followed, intrigued, and obviously pleased I had abandoned my quest to know his age.

We weaved through the people and alleyways, but it wasn't until we reached the worst part of the city that Drake's concern showed.

"I don't know what motives you had for venturing this far from the castle, but you must promise not to do so again."

"I hate to remind you that I can still take care of myself."

"Under other circumstances, I would agree, but you cannot summon earth or wind, and you have no fire. Please, promise me you'll be more careful."

"I'll be more careful." I conceded. He was right after all. The threat we faced was real.

I rounded the corner and the small stone house with the blazing chimney came into view. I beamed.

"What are we doing here? Who lives here?" he stiffened beside me as I knocked. After a brief pause, the door opened, and I stepped inside. Drake hesitated by the threshold, then removed his hood. When I turned around, he was motionless.

"Mother..." Drake stilled.

The woman closed the distance, throwing her hands around her son. Drake stared at me, a million questions in his gaze, but when his arms encircled his mother and grasped the woman to him, my throat tightened.

I had never seen him so overcome with emotions. His eyes shone as he struggled to contain them.

"How?" He whispered, trying to understand.

I closed the door behind them as the woman guided him to a seat by the fire.

"I've missed you so much." The woman took Drake's hand, and he reached with the other to wipe away her tears.

"I'm here now." Drake stared at the burning logs, his mind somewhere else, but I watched his eyes change, and knew the darkness was knocking.

"It was Dagasti, wasn't it?" He said.

"How did you know?" His mother asked.

"It wasn't hard to guess. He and Father always had their differences. It all just felt too convenient, too easy. At first, I didn't know what to make of it, which is why I have been urging *you* to stay safe." Drake said pointedly to me. Perhaps that explained his fierce protectiveness of me since we had arrived. "I also heard different versions of what happened that day. The elders refuse to speak of it, meaning Dagasti has a leach around their necks. I knew Dagasti was lying, but I never imagined you'd be alive..." He looked over his mother's face and kissed her hands. "How did you find her? Was she the one who masked your scent?" He glanced my way, waiting for an explanation.

"I had a vision. It appears the fates wanted me to find her." I explained. "As for masking my scent... I don't know why you couldn't track it." Drake was lost in thought for a moment. "I'm sorry if I worried you. I couldn't tell you without being sure of it myself."

"Yes, that was reckless and stupid."

"Perhaps, but she is brave. She's good for you." His mother argued; it made me love the woman even more.

"Don't mistake her bravery for foolishness. Trust me. She has no sense of self-preservation."

"Just the same. You wouldn't be here if it weren't for her bravery or *foolishness* as you call it." His eyes burned into mine, and the silence exchanged between us was recognition enough of the sacrifices that had been made.

"You've said so yourself. The fates work in mysterious ways. Let's just be glad we're here now so we can figure out a way to expose your uncle." I said, hoping to steer the conversation to what was important.

"The only way to stop him is if you claim the throne." His mother said, and Drake glanced at me.

"I cannot do that. You know what that would mean."

"Yes, I do. You could rule like your father did. Help your people. Help put a stop to the war."

"It will also mean staying in Druleska and that wasn't our plan." He confessed, taking his mother by surprise. She glanced at me with confusion, but it was Drake who explained. "I came here to find a way to control my fire, but Belynda cannot live here. This is not her home. Her life is in the human world, and mine is wherever she is."

He glanced at me, and for a moment, I felt a wave of nostalgia as I remembered I would not see my family again. I could support Drake's claim. After all, my fate was sealed to end here.

"Drake. I want to stay with you. Your mother is right. You must take your place here. It is the only way to stop your uncle." His eyes bore into mine, searching.

"Belynda... no. You don't know what you're saying. What about your family? Your world? Everything you've ever known?"

"This could be my home. I'm sure once we figure out how to put an end to the war, we can revert to the old ways. Perhaps leave the gates to the human world open like they were long ago.

You remember Isabel's prophecy. I'm meant to restore the balance. What if that's what she meant?"

He seemed to process my words.

"You have already given up so much for me. I couldn't ask this of you."

He didn't have to.

"You're not asking. I'm offering. Besides, isn't that what we do for each other? Forever, remember?" I touched his face, and he pulled me in, brushing his lips against mine.

"Your father would have been so proud to see the man you've become."

The lines tattooed on his hands expanded at the mention of his father.

"How could he be when I cannot even control my fire?"

"You must fight it, otherwise Dagasti will have the upper hand. You are the ruler of fire. You are strong. If anyone can do it, it's you." His mother reassured him, placing a hand on his shoulder. The fire eased from his hands.

"Dagasti has men that are loyal to him. I'm certain the royal guard will follow."

"You are the rightful heir. They will follow you once they know the truth."

"The elders don't seem to think so. We make no moves until we can guarantee our success." Drake said.

"I have kept a few loyal men; they have served me well. I'm sure it wouldn't be difficult to find allies amongst our people."

"No. Dagasti is up to something, and until I figure out what it is, we don't make a move."

"Very well." His mother agreed. "Just be careful. Dagasti is smart. I wouldn't trust anything he says."

"He might confide in me if he thinks I'm the obedient nephew willing to do his dirty work and help his cause."

Kylram shook her head in fixed denial.

"No, my son. You do not know him like I do. Trust me when I say you are only a threat to him. Do not let your guard down. Your father made the mistake of underestimating him and look at what happened. Trust me, he will not hesitate to drive a knife through your heart like he did to your father."

I saw the storm in Drake's eyes at the mention of his father. Dagasti would pay one day for his sins. Drake would make sure of it.

"I will be careful, I promise. We will meet again in a few days' time. If I do not figure out what Dagasti wants by then, we will leave for Upherya."

"Upherya?" His mother questioned. "We shouldn't run. Your right is to claim the throne."

"I know you think taking claim to the throne is the solution, and perhaps it will be in the future, but not now. Not when we are so vulnerable. My uncle has an army. We only have each other. Besides, I would feel much better knowing that Belynda is far away from Dagasti. I have a feeling that whatever plan he has, it involves her, and I don't plan to wait long enough to find out."

DRAKE DIDN'T SAY much on our way back to the castle, yet it was a comfortable silence as I, too, had a lot on my mind. As we entered the gates, he dropped my hand and peered down at me with apologetic eyes before strolling ahead, leaving me to trail behind. I knew why he did it. To everyone watching... I wasn't important, only the blood witch he kept as his pet. Now I knew why he did it, to quell the monster we were fighting. So, I kept my head down and played my part.

When we entered the grand hall, he glanced around then turned to me.

"I'm sorry. You don't deserve this." I searched the empty halls. When I saw no one was about, I lifted my hand and placed it over his heart.

"I know why you must do it, and I'm sorry I didn't understand you sooner." He took my hand, and brought it to his lips, planting a gentle kiss.

"Is it alright if I call you to my chambers this evening?" He asked. I wanted to roll my eyes at the absurdity of his request but glared back at him instead, feigning a cold expression.

"Well, isn't that all I'm good for anyway?"

"You know that's not-"

I laughed, placing a finger over his lips to silence him. "I was joking."

He smiled, then, relieved.

"I will wait for your summons. My *Lord*." His eyes darkened at the formal address, evidently enjoying the use of his title.

With blinding speed, he disappeared down the corridor. A moment later, three maids came down the stairs. One of them was Tolly. When she spotted me, frozen by the entrance, she marched my way, and left the two other maids behind.

She smiled with a wink.

"I take it you had a nice day out, my lady?" She asked, maintaining formalities in front of the other girls.

"I did." I smiled. "And I require your assistance, Tolly." Beaming with excitement, she turned to the other two maids.

"I'm afraid you'll need to finish on your own. My lady needs me." The two girls disappeared towards the South wing, and the moment they were out of view, Tolly smiled conspiratorially.

"Am I allowed to ask how it went?"

I smiled and pulled her along toward my chambers. "I will receive an official summons tonight."

"He told you this?" She asked, and I nodded. "Then I have the perfect dress for the occasion." She beamed as we took the stairs to the tower.

After recounting last night's events, excluding the details of our lovemaking, Tolly returned to her chores, and I took to the second book.

A rasp sounded at the door as the darkness grew deeper into the horizon.

"Enter." I stood up quickly, knowing it wasn't Tolly.

"My lady," Rommina curtsied. "You have been summoned to the prince's chambers this evening." My heart soared. He had kept to his word.

"Thank you, Rommina."

"My lady." Curtsying again, she left the chamber. Ten minutes later, there was a soft knock before Tolly entered.

"I heard," she said, "it's all the staff talk about."

"Why is my visit to Drake such an event? Surely it's not a secret that I am his mate..."

"It's not, but everyone is trying to figure out exactly what you mean to the master."

"I don't understand."

"You're a mystery to everyone, and a blood witch at that. Everyone waited to see when he would call on you, but the days passed, and he never did. So, when he called for another girl, many concluded that you had followed him here because you served him, but then he sent the girl away untouched... and that offered new possibilities as to what your relationship meant. Now many believe he is in love with you. So, you see why you and the Prince are the talk of the staff. They had bets to see how long the master would last before summoning you."

"Tolly, you must never speak of what you know."

"No, my lady, I would never. I promise."

"I know I can trust you, but the less others know, the better."

She nodded in understanding.

Turns out the dress Tolly had in mind was not a dress at all; it was a long garb crafted of a sheer gold material. It left little to the imagination. I glanced at the curve of my breasts in the mirror.

"I can't wear this."

"If you don't want to give the servants more to talk about, then I suggest you follow traditions."

I sighed. She was right. My hair flowed over my shoulders in beautiful waves, and my skin glowed beneath the light. This was for Drake, after all.

Tolly placed a robe around me, and we made our way to his tower like we had the night before, only tonight I had an official invitation to the royal chambers, and we were not sneaking past the servants.

Everyone who crossed our paths smiled and bowed before scurrying away.

At the base of his tower, Rommina waited for me with her usual lifeless expression.

"My lady," Rommina greeted before marching up the steps. Tolly squeezed my hand and winked before I turned to follow Rommina up the stairs that led to Drake's chambers.

I stood awkwardly behind Rommina as she knocked on his door.

"Enter." His dark voice boomed. Rommina pushed open the door and curtsied.

"My lord," I kept my eyes cast downwards, yet I felt his gaze peruse over me.

"Leave us." He commanded. Rommina all but zoomed out of the room, closing the door behind her.

With my gaze remaining at his feet, I curtsied before him, and fought the smile that threatened to expose me.

"My Lord," I said in a sultry voice. His growl was at my ear in a moment as he lifted my chin to meet his eyes. He pushed the hood away from my face.

"Is that the game you wish to play?" He whispered, his breath against my ear. I quivered.

"Yes, my Lord."

He groaned against my skin.

"Do you have any idea what I want to do to that mouth of yours every time you address me in such a way?"

"No, my Lord." I stoked the fire. He strode behind me and pulled my body flush against his. The hard strain on his pants prodded against my behind, and I sucked in a breath as his lips found the hollowed space beneath my ear.

"Do you feel what you do to your master?" He pressed his hardness against me.

"Y-Yes," I whispered.

"Yes, what?"

"Yes, my Lord."

He snarled against my ear.

"Good girl. Now, turn around. Let me see you."

I faced him, unclasping the cape and allowing it to fall to my feet. His eyes burned a path over my skin.

Taking a fist full of the gown, he tugged me to him and brought his face close to mine.

"Was this your idea as well?"

I smiled up at him.

"No. It was Tolly's. I went along with it to keep up pretenses." He studied my breasts and smiled.

"Remind me to thank her for sticking to traditions. I have fantasized about you like this for some time." His admission reminded me of the night I asked whether to pack a bag; I recalled the desire seeping from his voice as he said he would make sure I had something to wear. I knew then his thoughts were wicked...

His hands trailed over the gown, tracing my hips and the sides of my breasts. His thumbs teased over the peaks, eyes burning with desire. "Are you certain you want to play this game?"

"Yes, my Lord," I said, burning to know what he was like without reservations. Something told me I could make him lose himself tonight.

"This game... it could be dangerous." He whispered, warm breath fanning across my face. "You must tell me if it's too much for you."

"I'm here to serve you, my Lord."

He sighed and took my chin in his hand.

"Are you sure you can handle the monster? The darkness?"

I nodded with a smile, encouraging him. His eyes darkened and my core ached.

"Say it. I want to hear you say it." He ordered.

"Yes, my Lord."

His lips assaulted mine, grasping my bottom lip between his teeth and biting gently.

He pulled the leather belt from his pants and secured my hands in front of me. I smiled, amused, and he noticed.

"I thought you wanted to play?" He questioned, raising a brow.

"I do, my Lord."

He smirked, pleased I was still following along.

"On your knees." He ordered, and I obeyed blindly.

His hardness strained against his pants, and I bit my lip in anticipation.

"Are you going to be a good girl for your master?" He fisted my hair, and tilted my head to meet his dark eyes.

"Yes, my Lord."

"Good."

Loosening the grip on my hair, he slowly unbuttoned his pants. I admired his skillful fingers, noting the fire burning in his eyes. Completely at his mercy, waiting on his every command.

My cheeks burned as I watched his sex spring taut before me.

"Do you want a taste?"

I smiled at such a question.

"Yes, my Lord."

He lifted my chin to meet his eyes.

"Then *beg* for it."

"Please, my lord."

"Yes?"

"Let me taste you," My words were a breathless plea, and he roared.

He took a step closer.

"Take me."

At his command, I leaned forward and licked the glistening tip; he shuddered as I brought my lips around his smooth skin.

With my hands still bound, my lips tightened around his length, taking him in. His hips moved, thrusting into my mouth with deliberate strokes. My core pulsed with every assault.

Each thrust drove him deeper, and I accepted the challenge.

"Oh, you are a greedy girl, aren't you?" The question didn't merit an answer as every time he pushed against the back of my throat, I encouraged it.

Hand fisted in my hair, Drake held me in place as he drove his hardness deeper into my mouth.

"By the fates... The sight of you." He ground his hips forward, pushing deeper, and showed no mercy. He plunged into my mouth, securing me in place, and didn't stop until I choked.

"Fuck. I'm sorry." My eyes begged him not to stop, not to apologize, as I tightened my lips around him.

"You want it rough? Is that it? You want me to bury myself in you?"

He found the answer he needed in the desire he must have seen reflected in my eyes. The dark lines of his tattoos fluttered above his skin. The darkness was unwinding.

His fist tightened in my hair, but he didn't apologize this time. Relentlessly grinding his hips forward, he buried himself into my mouth. I choked, and while he eased somewhat, he didn't stop.

Darkness swam across his skin as his hips buckled with a final thrust, holding me in place as warmth spilled into my mouth, forcing me to swallow.

"Is that what you wanted?" His voice was raw, consumed by desire as he eased himself out of me.

"Yes," I admitted shamelessly.

"Yes, what?"

"Yes, my Lord." I amended, pleased we were still playing. The aching between my thighs needed to be eased somehow.

"You have been a good girl. And I'm feeling generous tonight, so I will reward you." He adjusted himself, taking my arm, and pulling me to my feet. Guiding me to one of the stone pillars, he pressed my back against it and raised my hands high above my head. The belt securing my hands was hitched onto the metal clamp above.

"Is that alright?" He asked.

"Yes, my Lord."

He smiled and closed the distance, a predatory look in eyes. The fire between my thighs burned.

Lifting my dress, he slipped a hand between my legs while his eyes burned into mine.

His fingers found my folds and I quivered against his touch.

"You are so wet."

I gasped as his fingers teased my core.

His other hand pulled at one of the strings securing my gown, and exposed my shoulder. His lips left a fiery trail from my ear to my neck and down to the exposed skin of my shoulder.

His fingers abandoned their assault on my core, and I groaned in protest.

"Please," I begged, and he smiled.

"I make the rules here, remember?" He teased, exposing the other shoulder by pulling the delicate material further down, exposing my breasts, navel, and thighs until the garb pooled around my feet.

He kneeled before me and I stopped breathing. Lifting one foot, and then the other, he removed the gown from the ground. His warm breath fanned over one leg, followed by a trail of warm kisses as he proceeded to the other, burning and teasing as I writhed against the restraints of my hands.

This God kneeled before me, eyes heavy with desire as he traced his lips over the rise of my stomach and the valley between my breasts.

His hands tightened around my behind as he bit and kissed his way over my body in a slow and merciless assault. I wasn't the only one affected. I noticed the straining bulge in his pants fighting to break free as he stood.

Drake kissed my lips and smiled against them. He was nowhere near ready to release me from the aching prison I was in. Spinning me around to face the pillar, he moved my hair to the side, and kissed down my neck and shoulders.

His teeth graced the skin of my back, and I sucked in a

breath. When he rose, I felt his burning erection against me, and my core pulsed in response. He had freed himself of his clothes, pressing his body flush against mine. Skin against skin, I felt him against my behind, and I pressed back against his hardness. Urging him.

Circling a hand around my waist, his skilled fingers found my folds; he teased and probed my wetness, then withdrew his sodden fingers. My body jolted with surprise when he guided them to my behind, pressing them between my cheeks. The sensation was strange and new, but every nerve in my body ached to be filled and consumed.

I pressed against his fingers as they teased at my tight entrance.

His fingers moved back to the sleekness between my folds, then to my behind once more. The sensation was maddening.

"Drake, please." I pushed against him as one of his fingers probed before sinking in. It was strange. An odd sensation, and so tight, yet it felt good.

He pulled his finger out, bringing it to his mouth before returning it to my tight entrance. This time, the intrusion felt fuller, and I realized he had added another finger. Invading me.

"Mhhh. You are so tight..." He rasped, his hardness throbbing against me.

"Take me, please. I beg you."

"Where do you want me?" His fingers returned to my dripping folds, teasing. "Here?" he asked, before moving them to my behind. "Or here?" I sucked in a breath.

"Both," I said without thinking, overcome by the sensation. Everything felt so intense; I felt like I would die soon if he didn't do something. I was desperate to ease this throbbing ache.

"You really are a greedy girl." He whirled me around, and in a swift movement, lifted me. I clasped my legs around him as he pressed my back against the pillar. He slid into me smoothly, and I moaned as he rocked my hips, sinking in and out of me.

He was killing me. My inner thighs were sodden. Flames burned in his eyes as he watched our bodies connect.

His fingers moved to my tight entrance.

"Do it." I urged him.

"It takes time, love. I don't want to hurt you."

I felt disappointed that he was no longer playing; my body craved the darkness.

"I'm yours, my Lord," I said, testing him. He groaned. "Take me. My body is yours." I urged. "Don't hold back." The feral growl that escaped his lips told me the darkness had come to play.

"You will beg me to stop." He growled against my ear as his fingers plunged deep inside of me from behind. The sensation was unequal to anything I had ever felt before: full, intrusive... exquisite.

The darkness inked on his body stormed around us, as his fingers moved in and out, keeping the same pace as he buried himself in me.

He eased out and removed my legs from around him, then turned me, pressing my stomach against the bitting stone of the pillar. I held my breath in anticipation.

"Remember you begged for this..." He groaned against my ear. "The monster will not listen when you beg me to stop." He pushed himself between my cheeks. "He will plunder that tight little ass and become deaf to your cries. Is that what you want?"

"Yes. My Lord." Whatever warning he offered was lost to the heaviness that had been building up between my thighs.

Biting my shoulder, I arched into him as the tip of his hardness pressed between my cheeks. As he pushed against my entrance, his hand snaked around me, and his fingers found their way to my folds. He teased my core in a welcoming distraction, while slowly easing himself inside.

I held my breath and pulled on my hand restrains, as the fullness of him tore though my entrance.

"This is going to hurt love... " His warm breath fanned behind my neck. "But you asked for it..." He grunted, sinking in further, "And I will gladly oblige..." His fingers increased their assault over my sleek folds. "There is no escaping now... this tight little ass... is mine." I whimpered, as he pushed in, expanding me, breaking thought. The uncomfortable sensation, eased as the assault of his fingers continued against my core. That strange feeling was all I could concentrate on, and my body pushed back against his, urging him to bury himself in me.

"You are so tight." He roared, sinking deeper. His hips moving in circles, teasing, allowing me to adjust to his fullness.

"Just do it, please." I pleaded, and he growled.

"You are urging the monster, love, and that is dangerous." His breath fanned against my neck as the fire around us flowed, then without warning, his hips drove hard and I cried out as he buried himself fully.

I fought against my hand restrains at the sharp pain but he stilled for a moment allowing my body a reprise. His fingers circled around my aching folds, and after a moment, the pain dulled and the fullness of him became bearable.

I hissed as he eased himself out, then in again. The discomfort slowly disappeared, and the fire in my core intensified. Once again, my body adjusted to the shadows of his consuming darkness.

"You fit so tight around your master." His voice vibrated on my skin as he plundered without restrains. "Is this what you wanted?" I met his thrusts.

"Yes, my Lord. Please don't stop." I begged, as I felt the building sensation form deep in my thighs.

He roared, pressing me harder against the pillar; the stones chaffed against my breasts. His hand still tormented my core and served as his anchor to bury himself deeper with each thrust from behind.

"Let go... Come for me. Let me feel you." His fingers circled the apex of my sex and sunk again into my folds, begging for my release. I was freed at last.

I screamed and buckled around his fingers as I came undone. He took my hips and forced me against the stone pillar, his fingers digging against my behind as his last thrusts tore through me finding his own release. His warmth trailed down my thighs as he eased out of me.

I COULDN'T MOVE. Honestly, I wasn't even sure I was alive. I felt my body sag against him, as he freed my hands and carried me to his bed. I had nothing else to give tonight. He had taken all of me and I had taken all of him. As he cleaned me and pulled me into his arms, I allowed myself to drift into a warm and peaceful slumber.

IO
RECKONING

I STIRRED IN BED THAT MORNING, and everything ached, but I smiled as I recalled the events from last night. Clearly, he had been holding back, perhaps for fear of hurting me, which seemed ridiculous. He was incapable of that.

I glanced at myself in the mirror as Tolly adjusted the back of my dress. She didn't have to ask about last night. My smile said it all.

A knock at the door startled us.

"Come in," I called. I turned, surprised to find Drake standing in the doorway. Tolly curtsied.

"Tolly, isn't it?" He asked, and her cheeks flushed.

"Yes, my Lord."

Drake's eyes flashed to mine, and I smiled: another reminder from last night.

"Would you mind leaving us, please?" He asked politely.

"Of course, my Lord." She curtsied, stealing a peak at me from under her lashes before disappearing beyond the chamber door. As soon as she was gone, he was before me.

He braced his hands around my waist, pulling me close. I beamed at him.

"What happened to keeping our distance and ensuring our relationship is *discreet*?"

He smirked.

"I just had to see you, make sure you were alright. After last night..." his voice dropped to a whisper, and I felt my cheeks redden as he ran his fingers over my skin.

"I've never been better or happier. Really." I said, and though his eyes lightened, the lines on his forehead furrowed. "What is it?" Something was clearly on his mind.

"I want you to know how hard it is for me to stay away. I am a monster for doing this to you, but I need you to tell me you understand. I cannot endure this charade if I know that you are not ok with this."

I touched his face. How could he think so little of me?

"You need to do whatever you think is best. Anything to stay alive and to keep us both safe. Even if that means playing a part you despise. Believe me, I understand. Sometimes we must live with the guilt of our choices if it means protecting those we love." I said, the heaviness of my secret weighing down on me.

"I also need you to promise me you will stay safe. No more missions outside the castle." His eyes pleaded with mine.

"I promise," I said without hesitation. "I have books to keep me occupied here. Besides, after my last encounter with your uncle, he is the last person I want to run into," I admitted, and his eyes narrowed.

"What did he do?"

"Nothing. Dagasti didn't touch me." I said, trying to conciliate his darkness. I shivered, recalling his uncle's fingers against my skin. "He was just unpleasant. He insinuated I could warm his bed if I tired of you."

Drake growled.

"Don't worry. Dagasti is not my type." I tried to ease the fire flickering behind his eyes.

"This is my fault. He wouldn't be chasing you like a vulture if I had made it clear to him that you were off limits."

"You know that's not true. If you had shown him how much I meant to you, it would give your uncle more incentive to come after me. Dagasti seems like the kind of man who enjoys a challenge." He sighed, running a hand through his hair.

"I don't like that he is lurking so close."

"I'll be fine here. Just try to find out what you can about his plans, and then we can leave for Upherya like you said."

He paced about the chamber before returning to my side.

"I would never forgive myself if I let anything happen to you." He said, eyes bottomless pools of darkness.

"Nothing will. I'll be safe here. Go." He kissed my cheek, and then my lips, before glancing at me one last time before vanishing through the door.

DAGASTI

If I had to listen to one more ridiculous audience from these peasants with their trivial requests, I would have their heads.

"My lord, may I have a minute?"

I motioned for the guard to approach the throne.

"You wanted me to keep an eye on the prince, sir." He whispered, leaning in to not be overheard.

"We will continue another time. Leave us." I ordered, instructing the guards to escort the waiting villagers out of the throne room. I had had enough of them for one day.

I turned to the man standing before me, his eyes alight with interest.

"Do you have something important to share about my nephew?"

"My lord, there are rumors amongst the staff that the prince is in love with the blood witch." The man had my undivided attention. I already had my suspicions, but proof was what I needed.

"I don't want gossip. I want evidence." I roared, and the man shuffled.

"Sir, he rejected the odalisque that visited him despite summoning the girl himself. He didn't touch her. He refused to."

Interesting... Yet it still didn't prove his love for the blood witch. He was lying to me, and I knew it. I had to test him and I knew exactly how.

The doors to the chamber opened, and the devil himself strolled in.

"Good morning," his words were clipped, and I knew it irked him to see me sit upon his father's throne. *His* throne by right. I smiled.

"You can go now." I dismissed the man and turned to my nephew, the boy who thought he could fool me. I knew that witch was vital to him the minute he marched through those gates with her by his side. Oh, but I would play his game, and bide my time until I found the stone in the king's trove. Then the realms would burn, and so would he. The little dove, however, would be mine to keep.

"Are you ready to head out?"

"I think I've had my share of audiences for the day. Our visit to the borders can wait, but perhaps you would like to join me for supper tonight? You should bring your pet along, too. I'm sure she's bored out of her mind. It's no wonder Callix has been keeping her company." I sneered, testing, and baiting him, but he didn't move. He didn't react. I learned nothing from him which proved he was either good at this game or didn't care for the blood witch after all.

"I will be sure to pass the invitation along. As I already told you, it's her choice where she goes and who she sees."

If he cared for the girl, he gave no indication. But I would push his limits tonight. Oh, I would make sure of that.

BELYNDA

I cringed when Tolly brought in Drake's note to accompany him and his uncle for dinner.

A bad feeling settled in my stomach, and I wanted to trust my instincts. They were usually right. But declining the invitation also seemed like a bad idea, so I had no choice but to accept and join them.

I DESCENDED the stairs of the tower that evening with unease. The cold evening air bit against my skin, and I hugged myself to ease my shaking frame. My heart rate spiked, yet I had to get a grip of myself before I marched into that dining hall. Following the sound of rushing water, I found myself once again at the promenade with the gargoyle fountain.

I wouldn't be alone with Dagasti. In front of Drake, there was no way he would attempt anything foolish. That's what I told myself, anyway, but deep down, I knew he was capable of anything, and that's what scared me.

Sitting at the edge of the fountain, I ran my hand through the warm water, letting it flow gently through my fingers. For a moment, my heartbeat slowed to an even pace; the water was electric, prickling the hairs on my arms.

Staring at the water droplets on my fingertips, the element

called to me. Droplets rose from my skin and danced around my hand in circles, and with every turn, I regained control. The water droplets floated above my palm before falling to the ground.

"My lady?"

I whirled to face Rommina who stood under the archway of the terrace.

"Supper is ready." She said with an odd look.

I followed the woman through the corridor, staring at her back. Had she seen me using water magic? If she had... I didn't trust her to keep my secret. I hesitated before the dining hall doors. What had I done?

"Rommina."

The woman paused and turned to me.

"Yes, my lady?"

I stared at her briefly but decided that saying anything would likely make things worse. There was a chance she hadn't seen me, so I smiled and shook my head.

"Don't worry. It's nothing. Nothing at all."

She bowed her head and pushed open the doors into the glowing dining hall.

My eyes fell on Drake first; he looked impeccable like the prince he was. Rising from his chair, he sauntered to my seat, pulling out a chair so I could take my place.

"Dagasti," I greeted, bowing my head a fraction. "Thank you for the invitation." I added out of polite necessity as Drake returned to his seat.

"I'm glad you decided to join us." He said. His smile was sinister as he attempted to conceal it, taking a sip from his cup.

The servants entered with the trays; I was glad for their pres-ence as they stayed, hovering behind us in case we needed assistance. Knowing there were others in the room offered my mind some peace.

We ate in silence; mostly, I stayed silent. Dagasti and Drake engaged in mundane conversation about their recent trip to the borders, which I imagined was where he had disappeared for errands a couple of days ago.

The servants filled Drake and Dagasti's cups several times during dinner. I glanced toward Drake, unsure if drinking was really a good idea under the circumstances. But he accepted a drink every time; refusing his uncle was likely not an option either.

As the servants removed the trays and served dessert, Drake's eyes scanned my face. Whatever was in his cup was starting to affect him as lust filled his gaze.

"I think I'll have my dessert later," Drake said, glancing at me briefly, and then at his uncle. Drake smiled and the devil smirked in return.

"I actually have a special surprise for you." His uncle waved his hand, and Rommina disappeared from the dining room. A few minutes later, she returned with a beautiful woman following behind her.

Drake straightened in his chair, and I didn't miss the way he stiffened at the sight of her.

She was beautiful, exotic even. Her long dark hair reached past the middle of her back, and her tight black corset snatched her waist and enhanced the swell of her breasts. It didn't take a genius to figure out what Dagasti's intentions were. I swallowed as the woman sauntered towards Dagasti, smiling at Drake from across the table. I should have trusted my instincts. This dinner was a bad idea.

"Kore, you remember my nephew?" Dagasti said as the woman perched on his armrest, draping an arm around his shoulder to whisper in the man's ear.

Dagasti's laughter boomed around the chamber.

"She seems to think you have forgotten her."

I glanced in Drake's direction, but his eyes remained locked on the woman. Leaning forward, his forearms rested against the table as he offered a seductive smile.

"How could anyone forget Kore?"

My fists clenched under the table while I reminded myself that he was only playing Dagasti's game.

"Perhaps you can catch up tonight. I'm sure my nephew has nothing better to do." Dagasti offered, glancing at me, then at Drake.

I tried. I really did everything in my power to contain myself, but the anger burning in my cheeks could not be concealed.

"We could have fun. Just like old times." The woman cooed, and it took every ounce of self-control to remain in my seat and not wrap my hands around her throat.

"As tempting as it sounds, I'm afraid I'll have to decline. Despite what my uncle says, I do have a prior engagement." Drake stood, surprising everyone. "Kore, it's always a pleasure to see you. Perhaps another time?" The woman nodded. "Uncle," Drake said, excusing himself. He left me staring after him as he disappeared out of the chamber, leaving me alone in the den of Dragons.

"Don't worry. I'll make sure you're entertained. Warm and sated." Dagasti traced his hand down the woman's spine and glanced at me. "Perhaps you would like to join us?"

My heart lurched in my chest.

"I don't think I'll be good company. I would rather retire for the evening, if you don't mind." He stared at me until Kore's fingers traced his chin, returning his attention to her. The woman kissed him, and he pulled at her hair, devouring her lips. When he released her, he stared back at me with wild eyes.

"Your loss, dove."

I didn't excuse myself or stick around a moment longer. I flew out of the dining hall, running down the corridors and up the tower. Relief flowed through me as I opened the door to my chambers and noticed Drake's silhouette standing on my balcony.

I locked the door behind me and ran to him. He turned at once, pulling me into his arms.

"I'm sorry." He buried his face against my hair. "I would have declined dinner if I had known he planned to pull something like that. I'm sorry you had to see that."

I nodded, allowing him to shield me in his arms.

"Drake... what's Kore to you?"

His hand paused at the small of my back before he pulled away, gazing down at me.

"Belynda, I had a past. Before I met you and before I met Isabel. I cannot change that." His frown intensified. "Kore was one of my mates." He admitted, and I had to ask.

"How many mates can you have?" His jaw tensed. "How many *have* you had?" I amended, realizing that perhaps I didn't want to know the answer.

"We can have as many as we want." He confessed with a pained expression. "And I... I've had too many to count." He peered up at the night sky, trying to hide his guilt. "I'm sorry for hurting you like this."

I sighed and reached for his hand.

"I'm not mad. You're immortal, a Dragon and Prince of the Fire Realm. I would be a fool to think you don't come with a long history."

"She means nothing to me." His eyes pierced through me. "You need to know that."

I smiled up at him.

"I do. I wouldn't be here if I didn't," His fingers trailed

through my hair as I spoke, "but I must admit, it took every ounce of self-control not to get up from that chair and wipe that smile from her beautiful face."

Drake smirked.

"You know… jealousy is very powerful indeed." He said. It seemed like he wanted to add more, but didn't. Instead, he kissed the top of my head and embraced me once more.

"I have a feeling Dagasti is onto us," Drake said.

"I don't know… you were pretty convincing back there."

He pulled away and walked back into the chamber.

"Regardless, I think it will be safe for me to keep my distance, at least for tonight."

Drake walked to the door, and I was saddened to watch him leave already, though I understood why.

"Will I see you tomorrow?"

He paused at the threshold.

"I have plans to visit the elders tomorrow, and I don't think it is a good idea to sit through another dinner with my uncle… so, no."

I buried the rising sadness in my chest.

"Ok," Was all I could say without crumbling.

"You are my life." He said. His words were a breath for my dying soul.

"I love you… be careful." I whispered, and then he walked out the door.

DAGASTI

Her dress flowed behind her as she fled from the dining hall. Kore teased my neck, and though I had promised to take care of her tonight, my mood had soured.

Rommina entered the chamber and filled my cup.

"My lord, may I have a word?"

I pushed Kore away, and she pouted.

"Leave us. Now."

She stood from my lap and sauntered away, swaying her beautiful behind... perhaps I might change my mind after all.

"You better have a good reason for interrupting my evening." I said, glaring at Rommina.

"It's the blood witch, my Lord. I saw her this evening..." She said, voice trembling.

"Out with it, woman."

"Sir, she is a water elemental."

My eyes narrowed, and I sat up straight.

"What do you mean?"

"I saw her by the fountain, my Lord. She could manipulate water."

"Are you certain of this?"

"Yes, sir. I saw her with my own eyes."

"Did she say anything?"

"No, my Lord, but she did look startled. I'm certain she didn't mean to be seen which is why I thought you should know. She could be lying to the prince as well." I very much doubted that, though he truly was a fool if he thought he could lie to me. I would take the blood witch. His blood witch.

If they had lied about the loss of her powers, then she could open the portal to Xelraa again. For once, the fates seemed to be smiling upon me.

"Speak of this to no one. You may leave."

A blood witch, with water element powers... meant she was quite special indeed. I smiled, realizing why Callix had lingered. The bastard... he must have sensed her power yet chose to keep it to himself. I knew he wasn't to be trusted...

I had to find that amulet. No one would rest tonight, not until every last coffer of the trove was turned and every jewel checked.

I strolled out of the chamber and called for the royal guard. We were so close; I could almost feel the pull of the Nightshade's Talisman. Once I had it, the little dove was going to help me release its darkness. She would be mine... The realms would finally kneel before me.

DRAKE

Cronis glanced at me as I entered the elder's temple.

"You again." He said, peering over the scroll.

"Are you not pleased to see me again, old man?"

"Not when you seek answers I cannot give."

"Refusing to speak the truth doesn't make it less real."

The old man glanced at me and pushed the scroll away.

"We are not warriors. Simply keepers. We cannot fight your uncle. Not even you can go against Dagasti, not with the royal army by his side."

"Then how can I claim what is my birth right if I cannot even gain your support?"

"You're wrong. You have our loyalty and our support. What you lack is an army; without one, I'm afraid a throne cannot be reclaimed."

"Then at least tell me of Dagasti's plan for the kingdom." They had to know. Dagasti would never confide in me, and I suspected time was running out. Cronis leaned across the table.

"Dagasti has been digging in the treasure trove caves, yet no one knows what he is searching for."

"But you have an idea." I pressed, and the old man cleared his throat.

"Mere speculations. But yes. We fear Dagasti might be going after the Nightshade."

I gaped at the old man.

The serpent bound stone. The one thing legends warned us to steer clear of.

"What happens if he finds it?"

Cronis straightened with a sigh.

"You know your tales, boy. Remember what they foretold."

I hated when he answered in riddles.

I tried to remember the old legends, and only one song I remembered as a boy came to mind.

> *"Pillaging through light, the embers of darkness arise. A force*
> *of demise rendering will and life, sprung from Night-*
> *shade's magic wake where a fate awaits plight. Falling*
> *swiftly on fortune accorded this strife. A steel of courage*
> *seeks its peak as hearts of true belief make ready the keep.*
> *For when Hell is raining down and ruin wantonly sings.*
> *Honor and strength must face the only thing it brings.*
> *Together we stand, shield to shield, sword in hand. Our*
> *bolder-than-death vow, a relentless stand. Memories of*
> *love, from any age. No greater strength remains at this*
> *stage. Our kinship's light lit its truth the day. We shall*
> *survive together, no matter what comes our way."*

I whispered the words of the almost-forgotten song. I frowned, facing the old man.

"It doesn't make sense. What does it all mean?"

"It is called the song of despair for a reason. The Nightshade Talisman will bring about darkness and destruction, an army of Darkling's at Dagasti's disposal."

"Do you think he will succeed?" I asked. The somber look on his face offered no hope.

"I'm afraid it is only a matter of time before he does."

"What if we find it first?"

"No. Don't you remember anything we taught you? That is not your path. Your soul will turn to the darkness if you so much as touch that stone."

If the old man was right and there was any possibility that Dagasti could unleash such evil, then I had to get Belynda out of here and leave for Upherya at once. We needed to find a way to reopen the portal and send her back to the human world. Anything to keep her safe. I would rather fight against Dagasti than alongside him.

"Thank you, Cronis."

"You will sit on your father's throne one day, my boy. I just hope I'm alive to see it."

I bowed to the old man before leaving the temple.

I couldn't risk Belynda being here, not while Dagasti unleashed a soul-devouring army.

DARKNESS COVERED the kingdom skies as I strolled through the castle doors. The night guard shift seemed to have been stripped to a minimum; it was the perfect time to leave.

I stood outside her chamber, listening to her and Tolly's quiet laughter. I should have been happy that she had made a friend, but it saddened me. I had to rip her away from yet another person she cared about.

I knocked , and silence followed.

"Enter." Her melodic voice made me smile. As I peeked through the door and she spotted me, her face lit up.

"Excuse me, my Lord." Tolly walked past me and closed the door behind her.

"You came!" She beamed, closing the distance between us. "You said I wouldn't see you today." I pulled her into my arms, breathing in her scent and allowing it to fill my soul.

"I know, but we must leave."

Belynda drew away from me with a worried look.

"Already? Is everything alright?"

I shook my head.

"We leave now. Tonight. Come, I'll help you dress and explain everything on the way."

I tightened the last of the laces at back of her dress, and though she tried to hide it, I saw the fear on her face through the mirror, and it tore my soul apart. She slipped on her boots and glanced around the room, with a saddened look.

"I'm ready." She forced a smile.

"Come." I took her hand, and we descended the tower.

"When are you going to tell me what's going on?" She whispered as we crossed the entrance hall.

"Once I reach my mother. When we're out of the castle, we will speak." I whispered. "But we leave for Upherya tonight."

I felt her hand tighten around mine as we stepped from the castle doors.

II

POWER LUST

SOMETHING WASN'T RIGHT AND I sensed it the moment we crossed the courtyard. It was awfully quiet. I tightened my grip around her hand. Instantly, she knew.

"What is it?" Her voice trembled, and fear gripped my soul. If I allowed anything to happen to her...

"Something is wrong." I pulled her behind me as the guards slipped from the shadows. "Say nothing," I whispered as they circled us. Dagasti would not allow us to leave. Not without a fight.

"What's happening?" She demanded, but I remained still, calculating my next move.

"What is the meaning of this? You will let us through. That is an order. Put your weapons down." My voice boomed over the darkness, and the guards halted their approach but did not retreat. I could shift and wipe them out quickly, but these men were likely innocent. They didn't know the ruler they served.

"We have orders, my lord."

"And what orders are those?"

"We are not to let you walk out of those gates." Belynda tugged on my arm, and I glanced her way, hoping to ease the worry on her face.

"I don't care what the orders said. You will stand aside."

The line of soldiers quivered, but they did not retreat; then, I caught his scent, and I knew we were trapped.

"I am the Prince of the Realm. You will heed my orders." I roared, the darkness dancing across my skin.

"I thought you said you were not interested in your claim." Dagasti's voice spoke from behind the line of guards.

"That was before I knew the truth." My voice boomed. In that moment, the truce I had asked my mother and Belynda to make would not come to fruition.

"And what is the truth? Enlighten me."

"You are a traitor. A murderer. You betrayed my father. My parent's blood is on your hands, not the hands of the air people as you have everyone believe."

"That is an unfortunate truth. Your father was weak." Dagasti admitted, and dread coursed through me, the guards did not flinch. They would stand with Dagasti which meant they knew... I was no longer sure if they supported him out of respect or fear, but I should have taken their heads when I had the chance, without hesitation.

"My father was a good man. He was your own blood. He was loyal to his people. You... I don't know *what* you are." I spat. Belynda's hand tightened around mine, anchoring me to my sanity.

"I am a visionary, unlike your father who fantasized about peace. Your silly infatuation with the guardian girl cost us, and yet your father did nothing. It's time we take back what is ours. I will expand the empire your father created. Do what he was too weak to do. I will rule them all and make them bow to me."

"You are a madman. You will bring what is left of this kingdom to ruins."

"No. I will bring our kingdom to glory." He roared. Dagasti was insane.

"How exactly do you plan to do that? Do you think Abryas and Upherya will lay down their swords willingly? What about Callix? Exactly how do you plan to take over his Realm?"

"Without thinking, you have brought me the key to unlock my secret weapon. This is the fate's plan." He glanced at Belynda. The darkness inside blinded me.

BELYNDA

Drake streaked with lightning speed, taking down three guards in his wake.

"You pack of fools. Approach and contain him. Use the fire shackles." Dagasti's voice echoed over the chaos, and the men closed in around us.

"By the fates if you lay a finger on her, I will kill you all." Drake warned as fire broke over his skin. Drake became their target, but he took out the first guard with a direct punch to the face. I had never seen him fight in his human form, but he was just as skilled and lethal.

They came at him from all angles, yet only one landed a blow. I couldn't watch him fight while I stood idly by. I summoned the one element I could, creating a water bubble over the guard's head. The man twisted and turned, choking as the water drowned his cries. I extended the bubble, submerging the other guard that had moved to Drake. It wasn't enough.

They swarmed over him, and though he fought them off at

first, the moment the shackles were on him, his fire was subdued. It disappeared beneath his skin, and he was left defenseless.

"Let Drake go or your men will continue to suffer." I extended the water, and it swallowed another two guards. Dagasti simply laughed.

"Go ahead. They are worthless to me."

I assessed the guards. My power wasn't strong enough to contain them all. I wasn't even sure I could kill them with water... and their lives were useless to this monster of a man.

"Release them now," Dagasti ordered, noticing my determination waver.

The water bubble disintegrated, and the guards fell, heaving onto the floor. Dagasti approached. I could not outrun him.

"You are a coward."

"And you have much to learn." The monster taunted, smirking. "See, he's perfectly harmless." Dagasti swung a punch in Drake's direction, and I screamed. But Drake was swift and dived to avoid the blow, redirecting his force to ram his head against his uncle's, knocking him to the ground.

Dagasti dusted himself off, and the guards held Drake this time as the monster delivered a blow directly to Drake's face.

"Is that all you've got?" Drake mocked, spitting blood at Dagasti's feet.

"Please stop. Please."

Dagasti didn't listen. He delivered punch after punch, but Drake only goaded him more.

"You've gone soft, Dagasti. Is this how you plan to make the other Realms bend the knee?" Dagasti roared with anger and punched Drake again.

"No. My army of shadows will, and I will take pleasure in bringing you to the darkness first." Drake's grin vanished before his uncle delivered the final blow that rendered him unconscious.

I watched, horrified, as the guards dragged Drake away.

"Come, little dove." The monster cooed, and his men pulled me along.

"What do you want with me?"

"Oh, I have plans for you."

"Please let us go. You don't want to do this."

"But I do. I very much want to, and if you wish to keep your Prince alive, you will do as I say."

I stared at the man's back as we descended into the pits of darkness, a part of the castle I would have been content to avoid. The dungeons.

The high ceilings reminded me of the guardianship chambers. It was almost as if time was repeating itself, only this time, I was alone. The guards threw me behind bars and hung Drake from chains bolted to the ceiling. Whatever plans Dagasti had for us, he wasn't in a rush to pursue them which I realized the moment he and his guards disappeared.

Only one guard remained posted by the entrance. I assessed the prison yet there seemed no possible way to break the metal bars. Not without my powers. If Dagasti was right, and those fire shackles contained Drake's ability to shift, then we had no way out. Drake's mother had no idea what was happening, and even if she did, she could do nothing. Not without risking herself.

Drake stirred, and my heart skipped a beat.

His eyes scanned the darkness until finding me.

"Drake, I'm here." The chains rattled as he pulled on them, but it was useless. Drake roared and yanked his wrists. "Stop, please. You will only hurt yourself."

"I have to find a way." His snarl echoed around the stone walls, and the chains trembled but didn't falter. "This is all my fault. I shouldn't have allowed you to come here with me."

"Stop it. Enough. This is not your fault. I chose to come, remember?"

"I should have known what he was up to the minute we arrived. I knew something was wrong. I should have sent you away to keep you safe."

"Please don't do this now. This is not the time for blame. We just need to give him what he wants."

"He plans to raise an army of shadows," Drake said. The void in his voice warned of the danger this army of shadows posed.

"Then how do we stop him? Drake... what is it? What is this army?"

Silence returned to the chamber.

"I don't know... I have only heard legends of such power. Before the realms were forged. Before the first of your kind even took a breath."

"Then how do we even know he's telling the truth?"

"Dagasti is many things, but he is not lying about this. Remember when I told you and..." he caught himself before mentioning his mother, remembering the guard nearby. "Remember when I said I needed time to figure out what he was up to?" His voice lowered to a whisper.

"Yes."

"I went to the temple again and spoke with an elder. Dagasti has been pillaging the treasure trove looking for a talisman."

"A magic amulet?"

"Yes, though this particular one has a history. It's a stone bound to a serpent and has been in my family's trove since the Realms were forged. None of my ancestors dared to touch it. They said it was cursed. It was always well guarded, and as an heir to the throne, do you know what my first sworn duty was? To stay clear of the damned thing. Its power is believed to bind the soul of whoever yields it to darkness. My ancestors sang songs about the cursed necklace. They called it Nightshade."

"What does that mean?"

"It means 'he who has the power to command an army'. An army of Darkling's."

"And do you really think this necklace can do that?"

"I don't know. Like I said, it's all legend. But all myths have their truth, don't they?"

"What are we going to do?" I whispered. He roared, fighting against his chains. "Drake, stop."

"Belynda, do you think it's easy for me to feel this helpless? I'm responsible for your safety. I could never live with myself if I allowed anything to happen to you, and your family would never forgive me."

"No. You promised me. Please, I beg you. No more sacrifices."

The silence between us signaled his recognition of a promise that weighed heavy on his soul.

"I know what that promise means to you, but how can you ask that of me? Do you really think I could ever live with myself if I didn't do everything in my power to keep you safe?"

"I would never forgive you if you gave up your life again to save mine."

"And I would rather live in a world where you exist, even a world where you despise me."

No. He was taking back his words, but I couldn't allow it. How could I make him see?

The cell was eerily quiet, then, and I measured my words before speaking.

"Rest assured; I wouldn't exist in that world. If you go, I go, and that is my promise. I will meet you in the depths of darkness if that's what it takes."

"You would hurt yourself? Have you lost your mind?"

"You leave me no choice. What if it was the other way around? Would you want me to sacrifice my life? Would you be content for me to give my life to save yours?"

"Never!" He roared.

"So, you do understand..."

"Belynda..."

"Promise me, Drake, and this time you need to mean it. Swear to me on your father's name."

"I promise you no more sacrifices, but I won't let anything happen to you."

"This is out of our control; do you think I would ever blame you if anything were to happen to me?"

"I would blame myself."

"Please don't. I would want you to find a way to live your life. To find happiness again." Despite the darkness, I felt his eyes piercing into my soul.

"Why do I feel like there's something you're not telling me?"

"I wouldn't lie to you." My soul twisted with guilt, yet it was the only way to ease the pain. "I don't want us to repeat Isabel's story. Surely you agree that enough sacrifices have been made."

He remained silent, and I took that as his resolve.

"Now, tell me more about these legends."

We lost track of time as we remained alone in the cells. We knew nothing of Dagasti's plan or how he intended to bring about his army of shadows, but if there was truth to Drake's tales, then there wasn't much we could do to stop it. The shadows would spread, turning any man, woman, or child it touched. Their soul would be consumed by the darkness. If Dagasti found that Talisman, and its power was as the legends described... no one was safe. Not with Dagasti commanding such forces.

Dagasti said I was the key to unlocking his weapon but neither Drake nor I understood how that could be possible. I had no powers. The only element I could command was water, which was useless against these immortal creatures.

Drake fought against his chains with relentlessness despite many futile attempts. I chose to spend my time trying to summon Earth and Air but I, too, failed.

A guard brought me a tray of food, pushing it through the bottom of the rails.

"Eat," Drake ordered.

"Do you think I can eat or drink anything now? While I watch you starve?"

"You forget I can survive without food, but you cannot. Do not be stubborn. Eat." He pressed. I glanced at the tray and grabbed a piece of bread, forcing myself to chew then swallow.

"Do you know how long we've been down here?"

"I can't be sure. Perhaps two days. Maybe more."

"That means he probably hasn't found what he's looking for. How long does he plan to keep us in here?"

I began to pace; inside this cell, I felt like a caged animal.

"Something tells me we'll find out soon."

I grabbed hold of the rails, glancing at Drake. Then, I heard it. The trudging of footfall on stone.

The guard entered the chamber first, carrying torches. Dagasti followed; in his wake marched a throng of about forty armed men. They wore the royal guard armor and held metal shields to their chests. These men were ready for battle.

"Bring her to me," The monster commanded, and I moved away from the rails until my back hit the wall. The two guards opened the cell and reached for me, but I didn't go willingly. I lunged at them, kicking, biting, and screaming. But it was no use.

"I can see why you like this one. There's fire in her."

"I swear if you lay a finger on her, I will end you." Drake snarled. Dagasti grinned.

"Finally, some honesty on your part." He smiled. "She will be safe. I promise. All she needs to do is open the rift into the Dark dimension again." I glanced at Dagasti, then Drake.

"Is that why you need her? She cannot do that."

"She did it once to free you. She can do it again."

"Drake is right. I can't. I don't remember the spell, and I can't summon all the elements to draw power from them. You're wasting your time." It was unlikely, but perhaps he would let us go. He was mistaken; I was no use to him.

"No. You are wasting my time." His smile was twisted; he wouldn't give up easily. He turned and jabbed Drake in the stomach.

"No!" I shrieked.

"Perhaps what you lack is an incentive."

"I'm telling you the truth. I can't do what you're asking." The monster didn't listen, but punched Drake again. His chains rattled in the chamber's silence, and though Drake did not beg, I did.

"Please. Stop it."

"Open the rift to Xelraa." He roared.

I looked at my hands and closed my eyes, sensing the cold stones beneath me. *Earth... Wind... I need you.* I willed their power to flow through me, but nothing happened, like I feared. Tears brimmed in my eyes and I stared at the monster again.

"I can't..." He pulled a blade from his vest and tore Drake's shirt.

"What if we carve a little?"

"Nooo!" I shrieked as Dagasti plunged the tip of the knife into Drake's chest. This time, Drake's chains rattled as he fought his restraints.

"Stop it! I beg you."

"Don't beg me. Open the portal." His sinister smile grew as the blade slid down Drake's stomach. Dagasti withdrew the blade, licking the blood clean off the tip. He was a sick man.

I pressed my hands against the floor, commanding the stones beneath me to move. For a moment, I thought they did. Then I realized it was my body that trembled, pulsing with rage.

I allowed water to surge through me; perhaps that would be enough. Dark waves crashed in a violent storm inside me as I recalled the words I had spoken the night I released Drake.

"Guardians of the shadow realm, I command you to release Xelraa. Unveil the portal of the dark shrine: the forgotten gates. I command you." A tendril of air snaked through the chamber, and everyone froze. A spark ignited under the umbral of the arched columns, and though it lasted only a second, everyone saw it.

Dagasti walked to my side, a determined glint in his eye.

"That's it. Do it again." He commanded.

"Belynda, don't." Drake urged through gritted teeth. I watched in horror as a trail of blood trickled down his body.

"Guardians of the shadow realm, I command you to release Xelraa. Unveil the portal of the dark shrine: the forgotten gates. I command you." This time, nothing happened. There was no gust of wind. No spark. Only rage and madness behind Dagasti's eyes.

"I see, perhaps something sharper..." He motioned to one of the guards, who stepped forward and offered Dagasti a small wooden box. The monster opened it, and I froze at the sight of the gleaming blue blade in his hand.

"No!"

Drake noticed, too. I saw the fear in his eyes as he took in the glimmering blue of the crystal blade. I had seen only one other like it. It was forged from blue firestone, like the blade that had taken Drake's father.

I became fire, water, earth, and wind. I rose to my feet, heading directly for Dagasti, but his men grabbed me before I could reach him.

"You will never see those gates open if you hurt him. I promise you." I raged.

"Do you think I will stop with him? I will kill everyone you ever cared about if that's what it takes."

"Belynda, I don't care what happens to me. Don't do it."

I shook my head, refusing to listen to him. Pressing my hands against the cold floor, I screamed at the top of my lungs.

"YOU WILL YIELD TO ME!"

The stone floor and walls trembled. I felt it then. I felt the raw strength of the earth as it rattled in the chamber, and the wind as it howled around me, charging my blood.

"Guardians of the shadow realm, I command you to release Xelraa. Unveil the portal of the dark shrine: the forgotten gates. I command you."

The spark under the umbral widened into a black hole. It fed off my energy as the pulsing grew.

"Yes. That's it. You see, little dove? So little faith in yourself."

"Let him go. Now."

"Oh, but what's the rush?"

"You promised." The dark portal was fed from my rage.

"I said I wouldn't hurt him if you did as I said, and I meant it, but we're not done yet. Now, open a portal into the other Realms."

"Dagasti, you don't know what you're doing." Drake thundered.

"But I do. My men will no longer suffer trying to breach the borders. I will plant the seed of darkness inside all their kingdoms and watch as it spreads like a disease. They will bend the knee and beg for mercy."

"What about your alliance with Callix?" Drake questioned.

"Did you honestly think I would sell my soul to the water lord?" Dagasti smiled. "I'm afraid he will, too, be treading water. Ironic, isn't it?"

"If I do as you ask... you promise to let us go?"

"Belynda, don't."

I ignored Drake's plea and stared only into the monster's eyes who turned the blade in his hands.

"I don't think you should be bargaining when I hold his life in my hands, but I'll concede. The portals for his life."

"Don't do it." Drake pleaded. "He's lying." Drake pulled on his chains, twisting, and contorting with rage.

I knew what my decision would cost; so many would suffer, but I wasn't a hero. Drake had often warned of what he would do to save me. The worlds he would devastate. I would always choose us. Him. I saw the face of death staring back at me, and without a doubt, I knew that Dagasti was the one in my visions.

"*Dimittis Onulic.*" As I said the words, a new rift opened in the far corner of the chamber. A portal to Abryas, the Earth Realm.

"Belynda, don't..." Drake yanked on his chains, and I turned to him for a moment. I hoped my eyes conveyed what my lips dared not speak.

"*Dimittis Viscerai.*" The words left my mouth, and another spark emerged behind us. The portal to Upherya, the Air Realm.

"Form," Dagasti commanded, and the armed men assembled into three groups.

"*Dimittis lepdieum,*" I said at last. The blast sent water spurting into the chamber as the portal to Serfier, the Water Realm, opened. Water rushed through the portal, filling the chamber quickly, and I glanced between Drake and Dagasti with panic.

"Blasted Callix!" Dagasti cursed. "Close it. Shut the damn

portal." I released the gate of Serfier, and as the portal disappeared, so did the water.

"No one has ever breached the Water Realm. Did you really think you could?" Drake taunted, pleased by his uncle's failure. Dagasti's eyes darkened like the sky of an impending storm. He roared, streaking to Drake's side with blinding speed, and plunging the glass knife into his shoulder.

"NOOO!" I shrieked as Drake roared in agony. Dagasti yanked the blade out.

"You open your mouth again, and it will be your heart next time." The monster warned.

"Please stop. I did as you asked."

"Yes. You've done well." The monster retrieved a necklace from under his vest, and Drake and I stared, frozen at the glowing Talisman. It was the stone Drake had spoken of, bound into a coiling serpent. *He had found it... the Nightshade Talisman.*

"Nooo!" Drake roared.

Dagasti gripped the stone, and as he neared the portal to the Dark dimension, he whispered foreign words to me.

"*Vesu induerso, secti du mort.*" The darkness didn't wait... it slithered through the rift like a black fog with tentacles, probing any space in its path. It circled Dagasti's men, who stood by the Earth portal before blanketing them. Their bodies stiffened; eyes consumed by shadows.

"Go," Dagasti commanded, and they marched forward, disappearing through the gate as the darkness followed.

The slivers of fog trailed over the rest of the armed men, shrouding them in darkness. At Dagasti's command, they marched through the gate into the Air Realm and ripples of darkness trailed behind. The monster's eyes found me, and he smirked.

"Don't worry. Your world will be next."

"Over my dead body." I challenged.

"That we can easily arrange."

"Dagasti, I will kill you." Drake roared, wrestling against his chains.

The monster held the jewel around his neck, and the darkness moved, plundering, pillaging the soul of every man it touched in the chamber.

The monster smiled at me; his intentions were clear. Drake had been right. He would never let us go. The dark shadows veered towards Drake, and my fists clenched by my sides. I didn't think.

"*Dimittis Gaia.*"

Dagasti glanced at me with confusion as the void expanded on the roof where Drake's chains were connected.

"I love you."

Drake's eyes met mine for a brief moment before I flung my hand, thrusting him with a gust of wind through the rift, which had swallowed his chains. I closed the portal as soon as it absorbed him, but I didn't have time to fend off Dagasti. His fist smacked my face, then everything went black.

12

MORTAL ALLIES

A *CALL IN THE MIDDLE OF THE NIGHT* never meant good news. I bolted from bed and answered immediately when I recognized the private number from the chamber.

"Sir. We've had a breach. It's the fire-bound."

"Where? When? Is Belynda with him?" I slipped on my pants and t-shirt.

"No, sir. He's alone. Gave us a fright when the portal opened just a few minutes ago."

"I'm on my way."

"Sir. You might want to bring in a doctor. He looks like he needs some medical assistance."

I ended the call, strapping my gun to my belt, and slipping on a jacket. I was dialing Seymor as I jumped in the car.

"Tyrus? What's wrong?"

"You need to meet me at the chamber. Drake has returned. Alone; he might need medical assistance." The line was silent for a moment.

"I'm on my way."

Meet me at the chamber. NOW...

I texted before pulling out of the driveway. A minute later, my phone buzzed. I knew it was Oliver, but I didn't have time to explain. I pressed my foot on the pedal, speeding up the mountain roads.

DRAKE

Pain seared through me as I collided against the stone floors. I roared, staring at my surroundings, and the reality of what she had done. The portal closed a second after me, and she didn't follow. How could she...?

"No..." I punched the stone floor, and it cracked. I hit it again and again and again until blood stained my knuckles. Fire consumed my insides and clawed at my soul, yet I couldn't shift. The monster demanded retribution, but it was imprisoned. Chained...

The metallic screeching of the shackles bounced off the chamber walls as I rammed them against the floor. It was useless as it only bit further into my skin, yet the pain was the only release I could offer the monster that burned to come out. I had to go back. They had to find a way to reopen that portal.

"Please calm down. Tyrus is on his way." The guards hovered but maintained a good distance, arms raised to show they weren't a threat. I already knew that. I was the real danger... to them, to myself. With the seething monster inside, no one was safe.

Felsia and Celest stormed through the chamber doors; Seymor, Oliver, and Tyrus followed closely after.

Their eyes reflected the horror etched before them. Though it wasn't the sight of my blood spilled across the marble floors that triggered it, but the lack of her presence.

"Please don't come any closer," I warned. Celest paused before the blood, but Belynda's mother wasn't deterred.

"What happened?" She demanded, expression haunted.

"I need to go back. You have to do something. Find a way. Send me back now." I pleaded, glancing between them. I crumbled to my knees. How could I tell them? How could I explain when I was supposed to protect her?

Seymor ignored my warning and marched to my side, kneeling close to me.

"You know we don't have enough power to open that portal again, but I promise you, we will find a way. Now tell us everything. From the beginning." He placed a hand on my shoulder, surprising me.

By the time I finished recounting the events, Celest was frantic. No one outright blamed me, but they didn't need to. I blamed myself. I was responsible for this.

"I suppose if you couldn't get out of those yourself, cutters won't do the trick either..." Seymor remarked, inspecting the iron shackles.

"There is a spell in the vault that can remove these. Let me look. Celest, why don't you help me?" Felsia offered, and the two women disappeared through the chamber halls.

"Leonor will be here shortly. She's the doctor. I'm sure she will be able to take care of those." Tyrus offered, glancing between the blood on the floor and my wounds.

"There's no need. I will heal as soon as these chains come off."

"Do you think he will hurt her?" Oliver asked. He kept his distance, and for the first time, I felt no resentment toward him.

"She's worth more to him now that she's regained her powers."

"But that doesn't mean he won't hurt her to get what he wants." The boy concluded, voicing what I dared not.

"Let's not get ahead of ourselves." Tyrus cut in. "If she's as valuable as he says she is, then I don't see why he would harm her."

"I just don't understand why she didn't open the portal again to save herself?" Seymor paced before us. "She did it for you. She could have done it again."

"That's why we need to find a way to open that portal. If she could have followed... she would have by now."

The chamber spun as I pushed up from the floor.

"Easy there. I think you've lost a lot of blood."

"I'm fine." I thundered.

"You're not. Listen to Tyrus." Felsia's voice cut in as she reappeared with Celest in her wake. "Let me see those chains." She knelt before me, and I offered her my hands. She studied the iron manacles.

"Did you find the spell?" Seymor hovered next to Celest, who held a book.

"Yes. It should be easy enough."

"Fetch us a cup of water, will you?" Felsia asked Oliver, and the boy disappeared at once.

"These are Fire Shackles. The only way to unlock the chains is with the key forged in the same fire as them." I explained.

"We obviously don't have a key, but we have magic." Celest kneeled on the stone floor next to Felsia, and this time, ignored the blood that soaked into her sleeping gown. She flipped through the pages of the book. "Here." Celest turned it in Felsia's direction as Oliver returned with a cup in his hands.

"I think if we use the opposite element, it might do the trick."

"Water?" I questioned. "It just won't do."

"Not by itself, of course." Belynda's mother placed her hand over the water and read from the book.

"*Protactu, Recticum, Unnonum, Septalis.*" She repeated, her hand hovering above my chains as she repeated once more.

"*Protactu, Recticum, Unnonum, Septalis.*"

As she poured the water over the shackles, the water hissed and dissolved to vapor, and with it, the iron started to fragment. The monster could already taste its freedom, but I would not allow myself to lose control around these people. I pulled my hands from Felsia's hold and struck the chains once against the stone floor; this time, they shattered.

I lay on the floor, forcing my breathing to ease as the monster scratched and gnawed inside. I needed to heal. I had never felt so weak, yet losing control and endangering Belynda's family was not a risk I was willing to take.

"Please give me some room. I need to heal." I felt the darkness slipping from my pores, but they listened and retreated from the monster.

"Drake, not in here. You can't." Felsia warned...

"I know," I said through gritted teeth, fighting the fire from consuming me. Flames seared the wound that trailed from my chest to my stomach, but the pain would not ease. The wound inflicted by the blue fire blade still bled. I gripped my shoulder and roared. "It's not healing."

"Easy." Seymor approached. "Just breathe."

"Stay away." I urged him.

"It's alright. I trust you. Just breathe."

He was insane. Madness must run in the family.

"Where is Leonor?" He demanded, and Tyrus got on his phone.

"That's it. Focus on your breathing." The old man continued

to take measured steps toward me. I remembered my mother's words. I was forged of fire; I was the ruler of it. It did not rule me. I forced the monster to retreat, dowsing the fire to a low simmer.

"She's just arrived," Tyrus confirmed as Seymor reached my side and kneeled over me.

"She'll give you something for the pain. Trust me. You will be alright." Never in my immortal life would I have expected to be at the mercy of the guardianship again. But here I was: powerless. Yet, despite my aversion to showing any gratitude to these people, my emotions were conflicted. I glanced at the woman who had sacrificed herself to give me back my human essence, at the boy who had lost his father to my wrath yet stood before me, and at the old man who hovered above. I extended my hand, and the man took it.

"Thank you," I said as the doors to the chamber opened.

The healer lady paused as she caught sight of the blood, then glanced at Seymor.

"I assure you, it is a lot less serious than what it looks." I offered, trying to ease the woman's mind.

"Let me be the judge of that." The woman didn't hesitate. Kneeling at my side, she ripped the rest of my shirt to expose my stomach, then tore the sleeve off my bloody shoulder.

She ran her fingers over the still-tender skin on my chest, inspecting the closed wound.

"Why isn't this one healing?"

I winced as she added pressure to my shoulder.

"Blue Fire dagger." I hissed through gritted teeth. "It's lethal for immortals. My fire cannot heal it."

"He'll be alright. I just have to stitch him up." She told Seymor; she looked down at me and smiled. "Although I'm afraid this one will leave a scar."

I stared at the ceiling of the chamber as the healer did her craft. What was one visible scar compared to a million unseen? My jaw clenched as I thought of Belynda and Dagasti back in Druleska.

"There. You'll just have to take it easy for a few days. This one will heal slowly. Like a mortal wound."

"A few days? Belynda might not have a few days…" I pushed away from the floor, ignoring the sharp pain tearing through my shoulder.

"I assure you, we will open that portal again. But we need to gather the necessary people to harness that power. In the meantime, you do as the doc says. We'll take care of the rest."

"You cannot expect me to sit idly by."

"You will. For her sake, you will regain your strength so you can fight. If what you said is true, then the only one who stands a chance against your uncle… is you." The old man argued.

"Come now. Let's get you home where you can rest and get cleaned up." Home… I didn't even know where that was anymore but knowing that this was hers… made it my own somehow.

THE WATER RAN red as I stood beneath the shower. It seemed like only yesterday since I was last here. I closed my eyes and could still feel her with me: her delicate body trapped between me and this wall. I flexed my hand as the darkness eased off my skin. Taking a deep breath, I commanded it to yield.

I couldn't shift. That was the doctor's order, at least not until the wound healed.

It felt strange being in Belynda's room without her, yet her scent was everywhere. I breathed in the clothes in her closet. It was a bittersweet torture.

Footsteps pounded up the stairs, so I searched for my clothes and pulled on a pair of pants. A soft knock sounded at the door.

Felsia and the doctor stared back at me.

"May we come in? Leonor wanted to wrap the wound before she left."

"There's no need to trouble yourself further. I'm perfectly alright." I declined curtly. I was not used to being pitied.

Leonor didn't listen, but breezed into the room. Felsia followed.

"Sit." She ordered.

"I assure you it's unnecessary."

"Humor me." The woman would not take no for an answer. My jaw clenched and I held my tongue, reluctantly sitting by the window.

She inspected the wound and dabbed a liquid over the stitches. It stung, but I didn't move.

"Does this hurt?" She asked while applying some sort of unguent.

"I've had worse," I said, yet even my most lethal wounds had always healed fast. This lingering discomfort was bothersome.

"I'm going to wrap it. Make sure not to get it wet. I will return the day after to check and change the bandages."

"Two days?" How long would this last?

"For now, yes. If you follow my instructions, we might be able to remove the stitches in a week's time. But even then, you must take it easy for at least another week." I fought the urge to burn everything in my path, but stayed silent...

Two weeks... two weeks...

I slipped on my shirt and stood. The two women must have sensed my darkening mood as they didn't linger for long.

I lay on Belynda's bed, brooding, and surrounded by her scent. Drowning me. Burning my soul. I had never been one to pray, but as I closed my eyes, I found myself pleading to the fates to keep her safe. She was all that mattered.

. . .

THE SLOW PASSING of time was the one thing I would never be used to in the human world. Seymor managed to contact the elementals, and their enthusiasm to help was humbling. They even asked to come with me. Given our history, I had reservations. However, I had no idea what awaited me when I returned to Druleska. A few allies would undoubtedly help even the odds.

SEVEN DAYS, six hours, and twenty-six minutes. As an immortal, I could not fathom how humans chose to live like this. A constant ticking at every turn: a slow, torturous reminder of the impending fragility of their lives. I had never felt more human in my entire existence.

"There. How does it feel?" Leonor clipped the last stitch and smiled, pleased.

"It's perfect. Can I go about my business without everyone fretting now?"

Her brow creased; that was never a good sign.

"I won't add a bandage, so you will be able to start moving that arm, but no shifting or heavy straining yet. That's an order."

IT WAS NO LONGER the slow recovery that troubled me. It was the guardianship's inability to acquire the power needed to reopen the portal.

This time, Seymor enlisted the rest of the council members, but even with the elementals, it wasn't enough to create a spark.

"We're running out of time." I growled, pacing the guardianship's chamber.

"We could still bring in Ben," Oliver said, and the council turned quiet.

"You know that's a risk. Benjamin will never agree. He only seeks revenge, not redemption." Seymor argued.

"If his power can make even the smallest difference, then you must try." I pressed, and Seymor paused to reconsider.

"I will speak with Ben." Oliver offered, and when no one argued the decision further, he marched out of the chamber with solid determination.

OLIVER

After years of friendship, it wasn't hard to guess where he would be. Confronting him in his home would violate the covenant as his mother was unaware of their family ties to the guardianship.

Patiently, I waited in my car outside the ice cream parlor. I waited for the last of the customers to leave for closing, then made my move. The bell on the door announced my entrance.

"We're closed." He called from behind the register. He didn't look up, not even when I flipped the sign to closed.

"We need to talk."

He glanced up once recognizing my voice, his face transforming from surprise to suspicion.

"What are you doing here?"

I turned and locked the door behind me.

"I'm only here to talk."

He walked around the counter.

"I have nothing to say. You're dead to me. You died the same day my father did."

"Don't you think it's time you stopped blaming me for what happened?"

"You think you can come in here and expect anything else? What do you want, Radcliff? Forgiveness?"

"I did nothing wrong, and you know it. If I am to blame, then so are you. Maybe things would have turned out differently if you hadn't gone to my father after I asked you not to. You betrayed my trust. Our friendship. All because of your lust for power, just like my father."

"I betrayed you?" He seethed, closing the distance. "You were the one who misplaced your loyalty."

"Can't you be reasonable for once? Belynda was the same girl you grew up with. She was innocent. How could you stand there and be oblivious to all your father and mine stood for? Murder."

I didn't see it coming. His fist connected with my jaw and I staggered back. There was so much hate directed in that jab. Oh, he had an itch... I was no longer in school or in a place where the covenant would be violated, so I returned his blow without reservation. He was on his feet in a second, hurling towards me like a rabid animal.

That's it. Let it out. He punched my stomach, and I threw another punch at his face.

"Is that all you've got? Do you want your revenge? I'm here. Take it." I goaded, and he came at me with everything.

Knocking me off my feet, he fell on me with fury, punching my ribs and my face without mercy. I allowed it, rolling over to spit out blood and gasp for air before delivering one last punch. Ben collapsed onto the floor next to me.

I kicked him for good measure, and he returned it, yet neither of us moved. This was exactly what we needed.

Pain seared through me as I tried to stand.

"Damn you, Ben. I think you broke my ribs." He laughed, and it was contagious. We seemed insane, but we had been friends, brothers even. We understood one other.

"I'm sorry." I offered a truce as our laughter died. The silence dragged before he shifted to his feet and offered me his hand.

"I'm sorry too." He finally apologized. I knew we could work things out.

"Are you sure you don't need a doctor?" He teased.

"You know I let you win, right?"

He snorted.

"That's what you always say, Radcliff." He moved to sit on the counter, wiping his broken lip on his apron.

"Now, can we talk?" I asked. This time, he seemed open to listen. I recited all recent events to him without revealing too many details, but the look on his face was not promising.

"I'm afraid you've wasted your time coming here. I promised myself that I would never return there."

"Surely, if we have buried our demons, can you not do the same for them? Your choice might tilt the balance. This is what you have trained for all your life."

"No. You won't change my mind. This..." He motioned between us. "Doesn't change a thing."

It was out of my hands. I couldn't force him to help. That decision had to be his.

"I see..." I stood up from the chair and winced. "I'm sorry for the mess." I offered.

"No worries." He jumped from the counter and followed me. "Have they tried using a Psypher?"

I froze. My father hadn't mentored Ben for no reason. He was smart.

"No. I don't think so..."

"They might be able to harness their power, then use the Psypher to increase it."

"I know my father tried to open the portals for years by using one, yet failed every time."

"He didn't have the spells to open the portals then; he had no idea what the magic names were. That's one of the reasons he sought out the Sacred Book. But now, you have the missing piece. A Psypher might do the trick."

I looked at Ben and offered my hand. He shook it.

"Thank you for the idea. Regardless, the offer still stands if you decide to join us..."

"Radcliff, go home."

I grinned as he closed the door behind me. He would come around. Eventually.

DRAKE

It turns out Oliver's visit to the kid was not a waste of time after all. Using the Psypher seemed the only promising option, and Seymor had mobilized all guardianship connections to find one.

The wound was healing nicely, but for the first time in my immortal life, I knew how it felt to heal as a human. I was able to bring movement back to my arm and shoulder, but not without effort. The sound of tires on the gravel in the driveway alerted me. Seymor and Tyrus. I had become relatively familiar with their scent after waiting impatiently every day for an update.

I streaked down the stairs, and the young guardian, Sylvie, jumped as I sped past.

"By the fates, you gave me a fright!"

"My apologies. I forget my manners." I said.

"No. It's alright, truly. It just takes some getting used to, that's all." She smiled and disappeared into the dining room as Seymor and Tyrus stepped inside.

"Did you find it?" I asked.

The wrinkles around Seymor's eyes creased as he smiled. They had done it...

"We did." He confirmed, but there was more. I could tell.

"But...?"

"There is a slight problem."

"Of course there is." The sharp edges of my darkening mood peaked, but I pushed it down. "How much longer do we have to wait? Every minute that passes, the risk for Belynda's safety increases. Her life is on the line."

The metal ornament on the stair's baluster bent within my tightened fist.

"We know that, and believe me, we're doing everything in our power to make it happen as quickly as possible, but some things are out of our control. You know that."

I did know it. All of this was my fault... these people should have blamed me, and instead, they had shown nothing but patience and understanding, yet here I was making demands.

"I know you've done your best; I just feel...helpless." I said, motioning to my arm.

"We know, but you're doing exactly what you must. Healing. Worry about regaining your strength... and we will make sure to open that portal."

"Dinner is ready," Celest called from down the hall. "Tyrus, you're welcome to stay." She offered.

"Perhaps some other time. I have to prepare. Get everyone ready to receive the Psypher. We only have a small window as it is."

He excused himself, waiting for Seymor to hand him a stack of papers before he was gone. I appreciated his no-nonsense attitude.

"What will it take to get that Psypher?" I asked as we sat down at the table.

"The artifact is on display at the National Museum. That's the setback."

"I'm sure we have connections there. Can't we have the piece pulled?" Belynda's mother inquired.

"We do, and that is precisely what we are doing. But we can only retrieve it when the curator closes the exhibit for maintenance. Once we are notified, we have a twenty-four-hour window to collect it from the restoration department, bring it to the chamber, and return it to the Museum's repositories."

"How long?" I wouldn't like the answer, but I needed to know.

"Two weeks... three perhaps."

I stood from the table and stormed out the front door before I said something I would regret. My frustration consumed me.

The front door opened then closed behind me, and I didn't have to turn to know who it was. Celest was hesitant, placing her hands on the porch rails beside me.

"How are you holding up?"

I didn't know how to answer. Though as I looked at her, I realized I wasn't the only one worried for Belynda.

"How do you and Felsia do it? How do you manage to keep a level head when Belynda is... when she could be..." I tightened my fists, unable to finish my train of thought, distracted by the images my mind conjured.

"Is that what it seems like to you? That we are at ease with this situation? Trust me, we are far from it."

"You hide it well."

"That's because we are used to dealing with our emotions, which is something I take doesn't come easy to you." She noted.

"That's an accurate assumption." I tried to compartmentalize the part of my brain itching to break free, fighting the rising fire.

"Would you like to talk about it?" she pressed.

"I don't know how," I admitted but found myself speaking, nonetheless. "I'm frustrated for obvious reasons. I feel helpless, but there's a part of me that's angry. Mostly at myself for allowing this to happen, but at Belynda, too, for being this... *foolish* when she could have saved herself." I eased my fingers from the wooden veranda and noticed the burned fingerprints left on the rails.

"It's ok to feel angry. I admit I was angry, too, but we can't blame ourselves for the decisions others make. How do you think Belynda felt when you sacrificed your human essence to save her? In the year you were gone, she was like a ghost in this house. Not eating, not sleeping; neither her mother nor I knew what to do."

Something twisted in my soul as I pictured her suffering.

"I don't know what I will do if something happens to her," I admitted. As I said it, a heaviness lifted from my chest.

"Nothing will happen. Belynda is strong and hardheaded, just like her mother." Celest said. I found myself smiling despite my mood.

"That she is. But her tenacity only makes me worry that she will never go out without a fight, or worst... that it might get her killed." The darkness inside me burned as I admitted my worst fears.

BELYNDA

Slowly, my eyes adjusted to the darkness. I was still in the dungeons, though I wasn't sure how long I had been unconscious. It was enough for them to bestow a pair of fire shackles on me. Whatever magic forged them was powerful enough to contain all the elements because I could no longer sense them.

Every attempt to draw on their power failed. Slowly, my body weakened as the days passed. Drake had been right. I had to eat. It wouldn't serve me to wither away in this cell.

I slithered over the cold stone floor towards the fresh tray of food and took a piece of dried meat. I bit into it and lay on my back, staring at the arched stone ceiling.

"My lady... my lady." The low hiss pulled me from my lethargic state. I turned over on the cold stone floor, disoriented.

"Tolly?"

The young girl kneeled by the bars.

"My lady, I'm sorry, I don't have much time. The guard on shift owed me a favor."

"Tolly, how long have I been here?"

"Close to ten moons, my lady."

I sat up, using the bars for support.

"Tolly, I need to get these off. Your friend, the guard, does he have a key?"

"No. I'm sorry. Master Dagasti is the only one with the key, but I brought you these." She pushed a parcel through the bars. Inside was a clean dress and a new cloak. "I figured you'd need a change of clothes. There is a blanket also." I felt the strangest sensation of Deja Vu as I noticed the blue material of the dress.

"Thank you. Won't you get in trouble for this?" I didn't want anyone else to suffer for me.

"I think the Master has more important things to worry about."

"Why do you say that? What's happened?"

"The Fire Army has gathered; they are all marching to the other Realms. No one knows for sure, but there are whispers that he controls an army of darkness."

I stared at my hands, unable to meet Tolly's eyes. It was my fault. I was the one responsible for opening the portals.

"You have to go." Called the guard at the entrance.

"I'm sorry. I wish there was more I could do." She placed her hands over mine.

"Thank you, Tolly. You've done more than enough. Thank you for the clothes. Now go."

The girl slipped out of the chamber, leaving me alone once again with only the dancing shadows from the candles for company. Droplets of water fell from the roof of the chamber, water that had slipped from the portal I had attempted to open into the Water Realm.

I pulled the dress from its wrapping, but quickly enough, I realized I wouldn't be able to change. Not with my hands bound in these shackles. I slipped the blanket around my shoulders and continued to stare at the dancing shadows against the wall.

I lay on the stone floor, facing the back wall of the cell. The guard's footsteps padded against the stones, but I didn't have the strength to turn. The metal food tray scraped against the floor. Closing my eyes, my head fell back, and I searched for oblivion.

Eat... The voice was like a gentle caress in the distance. My eyes fluttered open, then closed. *Fight...* There it was. Persistent. It beckoned like the voice at the fountain, a whisper in the wind...

My eyes adjusted as I rolled to face the chamber. No one was there. Only me and the puddles of water glimmering on the floor.

I coughed as warm liquid from the broth trailed down my parched throat. Perhaps the voice was simply my subconscious reminding me I wasn't a coward. I would fight. I had dreamed of my death, and my time wasn't up yet. I had more life to live. I stared at the shackles, ramming them against the floor. This wasn't permanent.

I studied the guard's shifts to keep myself from going insane. One guard brought the food and relieved the one standing post; another came much later to change the chamber bucket, but he didn't switch shifts. The following food tray arrived, and posts were traded once more. Guiding myself by their shifts, I created a way to keep track of the days. I couldn't be entirely sure, but it was better than living in a constant stupor.

Perhaps Dagasti hadn't returned yet because he knew he couldn't control me. Once I was out of these shackles, I could open a portal and vanish, yet something told me he had other plans.

I COUNTED. The bars of my cell, the stones on the roof... anything to pass the time. If my calculations were correct, two more days had passed, and everything remained the same. It was hard to stay sane in a place like this, and I wasn't sure I could last much longer.

There were voices out in the corridor, but I could barely make out their exchange. My heart skipped a beat. There was a familiar twinge to that voice. The footsteps loudened, and I stood, gripping the rails.

"You... What are you doing here?"

It was the last person I expected to see, blue eyes regarding me with a taunting smile.

"I thought you might want some company. It can get quite lonely down here."

I glared at him through the bars as he strolled over the puddles of water then leaned against the cell.

"I'll take my chances."

"You must have been very naughty to end up in this place." He taunted.

"Playing ignorant doesn't suit you. You know damn well why I'm here, and if you've come to gloat, you can leave."

He pushed from the rails and strolled to where I stood, barely a foot away.

"I wish I could," he said under his breath.

"You wish you could what?" I squeezed my hands against the rails, staring into his dark ocean eyes.

"Leave. I wish I could leave." He broke eye contact and whirled, pacing the chamber.

"What's stopping you? Dagasti?" Though that was unlikely. Dagasti had made it clear his presence wasn't welcome the last time when he saved me in the portrait halls. He paused and glanced at me, neither confirming nor denying my assumption.

"Circumstances," he said before resuming his deliberate pacing.

"What are you doing here? What do you want with me?"

His eyes locked with mine, then, and his forehead creased. He smiled.

"I promised myself I wouldn't interfere. Not again. Yet here I am." He rubbed his chin as he circled back in my direction.

Drake disliked this man, but what if he could help me? I tried to rationalize it, but this seemed too easy. How could he stroll in here so freely? He was clearly working with Dagasti, but the way he spoke of Drake's uncle gave me the impression he didn't care for him either. The bottom line? I didn't know if I could trust him.

"So, you will help me?" I asked as his steps slowed.

"I never said that..." His eyes shifted towards the hall. "I must leave."

"Wait... I don't even know your name..."

The blue eye god glanced back towards me and smiled without saying another word. He disappeared, and a few minutes later, I heard a guard resume his post.

I didn't know what to make of this man. He treated me like a pariah, and had saved me on more than one occasion. Now he's back, but is he a friend or foe?

• • •

ANOTHER THREE DAYS PASSED, going by my calculation of the guard shifts and the two daily meals I was served. My clothes were filthy; I was in dire need of a bath, or at the very least, a wash.

"Hello?" I called, hoping the guard could hear me. "Hello... is somebody there?" There was no response. "What must a girl do to get a bucket of water around here?" I yelled and kicked the bars, seeing as there was no one around to even care. I took a sip from the bitter liquid in the chalice.

A guard strolled in, startling me. He wasn't a part of the schedule I had mapped.

"This was just brought down for you." The scrawny man fumbled with the cell's lock, opening it enough to place the bucket he carried.

I stared at the water... someone had heard me...

"Who sent this? Did you hear me ask for water?"

The man locked the cell without bothering to respond. Something told me this wasn't a kindness he had bestowed upon me, but if not him, who? And how did they know? Had they heard me? Whatever the reason, I was grateful.

I smiled as the guard left the chamber.

"Thank you," I said to no one in particular. To my guardian angel, the fates, or whoever had made it possible.

I couldn't remove the dress with my handcuffs on, so I tore off the sleeves, ripping down the dress's bodice until it fell to the floor in pieces. I took off my boots and rubbed my feet. They ached after so long dormant.

The water was surprisingly warm. I used one of the shredded sleeves to wash as best as I could. Then I looked through the parcel Tolly had brought and put on the undergarments; it was one of the new pieces she had made for me. I eyed the soiled and torn dress on the floor, then the new one Tolly had brought. I had an idea.

I couldn't slip it on with the sleeves, but if I could remove them altogether, all that would remain was the corset and skirts with their front ties. I smiled, grateful for Tolly's choice of gown. Once the sleeves came off, I stepped into the skirt and bodice, pulled it up, and tightened the corset at the front. A part of me felt human again. I was still a fright to look at, but at least I felt I could live within my skin.

As the heaviness reached my eyes, I felt relaxed for the first time in days, even somewhat content, despite my situation.

I DREAMED OF DRAKE, his warm touch, and those light silver eyes. They urged me on, smiling, and I followed him through the line of trees at the lake's edge. *Beautiful...* the voice in the wind called, and I turned towards the night sky, watching Drake soaring below the night clouds. The shimmering lake beckoned, calling me as I strode to the water's edge. Cold water brushed against my toes. The moon was right above, and as I peered at the crystal waters, my reflection glimmered back. My skin looked pale, almost glowing. *Beautiful...* the voice traveled through the wind. Then, the ground shook as the Dragon landed behind me. I spun to see Drake striding towards me, outstretching a hand, but when I glanced at his eyes, they were no longer silver... No. They were the deepest color of blue, and it was no longer Drake who stood there.

I WOKE UP WITH A START.

"Not sleeping well?"

I glanced around the cell, unsure if I was still dreaming. I wasn't. His voice was not a figment of my imagination. I rubbed my eyes and stared at the intruder of my dreams, here in flesh and bones.

"Why do you ask?"

Was it a coincidence that I had dreamt of him? I was no longer naïve when it came to understanding these immortal men. Anything was possible.

"You look tired. That's all." He offered. I stared at him with wariness, but he seemed nonchalant.

"I slept great, actually."

I studied his expression, but it gave no indication that he had any involvement in my dream.

"I'm glad you're making the best effort, despite your accommodations," he said sincerely.

"Are you ever going to tell me your name?" I asked. He smiled.

"I prefer the enigma. Don't you?"

"No. I prefer the truth." I stood up, but he wasn't fazed by my outburst. On the contrary, he seemed to find it amusing. I decided to name him myself. "You look like a Teddy to me. That's what I'll call you... Teddy." I teased knowing he looked anything but. If I was being honest he looked like he could take the name of a God. Hades, or Ares sprung to mind, but I wouldn't give him that satisfaction.

His laughter bounced across the stone walls. It was a melodious sound, and I found myself grinning.

"My you have an interesting imagination. Really. I would rather you didn't."

"Then will you tell me your name?" I pressed.

"You can call me anything you'd like, but not that. It sounds... debasing somehow."

I smiled.

"Ok. How about Bubba?"

He turned the other way, then, yet I didn't miss how his fingers covered his mouth to conceal his laughter.

"How about we skip this name game?" he offered as his eyes scanned my new dress. "You changed." His eyes rested on the corset, lingering over the swell of my breasts. His smile was shameless as my eyes met his.

"Don't use my clothes as a distraction to change the subject."

He grinned, and I knew I had been right in my assumption.

"Who are you?" I asked in earnest. "You don't look like you're from around here," I added, desperate for some answers.

"May I ask what brought you to that conclusion?"

"Have you looked at yourself?"

He glanced down at his crisp white shirt and perfectly pressed slacks.

"You have me all figured out then..." He strolled towards me and I took a step back. He froze, some dark emotion flickering across his face before vanishing altogether. "I must go."

He strolled out of the chamber, leaving me in utter confusion.

Something told me he could help me leave this place, and my instincts were rarely wrong.

The next day, I waited for my nameless friend to appear, but he didn't. Not the next day either.

As I stared at the stones in the ceiling, I thought about Drake and my family back home. I missed them desperately. Tugging the cloak tighter around my shoulders, I wiped the tears that streaked down my face.

After a couple more days, time started to blur. The schedule I had developed and followed no longer seemed to matter. The guards came and went, but there was no sign of the blue-eyed God or Drake. Even Tolly seemed to have forgotten me in this dark, hellish place.

For the first time when I closed my eyes that night, I asked the fates to end this. I pleaded for mercy.

I STARED *at the molting rocks and the rivers of red lava flowing down the slope, melting everything in its path. The wind sizzled behind me as an orb of blue and white streaks formed. Drake emerged through the portal; he looked so real; I ached to run to him, but this dream felt different.*

He wasn't alone. Shortly after followed Amirth, Rashe, and at last, Alexia.

Drake looked straight at me with surprise, and for a moment, I wondered if he saw me. He moved towards me, but his stride didn't slow. He walked right through me as if I were a ghost, tingles erupting in my body. This was no dream... it was a vision. I spun and found Drake with his mother.

"How did you know where I'd be?"

She pulled him into her arms.

"I got Belynda's message. She said I would find you here."

My surroundings blurred as an intense ringing blocked my ears, and then my sight was lost.

13

WHISPERS AND DREAMS

I ROLLED ON THE COLD FLOOR AND heaved the contents of my last meal. The visions always took their toll on me. I refused to let myself die here. Drake was coming for me, and the vision was clear... I would be the one sending the message to Kylram, yet how was the question...

The cell walls were closing in, squeezing, and suffocating me as I paved a path across the stone floor.

The guard from the second shift walked in with the food tray. I couldn't trust him to deliver the message, but perhaps he could get the one person that might.

"I would like to speak with the castle guest who has been visiting me." The guard pushed the tray through the partition at the bottom of the cell, staring at me like I was insane. "You know who he is... the man with sapphire blue eyes." I pressed. The guard's confusion visibly grew on his face.

"You're a mad woman." He sneered. "No one's been down here. No one's allowed but us. Those are strict orders from the Lord King."

Was he serious?

"But you've seen him. You have."

The guard backed away from the cell slowly.

"Human blood witch... Stay away."

Stunned, I stared after the guard as he fled from the chamber. Though I was the one locked behind bars, not him. It wasn't like I could use my magic against him.

Had I imagined the sapphire eyed guest, a figment of the mind to quell my boredom? I had heard stories back in the human world of men who had begun to hallucinate after being confined for too long.

I thought back to the last time he visited, and the strangeness of his timing with my dream. Oh god... A heaviness settled in my chest. I was losing my mind.

"Let me out!" I shouted, slamming the shackles against the metal bars. "Please, let me out of here." I took the empty bucket and tossed it against the wall, watching as it splintered. The food tray went next, clashing against the metal rails.

"Bastards... Get me out of here!" Tears choked me. It was no use.

I cradled my head on my knees, allowing my cries to ease the desperation. I would never leave this place. I was no longer sure of what was real. Perhaps I imagined it all: the sapphire eyed god, the dreams... The fates were indeed dark and twisted. My visions of death at the hands of that Dragon seemed like a mercy now, compared to dying here alone.

As the tears stopped, a wave of calm and contentment washed over me as I accepted my fate, and was once again swept into oblivion.

. . .

THE PAST CAME TO VISIT. I was a little girl again, and my mother took me to the ocean for the first time. It was beautiful... the waves chased after me, then I chased the receding water back to the ocean. A dance of sorts. There was only laughter and the serene sound of the ocean. It was peaceful... *Calling... Whispering.*

"YOU CAN'T GIVE UP. Listen to me."

My eyes fluttered, but I refused the apparition before me.

"Not real..." I muttered, forcing it away.

"I'm right here. Get up." When my eyes opened, there was the sapphire eyed God. I refused to give in to my delirium.

"Go away. You're not here. Not real..."

I closed my eyes and covered my ears, trying to block the illusion from my senses. A surge of freezing water sprayed my body, like a million pinches forcing me to my feet in shock.

An empty bucket of water was in his hands, and his grin was unapologetic. I wiped the water from my face, staring into his dark ocean eyes.

"Are you really here?" I whispered. The deep blue of his eyes danced like the waves in my dream. There was something about him... something deep and hidden, but whatever it was, I felt it under my skin... pulling, calling just beneath the surface.

"I am here. I am real." He paced slowly... closer.

"The guard didn't believe me. He hasn't seen you. How is that possible? How do I know you're real and that I'm not losing my mind?"

He smiled, leaning against the bars.

"Are you losing your mind?" he asked, amused.

"I'm serious."

"So am I." he said, though he was anything but.

"You're really here?" I asked, lowering my voice as I reached for his hand resting on one of the bars. I allowed my fingers to brush over his. He nodded and glanced at our hands. Waves danced behind his eyes before his smile vanished, and with it, so did his hand.

"You look a mess." He said, taking a step back. I stared at my soaked clothes and frowned.

"You almost drowned me. Was that necessary?"

His sapphire eyes scanned my body, and the corner of his lips pulled up into a smile.

"It worked, didn't it?"

I glared at him but bit my tongue; he was my only chance of getting that message to Drake's mother. If he wasn't a figment of my imagination, I doubted my dream was. Even then, I couldn't take my chances. I wasn't going to allow these four walls to brand me as a lunatic.

"How do I know I can trust you?" I stared into his eyes for good measure.

"You don't. But I've told you, there are worse evils than me." I knew he was many things, but something told me he was honest. He always had been. From the moment we met, he never claimed to be good or righteous, never declared he was on my side or that I could be safe with him. Though he always seemed to speak the truth, and right now... that was enough for me.

It was risky. If he betrayed me, it could cost Drake, his mother, and the elementals their lives, but something inside begged me to trust him. Even if his intentions weren't clear, he had saved my life more than once. His strange visits had kept me sane in a place like this. Yes, there were risks, but I chose to trust him. I had to.

"Would you deliver a message for me?"

The words escaped my lips in a whisper.

"If it's in my power to do so... I will." He looked into my eyes, and I felt relief flow through me.

"Once you reach the outskirts of the village, around the red dragon inn, you will find a small stone house with a chimney and a blue-painted door. The woman that lives there has midnight hair and silver eyes. Let her know that the message is from me. Tell her she must meet her son where the rocks melt into fire." His brow creased with confusion at the odd request.

"Ok." he replied.

"Ok? No questions? No remarks? Are you sure you can do this?"

"The edge of town, the red Dragon, deliver the message. Relax. I can do this."

I gripped the cell bars, realizing I had no choice but to trust him.

"Thank you for doing this," I said and prayed to the gods that he was honorable and kept his word. I hoped I didn't end up regretting this.

"I'll be on my way then," he said, but after a few paces, he turned. "Oh, and whatever you do... don't eat the pudding."

I eyed the new tray of food on the floor.

"Is it poisoned?" I asked, and he laughed.

"Not that I know of, but it's the most awful thing I have ever tasted. Bad enough to decline an offer to dinner. It was one of the reasons why I excused myself from the dining hall the day we met." I recalled his hasty departure that day, though I had thought it was because of my arrival.

I found myself amused by his confession. Something told me he wanted to set the record straight; perhaps he didn't want me to think he disliked me.

"Can I ask you something?"

"I'm already doing you a favor... now you want to ask questions too?" he said, yet his manner was playful. I ignored his remark and asked anyways.

"What are you doing here? Why are you helping him when you know he's bad?"

"I never said I was helping him." He rebuked with finality. Then he turned and vanished from the chamber.

His words, however vague, left me with hope. Deep in my bones, I knew he would deliver that message. He was perhaps the one person left in this place who could help me. Even though I knew nothing of him or his reasons for being here, I was grateful that the fates had placed him in my path.

DRAKE

"Again," Amirth called while motioning Tyrus to advance.

The man was surprisingly strong for a mortal. A few days ago, I had experienced his brutal force firsthand after the healer gave me the ok to train; she stressed I needed to rehabilitate the muscles in my arm. I still couldn't shift, but at least I could punch things: a way to release some of the built-up tension and desperation in my body.

Five more days... I repeated this every day like a chant. Five more days until we have that Psypher. Five more days until we open that portal. Five more days until I go back for her... and Dagasti. Then his days will end.

Tyrus lunged, but the girl blocked his punch, diving and twisting in time to deliver a kick to the man's side. There had to be some inhuman abilities in that man. He didn't break. He lurched for her again, but this time she forgot her footing, and was swept off her feet with a low kick before she landed against the ground.

"Damn it!" she bellowed. Tyrus offered his hand.

"That was good. You're getting better." He praised, and his admission wasn't wrong. The girl was tough; I had to give her that. She could certainly stand her ground against Dagasti's men, even without using her powers. Alexia and Rashe could hold their ground, too, but Amirth was a force to be reckoned with. She was a warrior, a gift not very common of the elven people from which her earth powers came. The people of Abryas relied mainly on their powers, not their brutal force.

"Haven't you guys thrown enough punches for one day?" Called Felsia from the back porch.

"No. We saved the best for last," said Oliver, glancing in my direction. I glared at him as Amirth took a seat on the porch steps beside Alexia and Rashe.

"Are you sure you want to do this again, old man?" I teased Tyrus; with only one hand, I could defeat him, and that's with my other abilities contained. Nothing but raw, brutal force...

Tyrus grinned, the challenge etched on his face. I didn't wait for his approach. I took the first strike. But he was smart and was buying his time. I landed a second punch and then a third, but before I could block, he took his chance.

He was a military man. I should have known he would exploit my weaknesses.

"Fuck!" I roared as he jabbed my bruised shoulder.

"First lesson, kid." He mocked. I grinned; age had nothing to do with it, for I was much older. Positioning himself, Tyrus prepared for his next assault. "Never enter a fight with overconfidence. Second, always protect your weak spots." I smirked; that was a lesson well delivered. The only one he would get to teach me.

• • •

THE EVENINGS WERE THE HARDEST, thoughts of her constantly invading my mind. When everyone returned home and the house calmed, I felt the emptiness of her absence like a growing dark void in the pit of my stomach.

I jumped from the bedroom window to sit on the front porch steps, staring up at the thousands of stars: a beauty many from Druleska never got to witness. The stars were something I had read about as a boy, experienced only briefly on my journeys to the other realms, during the peaceful times in which all realms co-existed and allowed passage. The very skies I glanced at first with Isabel, then Belynda...

I never expected it to be possible to love two people this much. Past and present, uniting in one soul. My time with Isabel was long ago, yet the memories were fresh. Vivid. Perhaps it was her essence still living inside Belynda which kept her alive.

Footsteps thumped inside the house. Concentrating, I instantly recognized the pattern of Felsia's breathing. I debated jumping back through the window before she saw me but decided against it. There were things I wanted to say but hadn't. In five days, I would hopefully be gone; if I didn't say what I wanted to now, I never would.

The front door opened, and Belynda's mother stepped out into the cold night, and closed the door behind her.

"Felsia." I said without turning.

"I forget no one moves or breathes without you knowing about it." She stepped onto the veranda. "I've wondered how that feels, to hear every whisper, every sound, in your head at all times."

I smiled to myself.

"It's natural to me. It's like you can hear certain things around you, but my range of sensitivity is wider. We learn from a young age to tune it out unless we are listening for something in particular."

"Fascinating. It must be impossible for anyone to sneak up on you."

"I've had my share of surprises," I admitted, recalling the moment Belynda had walked in on me in the shower, at a time where the Dragon threatened to take over. So consumed by darkness, I had not heard her steps or noticed her breathing, or even her scent. "Especially when I'm trying to concentrate like I have been recently to contain my fire. Or if someone is skilled enough to not make a sound."

Though I've known only one other capable of that... *Callix*. One of the many reasons I grew to dislike the guy. I frowned at the thought of him.

"Do you mind if I join you?" she asked from the veranda. I glanced at her, moving to offer her space on the step next to me. Pulling the shawl closer around her shoulders, she stepped under the blanket of night. "It's beautiful out here. I get why you like it so much."

"Yes. I'm certain this is one of the many things your daughter misses. There are no clear skies or stars in my realm: only rain, thunder, and darkness." I glanced at her, noting her furrowed brow as she stared at the blanket of stars.

"I don't know if I will ever get to see her again, but if you do... tell her I love her."

"You can tell her yourself."

"You and I both know that might not be true. What if you go back to find that... that she's-"

"NO!" I cut her off before she dared to say it. "I will bring her back."

"What if you can't?"

"I will sacrifice the entire kingdom if I must. I will get her back."

The crease on her brow persisted; she still doubted me, but I couldn't allow her to. Even acknowledging that thought meant it was possible. No. That wasn't an option.

"There is a way to know if she's alright." she murmured, and my heartbeat spiked for the first time in weeks.

"How? If there is a way to see her, tell me."

"It doesn't always work, but it did once for me. It might show us what we want to see."

"What are we waiting for?"

"It's nighttime, and we must speak with Seymor first. The Scrying Orb was taken from Stephen's home and delivered to the reliquary. While I doubt accessing it will be a problem, we need to wait until tomorrow at least."

I stared at the open field of grass across the road.

"Why didn't you say anything sooner?" I asked. I didn't dare look at her, for the darkness scratched beneath the surface of my skin.

"Would it have made a difference?"

"Yes! It would have given us hope to know she was... ok."

Felsia shook her head.

"What if she wasn't? What if you saw something you weren't ready to deal with, something you could do nothing about? This has been hard on all of us, but especially you. Knowing would have only driven us to despair, and we all need a clear head, and like you said, *hope*. I didn't dare consider it before; I was afraid to lose hope, just like you."

There was wisdom in her words, but it was a harsh truth to accept.

"Tomorrow then..." I said, jaw clenched. I tried to find comfort in the promise of it.

"Yes. We will try. Now go get some rest." She stood, taking the steps back up to the porch.

"Goodnight."

I knew the doctor's orders, but I was done listening. That portal would be opening in five days, and I had to shift if I ever expected a chance to defeat Dagasti. I listened for Felsia, and once she was back in her room, I streaked down the back of the manor toward the woods.

The monster knew. It rumbled, knowing that soon it would be free. Once I was concealed by the shadow of the trees, I discarded my clothes into a heap. Naked, I continued a few meters into the deeper part of the forest where only darkness roamed.

The currents of fire spread over my skin as darkness slipped from my pores. My shoulder throbbed, but my jaw clenched as I pushed through the discomfort.

The beast roared as the shift took hold, but we were both determined to ignore the pain. Wings fluttered behind me, and though it was an effort, we were stronger. I rocketed off the ground, the shooting ache intensifying with every stroke of my wings. Still, we refused to descend. I needed this as badly as the darkness did; it had waited so patiently to be released. The blanket of stars were even more magnificent up close as I soared higher to the mountains, disappearing under the moonless night.

The pain never eased; on the contrary, as I circled back to the woods and shifted, I could no longer move my arm. From the looks of it, my shoulder was dislodged from its socket. I pulled on my pants, roaring with pain. I could do this... Holding onto my forearm, I shoved my shoulder against a tree without thinking.

Cracking and my cry of agony ripped through the sleeping woods. *Bad, bad, bad...* I had never felt so human in my entire existence. How could they live like this? Lying on the forest floor, swallowed by darkness, I dared not move. My shoulder had popped back into place, yet the throbbing didn't subside. Placing my hand above it, I willed heat to flow over the wound. This had once eased Belynda's pain, but in my case, the heat only amplified it. Making my way slowly back to the manor, I braced my arm as I jumped on the porch roof, slipping through the open window into Belynda's room.

I applied the salve the doctor had left me, but it wasn't working fast enough. I wanted this ache gone. Numbed.

Ice, I thought.

I streaked downstairs, trying not to wake the sleeping house. Grabbing a few cubes of ice, I folded them into a kitchen cloth, and pressed it on my shoulder. *Fuck...* The fire beneath my skin clawed as ice suppressed the burning, the Dragon reminded of being buried beneath it. Heading back upstairs, I shook away the memory. This time, the ice was not my punishment but my salvation.

I closed my eyes as the ache began to subside. In a couple of hours, I might see her and know if she's ok. Sleep wasn't always necessary for me, but today, I needed it. I couldn't shift again anytime soon; rest would help hone my fire, and hopefully, speed up the healing process.

"I THINK Drake and I should do it alone," Felsia said. Seymor and Celest were at the breakfast table when I walked into the kitchen.

"I won't oppose the idea if you think it is wise," said the old man, picking up his steaming cup of coffee.

"We should have used it the moment I arrived." I cut in.

"I agree. If we had the chance to know how she was, why

didn't we take it?" Celest questioned; I was glad at least someone agreed with me.

"It's not that simple." Seymor interrupted. "Firstly, the Scrying Orb was made to show us the future and the past. There's no guarantee it will work the same way a two-way mirror does."

"I'm almost certain it will." Felsia chimed in.

"Ok, let's say it does work… knowing will only serve to torment us. If she's ok, we'll feel helpless; if she's hurt… we will feel worse. Nothing changes. Knowing makes no difference to her situation, not if we are unable to open that portal." For the first time, I saw his composure waver. "Believe me, I want to know that she's alright, but I also fear knowing. I don't know that I could deal with any other truth." He finally confessed, and for the first time, I realized how much Belynda mattered to him.

"I would be willing to embrace the darkest truth," I admitted, "even if all it does is prepare me to face him. Dagasti will pay. At the very least, knowing could help even our chances against him."

The old man seemed to consider my reasoning.

"If you think you might gain some advantage, then by all means. I won't deny you access to the Orb. I only want you to know the risks."

"It's a risk worth taking."

"Very well… I will call the reliquary and have your names added to the access list."

"Thank you," I said. He seemed to concede with a firm nod.

"Sit. Have some breakfast. I'll go change, and we can head out right after." Felsia declared. She left the kitchen while Seymor excused himself, disappearing down the corridor and into the office.

Celest and I sat for breakfast on our own, though it no longer felt uncomfortable like it had done once.

"For what it's worth... I agree with you," she said, taking a sip from her mug. "I would rather know."

"You can come with us if you'd like." I offered. She smiled.

"I think I'll only be a nuisance. Felsia knows what she's doing. Besides, she was adamant this was something the two of you should do on your own."

"You have as much right to be there as she does," I said. I didn't miss the glassy sheen in her eyes or the pause she took to swallow.

"We've come a long way, haven't we?" she noted.

She was right. At one time in my life, I thought I would never trust this woman. Though now I saw her for who she was: a mother to Belynda. For the first time, I felt... sympathy.

"Yes," I conceded. "I believe we have."

"Are you certain this will work?" I asked. I followed Felsia into the secured building, though it looked more like a cathedral.

"It has to."

"That's not very reassuring."

"It will work. It did for me once, so I see no reason for it not to work again."

"What did you see before?" I asked; her pace slowed before reaching the checkpoint. She turned to me.

The woman's eyes, now aged by magic, regarded me for a moment.

"I saw what it would take and what I would have to sacrifice..." She didn't have to finish the words for me to know the sacrifice she spoke of. What surprised me was knowing the risk she had willingly accepted to return my human essence.

"Thank you." I said the words I had been meaning to say, but had been unable to. It felt liberating, somehow. This woman owed me nothing, and yet she had been willing to sacrifice her life for mine. She smiled and turned back towards the desk.

"Hershton." She said; she produced two ID badges to the man behind the computer.

"Here you go. I assume you know your way to the lower archives?"

She smiled and took the cards.

"Yes. Thank you. We can manage from here."

I followed her down the ornate corridors.

"What did Seymor mean about the Orb not being like two mirrors?" I asked, recalling his warning.

"Two-way mirrors show you a reflection of the present time, while letting you glance like a portal into any place, but only in the present. Whereas the Orb can show us the future or the past."

"We will be at the mercy of the Orb then."

"It will work."

I admired her tenacity; it gave me hope.

The elevator descended a few floors underground, opening into a vast hall. Felsia knew precisely where she was headed, disregarding all directions as she weaved through the corridors left and right. She paused outside a set of large metal doors, guarded by a sensor pad. She tapped against it.

The camera above the door blinked red, the doors opening into a barely lit chamber.

"Come."

She stepped inside, and I followed. The room came to life as we crossed the threshold. The metal doors locked behind us and the sound of the bolts latching stirred the fire within me. The idea of confinement threatened the beast, and Felsia must have noticed my sudden stiff posture.

"It's alright. It closes only for the preservation of the artifacts. They must maintain a certain temperature, but we can leave anytime we like." I clenched my jaw, shoving my fire into submission.

"Just lead the way."

She took the first path on the left.

"Exhibit six-thousand and forty-nine is in bay Z. That's where they keep special magical artifacts, meaning we only have a small interval of time to interact with the Orb."

"I don't understand. Isn't this under the guardians' ownership? Why would your access be limited?"

"You saw what Stephen became. Many of these artifacts were recovered from a secret archive that he kept at his property. It was actually Seymor's idea to establish rules, and I agree with him. If we don't have order, we leave room for someone else to follow in Stephen's footsteps."

"What if we don't have enough time?"

"We will. Once the chamber decompresses, we're allowed thirty minutes inside. Mainly, it's for the artifact's preservation. We should have enough time, but we can always return if there's not."

We turned into a corridor lined by glass doors.

"Here it is." Entering a number in the keypad, the glass door opened. As soon as the doors bolted behind us, we were shrouded by a cloud of mist. My senses flared at the pungent smell of chemicals.

"Decontaminants." Felsia offered in explanation. As the fog dissipated, another door opened, closing quickly behind us.

"Come. We need to hurry and find the Orb. We don't have much time."

It took her a minute to locate it. The white marble ball rested on a pedestal, shining beneath a bright light.

"Look at my watch. If I'm still connected with five minutes to spare, pull me out. It will give us enough time to exit the room before we're locked in here."

"What if I try?"

"No. It's better if we don't waste time. The Orb has worked for me, but we don't know if it will work for you."

"Fine. Just do it." I said, exasperated.

"Remember, five minutes to spare." She reminded me.

"Yes. We're wasting time."

She brought her hands around the white marble Orb, and as soon as her fingers pressed against the surface, her eyes turned frosty white.

For the next fifteen minutes, I watched her. She didn't move. Or react. I glanced at the watch on her wrist as the small metal hands ticked on.

"Come on, Felsia... Give me something." I whispered, but she remained frozen. In five minutes, I would have to pull her out.

As the last minute drew closer, I counted down the seconds with trepidation. I placed a hand on her shoulder and shook her.

"Enough."

Instantly, her eyes shifted back to blue, and met my stare.

"I need more time." Her eyes glazed over again, while the hands on the clock ticked ahead.

"We must leave." I shook her, and then again. Her eyes focused on me momentarily.

"Drake, more time, please." As Felsia's eyes clouded again, I knew something wasn't right. If I had to, I would allow her every last second. As the small metal hands of the clock circled for the final minute, I counted down. Thirty seconds before the doors locked us in here. *Twenty. Fifteen. Ten.*

I'm so sorry. Without thinking, I grabbed Felsia and tossed her over my shoulder, streaking through the doors as they shut behind us. I placed her on her feet, and she stared at me with confusion as a cloudy decontaminant mist fogged the room. The exterior door of the vault opened a minute later; she wavered on her feet, so I took her arm to guide her outside.

Felsia leaned against the wall as the vault doors sealed behind us and the red light of the camera switched off.

"What happened?" I asked. She shook her head as if trying to disassociate from whatever horror she had witnessed. "What did you see? Tell me!"

This time, her eyes focused.

"Not her... I couldn't see her."

"You saw something, I know you did. Tell me."

"The future. The war. The darkness... but not her." Her eyes were wild; whatever she had seen was much worse than anything we could have imagined. Stopping Dagasti would not be easy. "But you will make it back."

"You saw me?" I took her arm, and she stared at me. "You saw me but didn't see her..." Her eyes told me the words she dared not speak: the truth we both knew but refused to accept.

"Drake, it doesn't mean anything."

"You know it does..." I whirled and punched the wall. "Tell me, Felsia. *Tell me* what you saw."

"There's something you should know."

Slowly, I turned to face her, and for the first time in a long while, fear gripped my darkened soul. "I didn't see Belynda, but I know you will see her again."

Her confession eased the heaviness in my chest.

"How?"

"You asked me before what I had seen the last time I used the Orb." She moved from the walls, staring down at her hands. "It wasn't just my sacrifice I saw." Her eyes found me then, tears brimming her eyes. "She knew she wouldn't be coming home. Belynda saw it too. She had a vision."

"What do you mean she knew she wasn't coming back?" I yelled. "What did you see? Tell me!" It felt as though the walls were caving in around me, suffocating the flames in my chest.

"Her death." Bracing my hands against the wall, I pressed my face against it and closed my eyes. Every single noise in the building hit me at once.

"She knew…" I repeated through gritted teeth. Ripples of black sand danced over my skin, and I punched the wall again, forcing the beast to yield. All I wanted was to burn.

But it all made sense… her insistence, forcing me to promise. I was such a fool… blind not to realize her desperation. I should have known. She had bargained with me for a promise… a promise she knew would cost her life.

"That's why she chose to send me back. She knew…" I said through gritted teeth. "I should have seen the signs… the bracelet that stopped me reading her thoughts, her rush to experience things, her demand for a promise…"

I fell to my knees, unashamed of my weakness. Everything inside me had frozen. For a moment, I was back under that frozen lake. Unable to breathe. Dead, yet alive somehow.

"I made a promise…" I whispered, though I would burn for taking that vow. "She made me promise I would never sacrifice myself to save her." I admitted. I felt Felsia's hand on my shoulder as she kneeled before me.

"And she would never forgive you if you broke that promise. You know that."

"I know, but I would never forgive myself if I kept it. How can I live with that?" I looked at her, desperate for answers though neither of us had them.

"All I know is," Felsia said, "I was destined to die that night you came back, but somehow, she was able to change that…"

I stared into the woman's eyes, finding a sliver of clarity.

"Are you saying there is a chance?"

I stood, helping her to her feet.

"I'm saying that Belynda keeps surprising us all. If she was able to change my fate, what's to say she cannot change hers? Remember Isabel's prophecy. Only in death will she ever know her true powers…"

Now more than ever, I chose to believe in Felsia's words. I needed to accept them as truth; it was the only way for me to survive this.

"So, if your visions are correct, I will be with her. Somehow."

"Yes." She confirmed. I felt the heaviness of the truth settle into the pits of my soul. I would have to be content with that. For now.

"Then tell me about the war. Do we have a chance to defeat Dagasti?"

"Not here."

She pushed away from the wall, and I followed her through the labyrinth of corridors.

THE SCRYING ORB foretold the dark army's wrath of devastation throughout the realms. Felsia saw the kingdoms unite against Dagasti's forces. Yet still, no matter how hard she tried, the Orb showed no resolution in our favor. It offered nothing that would make us hope for victory or, at the very least, help to defeat him.

Felsia had made it clear that Celest and Seymor were to remain in the dark about Belynda's future. At first, I argued in Celest's defense, but eventually decided Felsia was right. It would only bring anguish to Celest; as Seymor had said, nothing would change by knowing.

Cold water trickled down my body, easing the pain I had managed to conceal until now. Black lines broke across my skin, and I allowed myself the slightest reprieve; it wouldn't be prudent to change again. The doctor had been right. Now more than ever, I regretted yesterday's impulsive decision to surrender to my fire. It would take all my immortal strength to keep Belynda alive, and even that might not be enough. With Dagasti's army, I could no longer afford to be weakened by this mortal wound.

I resented the time I wasted keeping up pretenses in Druleska. If I had known how short our time was, I could have been with Belynda, I would have spent every second with her. If only she would have confided in me... But who was I kidding? In her place, I wouldn't have wanted her to suffer from the truth. That secret would have gone with me to my grave, just like she had planned.

As the cold water eased the fire burning beneath my skin, my resolve sunk into the depths of my soul. I would keep my promise. Against my better judgment, I would keep it. Even if it broke me apart... I would honor the vow I made while praying the fates had other plans. But first, I must hold her in my arms again and tell her I know the truth. I must have her look me in the eyes while she tells me how foolish she has been to keep this to herself. I will worship her body and soul and make every last minute count. If her destiny means leaving me, then I will uphold her decision and know that, soon after, I will follow, but not before taking as much of Dagasti's army with me as I can. If the fates allow... my uncle, too.

. . .

WHILE RESTING on her bed that night, I chose not to view her scent as a torturous reminder that she wasn't here but rather as a memento of her essence, and of our short time together. I breathed, allowing it to saturate my being.

"Come in," I called before Felsia had the chance to knock.

"I brought you supper."

I streaked from the bed and took the tray from her hands.

"Thank you. You didn't have to. I could have gone downstairs."

"I know but I'm sure you prefer to be alone." She wasn't wrong.

I placed the tray on the small desk by the dresser, then noticed the ice pack under the folded napkin. I faced Felsia who studied me.

"That's for your shoulder. If you keep it iced over the next few days, it will help."

"I'm fine, really."

"Unless you prefer I call the doctor?" she pressed. I glared in return.

"I will use the damn ice."

She smiled.

"Let me take a look at it." She said, leaving no room for argument. It would be no use. She was stubborn like her daughter.

I sat by the window as she inspected my wound.

"It's swollen. I take it you violated the no-shifting instructions?"

"We're only a few days away from opening the portal. I needed to know that I could shift."

"You should be fine, but don't attempt it again. Try to delay it for as long as possible. I know this must be torture for someone like you. You're not used to knowing pain or treating wounds... or scarring."

"I have felt pain," I corrected, "and not all scars are visible."

"I'm sorry. I didn't mean it like that. I meant that you have the ability to heal quickly. I understand this must be frustrating for you, at the very least."

"You have no idea."

I watched as Felsia applied some salve to the wound. "Why did you do it?" I asked. She turned to me with a look of confusion, so I clarified. "Sacrifice yourself to help me... If you knew what it would cost you, why did you do it?"

Placing the salve on the dresser, she turned to me.

"I've always trusted my visions. I know the fates have unusual ways of mapping out our paths, but I learned to accept that if that's what is required, there must be a bigger purpose. I knew you would play an important part in the future, therefore my loss would be inconsequential. I did it for Belynda too." She added. "She loves you very much, and although I was grateful to have my time with her, it was heartbreaking to watch her mourn for you. The look on her face when she saw the tablets had failed was what hardened my resolve."

"I don't deserve it," I admitted, and her eyes softened.

"Is that why you sacrificed yourself to save my daughter?"

"I did it because I cannot imagine my life in a world where she does not exist. But perhaps a part of me knew I deserved my fate. I'm not the innocent man that once accepted his sentencing without a fight. Xelraa changed me. It turned me into a monster. A small part of me did feel as though my sacrifice would somehow atone for all the wrongs I did."

"Did you kill out of cruelty? Did you kill to possess? Or kill for greed and power?" she asked. No one had ever asked before.

"I did it to survive," I admitted.

"I would kill to survive too." She confessed, surprising me. "Does that make me a monster? Or a fighter?"

"You chose to die in exchange for my freedom." I said pointedly.

"So did you. You chose to save my girl, and that says a lot about you in my book." Pausing, she pressed the ice pack into my hands. "I would do it again. Even knowing what you've done, I would do it again. You are not the monster you claim to be."

She walked to the door, and I stared after her, humbled and with much to consider.

"Thank you."

"Don't mention it."

Closing the door behind her, I realized the truth: these people, these mortal allies, were my family. This world felt like home and had half of my heart. The other half lived on in Druleska, and would only be whole with her beside me.

14

REDEMPTION

T*HE CHAMBER HUMMED AS EVERYONE* gathered, awaiting the arrival of the Psypher. Even the elementals seemed eager to embark on this deadly journey, though I felt conflicted. Until recently, rescuing Belynda had been the only thought that kept me going. Now I knew crossing that threshold meant I was one step closer to losing her.

I attempted to drown out the voices, but it was impossible; I was the main focus. The sharp stares of the summoned council members followed me with unspoken questions. Everyone had an opinion or a theory I had no answer to.

"Nervous?" Oliver asked as he came to stand by my side, away from the multitude of people. I glanced down at the kid before turning my eyes back to scan the room.

"Irritated is the word you're looking for."

"I know they can be a nuisance, especially Thomas, Felix, and Meerim."

"They're not happy to be here."

"Oh, I know. But they still have a responsibility to the covenant. Whether they like it or not, they have a duty."

"As long as that portal opens, they can brood all they like. But one thing is for certain. They will present a problem for Seymor, sooner or later."

"He can handle it. Besides, he has the majority on his side. If they step out of line, they will be removed, and trust me, that is the last thing they want."

"Time will tell, but a bad apple always corrupts the rest."

"Well, I'll be damned...." Oliver's voice trailed and I followed his line of sight to the entrance of the chamber. It was Benjamin. He spotted Oliver, and I didn't miss his hesitation as our eyes locked. My presence didn't stop him from approaching.

"What made you change your mind?" Oliver seemed pleased he was here. Belynda had said they were childhood friends, and it had been his idea to use the Psypher. But the truth still remained. I was responsible for his father's death. He didn't trust me, and I sure as hell didn't trust him.

"You invited me." Benjamin offered, glancing my way.

"Well. I'm glad you came. You haven't officially met. Drake, Ben. Ben, Drake."

The kid surprised me by extending his hand. I stared at it briefly as I tried to understand why. Was this a truce? Or was he like me, searching for redemption?

"Benjamin." I shook his hand firmly.

"How are the ribs?" The kid asked, turning to Oliver with a grin.

"I told you I let you win."

I felt out of practice to join in with their friendly banter.

"If you'll excuse me," Felsia spotted me, and pulled away from her conversation with Victor and Celest.

"Have you heard from Tyrus or Seymor?" I asked impatiently.

"They're almost here. Patience. We've waited this long…"

"I have no choice."

"Are you always this exasperating?" she said, and I had to smile at her bluntness.

"If I recall correctly, your daughter accused me of the very same thing. So, I must be."

Felsia's smile was warm.

"Come. There is something I wanted to give you."

I followed her out of the chamber and down a small corridor that led to a large study.

I froze. Isabel's sword rested on the table, covered, and bound securely.

"For an uncertain future…" She said.

"Do you honestly believe she has a chance to change her fate?"

"Anything is possible." Taking the sword Felsia placed it in my hands. "If she succeeds, make sure she is prepared for what's to come."

"Seymor has arrived." Said Celest, appearing by the doorway.

"We'll be right there," Felsia said.

Celest returned to the chamber.

"I'm not good at this." Felsia blinked up staring at me.

"I don't think anyone is good at goodbyes," I smirked, "but thank you." I tried to convey my gratitude in those two singular words.

"Be careful, and please, give Belynda my love."

"I promise."

I followed her out into the chamber to find the circle assembled.

"Felsia." I paused, and she turned to me. "Whatever happens, make sure that gate is never again opened. You know what it could cost this world. Belynda would never forgive herself."

"I know." She said. "Now go raise hell."

I grinned. The woman had strangely grown on me. There was so much of her in her daughter...

The circle formed around the elementals and I. At the center, resting on the stone floor, was the Psypher—a triangular-shaped artifact, the edges etched with symbols.

"Remember to assume attack positions the second you pass through. We don't know what will await us."

The elementals nodded in understanding.

"Thank you for everything." I said to Tyrus, shaking his hand firmly.

"Remember what you learned." He replied, grinning.

"Sure, old man."

Seymor and Celest broke from the formed circle to approach me.

"Good luck," Seymor said, offering his hand.

"Thank you. We're going to need it." I glanced at Celest whose eyes brimmed with unshed tears.

"Get her back to us, will you?" she whispered. I glanced at Felsia briefly, the only one present who knew the truth of the future.

"I will." I forced a smile, and as they all returned to their positions, I looked at Oliver.

"Bring her back..." He said under his breath. I nodded in understanding.

Turning around, I willed my fire to flow through my hands.

"Amirth," I called. She was already summoning the earth's power. Alexia and Rashe followed as the force of the elements descended over the Psypher. The writings lit up as the artifact absorbed the energy. It sucked our powers in waves, demanding more, but then the sides of the small pyramid bloomed like a flower, and I felt the pull yield. The inside looked like a thousand glowing crystals.

"*Dimittis Voltratti.*" The circle said, voicing the magic door's name. The crystals on the Psypher pulsed.

"*Dimittis Voltratti.*" They repeated as the crystals grew.

"It's working," Amirth said.

"*Dimittis Voltratti.*" This time, bolts of electricity formed across the pyramid.

"Get ready. I will go first." I said, holding the sword tightly.

"*Dimittis Voltratti.*" This time, the energy singed, and the rift into my world opened. I didn't wait. I dove into the light, and a second later, I was home. Surrounded by the Mountains of Volten. I spun to see Amirth, followed by Rashe, and lastly, Alexia. A moment later, the light disappeared behind us.

The Mountains of Volten... glancing around, I was confused by the familiar scent in the air until I saw her. Stepping from behind the boulders, I rushed to her.

"How did you know where I'd be?"

My mother pulled me into an embrace, and I held her tightly to me.

"I got Belynda's message. She said I would find you here."

I stared at her in disbelief.

"How... Where is she?" My mother shook her head.

"Not with us. A vision... She must have seen you coming."

My happiness wavered as a group of armed men stepped from behind the stones.

"They are with me." She said.

"Good. We'll need all the help we can get. Did her message say anything else?"

"No but the boy that delivered the message said it came from a dove that lives inside the castle dungeons."

"He's still keeping her there…"

"I'm sorry." My mother said, taking my hand.

"This is not your fault."

"I know, but I should have realized something was wrong the moment I didn't hear from either of you."

"It was better that you stayed away. Dagasti has gone mad."

"We both know he was never in the right mind. He's using the amulet to spread the army of darkness."

"How do you know?"

"News travels fast around here. He managed to breach the lower lands of Abryas and Upherya."

"I assume it won't be easy to breach the castle without a fight?" Amirth said, then, reminding me that introductions were in order.

"Amirth. This is my mother."

"Your highness." The warrior girl bowed before my mother with admiration in her gaze.

"There is no need for that, child. Call me Kylram."

"That's Rashe and Alexia. These elementals have offered to help us."

"Thank you for coming. You are all welcome here."

"Thank you," said Rashe. I glanced at the boy, surprised; I had barely heard him utter a word since we met. Then again, he was a fire elemental who was finally home.

"Amirth is right. Slipping into the castle might be a problem."

"Perhaps not. Dagasti has mobilized most of his army to Upherya. The people of Druleska do not pose a threat to him."

"He's not going to leave Belynda unguarded. She is his prize. He used her to open portals to those realms. That's how his army got through." I confessed. "It's my fault. She only did it to protect me."

"He used you both. We just need to get Belynda out before he does more damage to the realms or to her."

"I agree. But first, we need to move. You know the Dravonis will sense a portal has been opened. We don't want to be here when they come to investigate."

"Septo. Erase our scent and follow us." My mother called to one of her men. A phoenix, I realized, for masking was a skill they possessed.

"Yes, my Queen." The young man transformed, his fiery golden wings fluttering as he circled a few times around us.

"We will cross through the mountains."

"Mother... the giants present a bigger threat than Dagasti's men. Are you sure that is wise?" She smiled.

"I have guaranteed us safe passage through there."

"You managed that?" I asked.

"Do you doubt me, my boy?" she teased, taking my hand.

"Never. Father always said you were fierce. He would be proud."

"He would be proud of you as well."

"I find that hard to believe. I left to preserve the peace, and by doing so, allowed my uncle to take what wasn't rightfully his at the expense of my father's life. I don't think my father would be proud of that."

"You're wrong. Your father respected your decision to be with Isabel. He understood the sacrifice you chose to make. He played no part in the council's decision because you had already made up your mind, and he respected the courage it took for you to do so."

"Perhaps I was a fool then," I said. For the first time, I realized what my so-called courage had cost everyone. Isabel's life. My father's...

"You don't really mean that." My mother whispered, pausing to stroke my face.

"I don't know anymore. I've always thought I was doing the right thing, but perhaps everything would have been different if I had chosen to fight instead."

"That was the path the fates had destined for you, and you couldn't have changed it, even if you wanted to."

At her words, something tugged inside my heart. I prayed she was wrong, for I was counting on Belynda to tilt that balance.

THE SILENCE STRETCHED to the edge of the mountains; no one in their right mind would dare trespass into the giant's domain.

"Are you sure about this?" I insisted. My mother ignored me, stepping into the dense forest.

"What exactly are we getting ourselves into?" asked Amirth, catching up to me.

"Giants," I said.

"Bad?"

"I hope we don't find out," I answered, watching as they followed my mother and her men into the forest. Looking behind me, I spotted the phoenix in the distance masking our scents. No one would be following us up the mountain. They would have to be insane to do so. Like my mother, and like I had been once before when I was young. I sighed and followed after the elementals.

The path was familiar. One thousand years was not enough to erase the memories I had built here: the place where Isabel and I had met, away from my family and hers, away from judgment. The scent of fresh water wafted in the air as the wind carried particles of moisture from the waves.

This place had been a sanctuary for Isabel and I. It had been the place Callix, and I would meet as boys. Still, I could not understand what went wrong or why he chose to betray us. He was the only one who knew of this place. The only one who knew where Isabel and I met. That was our secret, and I would never forgive him.

"This place is beautiful." Alexia glanced around, awe-struck, before setting her things down under a tree.

"It's lost its charm."

"I remember when you and Callix used to meet here." My mother recalled, coming behind us. "You gave your father and me a fright the first time. You disappeared for days."

I would never forget that day. It was my first time visiting the Water Realm, and I didn't want to leave. Callix and I were young and stupid, then. We thought little of the consequences. What was a few hours in the Water Realm for us turned out to be days in Druleska. My parents were furious when I finally turned up and Callix was banned from visiting for a while after that. However, eventually, he returned.

"Much has changed. He's not the Callix I once knew."

"Was his realm breached too?" Mother asked.

"Dagasti tried but failed. I knew he wouldn't be able to. Serfier is impenetrable. But what I don't understand is what sort of truce Callix has with him? Dagasti was very direct when he asked me to stay clear of Callix. He didn't want our differences to jeopardize whatever agreement they had."

"Whatever understanding they had must be broken if Dagasti attempted to enter his realm by force."

"I would assume so."

"My queen, the trace is clean. No one will follow." Septo reported.

"Thank you. We will rest here for the night."

"I think I've waited long enough. The more we delay, the longer she is there."

"The elementals are still human. They're tired, and we should be thinking with a clear head. We will let them rest, then we will sit and go over the plan. You are no use to her dead."

I kept forgetting how headstrong my mother was. She was right. She would make a wise ruler.

"Fine. Amirth. Make camp. We continue tomorrow."

Gripping the sword in my hand, I streaked around the lake, heading through a curtain of water: The Falls of Whispers. The sword would be safe here. I hid it under loose rocks and sat peacefully, knowing no one would find me. I collected small pebbles from the ground, tossing them one by one into the water and watching them disappear, as I had done long ago. There was no splash or ripples. Foam formed at the water's surface, swallowing the stones whole.

A small pebble hit my chest, and I bolted upright, staring into the water. Waiting...

Another stone hit the back of my neck, and I stood, my fists tightening by my sides. No other was as stealthy or as determined to die by my hand.

"Show yourself," I demanded.

"You can't throw stones at my door and expect me not to come calling."

"Callix..." I streaked towards him, striking him down. He didn't hesitate to return the blow and I pulled the sword from its hiding place, removing the bindings. How dare he show his face here? I surrounded myself with fire, fueled by rage as a bright flame licked the sword's blade to protect it from Callix's powers.

"This was not the welcome I was expecting. But if you insist," Callix summoned a water spear and held it above his head, aiming it right at me. Then he released a wave of water; he tried to sweep me off my feet, but I launched a fireball at him, countering the water and forcing Callix to dodge.

The clashing of the weapons echoed in the chamber behind the waterfall. Callix's skill and agility were unmatched. He deflected every move I made, then produced a vortex of water. I dashed, managing to deliver a kick before charging, tackling Callix to the ground.

The fight turned into a brawl, a flurry of punches and kicks. We moved in a blur, swinging and dodging until we were both gasping and tired.

"Is this the kind of gratitude I receive?"

I streaked again, grabbing him from behind by gripping his neck with my arm; he kicked my knees and jabbed my ribs, before twisting and freeing himself from my grasp.

"That's your problem. Always has been. You always say too much." I threw a punch and hit him square in the jaw this time. We were both exhausted.

"One thousand years," he gasped, "and you still blame me for what happened?"

"We should have never trusted you." I took another swing, but he moved out of the way.

"Speak for yourself. You know Isabel never believed it. I never betrayed you. You did. The very moment you directed your blame at me."

"You were the only one that knew. There was no one else to blame but you. You were blinded with jealousy because she chose me." I roared. "It wasn't enough to see us both happy." Dark waves stormed in his eyes as he came at me, landing a punch directly to my face.

"I told you I didn't do it," Callix repeated, and a lost part of me wanted to believe it. But how could I trust anything that came out of his mouth?

"What do you want? What business do you have with Dagasti?"

"My agreements with Dagasti do not concern you. I'm here to offer my help."

I laughed without a trace of humor.

"You will never change, you selfish bastard. What makes you think I need your help?"

"Dagasti plans to leave for Upherya in a fortnight."

I fought the instincts battling inside of me, urging me to throttle him.

"Do you think me a fool? You make truces with my uncle while the rest of the realms are at war, and you expect me to believe anything you say?"

"This is an act of selfless kindness. For her…"

"We both know there isn't a noble bone in your body. You stay away from her. Do you hear me?" His blue eyes raged; the storm rampant. Callix waved his hand, the spear on the ground melting to water.

"Suit yourself."

He walked towards the curtain of water, opening a portal with the wave of his hand. He paused before stepping through it, jaw clenched. "Did you ever stop to wonder how she got that message to your mother?" he spat before disappearing into the water.

I picked up the sword, feeling its weight in my hand as I carefully concealed it beneath the rocks once again. My shoulder throbbed with pain, a constant reminder of the irreversible harm I could have if I were forced to shift before I was fully healed. But deep down, I knew that the time for action would inevitably arrive. Soon...

Thoughts of Callix consumed my mind, causing a tumultuous mix of emotions to swirl within me. He claimed he had never betrayed me, but I couldn't bring myself to fully believe his words. The truth was, he had always harbored feelings for Isabel, and he made no effort to conceal them. It was something I had grappled with throughout our years of friendship. Callix possessed a rare quality—he always spoke the truth, regardless of the consequences or the pain it might inflict upon others. In our case, his love for Isabel strained the bond between us.

Back then, I didn't want to accept the possibility of his betrayal, and even now, doubts gnawed at the corners of my mind. But it was hard to ignore the fact that Callix stood to gain so much by exposing our relationship to the guardians. Who else would benefit from our downfall?

And yet, Callix knew about Belynda's message. He could have easily informed Dagasti of our whereabouts if he had intended to betray us. But then why deliver the message in the first place? The pieces of the puzzle didn't quite fit together, leaving me perplexed and uncertain.

There was one thing, however, that remained clear amidst the confusion. I was well aware of Callix's formidable abilities— he was capable of achieving anything he set his mind to. If he truly possessed noble intentions, why hadn't he freed Belynda from her captors? With his power, he could have rescued her in an instant. This contradiction further fueled my skepticism and mistrust towards him.

The fire of determination burned within me, fueled by the unwavering love and protectiveness I felt for her. Yet, amidst all the uncertainty, one thing I knew without a shadow of a doubt was that if Callix ever dared to harm Belynda, I would not hesitate to end him.

THE CAMP HAD SETTLED into a quiet stillness by the time I returned. The men who had accompanied my mother were scattered throughout, seeking privacy in their own secluded spots. The elementals, on the other hand, huddled close to one another around the crackling fire. But there was no sign of my mother amidst the group.

Taking in a deep breath of the cool night air, I immediately realized that the phoenix had done an exceptional job of masking our scents. It seemed almost impossible to track anyone in these circumstances.

"Have you seen my mother?" I asked, my voice a mix of concern and urgency.

"She left shortly after you did." Amirth replied. "She mentioned something about meeting the giants to secure our passage."

"Alone?" I exclaimed, a surge of worry coursing through me.

"Septo went with her..."

"He's only a boy..." I growled in frustration. "He can't protect her."

Without wasting another moment, I blurred through the trees and up the mountain, following the path I knew my mother would have taken. The adrenaline fueled my movements, but I made a conscious effort to slow my pace as my ears picked up a low grumble in the distance. I could sense the presence of giants nearby, and my instincts sharpened, urging me to be cautious.

My inner fire burned to be unleashed, but I couldn't afford to risk it unless it was absolutely necessary. The earth trembled beneath my feet, a clear indication that the giants were drawing closer. The thought of my mother potentially being in danger due to her own stubbornness ignited a mix of anger and concern within me.

Streaking through the dark forest, I followed the rhythmic thumping sound, fully aware that getting any closer would be like signing my own execution warrant. Yet, I held onto the knowledge that Felsia had witnessed my prowess in battle, granting me a glimmer of confidence as I pushed forward towards the light that emanated from a clearing ahead.

To my astonishment and horror, it wasn't just one giant but three. And there, amidst the towering figures, sat my mother, seemingly at ease and comfortable by the fire. I came to an abrupt halt at the edge of the woods, completely bewildered by the scene before me.

"My son..." My mother called out, extending her hand and beckoning me to join them. She had lost her mind...

I approached with deliberately slow steps, studying the towering figures before me. They appeared even taller than I remembered from my childhood encounters. Strangely, they didn't exhibit any hostility towards me. In fact, one of them raised a chalice in welcome. How my mother had managed to establish a truce with the giants was beyond my comprehension, but perhaps this newfound alliance was the edge we desperately needed. If we could convince the giants to fight alongside us, perhaps there was a glimmer of hope in our battle against Dagasti.

"Good evening." I offered courteously, trying to conceal my surprise and confusion.

"Groelus. This is my son. Drake," my mother introduced, her voice filled with a sense of pride.

"I believe I had the pleasure of meeting the young prince when he was just a young lad. Welcome to our colt." The elder said pleasantly. "This here is my son, Melias, and that grumpy old stump over there is my brother, Bilkas. He doesn't say much, but he has good blood. He's loyal."

I glanced at the three immense figures sitting around the fire, their presence towering over us even in their seated positions.

"Thank you for having us. It truly is an honor." I said in earnest, for I knew of no other who had managed to break bread with these creatures.

"Your father was a noble ruler. We lived in peace under his reign. It is we who are honored by your return. Dagasti has taken so much from us and from this realm. We have lost friends and family to the darkness because we refused to willingly join his army. He took some of our people against their will, but we will not be swayed by fear. We choose our allies carefully, and your uncle is not among them," Groelus spoke with a sense of conviction.

"My only regret is that I couldn't stop him sooner." I confessed, feeling the weight of responsibility on my shoulders.

"Your queen mother is a wise woman. The only way to halt Dagasti's rampage is by uniting the Realms, and if anyone can achieve that, it is you," the giant elder replied, his words filled with admiration and hope.

"Dagasti took my cousin, and now he fights for the darkness," Melias interjected. "If there is a way to defeat Dagasti and put an end to his spreading army, you can count on me."

"Thank you," I replied, casting a glance at my mother, who smiled encouragingly. Her support and guidance had played a pivotal role in my decision to pursue my birthright and claim the throne. Initially, I had resisted, considering the implications it would have for Belynda. At the time, abandoning her family and her world felt wrong, but now I understood why she had offered to stay. She knew she wasn't going back, and the reminder of that impending truth made my soul burn. But I was confident that if she perished, and I followed, my mother would make a great ruler.

For now, I would take my place and lead if I had to. My people needed change, and I would no longer deny my birthright. I was, after all, the only true heir: prince to the Fire Realm for as long as the fates allowed her to breathe; deep down, I knew that would seal my end too.

"When the time comes, my friends, I will be proud to call on you. We will surge through the darkness, come what may." I vowed, taking a seat by the fire.

"Then we proceed as planned. Tomorrow, we move up the mountains and position ourselves as close to the castle gates as possible." My mother said.

"I'm afraid there's been a change of plans. We will stay here and move when I say," I asserted, causing confusion to cross my mother's face. "Dagasti is set to depart for Upherya. I don't know how much truth there is to it, but perhaps we can send one of your men to investigate."

"How do you know?" She inquired, her voice tinged with skepticism.

"Callix..." I replied through gritted teeth. "He came to me earlier."

"And you're trusting what he says?"

"I don't know what to believe. He claims it was because of him that you received her message."

"Can you be certain he is telling the truth?"

"I can't, which is why I want to carefully consider our plan before rushing into a potential trap. Callix is aware of our presence here. I need to find out if what he said is true. If he's right, I'm willing to take that risk, especially if it increases our chances of rescuing her," I explained, my voice laced with determination.

"The Water Lord has proven to be a surprising ally. If his fore-warning hadn't arrived when it did..."

"Callix warned you?" I inquired, surprised by this revelation.

"Yes. If it wasn't for him, Dagasti would have taken more of my people." Groelus explained, offering an unexpected perspective.

"Perhaps there is hope for Callix after all," My mother remarked, her words brimming with compassion.

"Perhaps..." I conceded, allowing the possibility of redemption to enter my thoughts. While I wasn't ready to forgive him entirely, my mother's words resonated with me. There might still be hope for Callix, as long as he maintained his distance from Belynda and proved his loyalty.

We faced a daunting journey ahead, one filled with uncertainties and treacherous challenges. However, in that moment, I realized that even in the darkest of times, alliances could form unexpectedly, and redemption might find its way into the hearts of those who had faltered. Including me.

THE CAMP WAS enveloped in a quiet stillness as we returned. The elementals slumbered peacefully, and although sleep was not a necessity for me, I knew that allowing my wound to heal required rest. I found my mother sitting beneath a towering sycamore tree, her gaze fixed upon the somber gray skies.

"Do you mind if I join you?"

A warm smile graced her face as she extended her arm, inviting me to sit beside her. I removed my jacket and placed it gently on the grass, then reclined beside her, interlacing my fingers behind my head. Together, we stared into the vast expanse of the night.

"Do you want to talk about it?" She inquired, her voice gentle yet discerning. I could feel her unwavering gaze upon me.

"I'm not a child anymore, you know..." I responded, a touch of defiance in my words.

"I know," she replied softly. "But I'm still your mother, and I can sense when something weighs heavy on your mind."

"There is a lot on my mind," I confessed, the weight of my thoughts burdening my words. "Belynda. This war. And now, Callix. So many are counting on me and my claim to the throne."

"You're feeling the weight of your duty," she acknowledged, her voice filled with empathy. "I'm afraid that's the burden of a ruler. Worrying about those you love and the welfare of your people is inevitable."

"What if I fail them?" I voiced my deepest fear, the image of Belynda's pale, lifeless face haunting my thoughts. I squeezed my eyes shut, desperately trying to banish the chilling vision. What kind of leader would I be if I failed to save her?

Her hand gently rested upon my shoulder, radiating a comforting warmth. "Your father used to say... 'we fail by chance, not by will.' Soar and fight with all your might, and if all else fails, then you will know in your heart that you did your best."

Her words hung in the air, lingering in the depths of my consciousness. I pondered their meaning, recognizing that this time, failure might come by choice. It would be a surrender, a relenting at her request. A fulfillment of the promise I had made to Belynda, vowing not to save her. But no, I couldn't agree with that sentiment. If I failed to save her, it would tear me apart, knowing that I was honor-bound to stay my hand and refrain from intervening. I couldn't bear the weight of surviving while knowing I hadn't done everything in my power to save her. The thought was suffocating.

With that unsettling realization lingering in my mind, I

closed my eyes, preparing myself for the dark days that lay ahead. Knowing, the path forward was treacherous and uncertain.

BELYNDA

The days had blurred together, devoid of any visions or unexpected visitors. Instead, I relied on the comforting routine I had established as a means of coping with the darkness. But sometimes, even the routine felt insufficient in warding off the encroaching insanity. The one thing that kept me anchored was the knowledge that Drake was coming for me. I didn't know when or how, but the mere thought of his impending rescue provided me with strength to face each day, one after another.

After cleaning myself with the meager water provided and settling onto the cold stone floor, I picked at the stale bread, cheese, and dried meat on the tray. Oh, how I longed for Celest's fluffy pancakes or the comfort of my own bed. Simple luxuries that I had once taken for granted now seemed indispensable. The skin on my wrists was raw from the relentless grip of the shackles, a daily reminder of my captivity. Every day, I struggled against them, a futile rebellion, but it was a way to release my pent-up anger.

I often cried, too, although now I couldn't quite pinpoint the reason behind my weeping.

"Don't waste your tears. Don't give your captors that gratification." Startled, I jolted to my feet as I heard his voice, a voice I hadn't heard in what felt like an eternity.

"You've been gone..." I uttered, attempting to mask the desperation lacing my voice. But truthfully, I was desperate. Desperate for any form of companionship. The stranger's intermittent visits had been a lifeline, keeping me tethered to sanity, and a part of me yearned to see him. I counted the days, awaiting the arrival of either Drake or the stranger, yet disappointment settled within me as the days passed by without their appearance.

"The world is burning. I seem to be trying to put out fires everywhere." He said as though his words made sense.

"What do you mean?" I inquired, sensing the hesitation in his sapphire eyes as he glanced up at me.

"I've been busy. That's all." He explained.

"But you're here now. That's all that matters." I found myself replying, a hint of longing seeping into my words. I caught the way his lips curved into a teasing grin.

"Careful... one might assume you missed me," he playfully remarked. In that moment, my heart quickened its pace. I averted my gaze, attempting to hide the truth from him. But deep down, a part of me had missed his visits, missed the light he brought with him every time he entered the dungeon, cutting through the darkness that threatened to consume me.

"Did you manage to deliver my message?" I asked, attempting to shift the focus of our conversation.

"I'm hurt," he said, pacing closer to the cell. "I thought you missed my company, but it seems you're only concerned with confirming the completion of my services."

"No!" I rebuked his assumption quickly.

"No?" His fingers grazed his jawline, his piercing blue eyes challenging me.

"That's not all I wanted," I confessed. In that moment, his oceanic gaze seemed to warm my face, his smile illuminating the darkness of the room. It dawned on me how dangerous he had become, how much of a threat he posed to me... to my heart... to Drake and me.

I swallowed, watching as his smile faded and his eyes became a storm. Then, abruptly, he straightened his back and retreated from the cell.

"It won't be long now," he declared, facing the entrance of the chamber. "Be prepared to leave soon." With those words, he departed, leaving me in a state of bewilderment. *What was wrong with him? What did he mean? Was Drake finally coming?*

<h1 style="text-align:center">15</h1>

<h2 style="text-align:center">UPHERYA</h2>

THE CRISP AUTUMN AIR WAS TENSE as the impending battle drew nearer. The Warrior Clan of the Southern region of Upherya assembled in the clearing, their glinting armor reflecting the waning light of the setting sun. The Clan proudly flew their banners, embodying their golden wings as they gathered strength from their fierce leader who charged through their lines, sword raised high.

"Brothers... we stand together. Whatever you do, do not let any of them touch you. If they do, you're as good as dead." The leader proclaimed. "Remember, every face here today can become your enemy. We are the Borean Clan. We fight for this realm, our families, our wives, and our children. We do not fear the darkness, for we are warriors."

The horn blared in the distance. The darkness was coming.

ON THE FAR side of the borderlands, the Army of darkling's advanced. Under a blanket of complete darkness, serenaded by the loud pulse of drums, their line of spears, swords, and axes were unending. The bloodcurdling howls of the darkling echoed throughout the lands as they marched forward.

The two sides met in a violent clash. The Battlefield was alight with surging elemental energy as both sides fought tooth and nail. Powerful gusts of roaring wind collided with the howls of hungry darkling's, each desperate to consume the soul of their foes. A gigantic golden cloud of air-realm warriors bravely swarmed the overwhelming horde of darkling that had quickly gathered around them.

The Warrior Clan fought with courage; however, despite their efforts, the Army's numbers were too great and the dark-ling's powerful magic proved too strong. Paralyzed by fear, the Clan watched as their enemies swept through their ranks, touching each and every warrior. Wave after wave, the warriors were met by darkling's that materialized from the shadows, consuming their souls, and sending them plummeting into darkness.

The Borean Clan of Upherya ceased to exist, replaced by an army of soulless warriors now adorned with the symbol of the Army of darklings. As the swelling army marched Westward, the setting sun sank below the horizon, leaving nothing but the encroaching darkness of night in its wake.

EUROS

Darkness prevailed. The outer lands bore no resemblance to the vibrancy it once held. The darkness left corpses and decay in its path. Every last warrior from the Southern clans were either dead or had turned. Brothers I grew up with now fought against their own.

Our powers were yielding against Dagasti's forces. Soon, there would be nothing left of Upherya to call home.

"Euros." one of my men called. With a pained heart, I turned from the scene of devastation, bracing myself for the news he carried

"What is it?"

"The Borean Clan... they have confirmed it. Their leader... is gone," he delivered the news with a mixture of grief and resignation. The loss of the Borean Clan leader was yet another blow to our already shattered hopes.

A surge of pain coursed through me as the weight of the loss settled upon my shoulders. The realization that even the leader of one of our clans had fallen in this merciless battle deepened the sense of despair that gripped us all. Yet, amidst the darkness, a flicker of determination ignited within me. I knew I had to find a way to rally what remained of our forces and fight back against the encroaching darkness. Upherya may be on the brink of destruction, but I would not let our realm fall without a fight.

I glanced around me at the women and children who were spared.

For years, we had fought relentlessly against Dagasti's forces, fighting to keep them out of our borders. Watching this was sickening, but there was nothing else I could do for these people. My duty as the leader of the Hestians, Clan of the North, was to Upherya and the clans remaining.

"Have everyone gather what food they can. We'll return to the North at first light. Send word to the Astreans and Euresians that the South Clan has fallen."

"Right away, Sir."

. . .

THE TENSION in the room was palpable as the empty chair at the round table served as a stark reminder of the losses we had endured. The absence of our fallen brother weighed heavily on our hearts, fueling our determination to find a way to salvage what remained of our lands.

As the leader of the Northern clan, I found myself locked in a heated debate with Link and Phoenix, my trusted brothers in arms and the last two standing clan leaders for the East and West lands. The fate of our people hung in the balance, and our differing opinions clashed in the confined space.

"King Herod is no fool," I argued, my gaze fixed on Link and Phoenix. "He will not recall his men, nor will he be willing to lend his army to protect our people. We must face that reality."

"This war threatens their lands as well," Link countered, his voice filled with conviction. "Herod cannot fight on two fronts simultaneously. We can appeal to his sense of self-preservation and seek a truce, perhaps even form an alliance."

"That's assuming he even grants us an audience," I retorted, voicing my skepticism. "Herod has proven stubborn in the past."

"He will meet with us," Phoenix interjected, his tone carrying a hint of certainty. His words hung in the air, leaving us all curious as to how he had acquired such knowledge. I narrowed my eyes in Phoenix's direction, knowing there was more left unsaid. "He has already agreed to meet." He finally admitted.

I glared at Phoenix, a mix of anger and frustration bubbling within me.

"Damn you, Phoenix! How many times must I remind you not to act without the unanimous agreement of all clan leaders?" I roared, my fist slamming against the table in a display of frustration.

"Easy, Euros. We know you disagree, and perhaps you're right to think there is no hope for the Elvin King, but shouldn't we take the chance? If it means offering more protection for our people?"

I glared at the Astrean warrior, leader of the West Clan. For a man so young, Link was wise. Perhaps he was right.

"You know I would do anything to protect this realm."

"We agree, then. We fly to Abryas." Phoenix pressed, and I had no choice but to concede.

The room fell into a tense silence as we weighed our options. The impending threat of Dagasti's army loomed over us, and we knew we had to make a decision that would safeguard our people. Phoenix's unwavering determination clashed with my cautious approach, but we had to find a compromise.

"What about Link's people? Dagasti's army marches to the West," I pressed, seeking a solution that would protect all of Upherya.

Link spoke up confidently, his voice filled with conviction. "We have reinforced our magic barriers with the Lord's help. My warriors can hold the ground."

Frustration surged within me as I rebutted, "You did not witness what the darkness did to the Southern Clan. Our magic will not hold against the darklings, not for long..."

Phoenix, ever the resilient one, responded sharply.

"So, what do you propose? That we give up and surrender without a fight?"

His words stung, but I couldn't let my anger cloud my judgment. I took a deep breath, trying to find a middle ground.

"No. But we stand a better chance if we unite as one. Let's move the women and children to the caves in the mountains of Tirse and gather our warriors here in the North. If we are going to face this battle, let's give them a fight they won't forget."

"No. If we retreat, we leave Upherya open for Dagasti's

taking." Link offered, "My people will fight, and hold the army for as long as possible."

I glanced at Phoenix, knowing the tide was turning against me.

"The East will stand its ground as well," Phoenix confirmed, sealing my defeat.

Accepting the reality of the situation, I conceded.

"Very well. Then, at the very least, let's move the women and children to safety."

Link and I shared a moment of agreement, our eyes locked on Phoenix. "I agree," Link said firmly, and we awaited Phoenix's response.

I will prepare my people to move," Phoenix conceded, placing his fist on the table in agreement.

"We meet here again in seven moons, then fly to Abryas. I will order my men to divide. They will accompany you to help move your people."

"Thank you, brother," Link said, expressing his gratitude, his hand resting on my shoulder before he left the meeting hall.

As Phoenix stood, he extended his hand to me. I shook it, cautioning him, "Just don't do anything reckless..."

He grinned, displaying his trademark confidence. "Seven moons, Euros. I'll be here as agreed," he assured me before turning and walking away.

16

ABRYAS

I *KNEW I WOULD FIND HER HERE.* Watching the sleeping city always brought her comfort. The army of Darkness weighed heavy on her mind, as it did mine. As the King, it was my duty not to show it. Based on the reports from the borders, the losses were significant for Upherya. The breach to our borders although contained, was still a potential concern amongst the elders. Our magic was our only weapon. If the army breached our shields...we would be lost. I came behind her silently, though her eyes found me first.

"It's late to be roaming the halls." She said, offering a smile I knew was reserved for me only. Gently, her hand beckoned me to join her on the veranda.

"Why aren't you resting?" I braced my hands either side of her, my breath fanning the back of her neck.

"I couldn't sleep. Has there been any news?"

"The Borean clan was wiped out. The borderlands of Upherya leveled, and everything in the army's path along the South." She turned in my arms with a haunted look, and I held her tighter.

"Herod, you must remove the magic shields and your troops from Upherya's borders. They are no threat to us. Dagasti is. We cannot protect our people and fight two fronts."

"If we retreat now, we are cowards."

She turned in my arms to face me.

"No! You would be wise. You are the King, Herod. Every soul in this kingdom is counting on you to keep them safe. Their lives are in your hands."

I studied Leiwen's face masked with concern, sensing my wavering resolve. I hated when she was right, but it made me proud to have her as my Queen.

She was wise. I was the King of this realm, but Leiwen was the soul of Abryas. Her kindness and light had reached many elven towns in this kingdom, more than I could count. Even now, her kindness was reaching even our enemies in Upherya.

I had no doubt that her concern for our people was solid, yet I knew her better than anyone for I had shared her soul since the beginning of light itself. Leiwen empathized with the air people and our differences with the realm of Upherya was something she had always considered trivial.

"I will speak with the elders. Perhaps it is time we accepted an audience with the clan leaders." I conceded. Her expression softened as she returned to watch the sleeping kingdom below us.

As I held the one person that mattered most between my arms, I realized that a war like no other was upon us, and I would do everything in my power to protect my people, my kingdom, but her above anything...

17

ENDINGS AND BEGINNINGS

I WATCHED FROM THE TOWER AS THE rest of the Fire Army marched on my orders towards the borders of Upherya . The Southern clan had fallen easily and the number of darkling's soared. Now that I had control of the lower lands, it wouldn't be long before the darkling's swept the rest of the clans and claimed Upherya for me... for the darkness.

"Master Dagasti. Everything is packed."

"Send the caravan off without me. I will follow."

"But my lord..."

"Do as I said." I thundered, dismissing Rommina with a wave of my hand. There was one loose end to tie... Callix. He thought I was a fool; he thought he was using me while trading information with the rest of the Realms... but he was a bigger fool than I. I fed him only what I needed him to know. At first, I had doubts, but the giants validated my suspicions. They couldn't have known, not without forewarning. His realm was safe from me now, but it wouldn't be for long. If I brought him to the dark side, he would surrender his kingdom without a fight.

DRAKE

The elementals spent their day training while I watched. The men we sent to gather information confirmed what Callix had said; Dagasti had left for Upherya, and tonight was our chance to move in.

"You're not joining them?" my mother asked, standing beside me. "I recall a time when you never missed an opportunity to spar."

"I'd rather not. I have a lot on my mind." I said before walking away. I didn't want to concern her by discussing my still-healing wound. She was right, though; the fire inside me was restless; joining would have served as an escape, but I refused to make the same mistake I had last time. I needed to be ready; I could not risk weakening myself further.

Hiding behind the waterfall, I removed my shirt. I splashed water over my shoulders and face, hoping the cold water would extinguish the fire raging beneath my skin.

"That is one hell of a scar."

I turned around, growling.

"I thought my last warning was clear."

"I'm not here for you." He snarled. "I'm here for her."

I spun, but Callix formed a water blade and pointed it at me. It didn't stop me, though. I took a step forward, staring him dead in the eyes until the tip rested against my throat.

"I told you. She is of no concern to you." I hissed.

"Do not presume to order me around because I've shown her kindness."

"What do you want?" I spat, clenching my fists at my sides. I remembered the giants' words.

"It's a trap." He said. "Dagasti wanted me to believe he was leaving, but he's not. I thought you should know." He took a step back, and the water sword separated from my skin.

"Thank you for the message. As I said, we don't need your help."

His eyes darkened, and the water sword morphed into a water portal.

"There will come a day when you will beg for my help."

The water gate vanished as Callix stepped through it. I would die before I ever begged him for anything.

PERHAPS, I had not been the only one feeling restless; at my orders, the camp was abuzz with energy. Everyone was prepared to march within the hour.

We managed to make good ground, yet because of the elementals, we moved at human speed. The castle lights were a short distance away and the fire raging in me burned, urging me to fly into the fortress and take her. But I couldn't do this alone. Not with Dagasti's army looming in every corner.

DUSK WAS FAST APPROACHING, and I sensed the heightened anticipation among the elementals. They were eager for a fight, ready to unleash their powers in the upcoming battle.

"Whatever you do, do *not* let his men touch you. We don't know if the guards have been turned into darkling's, but it's best to be safe."

"Are you sure you want to do this alone? What if it's a trap?" My mother's worry was evident in her voice.

"I will get to her whatever it takes. If anything goes wrong, and I don't walk out of those gates with Belynda, you must take your men and the elementals and disappear into the mountains. Do you understand me?"

"You know I won't do that."

"Mother, do not argue with me on this. I beg you."

"I promise." After a moment of hesitation, she finally acquiesced.

Turning, she marched out from under the shadows of the mountains, towards the castle gates. The men, resolute and prepared for battle, followed in her wake.

"Amirth. Look after those two, will you?"

"I always do." She smiled, then ran to catch up with Rashe and Alexia. I stared after them until the last one disappeared from sight.

AMIRTH

The path leading to the castle gates was strangely clear, indicating that Dagasti had likely consolidated his remaining soldiers within the castle walls. Sensing an opportunity, I whispered to Alexia, "Give me a lift, will you?" Recognizing my intent, she summoned a powerful wind vortex that lifted me off the ground and propelled me up the stone walls, allowing me to scout the area.

From my vantage point, I surveyed the scene and counted twenty-five guards, but there was no sign of Drake among them. I motioned to Alexia, signaling her to bring me back down using her wind vortex. Once on the ground again, I relayed the information to the others. "I counted twenty-five men, but there could be more."

"We can take them. Let's give Drake a little more time before we stir up the castle." The queen declared with confidence.

"I think if we separate, we might have a better advantage. We could surprise the guards from behind once they advance toward you." I suggested, considering our options.

"You're right. Be careful. I promised my son I would look out for you." Kylram glanced between the three of us. "I'll see you inside. You'll know when." The queen and her men ran for the gates while Alexia, Rashe, and I made for the Southern walls of the castle's courtyard.

"Here," I stared up at the shadow cast from the tower. "They won't see us up there."

Without delay, Alexia summoned her wind again, silently lifting Rashe and me to the top of the stone wall. Gracefully, she joined us moments later.

"What now?" Rashe asked. I had never seen the boy this excited to kick some ass. Smirking, I replied.

"You heard the queen. We sit, watch, and wait." We positioned ourselves atop the wall, hidden within the stretching shadow of the tower, hoping that whatever the firebird had done to conceal our scent would hold. Otherwise, it wouldn't be long before the guards discovered our presence.

DRAKE

Stealthily, I moved across the stone walls of the castle. My ears were on high alert.

I reached the castle drains, and sure enough, there was a guard. Dagasti wasn't stupid enough to leave a single entrance to the fortress unattended. I removed the sword from its hilt and lunged for the guard. One strike was all it took, and he was down. His eyes were clear... he wasn't a darkling.

I searched the guard for a key, but there were none on him. So, I kicked the metal bars. They gave on the second try.

The drainage sites connected to the crypts beneath the castle.

If our plan worked, my mother's distraction would pull most guards outside, and provide me with ample time to reach Belynda.

The corridors inside the crypts were quiet. I listened for the slightest sound, but it was only the dead and me.

I streaked up the spiral stairs that lead inside the castle. Sharpening my hearing, I reached the main landing, but there was no sound in the corridors. Crossing the entrance hall, I slipped into the South wing unnoticed and reached the entrance to the dungeons.

I descended the spiral stairs, and the temperature dropped. I felt the presence of darkness instantly, as if it could almost be tasted. It sensed me, too, and I felt its approach, as I was sure it felt mine. I was ready for it.

Reaching the dungeons, I raised the sword. There was a moment of stillness before it charged into view with fierce intensity, eyes a dark void. I swung the blade, and the darkling hissed, circling me. His claws came dangerously close to my skin, waiting for me to make the first more. I directed my energy into a powerful uppercut; the darkling barely dodged the strike, but used its momentum to move towards me again. Only this time, I was prepared, and met his attack with a swift kick to the chest that sent him stumbling backwards. He recovered faster than I expected, but I was one step ahead. Jabbing a blow to the darkling's throat, I watched it collapse and still at my feet.

I took a few steps back, and with my foot, turned the darkling's body onto its back. The keys hung under his vest. I slipped the sword's tip into the key ring and brought it out without touching the abomination's flesh.

The darkling was strong, but it wasn't a fighter. I was lucky. A skilled fighter turned darkling was a force to reckon with.

A crushing wave of sadness overwhelmed me as I entered the dimly lit chamber. Belynda sat there, her head nestled against her knees, and the sight of her fragility pierced my heart.

"Belynda..." I whispered, my voice filled with a mix of relief and anguish. Her gaze darted through the darkness, and as soon as her eyes met mine, she hurriedly rose to her knees. Gripping the bars, she pressed her face between them, desperate for our connection.

"You're here... you're really here," she uttered, tears streaming down her face. With trembling hands, I inserted the key into the lock. As the bolt clicked open, it felt as if my heart started beating again.

Swinging the door open, I embraced her tightly, enveloping her sobs with the solace of my presence. Her scent wrapped around me like a soothing blanket. "Shhh, it's alright. I'm here now," I murmured, gently brushing my lips against hers, tasting the saltiness of her tears. "We have to go now. It won't be long before they realize I'm here."

Her eyes, still glistening with tears, glanced at the shackles restraining her wrists. "What about these?" she asked, a hint of desperation in her voice.

"I don't have the key, but your mother gave me the spell to remove them," I explained, my voice laced with regret.

"Please, do it now. I can't bear another moment with these on," she pleaded, her desperation tearing at my soul.

"I can't do it alone; we need a blood witch for the spell," I explained, feeling the weight of the situation.

"Can't I do it myself?" She questioned, her eyes shifting towards the glinting metal around her wrists.

"No, not while wearing the shackles. They block all powers, including your blood magic."

"Damn it." She cursed, frustration etching across her face. With a distant look in her eyes, her gaze shifted to the gleaming sword in my hand.

"You brought Isabel's sword." She whispered, her voice barely audible.

"Your sword," I corrected her. She lowered her head, a resigned expression crossing her face. All I wanted was to embrace her, shielding her from the weight of her visions and the cruelty of the fates.

"It's okay," I assured her, taking her hands in mine. "We will find a way to remove the shackles. I promise." I wiped away her tears. "But right now, we must go," I pressed, with urgency.

Belynda gazed up at me with resolve, then took my hand.

She followed me out of the chambers, but I remembered the dead darkling ahead.

"Close your eyes," I warned, and for once, she did as I said. Taking her into my arms, I hastened past the corpse and up the stairs to the castle's main landing.

I returned the way I came, tracking back through the South wing. But as I neared the entrance hall, my ears detected commotion. I pulled back into the portrait hall and placed Belynda on her feet, motioning for her to remain silent.

AMIRTH

The moment the horn sounded, our time for waiting in the shadows was over. In the distance, I could see Kylram and her men storming through the courtyard, meeting the guards head-on. However, the guards didn't yield in surprise at the sight of their supposedly deceased queen, as Kylram had hoped.

"Let's go," I urged, and Alexia gently lowered us into the courtyard. The instant our feet touched the ground, we broke into a sprint. Alexia used her powers to clear a path for us, dispersing the guards with a powerful gust of wind. Yet, our relief was short-lived as a fresh wave of soldiers poured out of the castle doors.

Reacting swiftly, I pressed my hand against the ground, causing a fissure to open up beneath the shifting guards, swallowing several of them. "Alexia, move!" Kylram's urgent cry pierced through the chaotic uproar. I instinctively threw myself into Alexia, knocking her to the ground just in time to evade a spear thrust. However, the spear grazed my arm, leaving a painful cut in its wake.

With unwavering determination, Alexia pushed herself up from the ground and flung her hand forward, sending the guard hurtling over the castle walls. "Move!" Rashe called out, his voice filled with urgency. Together, we managed to reach Kylram and the remaining men who were still standing, but the toll of the battle was escalating.

As the bells above the tower rang, signaling further danger, another swarm of soldiers emerged through the castle doors. We knew that facing them all would be futile, and the cost would be too great.

DRAKE

The swarm of guards rushed past us, their destination clear: the crypts. They knew...

As I surveyed the compromised entrance, I quickly assessed our options. Taking the tower seemed to be our best chance. If need be, I would shift and carry us through the skies to safety. However, when I moved to lift Belynda, she stopped me.

"I can walk." She insisted, her voice filled with determination.

"I don't doubt it, but you're weak. Let me carry you," I pleaded in a whisper.

"No. I'd rather walk. I've been trapped in that cell for too long; please don't deny me this." She implored. I gazed at her, realizing there was nothing in this life, or the next, that I wouldn't give her.

"Very well," I acquiesced, gripping her hand firmly as I led her across the grand hall towards the North tower. However, my steps faltered in surprise as a familiar scent reached my senses. He was always skilled at masking it....

His eyes shifted from Belynda to me.

"I swear, Callix, if you say a word... if you stand in my way..." I warned.

"I only came to make sure you got her out."

"And I told you to stay away. We don't need your help."

"Callix?" Belynda whispered at my side, confusion etching her face. He turned his gaze to her, and in that moment, I couldn't contain my anger any longer.

"I'm warning you," I growled, my voice filled with a primal edge. Callix grinned, but he moved aside, allowing us to pass.

Without wasting a moment, I stormed up the stairs of the tower, my focus fixed on our escape. I didn't look back; I didn't have time to spare.

"Callix...?" Belynda's quiet voice, carried a sense of surprise and curiosity. "As in the Lord of the Water Realm Callix?"

"There is no other." I confirmed, my tone guarded. "I thought you had already met?" I tried to push aside the resurfacing memories of that night when she returned, seemingly immersed in his scent. Dark thoughts clouded my mind, fueled by Dagasti's poisonous words suggesting Callix had kept her entertained. I knew it was a test, an attempt to poison my soul, and yet a part of me couldn't help but fall into the trap.

"No. Not by name. He never said who he was..." Her brow furrowed, making me wonder what game Callix was playing. "I thought Mer people were supposed to be ugly and despicable creatures?"

Despite the gravity of our situation, a fleeting laugh escaped me at her absurd assumption, though deep down, I wished she held such a disdainful view of him. "Just stay away from Callix. I don't know what his intentions are... and I don't trust him," I cautioned, my voice laced with a mix of concern and lingering doubt. But something else as well... jealousy.

BELYNDA

The revelation of Callix's true identity left me with a flood of questions. Why had he kept it a secret from me all this time? And what was his connection to Dagasti? If our circumstances were different, I would have pursued the blue-eyed God, demanding answers.

Mortified, I thought of all the ridiculous names I had given him. I had probably offended him, but somehow the thought made me smile. It was a relief to finally put a name to the face.

While I was unaware of the specifics of Drake and Callix's history or their differences, I had a strong intuition that Drake's mistrust of Callix had more to do with me than any shared past they had. Drake had admitted to his jealousy, and I could feel the tension between us as we stood at the foot of the stairs.

Nevertheless, I had complete trust in Drake. If Callix was his enemy, then he was mine as well.

But as I made this decision, a weight settled in my conscience. I couldn't help but acknowledge that Callix had been a friend to me, and the thought of him betraying me or as my enemy, weighed heavily on my heart.

I SHIVERED in the cold air as we climbed higher up the stairs. Drake noticed my trembling and paused, concern etched on his face

"Wait here. I'll be a second." He disappeared downstairs, reappearing a minute later. Something in my memory ignited when I stared at the blue cloak in his hands. My eyes brimmed with tears as I remembered a detail that had not been important before now. The moment was near, and I realized it as soon I saw Drake carrying that sword. Yet as I stared at the blue material before me, the heaviness of what I was yet to face crushed me from the inside out.

Tears streamed down my cheeks, and Drake cupped my face, forcing my eyes to meet his.

"Tell me what's wrong." He pleaded, and I found myself lost in his eyes. We didn't have much time.

"I'm scared," With a trembling voice, I confessed. Drake's brows furrowed with worry.

"I won't let anything happen to you." I met his eyes, silently pleading.

"No..." I whispered, my voice barely audible. "You promised, remember?" His eyes darkened at the mention of it. "Whatever happens, you will not sacrifice yourself again."

His jaw clenched, and for a moment, the black lines danced across his skin, the darkness threatening to surface.

"I know..." He said through clenched teeth. "You had a vision. You knew and still asked me to promise. You lied to me."

I had never seen him so angry. His voice broke, and I fought the knot in my throat. I couldn't find the words to explain myself or to make him understand. Despite his anger, he pulled me against him. He knew, and there was only one other person who could have told him. *My mother...*

"Look me in the eyes this time and tell me." He whispered, his voice filled with pain. "Tell me that when the time comes, you choose not to be saved. I will honor my promise. Even if it kills me." His words pierced my heart, and I fought back more tears as I gathered the strength to face him.

I pulled away slightly, gazing into his silver eyes, and in a hushed voice, I uttered the words that would forever condemn me.

"Do not save me."

His eyes silently pleaded with me to reconsider before his lips claimed mine. He broke away, and as he did, he looked at the binding bracelet blocking him from reading my thoughts. In that moment, I understood what his kiss had meant. My words alone were not enough; he needed to see the truth, to read it in my thoughts.

I reached up with my shackled hands, desperately trying to make him understand. How could I make him see the truth?

"I have accepted it," I insisted, my voice filled with resignation. "Things are as they should be."

"No, they are not. You changed your mother's fate. She was supposed to die the night you broke the tablets, and you stopped it. Fight this, damn it. If not for you, then for me." He thundered.

I stared at his face, feeling defeated. What could I possibly do to escape this fate? Did he think I didn't want to live? The weight of it all bore down on me.

"Do you think I wouldn't do everything in my power to change this if I could?" I whispered.

"It seems like you're giving up."

"I'm not giving up." I replied, my voice laced with weariness. "I just don't see a way out. It's exhausting to fight against the fates. I'm tired of making sacrifices."

"Your mother spoke of Isabel's letter and something she said."

"Yes. She told me, too. But believe me, if there is some magical way to prevent this... I do not know of it."

His fingers brushed my cheek gently, but then his attention snapped to the top of the tower. Time was running out.

"We need to move." He declared urgently. He kissed my hands, my cheeks, and lastly, my lips. "Come, we'll take the sky bridge. They're right behind us." He pulled me into his arms, and we hurried towards the top of the stairs. Drake froze before opening the door. Pressing me behind him, his fists clenched at his sides. When he looked down at me, darkness danced over his body.

"We're trapped."

He kicked open the door, and gray skies stretched before us. Closing my eyes for a moment, I felt the wind against my face, and then I saw them. There, on the connecting tower, stood Dagasti and his guards. The bridge was the only thing separating us from them. The wind whipped against my face, and the bells rang in the distance. Drake smelled the air and tightened his hold on my hand.

"Darkling's." Drake muttered, his brow furrowing. "Remember, they cannot touch you. Be ready to jump." He said under his breath. I glanced at the approaching soldiers and Dagasti, their intent clear as they moved towards the bridge.

"I promise I will be the last thing you see before you die." Drake roared, and his uncle leered in defiance as the vile man we knew he was. Dagasti reached for the talisman around his neck, but Drake didn't wait to be cornered this time. Without warning, he placed the sword in my hands, and hugged me before launching himself from the sky bridge.

The cold wind whipped against my face as we plummeted through the air. I closed my eyes, clutching the sword to my chest, while Drake's arms encircled me, holding me close.

"Fight for us," he whispered, his words barely audible amidst the rushing wind. I knew exactly what he meant. *Fight to live.*

AMIRTH

We watched them descend. Drake cut through the air clutching Belynda in his arms, but he struggled to shift with his wounded arm. A dark cloud surrounded them, and as they neared the ground, I held my breath and braced for their impact. Alexia noticed too and she reacted. She sent a gust of wind their way to slow their fall, and we finally took a breath of relief as the dark clouds were replaced by fire, wings and claws. We watched as he cut through the skies with Belynda in his claws. Only a minute later, another beast speared through the skies in pursuit of their trail.

"Let's go. We must go now. He's out. If we get separated, we'll meet back at the falls! Understood?" Kylram ordered.

"Rashe, go with them," I said, while Alexia and I held back the soldiers. We needed to give the others more time to escape before we made a dash for the forest edge ourselves.

BELYNDA

I opened my eyes and froze as the ground approached us. I held my breath, but the fire and darkness consumed him before we met the ground. Suddenly, I was flying, locked firmly within the grasp of the beast.

Below me, the ground was a blur of earth and sky, trees and hills, all melding together as the powerful creature tore through the skies. Drake was fast, but Dagasti was close behind. He came above us, and Drake dove sharply toward the ground.

"Drake!" I shrieked as we plummeted, but he didn't slow. He released me once I was a meter from the ground, turning in time to fend off his uncle's claws.

The sword clashed against the ground. Rolling onto the ashen floor, I winced against the pain in my side. I pulled myself up and collected the sword, staring at the dragons chasing each other with intricate maneuvers. They were powerful, twisting and turning out of each other's paths. Even the clouds seemed to be still in awe of their flight.

Sparks flicked from their claws as they struck at one other. They soared and dived with determination, and as I regarded my surroundings, I knew exactly how this story would end.

EVERYTHING UNFOLDED before me just as it had in my dream. The line of trees ablaze in the distance, the swirling ashes dancing against my skin. But there was something different, a subtle shift that I couldn't quite put my finger on. A strange pull tugged at me, a sensation I had experienced only once before. I turned my gaze behind me and froze in my tracks as I watched him emerge, from a shimmering water portal.

"You..." The words caught in my throat, a mix of surprise, confusion, and apprehension flooding my senses. He halted a few steps away, uncertainty etched on his face.

"You must come with me... It's not safe for you here," he urged, his voice laced with urgency.

I stared at him, my mind overwhelmed with questions.

"How did I not see you...?" I murmured, replaying the vivid vision in my mind. Callix had not been there. He was never part of my dream... I looked at him, searching for answers. "You were never in my vision... Why?"

"There's no time to explain. Come with me. Please." He implored, closing the distance between us. His intention to take my hands was met with my instinctive withdrawal, my sword pointed at him defensively.

"No. It was you, wasn't it? I trusted you, and you betrayed us." I accused, my voice trembling. His sapphire eyes darkened, and as I stared into them, I felt like I could drown in the sorrow myself.

"You don't know anything," he retorted, anger lacing his words.

"Because you won't tell me!" I yelled, frustration and hurt rising within me. "You lied to me. All this time, you *lied*. Why?" I locked my gaze with his, a mix of anger and desperation burning inside me. "Why didn't you tell me who you were?"

"It wouldn't have made a difference." His voice wavered, transforming into a raspy whisper. "You wouldn't had given me a chance... you hated who I was without ever knowing me." He whispered.

"You don't know that..." I sighed. "You made me feel like a fool," I confessed, watching as the tempest behind his eyes gradually subsided.

"Forgive me... That was never my intention, I assure you," he pleaded, his gaze shifting momentarily to the dragons soaring above us. He took a tentative step closer, and this time, I stood my ground.

"I've never lied to you. I might not have been forthcoming about who I was, but I've never lied." He murmured, his words hanging in the air. I could only stare at him, torn between skepticism and a glimmer of hope. Slowly, my grip on the sword loosened, and I lowered it, uncertain of what to believe.

"I want to believe you... I really do," I began, my voice wavering with uncertainty. "But I don't know if I can trust you." I shook my head, attempting to gather my thoughts.

"You don't have to trust me if you don't want to," he replied, his gaze unwavering. "But you know what happens next. If you don't come with me now... you seal your fate." His eyes bore into mine, yet his words were a reminder that there were still important details left unsaid.

"Will you tell me how you know all this? Why I didn't see you in my vision?" I pressed, searching for answers. His jaw tightened, his attention briefly diverted to the violent clash of the dragons in the sky.

"Water is linked directly to the fates; that's how I knew." He revealed, his words resonating with a semblance of truth. The connection between water and the fates was something I had come across in my studies of Serfier.

"How does it work? Did they send you to save me?" I inquired, hoping for a clearer understanding. His brow furrowed as he considered his response.

"The circumstances are more intricate than that, and we don't have the luxury of time right now," he urged, his tone pleading. "All you need to know is that I have your best interests at heart. I was the one who stole the Sacred Book from the guardianship. I retrieved the relics from the realms and entrusted them to the water elementals for safekeeping."

I stared at Callix, the realization of his actions sinking in. "That was you?" I whispered, my voice laden with astonishment. "You did all that for me?" Nothing seemed to make sense anymore. What drove him to steal the book and secure the relics, the very items necessary for opening the Ora tablets?

"Yes," he confirmed, his gaze meeting mine with unwavering determination. "But there is a reason behind it all."

"Why?" I pressed, needing to understand the motivations that propelled him.

"Like you, my fate is forfeited to the fates." He said, though I had the distinct feeling there was more he wasn't telling me.

"You still haven't explained why I didn't see you," I reminded him, my curiosity demanding an answer. The pieces were slowly coming together, but that crucial puzzle remained unsolved.

"You didn't see me because I refused to accept my fate," he explained, his eyes locking onto mine with intensity. "I didn't want..." He trailed off, briefly closing his eyes as if searching for the right words. When he opened them again, they focused on me. "I didn't think I would care enough to save you," he confessed, a flicker of sadness passing through his gaze.

"And now you've decided?" I asked, my voice laced with a mixture of hurt and skepticism. "What made you change your mind? How can I trust anything you say when everyone warns me to stay away? When you make deals with Dagasti. When you question whether I'm worthy or not?"

"You are worthy. I was a fool," he admitted, his face transforming with regret and remorse. "People often see only what they want to see, but you're different. You trusted me despite everything. My deals with Dagasti were made to benefit the wind people, to protect the Realms. It was through those deals that I managed to keep his forces from breaching Upherya's borders all these years."

"How do you know that I'm different? You don't really know

me... How can you be sure I wasn't just using you?" I challenged, sensing the tempest brewing within him.

"Were you?" he asked, his voice tinged with doubt. The storm in his eyes raged, revealing the inner turmoil he grappled with. He didn't believe it. Or didn't want to...

"No." I admitted, my voice steady and sincere.

THE SKIES CLOSED above us like a red blanket of fire. Falling ashes stuck to my skin like demonic specks of burning frost.

The cinders stirred above us with the vortex of winds, and I held my breath as the giant beasts sailed through the fiery skies above us. The dragons flew, twisting and turning in a dueling dance before crashing against what was left of the burning line of trees.

"Come with me," he pleaded once more, desperation coating his voice. The urgency in his tone revealed that he, too, had glimpsed what awaited us in the future, just as I had. He knew that time had run out.

"I can't," I replied, my gaze flickering to his outstretched hand. Drake's words echoed in my mind, urging me to fight for him. "I won't leave him." Stepping back, I resigned myself to whatever fate awaited me. If this was the path I was meant to walk, so be it.

"Don't do this," he implored, his voice filled with anguish. "You're making the same mistake she did. Choosing him will always be your downfall." His eyes blazed with intensity, but I had reached my limit of listening.

"Is that what this is about... choice?" I stared into his eyes, then glanced behind me towards Drake. "If, it's my life or him... I choose him." I said, and the storm moved behind his eyes, yet he made no move to stop me when I turned away, and ran towards the desiccated line of trees, towards Drake.

"Stop. Enough!" I called to the beasts. It was no use but I ran fearlessly toward the clashing dragons, sealing my fate.

"Please, stop!" I begged, my eyes locked on the grey-eyed dragon. In that fleeting moment, a chilling winter breeze swept through, piercing the fiery inferno surrounding us. Dagasti seized the opportunity and sank his teeth into Drake's shoulder.

My scream was drowned out by Drake's roar, but the pain didn't deter him. With a wounded wing, he circled back with unyielding force, clawing at Dagasti's wings and forcing him to the ground. I halted a short distance away from the battling dragons, witnessing Drake's merciless determination. He stood tall as Dagasti bowed helplessly before him.

Drake let out another roar, his wings extended dominantly over the fallen beast. Yet, as he glanced in my direction, I saw a fleeting darkness pass behind his eyes. He growled, then turned away. Just as I had seen in my dreams, Drake hesitated to take Dagasti's life. I held my breath, realizing that while Drake might have been aware of my fate, he didn't know the details. Otherwise, his uncle would already be dead.

The dragon bellowed, and a sudden jolt coursed through my body. Drake's gaze remained fixed on mine, and I didn't blink or move. I stood frozen, silent. I glanced down at the sharp tail spike protruding from my stomach, feeling all my strength drain away. The sword slipped from my grasp, crashing against the ground as my hands went limp. The once-blue cloak now stained crimson with my blood, but my focus remained on the fire consuming Drake's eyes.

Something had indeed changed. This time, Drake didn't turn to claim his uncle's head. Instead, he flew towards me, fire engulfing him as he transformed into his human form. Dagasti swiftly fled, disappearing into the gray skies.

As my knees hit the ashen ground, Drake's arms enveloped me. Tears welled up in his eyes, a sight I had never witnessed before, as he cradled me against his body.

"You promised..." I whispered, my hand reaching to stroke his ash-covered face. He gazed up at the sky, tracing Dagasti's path back to the castle, and let out a roar of anguish as he pulled me closer.

"I can't," he choked, his voice breaking. "Take my soul... my life. I don't want it without you," he pleaded, desperation lacing his words.

"Please, Drake... you promised... I'm not afraid." I pleaded on my last breath "I love you..."

The ashes swirled around me like waves of white and gray, obscuring my sight. The waves moved, and water coursed around my feet. Voices sang.

"Only in death... Only in death..." The wind whispered through dancing strokes of light.

DRAKE

The skies closed around me as I cradled her limp body to mine.

Her words echoed in my ears, *"Please Drake... you promised... I'm not afraid... I love you."* With her final breath, her words dissipated into the air like smoke.

"Nooo!" I screamed, my anguish piercing the air as I buried, my face against her neck. Fire danced around us, circling our bodies. Shielding us.

"Do something." Callix's voice cut through the darkness, and I pulled away the veils and flames that consumed us both.

"I made her a promise..." I replied, my voice filled with

despair. I slammed my fist against the ground, causing the earth to tremble beneath me.

"Then break it."

I glanced at her lifeless body in my arms: her ashen face, a sinister contrast against the flowing red blood pouring from her stomach.

"It was her last request..." I sighed. She would never forgive me. "I can't do it, damn it. I can't." I stared up at Callix.

"Will you let her die without a fight, just like Isabel?" He challenged

"Callix." I snarled. "Shut up, or by the fates, I will make you."

"Isabel didn't have to die. But she chose you."

"I would have never allowed it to happen. You have no right to blame me for that! You have no right to be here now. Go back to your realm. Leave us."

"I can't. I won't let history repeat itself."

"Just leave, Callix. Leave..." I pleaded, my hand trembling as I caressed her pale face. He remained stubbornly rooted in place. "Leave us!" I thundered, my voice filled with anguish.

"If you won't do it, let me take her." Callix's tone softened. "I will do it. I made no promises. Let me try..."

"No," I growled, my pride warring with the desire to save her. "I told you to stay away from her."

"Is your pride worth more than her life? You'd hang on to this absurd feud and let her die?" He spat, and my jaw clenched as I hesitated. "Fine, suit yourself."

Damn him! He turned while I stared at the girl lying dead in my arms, her moon-white skin lifeless. My soul burned.

"Wait..." I whispered, my voice barely audible. Callix paused, his back still turned to me.

"Save her," I whispered, staring at the man I had once called my friend, my brother, and now my enemy. Yet here he stood, offering to save the life of the woman I loved. His eyes raged with indecision. "Please." I begged. "By the fates, Callix, if you think you can save her... do it."

He turned back to face me, a mix of triumph and regret in his eyes. "I told you the day would come when you would beg for my help," he remarked.

I glared at him, swallowing my pride if it meant she would live. "Why are you doing this? Why her?" I demanded.

"She trusts me." He replied simply.

"I trusted you. Long ago." I reminded him.

"You didn't trust me. If you did, you would have believed me when I said I had nothing to do with it."

"No one else knew."

"That's the problem. It was easier for you to believe I could betray you than to imagine your secret was no longer a secret. You can hate me if you wish. It is not your forgiveness or approval I seek."

"You seek hers?" I narrowed my eyes, understanding that his insistence on helping Belynda went beyond a mere act of kindness. His silence confirmed my suspicion.

"I swear if you so much as lay a finger on her, I will find a way into the depths of your realm, Callix, and it will be the last day you take a breath." I warned.

"That presents a problem when I have to carry her out of here."

I growled, my jaw clenching as I tried not to throttle him.

"Damn you, Callix, just fucking take her."

My soul was ripped from my chest as he took Belynda from my arms. He cradled her against him.

I stared at his back as a water portal formed before them. He paused at the threshold and glanced at me.

"If you insist, I will take her." He grinned before slipping through the gate. Vanishing before my eyes.

WHAT HAD I DONE…?

I took a deep breath as my mother draped a cloak over my shoulders. Her gaze lingered on my blood-stained hands, but she didn't press for an explanation.

"She has to be okay," I muttered, my voice barely audible. It was all I could manage to say, my thoughts consumed by Belynda's fate. I had to hold onto the belief that she would be alright, even if I didn't know if Callix could save her or if I would ever see her again.

"Your uncle is likely healing…. He won't be long. I lost a few of my men. We can't stay here. We must hide in the mountains until we can travel to Upherya," my mother spoke, her voice filled with urgency. "The only way to stop him is to unite the rest of the realms, and I think the clans will be more willing to accept a truce than Herod."

"My father would not have run. He would have stayed and fought for his home. His people."

"We both know this is not a battle you can win. Not on your own. Your father would have known it too. The people of this realm will be safe. Dagasti is not interested in Druleska. He only wants to conquer what is not his." My mother attempted to soothe my anguish.

"This realm is not his!" I bellowed, my anger rising.

"It is for now, my son. But it won't be forever." My entire body shook, and the robe fell to my feet as I stood. I didn't want to feel. Not anymore.

The flames took over my body, and instantly, the beast was

free. Wings stretched behind me as I shot from the ground and into the thundering skies. As I lost myself to the darkness, vanishing into the gray clouds, my thoughts were of her. I would see her again. If not in life, then in death, but before I met her there, there was one life I had to claim. The only one that mattered.

Dagasti would die. That was my promise to her.

Acknowledgments

To the friends and family, tired of me bouncing ideas off them. Thank you for being steadfast when I've wavered. I couldn't have made it this far without all of you. To my husband, especially for his patience and understanding of the time, sacrifice, and effort that goes into creating a book. My children, thank you for your beautiful ideas for making these fantasy worlds.

I would also like to thank the cover designer team. They never cease to surprise me. Also, my editor, for her patience and magnificent work.

Lastly, thank you for reading and supporting Vanished. A dream of mine...It is you, the reader, who makes all the difference. It is wonderful to have someone find your books and connect with the characters, their stories, and the worlds you've imagined. You are the main reason I write.

Thank you all for making the impossible happen and for being a constant.

ABOUT THE AUTHOR

Morgan Vela is a debut author of romantic fantasy novels. Her stories join with shifters, witches, and dragons and explore other realms—while magic fills the pages of her stories, romance guides her imagination.

I have made up stories in my head for as long as I can remember —I have seen dragons and magic-filled worlds since I was young. I have traveled long and far and lived many lives through the pages of books I've read. This freedom of believing in the impossible, even briefly, made me want to share my stories. And so, my journey began as a writer.

My debut novel 'Vanished' is in paperback at Barnes & Noble and Amazon. It is also available as an eBook through Kindle Unlimited. 'Vanished A Guardian Story' is Book One of the Vanished Series. 'Throne of Fire' is the sequel of the series, followed by 'Tides of Destiny,' book three, scheduled for release next January. The fourth book and last of the series, 'Shadows and Light,' is projected to be released summer of 2024.

A SNEAK PEEK
TIDES OF DESTINY

PREFACE

Beyond my knowledge will be your gifts but know that only in death will you discover your truest self.

Bonded through blood, water, and soul, together as one we shall be...

Isabel Adams Cromwell

CHAPTER I
TACTICS OF WAR AND LOVE

AS AN IMMORTAL, THE THOUGHT OF TIME NEVER HAUNTED ME BEFORE. Living in the subtle absence of it was liberating. There were no fears, no expectations, but peace is now a whisper of the past...those moments have vanished. The instant Callix disappeared through that portal with her; he robbed me of my sanity. All reason is gone. Adrift under the Sea of Varenver. Deep into the depths of the Water Realm.

Nothing seemed to matter anymore. Not without her by my side. Not while deprived of knowing if she was alive. If I would ever see her again.

Slowly, the hours had turned into days. Days which pooled into weeks...and now months. And still, there was no news of her. *No word from Callix....*

I often placated the desperation reminding myself that no news was better than the alternative...learning that she was gone...that we had both failed to save her. But just as often, different thoughts entered my mind. Thoughts of Callix's provoking words mingled with images of them...succumbing to their desires. Darker, vile thoughts that only served to taunt the monster now clawing inside me.

I paced about the leader's meeting room and out onto the open deck, staring at the fogged city below, sleeping still under the peaks of the morning mountain mist. Getting the warriors to agree on something was hard enough with a clear head, even less so with my judgment lost to darker thoughts and emotions.

"Drake..." Euros called as he marched into the round hall. He poured himself a cup of wine, extending the decanter in my direction as an offering, but I declined with a firm nod.

"I think we all need a clear head." The warrior drowned the liquid in one draw and slumped in his chair, running his hands over his face. Although sleep wasn't required for immortals, unlike the fire people, the air realm seemed to have adapted to the old customs, and it appeared the lack of it was starting to affect them. Although I was certain that wasn't the only reason for their despair. Watching their Realm shred apart by darkness. The loss of their people. The feeling of helplessness...which I shared, all added to their misery.

"Will Link be joining us? How is he holding up?" Euros braced his forearms on the stone tabletop adorned with the intricate carvings of their clan names and stared at his hands.

"Nothing will keep Link from fighting. He is the youngest of us all but perhaps the wisest. I don't know that I could accept the loss of my clan as he has. Thinking about it just..."

"We will defeat Dagasti," I spoke. The words clipped one by one from my lips like knives. Euros glanced at me, and the warrior looked defeated for the first time since arriving in Upherya.

"There was a time when I thought we could, but seeing my world shrivel under darkness...Watching that monster's creation sweep clear our valleys...take our people...I don't know that I can believe in victory. Not for us." I knew Euros only dared admit this to me, not his brothers. The warrior I had come to know would never show weakness or defeat, not when both Link and Phoenix looked up to him. Even though they made decisions as a group, it didn't take long to realize whose trust I had to earn when I arrived here.

I took the wine bottle and refilled his cup. He certainly needed it. When I returned the bottle to its place, I turned to Euros and stared at the man for good measure.

"This war is not lost. Not as long as we have breath and strength to fight. Giving up now, claiming defeat, will not give your people back what they have lost. So, you will drink that cup and pull yourself together. Especially for your brothers. Euros, if you cave now, everything will be lost." The man drowned the red liquid in one draw and struck the cup against the table with resolution.

"Who would have thought I'd be listening to you when it was your mate who placed us all in this predicament, to begin with." My fists tightened at my sides.

"If you truly blamed us, you would have never allowed me and my people to remain and fight by your side. You wouldn't be here admitting your darkest fears to me if you truly thought I was your enemy. Belynda only did what she did to save me, even against my advice and her better judgment. But I cannot blame her, and you know this much because I have told you time and time again. I would have done the same despite the cost if the situation had been reversed. I would have unleashed this army if the alternative was I could save her."

The chair scraped against the stone floors as he stood. He strolled across the room and came to stand before me.

"I have to admit, I did blame you at the beginning, but if I'm being honest, I don't know that I would have done anything differently if I were faced with the same choice. If it were one of my own and their life was in my hands...." I conceded with a single nod. That was as much of an apology as I would get from the man. Not that I was looking for one or cared if he believed us innocent or not, but it did make our stay here and our formed alliance easier if we managed to trust each other.

He walked to the open promenade, and I followed. We watched the mountain range rise like a wall, emerging under its magic after the sun's rising rays.

"Do you truly believe Dagasti's army won't attempt to cross through the mountains?"

"I would bet my life on it. The Hills of Tirse are protected by ancient magic. Powers that we can't even understand. We've seen the Darklings turn from their borders. If we could yield whatever magic shields those mountains, we could use it to guard our borders, but luck is not on our side. That is why we chose to send our women and children there. They will be safe. It is Phoenix's clan I'm worried about. Dagasti's only move is to march his army to the East. The only thing standing between the darkness and us now are those mountains and Phoenix's clan."

"Why not move all your people to the mountains, then?" His brow furrowed as he glanced at me.

"We will not offer this Realm to Dagasti freely. We will fight to protect it until the end. You said it yourself. As long as we take a breath and have the strength." I offered him my hand.

"Till death," I vowed.

"Till death." Euros declared as he shook my hand firmly.

"What did we miss?" Phoenix declared as he entered the round chamber. Link followed like a silent shadow, and I didn't have to read his mind to know the battle he fought now was one of guilt. These warriors had been trained since birth to fight to their deaths. Not to cower. Not to run or fear. Link could not forgive himself for surviving when so many of his men had died, and the darkness had taken others. If Phoenix had not knocked him out cold and ordered me to fly him out of the battle of the valley, he wouldn't be standing here now.

"Nothing. We were waiting for you." Euros fortified himself with the face of armor he often donned in the presence of the other leaders.

"Shall we." Euros took his chair, and Phoenix and Link followed. I didn't dare take the last empty chair at their round table. The open seat honored the Borean leader's memory—their lost brother. That was an honor only reserved for their clan leaders.

I brought the map and laid it before them. Resting my fists against the stone table, I stared at the warriors.

"I scouted the trail of the valleys a few hours ago. The army has divided." I pointed to the lower lands of Upherya. "Dagasti has ordered half of the Darklings back to the South, towards the borderlines. I'm afraid the rest continues to march East." I glanced at Phoenix, for we knew exactly what their aim was, to overtake the Euresians.

"What reason would Dagasti have to separate his army? It makes no sense?" Link spoke this time, and I regarded the young warrior with respect. Not many could bear witness to the loss of their people and still find the strength to stand here and keep a cool head despite it.

"That's what we need to figure out. Perhaps, Dagasti plans to return to Druleska to grow his army."

"I feel that is precisely what he intends...but not by going to Druleska." Euros spoke quietly. "He means to cross the Fjord."

"Why would he risk separating his army now when he knows Herod has managed to keep the Darklings from breaking the magic barriers across his shores?" I paced around the table, trying to understand the reasonings behind the monster's cunning mind.

"Perhaps he's found a way to breach Abryas." Phoenix offered, but it made no sense. Even if Dagasti had figured out a way to cross the magic barriers, why would he want to rush into Abryas with half his army?

"We know Dagasti will not be satisfied with Upherya, so yes, it is a given he intends to cross into Abryas. His first attempt to breach it didn't stand, so we can anticipate he will try again; the question is why now, when his focus has always been to sweep across Upherya. I think there is something we're failing to see."

"Let's think like Dagasti for a moment. What has driven him from the start?" Link added.

"Power to take over the realms," Phoenix said.

"Precisely, and if our army had succeeded thus far, taken claim over the South and West territories, what could possibly, make us split our men when the strategic move would be to claim the East, border the mountains, and at last take the North?" I noticed the deep frown set upon Phoenix and Euro's brows, for I knew my hypothetical strategy was not something they wanted to think about, even if they knew it was the truth.

"Perhaps, Dagasti has grown overconfident. He must think claiming the East won't be a challenge." Phoenix added.

"I wouldn't doubt it, and if that is the case, his oversight might just earn us some advantage." Everyone seemed to agree that this could potentially tilt the scale in our favor for once.

"If that is the case, let's not make the same mistake Dagasti has. We must focus on what we don't know...." Euros said, returning to what was pressing. "We need to follow the army that marches to the borderlines. Figuring out Dagasti's plan is just as vital as guarding our borders. We cannot afford any surprises." The warrior's agreement was unanimous. Euros was right. We couldn't afford to bring down our guard; on the contrary, something told me Dagasti was no fool. It rather made my skin prickle, not knowing what the man was up to.

"I will patrol and report back. It looks like you could all use some sleep."

"I will accompany you." Euros said, and I accepted, with a firm nod, knowing he wouldn't change his mind, let alone find peace to sleep. At least not until we discovered what Dagasti's plan was.

EUROS

The village had yet to wake, but I knew Amirth was up. I could hear the sword's metal clashing in the distance and knew it could be no other. The girl was relentless and a truly worthy adversary. But I would never dare admit that to her. She was as skilled as she was infuriating. A true child of the Earth... which was perhaps why we disagreed so much.

I tried to pass the training forge unnoticed, but I knew I was unsuccessful the second the echoes of the clashing metal stopped.

"What's got your panties in a notch? Didn't get laid last night?" I rocked on my heel, clenching my fists at my sides and biting my tongue before turning to face the demon girl.

"For lack of it, I had the pleasure of two. Perhaps you should try it sometime; it might help improve your aim." I jabbed her ego and smiled, pleased to see her anger flourish, but her tongue was as poisonous as a snake, so I braced myself for her clever comeback.

The small dagger flew through the air inches away from my

ear, taking me completely by surprise. I plucked the small silver blade from the wooden post behind me and turned, narrowing my eyes in her direction.

Her eyes became wide as saucers as I strolled towards her with determination. The sound of metal echoed around the walls of the Forge as the swords fell from her hands. I secured her wrists against the wall over her head and trapped her body with mine.

"Do you have a death wish, woman?" I whispered, anger seeping from every pore in my body. I was not in the mood to be trifled with. She had lost her mind, and I...

She pushed against me, and I eased away before releasing her hands.

"I was merely stating a point." Her eyes burned into me defiantly.

"And what point was that exactly?" I demanded, hovering above the earth demon set on claiming my soul if I allowed her.

"That there is absolutely nothing wrong with my aim." She declared, and as her words settled in, I found I could not stop laughing.

"Seems to me you rather just proved my point. Don't you agree?" She scowled, staring back at me, and I grinned. "Your better sharpen that aim. Here," I pulled her dagger from my back pocket and handed it to her. "Keep at it. Practice makes perfect." I winked at her and strolled out of the Forge quickly before she had the chance to bite back. Or worse...I knew if I stayed a second longer, she would make me eat my words, or worse, she would draw blood to prove her point. Surprisingly, I smiled for the first time in weeks at the thought.

"You're in better spirits, I see," Drake noted, materializing almost out of thin air. He knew I detested the stealthy way in which he moved about, but he had never once shown contrition or tried to alter this habit. In the short months we had fought side by side, I had come to know the Dragon Prince, and one thing I had learned was that his character and demeanor were as sharp and unbending as the steel of his Dragon claws. Something I had come to respect and appreciate on the battlefield.

"Perhaps your keen eyes are failing you."

"You forget it's not just my eyes that are sharp, but my ears as well." Yes, how could I ever forget…" If Amirth is a problem…you will tell me. I am responsible for the girl."

"I don't think she would appreciate hearing you say that," I added, having witnessed the temper of that girl, and Drake grinned.

"Just the same." He looked at the dusk-painted skies with a frown. "I know they can care for themselves, but I still feel responsible for bringing them here. Even if it was their choice."

"I understand better than you think. Amirth is no problem. I promise." *Just a thorn in my side at times.* I yawned.

"Good. But if I might offer my opinion…." I stared at the Dragon Prince with a now bemused expression and accepted the offer with a subtle gesture. "Don't tease her. I might feel responsible for her, but I won't be held accountable if next time she draws blood to prove her point." He advised, and I laughed. Wholeheartedly.

"Thank you. I will heed your warning. Although I feel I would welcome the challenge…." I confessed, and Drake frowned.

"That's exactly what I'm afraid of…" He muttered next to me.

We marched through the now-sleeping city toward the edge of the mountains.

"How are you holding up?" I dared ask, knowing how reserved the man was.

"I'm existing. Breathing. Waiting…" The revelation of his pain didn't surprise me; that was something he could never hide. But the honesty with which he shared his darkest emotions did. It meant he trusted me, and I deduced that privilege was not easily given or earned.

"I don't presume to know how the fates work, but magic can be complex, especially when interfering with the balance of life and death. Such an endeavor might take time. Besides, you know the flow of time is different in Serfier."

"Yes, that is all I have to hang on to for now. Hope."

"That is all we have." I conceded, knowing hope was precisely what every son and daughter of Upherya was hanging on to.

"Has your mother sent a message? Has she mentioned when she expects to return?"

"She will remain in Abryas for now. She feels the invitation of the Queen to stay with them will be to our advantage."

"Your mother is a wise woman. I trust her judgment. But I hold my reservations where Herod is concerned. This is a truce; neither side would have chosen."

"Indeed, but the unification of the Realms is necessary. Retrieving the ships and his men from your shores was an act of good faith. I believe he will make good on his promises."

"I hope so, for all our sakes. Now, let's track some darklings."

DRAKE

I envied the ease with which Euros took claim of his element. One draw from the Winds of Tirse, and the golden feathers materialized, glinting off the warrior's back. He sprung into the night sky as I removed the last vestiges of my clothes and allowed the fire to claim me.

We flew, side by side, bordering the hills and through the upper lands of the East clan, trying to avoid the Windless Cliffs. No amount of magic could allow a single person or object to fly over those cliffs.

We were forced to dive close to the water's surface as we reached the Fjord and left Upherya's guarded territory. I trailed behind Euros, lost in the shadow of our reflection against the water. Her memory invaded my thoughts, and I fought against the need to divert our mission across the Bay and plunge into Callix's domain. I resisted because I feared that was a battle I could never win, not against the ocean.

We planned to veer West before reaching the Bay, and cross, between the outer lands and what remained of the Southern clan region, but when I spotted the army in the far distance, I took a sharp dive, and Euros followed.

Yes, we expected to find the broken branch of Dagasti's army approaching the borderlands, but much closer to the West. We had underestimated their advance.

Euros glided just above my right flank, and I noticed his resolve, even before he dove towards the trees behind the valley, where the darklings marched. He had a death wish, but regardless, I followed. He touched the ground smoothly, and I eased my landing beside him. Euros tucked his wings behind his back, but I didn't change. It was too risky. He knew this.

I growled, and he turned to face me.

"I know. Stay here." I extended my left wing and blocked his path, and he glared up at the monster.

"Seriously? Remove yourself; that is an order." He was a bigger fool if he thought he could order me about or that I would step back and allow him to risk everything we had worked for. His brothers would never forgive me if I did. A part of me wouldn't either, so I didn't move. The monster bared its teeth and wrapped the warrior in a breath of smoke as a warning.

"Fine. Let's use the cover of the cloud banks. We will trail from a distance." He took a step back, and his wings uncurled from his back in midair as he disappeared between the foliage of the trees.

It didn't take us long to figure out what the Darkling soldiers were up to. Most of the trees of the bordering forests were laid to waste, cropped, and lined while the army worked with resilience to build a fleet. Euros was right, they planned to cross the Fjord, and we had to warn Herod. Dagasti, wouldn't go to such lengths unless he had a way to breach Abryas defenses.

We reached the Hills of Tirsia, still under the blanket of night. Euros didn't stop. He zoomed straight up through the mountains' mist to the round chamber. He was still furious, but he would get over it and thank me. I slipped on my clothes and streaked through the sleeping town and up the hills to the peak of the mountain, where the clan leaders gathered. As I anticipated, Euros was already there, standing at the edge of the open terrace, a cup of wine in his hand. I entered the chamber and marched to his side. He didn't turn, but I knew he had something to say.

"You have been welcomed among my people. We have trusted you with our lives, but by no means are you bound to remain here if you do not wish to. However, you will not defy my command again. Do you understand?" He turned to me then. "Do you understand?"

I marched to the very edge of the polished floors, which ended in an abysmal plunge into darkness. Pausing at the precipice, I took a deep breath, allowing the purest air to fill my lungs before I turned to the warrior.

"Perhaps, my benevolence has made you forget who you speak to." I offered with premeditated ease. "I am not your subject to command. You will show me the respect I deserve." I emphasized each word as darkness seeped from my mouth. "I have come to trust you and your people. I even glimpsed the beginnings of a friendship, but I will never bow down to anyone. You viewed my actions tonight as a defiance when all I did was offer you a kindness. I could have given you leave to place yourself in danger. But I chose to stop you, for your brothers, for your people, for your own sake. The monster wouldn't hesitate. So next time you think to come at me, think twice, for I am not your enemy."

I strolled past him and into the cover of the room.

"Thank you." I paused. "You're right, and I don't often admit that." I knew that much, so I conceded and turned to Euros.

"I think we should leave for Abryas at first light."

"Yes, I will speak with Link and Phoenix." I acknowledged with a firm nod, and he returned the gesture, but it appeared we had both said enough for one day. As I streaked down through the mountain mist, I knew only one thing was certain...Euros would never underestimate me again.

Morning broke over the horizon as Link, Phoenix, Euros, and I flew over the Shores of Galnora. We landed near the bordering woods, neighboring Grettos Cave, where the closest Elvin post held the defenses of the borders. They would send the news to the castle and allow us passage.

The woods extended before us, but none of the warriors moved. The magic shields were invisible but poisonous to Darklings, humans, and immortal creatures alike.

I lifted my head, breathing in the winds coming from the North.

"They've detected us. The golden army is approaching."

Phoenix picked up a small stone from the ground and tossed it to the distant forest line.

As expected, the stone disappeared through the invisible shield, but the poisonous magic hissed in ripples just where the rock hit the invisible barrier.

Phoenix picked up another stone, but I held his arm before he could through it.

"Don't forget we are uninvited visitors to them. Let's behave." Phoenix smiled but heeded and dropped the stone.

"We are doing them a favor by coming anyway." Phoenix motioned with his head behind me as the line of Elven soldiers emerged from under the shade of the trees. Their golden armor glinted under the filtering rays of the morning sun.

"Who are you? Speak your business."

"You raided our borders and shores long enough to know damn well who we are." Euros glared at Phoenix in a warning.

The golden line took a defense stand, and so did the Warriors in reaction.

"Stand down," I said, looking directly at Euros, for I knew his brothers would follow his lead.

"Your names and your business in Abryas." The leader of the golden company demanded once more. His eyes glowed, and as he moved his fingers at his sides, so did the invisible wall. It was subtle, but I could see the gentle ripples moving across the ground, separating us. They were pushing the barriers toward us.

"Stop," I said, and the Elven leader dropped his hands, and with it, the movement of the barrier stopped. "We are on urgent business to see King Herod. These are the clan leaders of Upherya."

"We are not aware of an invitation." The Elvin commander

raised his hands, and once again, the wall moved inch by inch toward us.

"There is no time. My mother is a guest of Queen Leiwen; have your men send a whisper; you will see your King will receive us." The barriers stopped advancing once more. The commander turned and instructed two of his men, who disappeared into the forest, hopefully, to deliver the message. The Elvins relied on the magic of the trees—their messengers or whisperers, as they often called them.

"We await the castle orders." Conveyed the commander.

"Remind me why we're doing this again?" Phoenix muttered, but no one said a word. He needed no encouragement.

One of the guards returned twenty minutes later with an answer.

The young boy turned towards the invisible wall once more, and with the parting of his hands, the barrier opened like a giant curtain.

"You may enter." The poisonous mist closed behind us, and the Elvin commander turned to us.

"My apologies. We have orders to accompany you to the castle gates. King Herod will receive you."

"Thank you." I offered, and we followed the young boy who looked not more than twenty. But I knew that was an illusion of the Elvin people. Youth. Most chose never to age. The fact that this boy was in a commanding position meant he was much older than most of his peers. Perhaps even as old as I.

We were not allowed to shift. That was strictly forbidden since the barriers put in place extended around and above Abryas like a protective dome. We rode North, fast without much rest for the following two days until the lush green hills surrounding the Elvin city and castle came to view.

The ornate golden gates into the city limits opened at the commander's request, and we rode through until the heart of the city and gateway to the castle.

As we dismounted from the horses, the young commander stiffened.

"My Queen." The soldier fell to his knees before Leiwen.

"Thank you, commander," Leiwen said.

"It is an honor, my lady." The young soldier rose and gathered the horses.

"Welcome. We are honored to have you." The young Queen said, looking at me and the three clan leaders. "Your mother will join us momentarily. I'm afraid Herod is detained, but he will receive you soon."

"Thank you for taking us in without notice. We wouldn't be here if we didn't think it was urgent."

"Of course. You are always welcome in Abryas." Leiwen offered, but I wasn't sure that invitation came as an extension of the King. He always seemed to be the one with reservations about forming alliances with Upherya. Leiwen, on the other hand, was their champion.

"Thank you," Euros spoke.

I was certain the warriors had noticed as well. She was the only Elvin in this kingdom for whom they held a modicum of appreciation and respect.

"Come. You must be tired." The warriors followed, but I stayed behind when I saw my mother descend the stairs.

"My son." She said warmly. "I've missed you." She kissed my cheek.

"So, have I." I smiled, pleased to see her. "I received your message. How long will you remain here?"

"For as long as the invitation stands. You know I'm safe here."

"Yes. I know. I wouldn't allow you to remain if I didn't think you were." She assented with her head in agreement.

"What has happened to you?" She noted. I pulled her hand from my cheek and kissed it, then offered her a smile to ease her worried expression.

"I'm fine. I promise."

"You can lie to others. You can even lie to yourself. But you cannot fool your own mother." I sighed in defeat as we walked through the gardens.

"I take it there has been no news?" She asked as we reached the fountains.

"Nothing but silence. I swear if I had Callix before me now...I would kill him with my bare hands." She placed her hand over my clenched fists.

"Just because Serfier is connected to the fates doesn't mean they do Callix's bidding."

"I know." I paced about the spring, and my mother followed.

"I have faith that she will be alright. We would have heard from him by now if it weren't so. I'm sure of it."

"It doesn't make it any easier." I stared, lost in the falling water. "I should have never kept that promise to her. If I hadn't, she would be here now."

"But you wouldn't!" My mother stated.

"I much prefer the alternative." I felt her hand on my shoulder.

"Never say that. I couldn't bare it. Without your help, Upherya would have been lost long ago too."

"You think I care about Upherya or Abryas?"

"You should!" She admonished. "If the Realms fall under darkness...if Dagasti wins...there will be no place for her or you. It will no longer matter if she lives or dies." I cringed at my mother's words. It was bluntly the truth, but not what I wanted to hear.

"Please. I need to be alone, mother."

As I stared at the walling waters, all I could see was Callix taunting me, and the monster took the bait. The lines of black sand danced around my clenched fists.

"Drake...This is not you." My mother squeezed my shoulder before walking away.

I flexed my hands, easing the darkness onto my skin, but the monster wanted retribution. *"It no longer matters if she lives or dies..."* my mother's words bit into my soul. *"If you insist... I will take her."* I rammed my fist into one of the stone statues as Callix's taunting words echoed in my head.

"You made me promise...Fight, damn you. Why won't you come back?" I stared at my reflection on the water's surface and the blue skies in the background and prayed to the fates, to any god that would listen. "I will give anything to have her back. My life, my soul. Just take it." I whispered.

CALLIX

"I will give anything to have her back. My life, my soul. Just take it." I moved my fingers across the still water in the large basin in my chamber, and with the ripples, the image of Drake's haunted look disappeared.

"You and I both...." I sighed, resting my hands against the marble pillar that held the basin.

"Sire. You called?" I opened my eyes and glanced at the nymph.

"How is she?"

"No change, Sire." My fists clenched around the marble basin. *She should have awoken by now. It shouldn't have taken this long.*

My footsteps echoed against the marble floors, but the vibrancy of these crystal halls had lost its light with my stormy mood, something the nymphs perceived as well. They thought I did not notice, but they ran at my sight, and I didn't blame them. The silence that stilled through the castle was haunting. Almost as if it had been placed under some spell, but it was all because of her... Because of me... Because of the storm, everyone could feel brewing inside of me.

The stone steps descended into the caves. Its iridescent walls illuminating her pale face. The sea witches stopped their prayers at my command and left the chamber.

Step by step, I plunged into the stone-carved well where her body rested—floating above the water like a sleeping goddess. The tendrils of her golden hair glowed about her peaceful face.

The radiant blue water moved around my waist as I reached a hand hesitantly. My fingers stroked the moist skin of her cheek, then I glanced at her pale lips and withdrew my hand. I allowed myself only that much without disturbing the process.... Against the desires storming inside of me. Against this all-consuming need... However long the wait might be...

ALSO BY MORGAN VELA

VANISHED SERIES

A Guardian Story

Throne of Fire

Tides of Destiny (Coming January 2024)

Shadows and Light (Coming Summer 2024)

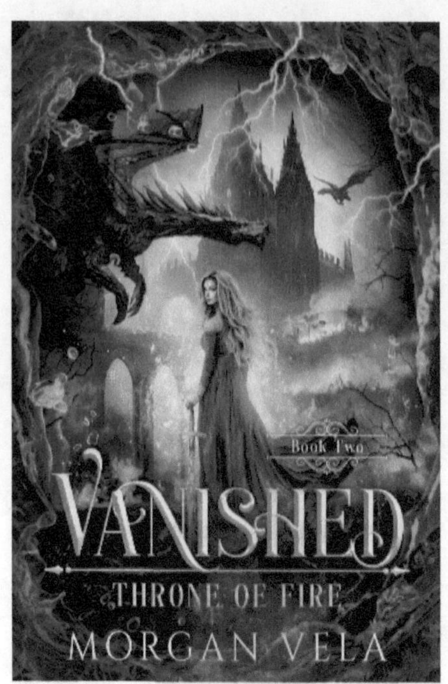

Book Two
VANISHED
THRONE OF FIRE
MORGAN VELA

STAY CONNECTED

www.ingramcontent.com/pod-product-compliance
Lightning Source LLC
Chambersburg PA
CBHW030912300726
48970CB00001B/121